JEWELS OF THE DESERT

Deserts, diamonds and destiny!

The Kingdom of Quishari: two rulers,
with hearts as hard as the rugged landscape
they reign over, are in need of Desert Queens…

When they offer convenient proposals,
will they discover doing your duty
doesn't have to mean ignoring your heart?

Sheikh Rashid and his twin brother Sheikh Khalid
are looking for brides…

Dear Reader

Okay, I confess, I'm fascinated with twins. I sometimes try to imagine my life as it would be if I had a twin. When I was a child, I always wanted to be one of a set of twins. The most fun would be switching places and fooling people—so I thought.

Alas, I am not a twin, nor do twins run in my family. But the fascination remains. This story is about twins—sheikhs, no less. The fact that they are twins does not play a huge role in the linked stories, but there is that mystique. Do twins think alike? Not always. Or each twin would want to marry the same person.

Sometimes, despite looking identical, twins' interests are vastly different, and the lives they lead are as individual as anyone's. In this story, the older twin—by seven minutes—leads a life of high-stakes oil and international business dealings. He loves the challenge of dealing in the world market. Just when he's about to sign a strategic contract things get dicey, and he needs help from an unlikely source.

Can two very different lifestyles be blended? Of course—if you have love. Please join me on this fun journey as Rashid and Bethanne discover the greatest gift of all.

Two brothers, twins to boot, find love and happy futures in totally unexpected ways.

All the best

Barbara

ACCIDENTALLY THE SHEIKH'S WIFE

BY
BARBARA McMAHON

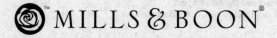

All the characters in this book have no existence outside the imagination
of the author, and have no relation whatsoever to anyone bearing the
same name or names. They are not even distantly inspired by any
individual known or unknown to the author, and all the incidents are
pure invention.

First published in Great Britain 2010
Harlequin Mills & Boon Limited,
Eton House, 18-24 Paradise Road, Richmond, Surrey TW9 1SR

© Barbara McMahon 2010

ISBN: 978 0 263 87350 4

Harlequin Mills & Boon policy is to use papers that are natural,
renewable and recyclable products and made from wood grown in
sustainable forests. The logging and manufacturing process conform
to the legal environmental regulations of the country of origin.

Printed and bound in Spain
by Litografia Rosés, S.A., Barcelona

Barbara McMahon was born and raised in the south USA, but settled in California after spending a year flying around the world for an international airline. After settling down to raise a family and work for a computer firm, she began writing when her children started school. Now, feeling fortunate in being able to realise a long-held dream of quitting her 'day job' and writing full time, she and her husband have moved to the Sierra Nevada mountains of California, where she finds her desire to write is stronger than ever. With the beauty of the mountains visible from her windows, and the pace of life slower than the hectic San Francisco Bay Area where they previously resided, she finds more time than ever to think up stories and characters and share them with others through writing. Barbara loves to hear from readers. You can reach her at PO Box 977, Pioneer, CA 95666-0977, USA. Readers can also contact Barbara at her website: www.barbaramcmahon.com

To Carol, Barbara, Kate, Diana, Lynn, and Candice.
Thanks a bunch.
Lunch is always great fun.

CHAPTER ONE

BETHANNE SANDERS lined up the aircraft with the designated runway and began the final descent. The new jet handled like a dream—all the way from Texas to the coast of the Persian Gulf. It was the first time she'd flown halfway around the world and she wished she could continue on until she circled the globe. When she left Quishari, it would be by commercial flight back through Europe.

Maybe she'd get another dream assignment like this one in the not-too-distant future. For now, she continued to scan the landscape as far as she could see as the plane began descending. Excitement built. The Persian Gulf was magnificently blue, from deep, dark navy to shades of azure and turquoise. The strip of sandy beach now visible was almost blinding beneath the sun. She had read so much about Quishari and heard so much from her father, she almost felt like she recognized the landmarks as she came in for the landing. Her heart raced at the thought of actually being here. It was like a dream come true.

Had this assignment not materialized, she still would have come—but it might have taken longer as the cost was exorbitant and savings accumulated slowly.

But fate had stepped in—almost like the answer to a prayer. She was delivering a brand-new Starcraft jet to Sheikh Rashid al Harum—and bringing in a priceless cargo. His soon-to-be fiancée.

Except for the shakedown trips around Texas, the only hours on this jet were the ones taken to fly it here. If the sheikh liked it and accepted delivery, he'd be the proud owner of the latest and greatest of the Starcraft line.

She hoped the sheikh's fiancée enjoyed the detailing of the luxury appointments and had enjoyed the flight. Bethanne had taken extra care to make the journey as smooth as possible. She found it vastly romantic that they were planning to marry—and neither had yet met the other.

A bit odd in the twenty-first century. Still, to have been chosen to be the bride of one of the fabulously wealthy sheikhs of Quishari had to be thrilling. Pictures had been exchanged, the parents had made the arrangements. How did a thirty-four-year-old man feel about having his bride hand-picked? Not too different from some of the online dating services—match likes and dislikes, find someone compatible, and there they were.

Would they kiss when meeting? Seal the deal, so to speak? Or would the woman be too shy to be bold enough for physical affection at the instant of meeting?

She had daydreamed on the long portions of the flight when autopilot had taken care of flying that she was being met by someone who would sweep her off her feet, make her feel cherished and special.

Or, alternatively, she'd also imagined her father striding along the tarmac, gathering her into his arms for one of his big bear hugs.

Blinking, Bethanne brought her attention back to the task of landing this multimillion-dollar jet.

The snowy-white exterior had already been detailed with stripes using the colors of Quishari— blue and gold and green. The interior resembled a high-end hotel lobby. The lush Persian carpet in golds and reds supported cushy sofas and armchairs, all with the requisite seat belts. The small dining area was elegant with rich walnut furnishings. The galley was fully stocked, and included a stove, oven and microwave in addition to the lavish below-counter refrigerator, wider than long, capable of carrying any supplies necessary for the sheikh's pleasure. Even the sole restroom was spacious.

Bethanne had shown Haile al Benqura all the features of the cabin before going to the cockpit for her preflight routine. The chaperone accompanying the young woman had not spoken English, but Haile had. She'd taken in everything with a solemn demeanor. Wasn't she the slightest bit excited? Apparently when the sheikh had mentioned something to the president of Starcraft, her boss had immediately offered to fly Haile from her home in Morocco to Quishari as a favor to the prospective buyer of their top-of-the-line private jet.

Bethanne glanced at her copilot, Jess Bradshaw. It was his first long-distance delivery as well and they had taken turns flying the aircraft to minimize delivery time.

"Want to bring it in?" she asked.

"No. We want this to go perfectly. I'm not as good at it as you."

She shrugged and then brought the plane down with a kiss against the asphalt.

"Nice job," Jess said.

"Thanks. This is a sweetheart of a plane. The sheikh is one lucky man."

She followed directions from the tower and taxied to an area away from the main terminal. The immaculate hangar was already swarming with ground crew; everyone had eyes on the jet as she pulled it into the designated slot. She and Jess

ran through the checklist as they shut down. She
wanted to dash out and breathe the Quishari air.
But duty first. She had scheduled several days
here to see if she could find her dad. And to see
the towns and desert that made Quishari famous.

"I'm glad we get to sleep on the way home,"
Jess mumbled, waiting for her to get up first. He
followed her from the cockpit to the outside door
of the jet. With minimum effort, Bethanne opened
it, watching as stairs unfolded. She glanced back
and saw the chaperone. Where was Haile? In the
restroom? Probably primping to look her best
when seeing the sheikh for the first time. Bethanne
hoped she hadn't been there when they landed.
Jess had announced their approach and told the
passengers to fasten seat belts.

The chaperone looked worried, her eyes darting
around the cabin, refusing to meet Bethanne's
gaze. Had she been afraid of flying? Bethanne
couldn't image anyone not loving it. She'd wanted
to be a pilot since she turned five and first been
taken up in the cockpit of a small plane. Of course,
wanting to follow in her father's footsteps had
also played a big part.

Two men waited at the foot of the stairs. When
the steps unfolded and locked in place, the taller
began to ascend. Bethanne watched him approach.
He was maybe six-three or four. Which Bethanne
found refreshing. Her own five-ten height usually

had her eye to eye with men. His dark hair shone in the sunlight, his skin was tanned to teak. The closer he came, the more she could see—from dark eyes that watched her steadily, to a strong jaw that suggested arrogance and power, to the wide shoulders encased in a pristine white shirt and dark charcoal suit.

Her heart began to beat heavily. She was fascinated by the man. Awareness flooded through her, as did a sudden need to brush her hair—she hoped it was still neat in its French plait. Studying him as he drew closer every step, she noticed the hint of wave in his hair. She wondered what he'd look like if he ran his fingers through his hair. Or if she did.

She swallowed and tried to look away. Fantasies like that would get her nowhere. This had to be Sheikh Rashid al Harum. Almost-fiancé to the woman in the back of the plane. Oh, lucky Haile al Benqura. She had undoubtedly fallen in love with the man from the pictures exchanged. Now she would be greeted and swept off her feet with one of the most gorgeous men Bethanne had ever seen.

"I am Rashid al Harum. Welcome to Quishari," he said in English as he stepped into the aircraft.

"Thank you." She cleared her throat. That husky tone wasn't like her. This man was rattling her senses. "I'm Bethanne Sanders. My copilot, Jess

Bradshaw." She saw the surprise in his eyes. Despite all the headway women had made in aviation, it was still considered primarily a male profession. She was growing used to seeing that expression—especially in locales away from the U.S.

Rashid al Harum inclined his head slightly and then looked beyond them into the cabin.

The older woman rose and began to speak in a rapid strained tone.

Bethanne still didn't see Haile. Was she ill? As the chaperone continued, she glanced at the sheikh, wishing she understood the language. His face grew harder by the second. In a moment he turned and glared at Bethanne. "What do you know of Haile's disappearance?" he asked in English.

Bethanne looked back into the cabin. "Disappearance? Isn't she in the restroom?" she asked, suddenly worried something was wrong. What had the chaperone said? Where was Haile al Benqura?

"Apparently she never left Morocco," the sheikh said in a tight voice.

"What? That's impossible. I showed her around the plane myself. She was on board when we were ready to leave." She turned to Jess. "You saw her, right? When you boarded?"

Jess shook his head slightly. "I don't remember

seeing her when I closed the door. A maintenance man ran down the stairs just as I was rounding the back to board. No one else got off the plane."

"There shouldn't have been a maintenance man aboard—there's nothing wrong with the plane," Bethanne said. What was going on? Where was Haile? "What did she say?" Bethanne gestured to the chaperone, still standing in front of the sofa.

The sheikh glared at her for a moment, then in a soft, controlled voice that did not soothe at all, said, "I suggest that you and I speak alone."

She stared at him, suddenly worried things had gone terribly wrong. He seemed to tower above her, anger evident.

"I'll check on things on the ground," Jess said with obvious relief. He eased by the two of them and hurried down the stairs. Once he was out of earshot, the sheikh turned to the older woman and spoke briefly.

She dropped her gaze and nodded. Gathering her few things, she walked to the back and sat on the edge of the sofa, gazing out one of the small windows.

"According to her, Haile took off before the plane departed Morocco, running to meet a lover."

"What? How is that possible? I thought she was coming here to meet you—your fiancée, or almost," Bethanne blurted out before thinking.

How could the woman choose someone else over this man? was Bethanne's first thought.

"So she is, was, to be. Her family and mine have been in negotiations for months over an oil deal that would prove advantageous to both countries. Included in that was the merger of our two families through marriage. Now my entire family—not to mention others in this country—expects the arrival of a woman who is to be my wife—and she is not on board."

Bethanne swallowed hard at the anger in his eyes. Surreptitiously wiping her palms against the fabric of her uniform, she raised her chin and said, "I'm not responsible for her leaving the plane. I thought she was on board. She was when I last saw her."

"You're the captain of the aircraft. What goes on is your responsibility. I hold you accountable. How could you let her leave?" His dark eyes pinned her in place. His entire demeanor shimmered with anger—controlled, which made it seem even stronger.

"How was I suppose to know she didn't want to come here? I thought everything was arranged." She would not tell him how romantic she found the scenario. Maybe she hadn't thought it through if the woman had fled rather than come to Quishari. "Though if I had known the circumstances, maybe I would have questioned whether anyone wanted to be *negotiated* into a marriage. I thought it was an old-fashioned mail-order-bride situation. But if the bride wasn't willing, I'm glad I did not have a part in bringing her here." She looked at the older woman. "She's the one you should hold responsible. Bringing them from Morocco to Quishari was a favor to you by our company."

"But the favor was not fulfilled. She is not here."

"I can see that. What do you want me to do about it now?" Bethanne said.

"The marriage would be an arrangement that benefits both countries," he said with a dismissing gesture. "That is not any concern of yours. The decision has been made. What is of your concern, is the fact Haile went missing on your watch."

Bethanne met his gaze bravely. It was not her fault the woman had deplaned. Why hadn't the chaperone stopped her? Or told someone before they took off from Morocco? What else could she say?

This was certainly not the happy arrival at Quishari she'd anticipated.

"The immediate need, now, is for damage control," he said after a moment. The sheikh looked back at the woman sitting so still in the back of the jet. For a moment Bethanne imagined she could see the wheels spinning in his head.

How could she have known Haile wasn't as interested in the marriage as she had thought? She would never have suspected a young woman like Haile would disguise herself and slip away between the time Bethanne went into the cockpit and Jess joined her. It couldn't have been more than five minutes. Obviously it had not been a spur-of-the-moment decision. It had taken planning and daring. Bethanne's romantic mind imagined Haile deplaning surreptitiously and finding her lover and both fleeing, whilst her father and his minions followed on horseback. She blinked. Her overactive imagination could get her in trouble.

"I'm sorry I can't help you," she said, hoping to ease the tension that was as thick as butter. Her primary goal was to deliver the plane, which she'd done. Now all the sheikh had to do was accept the delivery, sign the paperwork and Bethanne could begin her vacation in Quishari while Jess would be flying back to Texas on the next available flight.

"Ah, but you can help. In fact, I insist." He turned back to her. The serious expression in his eyes held her in thrall. What did he mean?

"How can I help? Fly back to Morocco and find her? I wouldn't begin to know where to look."

"Despite my family's efforts to keep the entire matter solely within the family, rumors have been flying around the country. I've ignored them, but

I know they speculate a special visitor will arrive soon. My coming to meet this plane would have fueled speculation even more. So, you're it."

"I'm what it?" she asked, wondering what would happen if there was no special visitor. Some gossip, more speculation about when his fiancée would arrive.

"The woman I came to meet. It's as if it was meant to be. What are the odds of having a female pilot bringing the plane—and one who is young and pretty enough to pass muster?"

"Muster for what?" Bethanne wondered if she'd fallen down the rabbit hole. Nothing was making sense.

"To pass as my special guest, of course."

She stared at him. "Are you crazy? I mean…" Ever conscious of the fact he was an important client of her company she didn't want to insult, she stopped. But he couldn't be serious. Thinking she could pass as a fiancée for a sheikh? He had to have half the money of the country. She'd learned that much about the al Harum family from her father. They controlled vast oil deposits and dealt in the world market for oil. They played a major role in the government of Quishari and had for generations.

Bethanne's head was spinning. He wanted to pretend she was his fiancée?

He spoke to the chaperone who came reluctantly to stand beside him. For several moments, he spoke in rapid Arabic. The woman glanced at Bethanne and frowned. The sheikh continued to speak and resignation settled on the woman's face. Finally she answered, bowing slightly.

Bethanne hadn't understood a word. But her mind had quickly considered and discarded one idea after another. The one fact that shone above all was she would be dealing with Rashid al Harum for days. Awareness spiked. She wished she had checked her makeup and hair before opening the door. Did he even see her in the uniform? Feeling decidedly feminine to his masculinity, she let herself consider the outlandish suggestion.

Special guest to a sheikh. They'd spend a lot of romantic moments together. Would he kiss her? Her knees almost melted at the thought.

"It is settled. Haile's chaperone will serve as yours for the time being. Her name is Fatima. She doesn't speak English but we'll get around that somehow."

"Wait a minute. I'm not—"

He raised his hand. "You are in my country now, Ms. Sanders. And my rules apply. Certain influential people are watching to see the young woman that I am interested in. It is fortunate that my family kept a tight lid on the negotiations. No one knows who I have selected. It would not be a good thing at this point to disappoint them. You are my choice since *you* lost my other one."

"That's totally ridiculous. How can you say

that? Maybe you need a few minutes to come up with an alternative plan."

"This suits me. Time is short. Please put on a happy face and accompany me down the stairs," he ordered.

"Wait a minute. I haven't agreed to anything."

"Would you prefer to fly this plane back to the United States immediately? Canceling the sale?" he asked. "And perhaps putting in jeopardy the relationship Quishari holds with Morocco?"

His implacable expression confirmed he was completely serious. She tried to comprehend if he really thought she could divert an international incident. She opened her mouth to refute it when a thought occurred to her.

She had another agenda in Quishari. She had hoped during her vacation to find her father. It wasn't exactly the kind of stay she'd envisioned, but maybe agreeing to his pretense for a short time would work to her advantage as well. Certainly the special guest of the sheikh would be afforded more access to information than a mere visitor. She had contacts to find, places to visit. Wouldn't it be easier with the help of Sheikh Rashid al Harum?

She closed her mouth while she tried to see how this odd request—no, demand—could work to her benefit. "What exactly are we talking about?" she asked, suddenly seeing the situation advantageous to her own quest.

"A short visit. We'll tell people you've come to meet me and my family. If they think you and I are making a match, that's their problem. After a few weeks, you leave. By then, I'll have the contract finalized and who cares what the rumormongers say. In the meantime, you would be my honored guest."

"I don't see how that would work at all. We don't even know each other." She had never been in love. Had dreamed about finding that special man, one who had likes and interests similar to her own. Never in a million years could she envision herself having anything in common with a sheikh. But there was that pull of attraction that surprised her. She couldn't fall for a stranger. Not right away. It had to be jet lag or something.

Still, he fascinated her. And she was pragmatic enough to realize she could get a lot of help in searching for her father.

The way he put things, it wasn't quite as if they were supposed to be lovers. They were to be still in the getting-to-know-you stage. The thought of getting to know him better tantalized. And people who were almost engaged did kiss.

Why did that compel her? she wondered as she looked at his lips, imagining them pressed against her own.

"Have you considered all the ramifications? What will you say when asked how we met? Why we are attracted to each other? My background is not that important that a sheikh would view it as any kind of advantage."

"Perhaps we could say we fell in love," he suggested sardonically.

She frowned. His tone suggested he didn't believe in love. The dismissing glance he gave proved the thought never crossed his mind. And it wasn't as if she'd fallen in love with him. A strong interest in an intriguing man—that's all she felt. Once she got to know him better, she'd undoubtedly find him a bit annoying.

"It's important even in an arranged marriage for the partners to at least be cordial to each other," she replied with false sweetness, wondering if she could spend much time in his company without coming completely unglued.

"Do you not think I can be cordial?" he asked in a silky tone, leaning closer. He brushed his fingers against her cheek as he pushed back a strand of hair. His dark eyes were so close she could see tiny golden flecks in them. The affinity she felt was drugging. She wanted to close the scant inches separating them and touch his face, feel his mouth on hers.

She drew a breath to get control of her senses. But the scent of his aftershave set her senses to dancing. She opened her mouth to offer a hearty no, then closed it.

Think.

It would help her look for her father. Using her un-expected position to gain access where mere visitors might not have was a bonus she never expected. Don't hastily reject this, she warned herself.

"Perhaps," she conceded.

"And you?" he asked. The intensity of his gaze had her mesmerized. She could no more look away than she could fly without a plane.

"I can be cordial. But not lovey-dovey," she said. There was a limit she dare not cross lest she be lost. One kiss would never be enough. She'd become demanding and forget why she'd come to Quishari if the tempting allure was given free rein.

Amusement flared in his eyes. "Agreed, no lovey-dovey. You must call me Rashid and I will call you Bethanne. In public you will appear to be devoted to me."

"And in private?" she asked, already wondering if she'd lost her mind to even consider such a bizarre plan. Still, if it gave her the answers she craved, who was she to say no?

"I'd settle for devotion, but can understand if you feel more reserved," he said. Laughter lurked in his eyes.

The amusement confused her. Was he serious or not?

"I will have Fatima accompany you to a villa I own by the sea. It was where Haile was to stay.

You'll have privacy there. Of course, I expect you to attend the celebratory functions that have been planned. And to convince my mother we have a chance of making this work."

"Your mother? You want to pretend to your mother? I think you're crazy."

Bethanne was not close to her own mother but lying to her would never be an option. Were the sheikh and his mother on no better terms?

The amusement vanished. "I want nothing to ruin the deal I still have pending with Haile's father. There are factions here who oppose the proposed arrangement. The finance minister, for one. He would consider Haile's actions an insult to our country. He'd love nothing better than to drive a wedge into the negotiations. As it stands, perhaps it is even better that things turned out this way. Al Benqura will feel guilty at the actions of his daughter so be more willing to concede some points still to be agreed upon. Help me and I will do something in return for you."

Mixed feelings washed through her. She could never pull off being a woman of interest to a dynamic man like Rashid al Harum. She'd be spotted for a fraud the first time she ventured out. Yet the thought of being escorted around by him had her stomach flipping over in giddy anticipation. She'd never have this kind of chance again.

She had only seconds to make a decision.

Jess stepped to the door. "Everything okay?" he asked.

Rashid did not look away from Bethanne. Her gaze met his, seeking assurance that if she complied with this wild scheme, it would end up all right for all.

"Everything is fine," she said at last, hoping she wasn't making a monumental mistake.

There was an almost imperceptible change in the sheikh's manner. Had he doubted her? Well, he should. If not for her goal of finding her father, she would have categorically denied his request. Or maybe thought about it a bit longer. She had trouble looking away.

The sheikh spun around. "There is no need for you to remain. We can get you on a plane within the hour to return to the United States." The sheikh summoned the other man still standing at the foot of the stairs. In only seconds, Sheikh Rashid al Harum had given him orders.

One less person who would know about the charade, Bethanne thought. She was still a bit bemused with the entire matter. This man knew what he wanted and went for it without hesitation.

"Bethanne?" Jess said, looking between her and the sheikh as if suspecting something was amiss.

"I'll be fine. Just a few details to work out. If you can get on a plane within the hour, you better take advantage of the flight."

"In the meantime, I will examine the interior and cockpit," Rashid said.

Jess came closer to Bethanne when Rashid went to inspect the rear of the plane. "Is everything really okay? What happened to the fiancée?" he whispered.

"Um, change of plans."

Jess still appeared doubtful, but he nodded and turned to retrieve his bag from where he'd stashed it. With one more look down the cabin, he turned and left with the sheikh's man.

The sheikh peered out of one of the side windows and watched as Jess entered the car that had been waiting and was soon heading for the main section of the busy airport.

He nodded as if in satisfaction and headed for the front of the plane.

"I assume you have your own bags," he said.

She nodded and pointed out the small travel case she used.

"You travel light."

"It carries enough clothes for me. Two more uniforms like the one I'm wearing. And some off-duty outfits. I have reservations at a hotel in the heart of the city," she said.

"You were planning to stay in Quishari for a while?"

"Yes. I've heard about it for years. Have pictures and books and pamphlets about the beaches, the history and the stark desert dwellings. I'm quite looking forward to learning more first-hand. I think I'm already in love with the country."

"Where did you learn this?" he asked.

"From my father, Hank Pendarvis."

For a moment she wondered at the change in attitude of the sheikh. His face tightened as it had when he learned of Haile's defection.

"Your name is Sanders," he said.

"My stepfather's name. My mother remarried when I was young and he adopted me. We do not get along. My father has been missing for three years."

"He is a thief. He stole one of our planes."

She blinked. "That's a lie!" Her father was not a thief.

"So you are the daughter of a thief." Rashid shook his head.

"No, I'm not. That's not true. My father would never steal anything—especially from your family. He wrote how he loved working for Bashiri Oil and for Sheikh Rabid al Harum."

"My father. Who died when he learned of Hank's theft."

Bethanne felt sick. Was it possible? No, not her father. She hadn't seen much of him over the years, but she had scads of letters. And he'd phoned her once a week for most of her life. Whenever he was in the States, he came to visit. They flew over Texas, had picnics in meadows and spent time at the beach together. She loved those visits when her father would tell her of the ideal life he enjoyed flying for the senior al Harum.

She raised her chin. "You are wrong."

Rashid uttered a word in Arabic she did not understand. But the intent was clear. He did not like this situation at all. Did he want to change the role she was to play?

He leaned forward, anger radiating from him. "My family has been hurt by yours already. Do not betray me in this charade or it will be the worst for you. I am stuck—temporarily—but do not think I shall forget for an instant."

"If you want my help, you need to make good your offer to do something for me in return."

"And that is?" he asked, his demeanor suddenly suspicious.

"Help me find my father."

He stared at her for a long moment, then stepped to the door. He gestured to someone on the ground and the man entered a moment later. He lifted Bethanne's carry-on bag and went back.

"Agreed. But if we find him, the law will take care of him."

"Not if he didn't steal a plane," she countered. She wasn't sure if she was relieved or stressed at the thought of being the sheikh's girlfriend. But if it helped her to find her father, she would make the best of it.

"So we begin," the sheikh said and stepped to the top step.

Bethanne followed, Fatima behind her. There were now several men in suits at the bottom of the stairs and they came to attention as the sheikh appeared. Bethanne felt caught in a dream. She glided down the stairs and before she knew it, she was in the back of a stretch limousine that seemed to take up a city block. It was a luxurious machine, gleaming white beneath the hot sun, with fancy gold Arabic script on the doors. When she stepped inside, Bethanne was delighted with the cold air that greeted her. Fatima rode in front beside the driver. Rashid slid onto the wide backseat with her. A few words and the driver had the glass wall slide up, separating them from the front of the vehicle.

She glanced at the sheikh as they drove away. He flipped on a cell phone and was speaking rapidly, the Arabic words beyond her. He didn't look like he was taking all the air in the car, but she felt breathless. Gazing out the window, she tried to quell her riotous emotions. She could reach out and touch him—had she the right? Clenching her hands into fists, she refused to give way to the clamoring attention his presence demanded. He thought her father was a thief. How dare he! She had best remember this was only a game of pretense while he went after that oil deal.

For her part, he agreed to help her find her father. It would be worth it in the end as long as she kept her head.

Fruitless daydreams of a relationship between them would contribute nothing. She had to keep focused and ignore the awareness that seemed to grow the longer she was around him.

Hank Pendarvis had disappeared three years ago. She feared he was dead. Her mother, long ago divorced and remarried, had tried to obtain information from the oil company for which he flew— the one owned by the sheikh—but her inquiries had produced no results. Bethanne had tried letters to people her father had mentioned over the years, but only one had gone through and that person had not known anything beyond Hank had flown away one day and never returned.

Bethanne missed the larger-than-life man, her secret hero from childhood. He'd been the one to spark her interest in flying, her passion for exploring new places, meeting new people. He would not have ignored her this long if he were alive.

Sad as it was to think of him as dead, she wanted closure. To know what happened to him. And if he were dead, where he lay. She tried to convince herself he was dead or would have contacted her. But the faint hope he was just caught up in something could not be quenched. Until she knew, she hoped he was still alive somewhere.

"We are here," Rashid said.

Bethanne blinked and turned her head to peer out his window as the car slowed and turned into the wide driveway that led to a beautiful white villa. A stunning expanse of green grass blanketed the area in front of the structure. It looked like an Italian home or French Riviera villa. Nothing like what she expected in an Arabic country.

"Wow," she murmured softly. The home was amazing. Two stories tall with a wraparound veranda on both levels, its white walls gleamed in the sunshine. The red terra cotta roof sloped down, providing cover to the upper veranda which in turn shaded the lower level. Tall French doors opened from every room.

The driveway curved around in front, flanked by banks of blue and gold flowers. The chauffeur slowed to a stop in front of wide double doors, with wooden panels carved in ornate designs. The heavy wrought-iron handles added substance. The right door opened even before the car stopped. A tall man wearing traditional robes stepped outside and hastened down the shallow steps to open the passenger door.

The sheikh stepped out and returned the man's greetings.

"Mohammad, this is Ms. Sanders. She has come to stay for a while as my special guest," he said in English.

Less than five minutes later Bethanne stood alone in the large bedroom that had been assigned to her. It held a huge canopy bed in the center, complete with steps to the high mattress. The chandelier in the center of the ceiling sparkled in the light streaming in through the open French doors. Gauzy curtains gently swayed in the light breeze.

Two sets of French doors gave access to the wide upper veranda. She stepped outside and immediately inhaled the tang of the sea mixed with the fragrance of hundreds of flowers blossoming beneath her. She crossed to the railing and gazed at the profusion of colors and shapes in the garden below. A wide path led from the garden toward the sea, a glimpse of which she could see from where she stood. Walking along the veranda toward the Gulf, she was enchanted to find a better vantage point at the corner with a clear view to a sugar-white beach and the lovely blue water.

The maid who had shown her to her room had thankfully spoken English. She told Bethanne her name was Minnah while she unpacked the few articles of clothing in the small bag and asked if Bethanne had more luggage coming.

At a loss, she merely shook her head and continued staring at the garden.

She'd have to suggest to the sheikh that a woman coming to visit would bring more than a handful of uniforms and an assortment of casual clothes. This stupid plan of his would never work. What did he hope to achieve? Save the embarrassment of people learning his intended bride had run away rather than go through with a marriage? Get the business deal completed without anyone knowing how insulting Haile al Benqura's actions had been?

She had no idea of how long he expected this charade to last. So any investigations for her father needed to be done swiftly in case her visit was cut radically short. The sheikh had canceled her reservations at the hotel. She wondered if she should make new ones, just in case.

After she'd changed and freshened up, Bethanne headed back down the way she'd come. The villa wasn't as large as she first thought. Probably only eight bedroom suites. She almost laughed at the thought. Her tiny apartment in Galveston would squeeze into her assigned bedroom here.

She didn't see a soul as she went back to the front door and let herself out. The limo was gone. The lawn stretched out to a tall flowering hedge of oleander, sheltering the house from any view from the street.

Following the lower veranda to the path she'd seen, Bethanne walked through the garden and out to the beach. There were several chairs and tables on the white sand near the edge of the garden. She could sit and relax after her walk.

In the distance she saw a large container ship slowly moving through the Gulf. Happily Bethanne walked to the water's edge, kicked off her shoes and started walking north. Her mind was already formulating where she could begin with her inquiries. When she returned to the villa, she'd summons the maid to begin with her. Had her father ever visited the house? Maybe the staff would remember him. She wanted answers and didn't plan to leave Quishari until she had them. Neither the difficulty of the task nor language barrier would stop her!

"What's got you upset?" Khalid asked from his position lounging on one of the chairs in Rashid's office at Bashiri Oil. The corner office had a splendid view of Alkaahdar and the Gulf. On the highest floor of the building, it rose above most other buildings in the capital city and gave an unimpeded view.

Rashid paced to the tall window and glared at the cityscape, annoyed afresh that his brother had picked up on his irritation. It was not new. Twins had an uncanny intuition concerning each other. Rashid could recognize his brother's moods in a second. Of course Khalid could recognize his.

He knew he had to contact Haile's father. The longer he delayed, the more awkward it would become. Did the man know yet his daughter had run off? Had he known about the other man all along and still expected Haile to consider marriage to him?

He turned from the window and met his brother's eyes. Khalid had the knack of instant relaxation. And then instant action when called for. He was slouched on one of the visitor chairs. Rashid noted his brother was wearing a suit again, instead of the more traditional robes. A concession to being in the city. First chance he had, Rashid knew his brother would head for the interior or the derricks along the coast to the south. Khalid was not one for society or social niceties.

For a second he debated trying the charade on his twin. But it would not take long for Khalid to figure things out. Besides, they had never lied to each other.

"It appears the glowing bride-to-be is glowing for someone else."

"Huh?" Khalid sat up at that. "What do you mean?"

"She never arrived."

"I heard she did and that she's blonde and tall and you whisked her away to keep her from the prying eyes of everyone."

"The rumor mill is even faster than I knew. That's the idea. Haile never arrived. I want to finalize the deal with al Benqura before letting the world know I've been stood up. You know what the minister would say if he found out. This deal's too important to me to let some flighty woman screw it up." Briefly Rashid outlined the situation.

"What does al Benqura say to his daughter's no-show?" Khalid asked.

"I'm not sure he knows."

"And the blonde you escorted from the plane?"

"I hope a substitute until the deal is done."

"Where did you conjure her up?"

"Turns out she's the pilot delivering my new plane—that was supposed to bring Haile. She thought Haile was on board and was as surprised as I was to discover she was not."

"Ah, yes, the new jet you're buying. The pilot is a woman? That's odd."

"Or providence in this situation."

"And she agreed to this charade? What am I saying, of course she did. How much for her silence?"

Rashid shrugged. "So far no monetary demands. But a twist I never expected. She's Hank Pendarvis's daughter."

"What?" Khalid sat up at that. "You're kidding. I didn't even know he had a family."

"And she's looking for her father."

Khalid sat up in his chair. "He took that jet some years ago."

"And disappeared. Apparently starting life anew, he cut all ties with his past. She wants to know what happened. As do we all."

Khalid shrugged. "Don't get in too deep," he warned. "I wouldn't trust her, if I were you." He shifted slightly and tilted his head in a manner that reminded Rashid of his own mannerisms when confronted by questionable behavior. "Are you sure she won't give away the scheme at the first chance? European tabloids would love such a story. And she has nothing to lose and lots of money to gain."

"So far she seems more interested in searching for her father than acquiring anything. But I will keep in mind her relationship to Hank."

Rashid glanced back out the window, but he knew he wasn't fooling his twin. That Bethanne would refuse to cooperate was a true risk. One he was willing to take to insure the finalization of the deal he had been working on for months. He needed the support of the ministry to finalize the deal of such magnitude. Otherwise he wouldn't care two figs about the minister's position.

He was not going to tell his brother how he had grown to regret agreeing to an engagement that had been so strongly encouraged between his mother and al Benqura. Haile had the perfect background to be his wife. And after his aborted attempt to marry the woman of his choice when he was twenty-two, Haile seemed more than suitable.

He also was not going to mention the flash of desire that had surprised him when he met Bethanne. She was so different from the women he knew. If asked for a type, he would have said he preferred petite and dark, with brown eyes and a lush figure. Bethanne didn't meet a single criterion. She was tall, blonde, blue eyes and almost as slender as a boy.

But that didn't stop his interest. Which hadn't waned even when learning she was Hank's daughter. There could be nothing between them. Not once the relationship was made known. In the meantime, he hoped they could carry on until the oil deal was signed.

"I hope you know what you're doing," Khalid said. "I'm off to the south for a few days. I want to check out the pipeline from the number four oil rig. There's a leak somewhere and so far no one's found it. If it catches fire, there'll be hell to pay." Khalid rose. "Maybe I should take the new jet and vet it for you."

"It's my new toy. Get one of your own."

Khalid's sarcastic snort of laughter conveyed his amusement. "Don't need one. I use the company's," he said, referring to the fleet of small aircraft the oil company owned.

"You don't have to have hands-on surveillance

of the rigs," Rashid said. "And if there is a fire, let someone else deal with it."

"Hey, that's my job."

He and Khalid had this conversation a dozen times a month. He glanced at his brother, his gaze focused briefly on the disfiguring swath of scar tissue running from his right cheek down his neck to disappear beneath his shirt collar. The oil fire that had caused the damage had eventually been extinguished—by Khalid himself. The devastation hadn't stopped him from turning his back on office work and continuing in the oil fields. His elite company of oil firefighters was in high demand whenever an oil fire broke out.

Both of them had inherited wealth when their father had died. Both had a strong sense of obligation to the family oil business. Rashid preferred to hire competent help for routine tasks. He loved dealing in the world markets. But his twin had always found the drilling sites fascinating. Not to mention finding the conflagrations that could ruin a site a challenge to extinguish. Khalid drove their mother crazy with concern.

The phone rang.

"Did she arrive?" His mother's voice sounded in his ear.

Khalid gave a mock bow and left his brother to the phone call.

"My guest arrived and is staying at Grand-

mother's villa," Rashid said. Another front to deal
with. His mother had been instrumental in the arrangement of the alliance with Haile. She herself
had had an arranged marriage and she wanted her
sons to follow the old ways.

"I can't wait to meet her. I know you were
hesitant about this arrangement, but it'll work out
for the best for all. Plan to bring her to dinner
tonight."

"Ah, I believe you misunderstood me, Mother,"
he said. The charade started now. "Haile had other
plans. My guest is Bethanne Sanders. Someone I
know from Starcraft." When concocting a mag-
nificent lie, it was best to stick as close to the truth
as possible.

"What do you mean?" He heard the bewilderment in her tone.

"I will be happy to bring Bethanne to meet you
tomorrow. For tonight, we wish to be together.
She's had a long flight and is tired."

"But Haile? What of her?"

"I'll explain when we meet," he said.

"Rashid, don't be impetuous."

He almost laughed. It had been years since he'd
been impetuous. His brief aborted love for
Marguerite when he'd been younger had ended
that streak. Now he kept careful control of his
emotions and actions. "Rest assured, Mother, I do
not plan to repeat the past."

When the call ended, he reached for the folder on the new jet. He needed to know more about the woman he had ensconced at the villa and quickly. His assistant had approved the requests for visas for both pilots. He took the photograph of Bethanne and stepped closer to the window, his curiosity raised. Blond hair, blue eyes, tall for a woman. A standard passport photo, yet the playfulness lurking in the depths of her blue eyes contrasted with the severe hairstyle, pulled back probably into a ponytail. He'd seen the anger flash in her eyes on the plane. And the shrewd bargaining to help find her father. Was Khalid right, she would be looking for some way to gain money or prestige from the charade?

She didn't look very old. Yet he knew she had to be experienced. Starcraft was an established firm that didn't take chances with the multimillion-dollar aircrafts it built.

How novel to have a woman pilot. Had that fact made the rumor mill yet? He put the photo back, wondering what the financial minister was making of the situation. Rashid had to make sure he did not learn the true circumstances until the deal was consummated. Or even then, if he could help it.

For a moment he remembered their meeting on the plane. She had caught his attention instantly. She was far different from anyone he knew. Wasn't it his luck she was off-limits because of her father. He would love to explore the attraction he felt when he first saw her standing proudly at the top of the stairs. But as the daughter of a thief, he could not let himself enjoy their relationship. He needed to be on guard for any nefarious activity on her part. The apple never fell far from the tree. Was she also not to be trusted?

Hank had worked for his father for many years when he stole the latest jet in their fleet. What had caused his actions? They'd probably never know unless they found him. But he'd watch his daughter. Their family would not be caught unawares a second time.

He was in a tight spot—balancing the minister on one hand, his mother's interest on another, and needing to keep his guest visible enough to satisfy curiosity, and secluded enough to insure she could not threaten the situation.

In addition, he was now committed to delving into the old business of the theft of their plane. Three years ago, when his father died, Rashid had stepped into his place at the oil company. Khalid had worked on locating Hank and the plane—with no tangible results. They'd accepted the loss and moved on. Would they have any more success now?

CHAPTER TWO

BETHANNE wondered how much of the beach she was walking on belonged to the sheikh. She had not seen any sign of other people as she walked, and she estimated she'd gone almost a mile. The water was warm on her feet. The sand swished around her toes as the spent waves swirled around them. She wished she'd worn a hat or something; the sun was burning hot on her head. She was reluctant to return, however. The walk was soothing and just touching the ground where her father might have once stood gave her a connected feeling that had been missing a long time. She could imagine she'd run into him and they'd both express surprise and immediately begin talking and catching up. Then she'd realize he'd been extremely busy and had not died alone and unlamented somewhere unknown, but had simply let time slip by. He had never done so before, but Bethanne clung to hope.

Finally she turned to retrace her steps. Glad she'd left her shoes above the tide line as an indicator of where to return, she studied the lush vegetation that bordered the beach. The villa was almost invisible from the shore. When she caught a glimpse of it, she also saw someone sitting in one of the chairs near the path.

Her heart rate increased as she walked closer. Even before she could recognize him, she knew it was Sheikh Rashid al Harum. Rashid. She said the name softly. He rose as she approached, watching her. Conscious of her windblown hair, sandy feet, khaki pants rolled up to her knees, she knew she must appear a sight. Why couldn't she have brought a dress that would look feminine and sexy? No, she had to be practical. What would he think?

"Did you enjoy your walk?" he asked.

She nodded, leaning over to roll down her pants and dust the sand off first one foot and then the other. Slipping on her shoes, she wished she had worn sandals. Glancing at her watch, she saw she'd been gone longer than she realized. It was approaching the dinner hour.

"It's quite lovely," she said, standing again. "I'd like to go swimming while I'm here."

"My brother and I enjoyed the beach when we were children. The villa used to belong to my grandmother. It's been a long time since I've gone swimming here."

End of conversation. She cast around for something else to say. But the topic she wanted to discuss was, of course, the charade he'd insisted upon. So—

"I don't think this is going to work," she said.

"Because?"

"I've had time to think about it. No one's going to believe you have fallen for some jet jockey from America. First of all, where would we have met? Then, let's face it, I'm no femme fatale."

His gaze skimmed over her. Bethanne felt her blood heat. She wished she could read minds. What did he think when he looked at her? When he again met her eyes, he smiled.

Bethanne's heart flipped over. The way his eyes crinkled with that smile had her fascinated. It changed his entire demeanor. He was the best-looking man she'd ever met. He had to know the effect he had on women. On her.

Flustered, she tried to appear unaffected, but suspected the color rising in her cheeks gave her away.

"You look like you could be most intriguing, with the right clothing."

"And that's another thing. I would not have come to visit bringing only uniforms and casual clothes! I expected to be searching for my father, not going anywhere where I needed to look like I could attract a sheikh."

He laughed. "Even in your casual clothes, people would know why you would attract a sheikh. But clothing is easily remedied. In fact, I took the liberty of having some dresses sent to your room. Please accept as a token of my appreciation for your help."

"Help? You practically kidnapped me." What had he meant by *people would know why you would attract a sheikh?* Did he like the way she looked?

"Hardly that. You agreed to help in exchange for my resuming the search for your father. I don't think we'll turn up anything at this late date, but I will make some inquiries."

Bethanne considered the terms. She was not going to stop believing in her father just on the sheikh's say-so. She knew her father would never betray anyone. Still, any help would be appreciated. "Okay, it's your party. If you think we can fool people, good luck."

"You underestimate yourself. No one will ever doubt that I could be interested."

"Nicely said. Maybe there is a ghost of a chance," she said. Her heart rate increased with his compliment. And the look in his eyes. Definite interest.

"Dinner will be served at seven. Perhaps you would join me on the veranda then?" he asked.

"Thank you, I should be delighted." She nodded

regally and swept by, wishing she wore a lovely dress and didn't have sand chafing her feet.

Bethanne gazed at the closet full of clothes five minutes later. Rashid's last words echoed in her mind. No one could doubt he could be interested if she wore some of these dresses. How had he arranged to have so many different ones delivered in the few hours since he deposited her at the villa?

Duh, money can accomplish anything, she thought as she fingered the light silks and linens. She pulled out a blue dress that matched her eyes.

Pampering herself with a luxurious bath and then paying careful attention to her hair and makeup, Bethanne felt a bit like she'd imagine Cinderella felt dressing for the ball.

Fatima had knocked on the door as she was slipping on the dress. She smiled and nodded, saying something in Arabic that Bethanne didn't understand. But the universal signs of approval were obvious. What had the sheikh told this woman about their charade?

The blue of the dress did indeed enhance the color of her eyes. During her walk the sun had tinted her skin with a light tan and the constant hint of excitement at the thought of dining with a sheikh had her on tenterhooks and brought additional color to her cheeks.

Descending the stairs shortly before seven, she wished Rashid were at the bottom to see her descend. The designer dress hugged her figure and made her feel as sexy as a French movie star. She hoped it would replace the image he had of her windblown and disheveled from her walk.

Reaching the ground floor, she headed toward the sound of male voices. She entered a formal sitting room a moment later, just as the butler left. She took a deep breath, dismayed to find her stomach full of butterflies and her palms growing damp. Why this sudden attack of nerves? He was the same. Nothing had changed. But she felt as if the stakes had been rachetted up a notch. She had to find her father to prove his innocence. It became important that the sheikh not think she came from a dishonored family.

As if sensing her arrival, the sheikh turned.

"Thank you for the dress. It's more than expected and quite lovely," Bethanne said quickly, her words almost too fast to understand. Her heart rate tripled and she gripped her poise and tried to act as if she were comfortable greeting Arabian sheikhs every day.

"It is of no consequence. I hope your stay in Quishari will be enjoyable. If you need anything while here at the villa, do ask."

"I look forward to seeing Quishari while I'm here. Since I assume I'll have some free time while you're at work, perhaps you could recommend a guide who speaks English? If I can hire a car, I can explore on my own. I've heard so much about the country for years. I can't believe I'm here." Or at least under these circumstances. Her father had loved Quishari. She knew she would as well.

"I shall put one of my drivers and cars at your disposal. Do allow me to show you the major sights of my country. I am anxious to try out the plane. If you would fly it for me, we can put it through its paces tomorrow."

"I'd love to. I am at your service," she said, feeling almost giddy with the thought she might actually fly where her father had flown. And find time to talk to maintenance men who might know what happened to him. She was a bit surprised the al Harum family had not done more to pursue the issue. Had they merely dismissed it as casual theft and written off a plane? she wondered.

Perhaps in the greater scheme of things, it didn't cost much from their perspective. But she would have thought Rashid the type to go after someone who had done him wrong and make sure justice triumphed.

"Then I will see that you have every opportunity to explore. I'm quite proud of our heritage and history. Some of the architecture in the old section of town is renowned."

"I look forward to seeing it all." In truth, she never expected Rashid to spend a moment with her if not in a public forum in an attempt to discourage gossip.

"Did the dresses fit?"

She loved hearing that deep, melodious voice with its trace of British accent. Why were Americans such suckers for accents? Her Southern drawl sounded out of place in the posh cosmopolitan sitting room with elaborate brocade sofas and antiques dating back centuries.

"The ones I tried on fit perfectly. I loved this one the best."

"It was the color of your eyes," he said.

She caught her breath. Had he noticed enough to request this special color? She searched his eyes for a hint of the truth, but though he looked at her for a long moment, his expression gave nothing away. He'd be terrific at high-stakes poker.

"I thought from your visa photo that you seemed young to be an experienced pilot. Now it appears you're far too feminine to fly planes."

"I've had plenty of training." She didn't know whether to be flattered at the subtle compliment or defensive for her abilities. Did he think women weren't as capable as men to pilot aircrafts?

"You graduated from the U.S. Air Force Academy, took flight training and flew a number of fixed wing crafts and helicopters while serving," Rashid said. "I read your background sent from Starcraft."

"You needn't worry I can't handle your new jet."

He laughed, amusement dancing in his eyes. "I never doubted it. You brought it safely from the United States. Come, dinner will be ready by now." He offered his arm to Bethanne. She took it, feeling awkward. She was more at ease in the casual restaurants she normally patronized than dining with an Arabian sheikh. But her experiences taught her how to meet every challenge— even this one.

Dinner proved to be less disconcerting than she'd expected. Once seated, the conversation centered around the new jet, its performance and the enhancements Rashid had ordered. After they ate, Rashid insisted they share hot tea on the veranda overlooking the garden. By the time it grew dark, Bethanne was glad to retreat to her bedroom. It had been a long day. One that had not ended as expected.

He bid her good-night at the foot of the stairs and even as she climbed them, he left the villa. The sound of his car faded as she shut her bedroom door.

Bethanne twirled around the large room in sheer joy. She felt as if she were a part of a fairy tale. Handsome sheikh, beautiful setting, lovely clothes and nothing to do but fly a plane at his whim. Could life be any better?

Falling asleep to the soft soughing of the sea relaxed Bethanne like nothing else. Before dropping off, she vowed she'd begin her search for her father tomorrow. But for tonight, she wanted to think about the dashing sheikh who chose her for his special guest—if only temporarily.

Minnah awakened Bethanne the next morning when she entered the bedroom carrying a tray of fragrant hot chocolate and a basket of fresh pastries and croissants. Breakfast in bed was not a luxury Bethanne enjoyed often and she plumped up her pillows and took the heavy silver tray on her lap with delight. There was an English newspaper folded neatly on one side.

"Thank you," she said as the woman went to the French doors to open them wide to the fresh morning breeze.

"I will bring you bathing suits after your breakfast. His Excellency suggested you'd like a swim before starting your day." The maid's English was practically flawless. "Later a driver will pick you up to take you to the airport. His Excellency is anxious to fly in the new plane."

"Sounds like a plan," Bethanne said, already savoring the rich dark chocolate taste of the hot beverage. The feeling of being a princess living in the height of luxury continued. But she dare not waste a moment.

"Before you leave," she said to Minnah, "did you know Hank Pendarvis? He was also a pilot for the sheikh. Or at least the oil company."

The maid tilted her head slightly as she tried to remember. Finally she shook her head slightly. "I do not know him."

That would have been too easy, Bethanne thought. She thanked her and resumed eating breakfast.

Selecting a one-piece blue swimsuit from her new wardrobe a short time later, she donned the accompanying cover-up and headed for the beach. A short swim would be perfect. It was warm enough to enjoy the water without the blazing heat that would rise later in the day. Fatima accompanied her. She had been informed of Bethanne's plans by the maid. For the time being, Minnah would act as the go-between. Bethanne wondered how she'd learned English. When they reached the beach, Fatima sat on one of the chairs near the edge, apparently content to watch from a distance.

Feeling pampered and spoiled, Bethanne relished each sensation as her day started so differently from normal. Shedding the cover-up near the chairs, she ran to the water, plunging in. It was warm and buoyant. Giving in to the pleasure the sea

brought, she swam and floated and thoroughly
enjoyed herself. She had a goal to reach and a job
to do. But for a few moments, she felt carefree and
happy.

At the airport an hour later, Bethanne's attitude
changed from bemused delight to efficient com-
mander. She talked to the ground crew through a
translator the sheikh had provided, reviewing
items on the checklist. She listened to how they
had refueled the aircraft. She did a visual inspection of the jet. She wasn't sure when the sheikh
would want to take the maiden flight, but she was
ready when he was. Now she had nothing to do
but await his arrival.

She beckoned the translator over. "Can you ask
among the crew if any of them knew Hank
Pendarvis? He was a pilot and probably flew from
this airport," she said.

He nodded and walked back to the group of
men.

Two spoke to his question and both looked over
at Bethanne. Breaking away from the rest, the two
men and the translator walked to her.

"These men knew him. He was a pilot for His
Excellency's father, Sheikh Rabid al Harum."

"Is he dead?" she asked bluntly, studying the
two men who had known her father.

One man looked away when the question was

posed in Arabic. The other looked sad and shook his head at Bethanne, speaking rapidly.

"It is unfortunate, but it appears he has vanished. Was he a friend of yours?"

Bethanne didn't want to reveal her connection to all and sundry. "An acquaintance. I heard he had a job in Quishari and hoped to look him up while I am here."

There was lengthy conversation between the three men, with a couple of glances thrown her way as the one man grew quite passionate.

Finally the translator turned to her. "The man was a pilot. One day he took a plane without permission. He never returned. It is surmised he either flew to another country or the plane crashed. No one has heard from him in almost three years. And the plane has not flown over Quishari skies since then."

She wanted to protest that her father was not a thief, but these men confirmed what Rashid had said. But it couldn't be. Her father was nothing like that. He was loyal to the al Harum family. Loved his job. He would not risk it to steal a plane, no matter what the provocation.

"Did they search for a crashed plane?" she asked, holding on to her composure with effort. Had no one been concerned when he disappeared? Had they so quickly condemned him as a thief that no one searched in case there had been an accident? Her heart ached. Her father had to be dead. He would have contacted her long before now if he could have. She refused to believe he stole the plane.

Another bout of conversation and then one of the men shrugged and turned to walk back to the group. The other continued talking and then watched Bethanne when the translator told her a search was impossible when no one knew where he'd gone. The desert was vast, uninhabited for the most part. Without knowing the direction he'd taken, it was fruitless to search.

"And no one knew why he took the flight?" she asked. How far could she push without giving away her avid interest?

"He was pilot to the old sheikh who died shortly after the man disappeared. His son had no knowledge of the reason he took the plane. There is no more," he ended sadly.

"Thank you." She forced a smile at the man who had conveyed the information. Refusing to let her dismay show, she walked back to the plane.

She wished she had some time alone to assimilate the cold facts. What would have compelled her father to take a plane if not authorized? He hadn't owned a plane, just flew for whoever hired him. Where could he have been going? Why was there no debris if he'd crashed? Someone flying over an accident site must have seen it. Maybe he'd flown off the normal route. Maybe he had not filed a flight plan and no one knew where to look. Yet, how could he have flown without filing a plan? She'd had to fill out enough paper to fill a box when requesting routes into Quishari. Even this morning when saying she wanted to take the jet up, she'd had to fill out a half-dozen forms.

She entered the plane and wandered through the sumptuous cabin. The interior had been designed to the specifications requested by Rashid al Harum. She sat on the sofa, encased in comfort. The microsuede fabric was sensuous to the touch, feeling like velvet. The thick Persian rug on the floor felt sumptuous beneath her feet. She'd like to take off her shoes and scrunch her toes in the luxury. It was like a fine drawing room. The only time she flew, when not piloting an aircraft, she was crammed into the cheapest seats possible returning to base. What would it be like to fly high above the earth in such elegant furnishings? Nothing like the flights she knew.

For a moment she imagined herself sitting next to the sheikh as they cruised high above the Arabian desert. He'd offer her a beverage. They'd sit close together, heads bent toward each other, enjoying each other's company.

Rashid Al Harum entered, ducking his head slightly to clear the lintel. He looked surprised to see her.

Bethanne jumped to her feet instantly, her face growing warm with embarrassment. Bad enough to be daydreaming, but to be caught sitting as if she had nothing to do was problematic.

"I'm sorry. I just took a moment to test the sofa," she said in a rush. She had no business imagining herself as a guest aboard this lovely plane. She was here to work!

"And is it as comfortable as it looks?" he asked, taking her presence in the cabin of the plane instead of the cockpit with equanimity.

"Fabulous. The seat belts are discreet. I feel like I'm in a small living room somewhere. I hope it meets your expectations." She stepped toward the front of the plane, hoping to squeeze by, but his presence filled the narrow space.

"If you're ready to depart, I'll begin the pre-flight checklist," she said, overwhelmed a bit by his proximity. It wasn't only his sheer masculinity, which made her feel quite feminine, it was the way he carried himself—with all the confidence in the world. And his good looks would give anyone a run for his money. Tall, dark and handsome was such a cliché—and now Bethanne knew exactly why. He looked like the dream of every young woman anywhere with his fabulous features, dark hair and chiseled lips that she'd like to touch hers just once.

Get a grip, girl, she admonished herself. They

would never have met in other circumstances. And the only thing he wanted to touch was the fancy furnishing of his new jet. Or the signed copy of the contract for the deal he was working on.

To further her efforts to return to reality instead of indulging in fantasy, she reminded herself the man thought her father a thief. But instead of putting a damper on things, it strengthened her resolve to find her father to clear his name. For his sake, and for hers. She wanted Rashid to think well of her no matter what.

He stepped aside and Bethanne squeezed by, careful to make sure she didn't touch however much tempted. Breathless with the encounter, she hurried to the pilot's seat and sank down, grateful for the few moments' solitude. She ran through the preflight checklist in the cockpit, hoping she could concentrate on flying and not have her mind winging its way back to the cabin and the sexiest man she'd ever encountered.

"Ready when you are," Rashid said, slipping into the second seat a few minutes later.

"You want to fly up here?" she squeaked.

"Why wouldn't I? Wouldn't a man want to spend time with his special friend?"

She glanced out the window at the scurry of activity in preparation for departure. The ground crew could easily see into the cockpit. Of course he wanted to bolster the conception they were involved.

"Okay. Ever flown up front before?"

"From time to time."

In only minutes they were shooting into the sky, the power of the rear engines thrusting them effortlessly into the air. Bethanne had no trouble focusing on the controls. The best part of everything was soaring above the earth. She had calculated the route south along the coast and had it approved by ground control. Flying for one of the top businessmen in the country gave her special privileges not normally afforded.

Slowly Bethanne leveled out and then gradually climbed to their cruising altitude. She prided herself on her smooth flights. The smaller planes were more susceptible to variations in air currents. Today was all about showing off how smoothly the jet rode.

Once they reached cruising level, Rashid nodded. "Good ride."

For a few moments, she'd forgotten he was there. Now, suddenly the space seemed to shrink. The scent of aftershave lotion the sheikh used tickled her nose and made her heart beat faster. She kept her eyes ahead, but could still envision every inch of his face as if he had put a photograph in front of her.

"Do you fly?" she asked.

"No. I leave that to the experts. But I sit up here with my pilot sometimes. I like the panoramic views which I don't get from only one side of the airplane. And I like the feeling of freedom. Must be one reason you enjoy it."

"The primary reason, I guess. It's fabulous." She wished her pulse would slow.

"Unusual profession for a woman, at least in Quishari."

"Not that many women pilots in the U.S., but we're growing in numbers."

"Did you always want to fly?"

She nodded. "From when I was a little girl. It was always magical to me. Soaring high above the earth. My dad—" She stopped abruptly. "Sorry, I'm rambling on."

"If I didn't want to learn more, I wouldn't have asked the question. Your father got you interested?"

She nodded stiffly, still feeling raw with what she'd learned this morning. She wanted to defend him to the sheikh. But she had only a daughter's loyalty to offer. She needed more facts.

"I, too, am following in my father's footsteps. He and my uncles built the oil company to the stature it is today before they died. The loss of them has been a tragedy for my family. My father built an empire through hard work and integrity. My brother and I and one remaining uncle are hoping to build it to even new levels."

"Lofty plans. From what I know, Bashiri Oil is already a leader."

"I hope to be remembered as my father is—someone with vision and the ability to achieve results."

Rashid was charming, Bethanne thought to herself. It was probably second nature to him, which would go a long way in achieving his ends.

"So how is our charade going? No accusations of impossibility?" she asked.

"No one would dare question my word," he said.

"Good."

"My mother expects us for dinner tonight. I accepted on behalf of both of us."

"She'll spot the incongruity."

"I fully expect her to question you about everything. It's up to you to make sure you allay any suspicions. One thing to keep in mind, if she discovers who your father was, she will never believe the relationship."

She resented his suggesting she would be less than worthy of being considered as a wife for the sheikh because of her father.

"I have done nothing wrong. And I don't believe my father has, either."

"Nevertheless, don't volunteer that information."

The sooner she found out the truth, the better, Bethanne fumed.

"Down there, circle around," he said.

Spotting a chain of oil rigs off the shore, she angled down slightly. "Are those the rigs you wanted to see?" One in the distance seemed to shimmer in the heat, gold flames reaching high. "Is that one on fire?" she asked in disbelief as they flew closer.

"Damn. I was hoping it wasn't. If Khalid is in the midst of it, I'll skin him alive."

She blinked at the vehemence of his tone. Who was Khalid? Did Rashid suspect the man had started the fire?

She contacted air traffic control to alert them to her altered plan, then began a wide sweep to the right around the chain of derricks. The last one in the line billowed flames, easily seen from their height. How frightening it would be if they were closer.

"How do you put out oil fires?" she asked, keeping a distance from where the heated air would be rising. Even at this distance they rocked slightly from the thermals.

"Best left to the experts. Which Khalid is. Not that it's any guarantee of his safety."

"And Khalid is?" she asked quietly, taking in his tenseness as he stared at the scene below.

"My brother."

"Oh."

Bethanne made the wide circle twice, then Rashid told her to return to the airport. "I need a phone."

"Don't forget this aircraft is equipped with the latest in satellite technology," she said, feeling a bit like an ad on television.

"I had, thank you." He rose and headed for the back of the plane.

"Whoosh," Bethanne said, feeling the atmosphere around her grow lighter with him gone. She hoped Khalid wasn't in the thick of things or he was sure to get the full brunt of his brother's anger.

How odd that his brother fought fires. They had more than enough money to hire the best. Why put his life on the line?

She wished she knew more about Rashid and his family. Her father had held the family in high esteem. He had enjoyed working for them, although he hadn't told her much about them. She couldn't deny she was attracted to the man, but it would be wiser to ignore that attraction. Where did she think it could lead? The pretense would end once Rashid finalized his important deal.

A short while later, she lined up the jet on the glide path the tower indicated. The landing was as smooth as silk. She taxied to the hangar and cut the engines.

"Now what?" she wondered aloud as she began the end of her light checklist.

"You return to the villa, I to work," Rashid said from the door. "Nice flight, thank you."

Bethanne felt a rush of pleasure at his words.

Not every multigazillionaire even noticed the people who worked for him, much less offered any praise for a job well done.

"Nice aircraft," she responded. "Were you able to use the phone feature?"

"It worked perfectly. The ride was comfortable. The appointments are just as I wanted. I'm sure I'll have years of use from it."

Bethanne pictured him lounging in the cabin for flights around the Middle East or as far as Europe. This model was the best plane Starcraft produced and she was pleased the buyer seemed satisfied.

"Was your brother at the fire?"

"Yes, and says he has it under control."

"Scary job."

"Dangerous, too. I have instructed one of my drivers, Teaz Suloti, to drive you wherever you wish while visiting. Teaz speaks English. Of course, you have complete use of the villa. The library has a number of books in English."

"Thank you."

"I'll pick you up at six-thirty tonight. We'll dine with my mother at her place at seven."

"Right. Shouldn't I know more about you if we're pretending to be involved?"

"Like?"

"Oh, come on. People who know each other and are attracted to each other want to know more about the other person. The early stages are questions and reminiscences and all. Did I misunderstand or do you want people to think we are on the brink of an engagement?"

"You are correct. I had forgotten."

"Forgotten what?"

"How people who are involved act."

She frowned. "I'm not sure I follow."

"Nothing you need be concerned with. I'll come earlier than planned and brief you on important parts."

"So I should have a dossier on myself prepared as well?" she asked.

"Not necessary. We have information on your visa request. I can wing the rest."

Bethanne settled back into the luxury seats of the limousine a few moments later, wishing she could have continued to spend time with the sheikh—if only to listen to his deep voice with its pleasing accent. She also had a bunch of questions. She knew so little about the man. She couldn't face his mother and not give away the show. She hoped he knew what he was doing.

When they reached the villa, she'd ask about her father to everyone she came into contact with on the sheikh's staff. Someone must have befriended him. He had a sparkling wit and genuine interest in people and places. Had they all condemned him without a fair hearing?

When they reached the villa, the driver opened the door and stood by, waiting for her to get out.

Once on the pavement, Bethanne stopped and looked at Teaz. "Did you know Hank Pendarvis?" she asked.

For a few seconds he made no move or response. Then he nodded abruptly—once.

"Do you know what happened to him?"

"He was the pilot for the old sheikh. He flew away one day and never returned." His English was heavy with Arabic accent, but Bethanne had no trouble understanding him.

"Do you know where he was going?"

The same stare, then a quick shake of his head.

"Thank you," she said. She started for the front door when a thought occurred. Turning, she saw Teaz still staring at her. "Do you know where he lived?"

"In the Romula section of old town."

She waited, hoping for more, but he said nothing. She had the address. Might as well go and see if she could find someone there who knew him.

"Maybe you could drive me there tomorrow if the sheikh doesn't need me." She'd love to see the old city. Match photos with the historic buildings. See a square with coffee cafés and stalls of goods for sale. Skirting Alkaahdar from the airport to the villa showed only the modern high-rises of shining steel and glass. She knew the older section would have been built in the more traditional Moorish architecture that she'd so loved in southern Spain.

"I am at your service," he said with a slight bow.

Entering the quiet villa, Bethanne paused at the bottom of the steps, then on a sudden whim turned and headed toward the sitting room she'd been in last night. A quick glance showed it empty. Moving down the wide hall, she peered into the dining room they'd used. The last room in the hall was the library the sheikh had mentioned. Books lined three walls. The French doors stood open, keeping the room fresh and cool. Stepping inside, she saw a large desk to one side. From the computer on top and the scattered papers, she knew it had been recently used. Who by? From their conversation, she'd surmised Rashid lived elsewhere. This was a second home.

She stepped in and crossed to the desk. She wouldn't open drawers and nothing was visible that would tell her anything about her father. It had been three years. Time enough to put away anything of interest.

"Where did you go, Dad? And why?" she muttered softly.

She sat in the desk chair, picturing Rashid sitting behind the desk, working on major deals for oil exports. What did he do for leisure? How come he was not married at his age? Most men she knew had married in their twenties. Rashid had to be close to mid-thirties.

Though she herself was still unwed.

She swiveled back and forth in the chair. Spotting the computer, she sat up and turned it on. Maybe she could search out what she could find about Rashid al Harum. She would not go to dinner unprepared.

Rashid leaned back as the car pulled away from the office. He was on his way to pick Bethanne up for the command dinner. He had thought about her questions, wondering what she felt important to know if preparing for a confrontation with a future mother-in-law.

He thought about Marguerite for the first time in years. How foolish he'd been not to recognize her type when they'd met. He'd fallen for her in a big way. Marguerite had been beautiful and sophisticated and very good at having fun. She'd often spoken about how much fun they'd have together.

Spending his money.

How gullible he'd been. No longer. He had agreed to the possibility of marriage to Haile as a way to connect the two families who had a strong mutual interest in oil. Now that was off the table, he could resume his solitary way of life. It would take another monumental deal to have him consider the institution again soon.

Lucky break, Haile's running away.

He wondered if his mother would ever see it that way. He'd have to be careful in what he conveyed to her this evening. She could accept things or constantly stir things up in her desire for answers.

How good an actress was Bethanne Sanders? Could he depend upon her? How ironic the woman he was looking to for help was the daughter of a man his family despised. If she was anything like her father, he was playing a dangerous game.

He entered the villa a short time later and paused in the large foyer. The stairs leading up were to his left. The space to the right led to various rooms and eventually back to the kitchen. The evening breeze circulated, keeping the house cool and inviting. Why didn't he stay here more often? he wondered. His grandmother had left it to him when she died last summer. She'd bequeathed another dwelling and surrounding land on the other side of the city to his twin. Khalid had yet to take up residence. Both too busy.

Fatima started down the stairs, surprised to see him. "I didn't know you were here, Excellency," she said. She clung to the railing and looked back up. "I can tell her you have arrived."

"Please ask her to join me in the salon."

Rashid waited by one of the French doors. The entire estate was cooler than his flat in the city. He liked living closer to the action, but he had forgotten how much he'd enjoyed visiting when his grandmother was alive. Only a few minutes' drive from the heart of the capital, yet the estate was serene and lovely, and quite different from the glass and steel of the high-rise where he had his flat.

When he heard the rustle of silk, he turned and watched as Bethanne entered the room. She looked lovely in a rose-colored dress that was most demure. Her hair was done in a neat style, up and off her neck. She wore no jewelry, but her modest attire would please his mother.

"Good evening," she said with a bright smile. For a moment Rashid wished she meant the smile, that she was actually happy to see him. It was a foolish, fleeting thought.

"You look lovely," he said.

"Thank you—it's the dress." She turned slowly and grinned. "I could get used to dresses like this. Most of the time I wear my uniform or shorts when hanging around at home."

He'd like to see her in shorts or a bathing suit. Or nothing at all.

Looking away quickly lest he give a hint of his errant thoughts, he walked to one of the chairs and gestured for her to sit in another.

She did so elegantly. What were the odds of having a suitable woman arrive just when Haile disappeared? One who seemed as at home here in his villa as she did behind the controls of the jet?

"So let the inquisition begin," he said whimsically.

She shrugged. "I looked you up on the Internet. There's quite a lot written about you and your brother. You have a lot of good press. Is that designed? Or are you genuine?"

"I'd like to say genuine. We are not given to excesses. We enjoy our work and do our best for it."

"Your brother is harder to find out about, but you are often in the press. But no special woman—hence the arrangement with Miss Haile, I suppose."

He kept his face without expression. At least the old press about his and Marguerite's disastrous breakup was old news, probably not in the top articles brought up when his name was entered in a search engine. He had his father to thank for that.

"So I know more about you than this morning. Enough to fool your mother? That I'm not sure. There's not much personal, like what your favorite food is or if you had a dog when you were a child."

He relaxed. She was not probing for intimate details, just basic facts.

"My favorite food is candied dates. My brother

and I had a wonderful dog when we were children. I miss him to this day. But my life is too busy and hectic to have a pet."

She settled and began a litany of questions, firing them off as if on an invisible checklist—favorite book, movie, activity, color. Did he consider himself close to his family? Did he have special friends she should know about? A hobby that consumed him? How had he done in school? What did he like about his job and what did he wish to change? Who did he admire most in the world?

It was a novel experience to be so questioned. Not once did she ask about material things.

Finally she stopped. "Ready as I'll ever be," she said, looking as if she were about to jump to her feet.

Rashid looked at her. "My turn."

"I thought you had all you needed from the report Starcraft sent," she said, looking amused.

"Ah, but I didn't realize all the nuances of information necessary for an almost-engaged couple's knowledge bank. I do not know your favorites or your passions."

"Favorite color—blue. Food, anything with dark chocolate. Passions—flying. I have no boyfriend, which is lucky for you or we couldn't be doing this stupid charade. I am not close to my mother—nor the man she married after she divorced my father when I was little. I love traveling and seeing the world. I have experience shooting down other aircraft."

She looked adorable as she recited her list ending proudly with her startling fact. He was fascinated by the play of emotions across her face. Now sitting on the edge of her chair, her animation was a delight. Would his mother like her? What was not to like? As long as she didn't find out Bethanne's father's name.

"I hope there will be no need of the latter while you are in Quishari."

She laughed aloud. "I should hope never again, but it was training I received and just knowing I could do it improves my confidence. If I get into situations that make me uncomfortable, I remember I could shoot down a plane if needed and probably no one else in the room could."

"A strange way to improve confidence."

"It'll help when meeting your mother."

He laughed at that. This American woman was intriguing. He had even more reason to thank Haile for fleeing. If nothing else, Rashid planned to enjoy the next few days with Bethanne by his side. Without expectations on either part, they were free to enjoy the other's company without looking for hidden nuances or motives.

He rose. "Come, we'll be late if we don't

leave soon. And tardiness is something my mother does not like."

"Tell me about her—I want her to be satisfied with the story we tell. Will she be hurt when the truth comes out?"

"Why should the truth ever come out?" he asked.

She looked at him in surprise. "Truth always comes out. You just make sure you put the right spin on it so she's not hurt by your deception."

"I would do nothing to hurt my mother."

"Good answer."

They were soon ensconced in the limo and on their way to the city.

"Where does your mother live?" Bethanne asked.

"In a penthouse apartment near the heart of the city, overlooking parts of the old section. She loves being in the center of things. It helps being close to friends since my father died."

"The soup is delicious," Bethanne said later, sipping the savory concoction. "So far I'm really enjoying the food here. I have a real sweet tooth and the candied walnuts really appeal. I shall have to buy a large package to take home when I leave."

Madame al Harum looked at her.

"And when do you leave?" she asked.

Bethanne smiled and glanced at Rashid. "Not for a long time, I hope."

She also hoped she was playing the role assigned her to his satisfaction. She'd been as gracious as she knew how when meeting his mother. She could tell at once that Madame al Harum did not like her. For one thing, she seemed to disapprove of tall, willowy blondes. She probably wanted a proper Arab woman for her son.

Then she expressed dismay that Bethanne was a pilot. It was too dangerous and too unseemly for a woman. Bethanne decided not to mention shooting down planes. She knew his mother would not appreciate that tidbit.

Dinner was easier. The food took some attention. She counted the minutes until they could finish and leave.

"And where is home for you?" the older woman asked.

"Galveston, Texas, right on the water. Galveston's an island that has been home all my life."

"What does your father do?"

"He's an antique dealer. But I have to say, history in Texas doesn't go back as far as here in Quishari. The old part of the capital city is thousands of years old. Texas has only been around for a few hundred years."

Rashid looked as if he were enjoying the meal. But Bethanne didn't think she was winning Brownie points with his mother.

"Tell me how you became interested in flying," Rashid said when the main course was served.

Grateful for the change of topic, Bethanne plunged right in.

"My father loved to fly and took me up in small planes almost as soon as I could sit up by myself." She smiled in memory. "It seemed logical when I got older that I, too, would love to fly. I actually learned when I was a teenager, to my mother's dismay. When I was accepted to the Academy, she really flipped. But I think Dad talked her in to letting me choose my own way. Anyway, I learned to fly a variety of aircrafts and here I am."

"So your father taught you to fly?" Rashid asked.

"No. That I had to do on my own. He was away more than home, actually. Probably why I'm following in his footsteps and seeing the world." She met his eye, holding it for a moment, silently refuting his ideas about her father.

"And that was your reason for choosing to attend a military academy?"

His mother's eyes grew large at that.

"Some of the recruitment material said join up and see the world. I knew I'd have the best education and pilot's training available. And I had a variety of aircraft to train on. I loved learning. And the service requirement enabled me to see Minot, North Dakota, in the dead of winter. Then a tour of Alaska. Can you imagine? I'm one who loves the sun and sea, and my two duty stations were the coldest in the U.S. I left the service when my commitment was up and landed a spot with Starcraft."

Rashid enjoyed watching Bethanne talk. He glanced at his mother. She had on that polite face she wore when tolerating others, but not connected to them. He felt a twinge of compassion for her. She would have been so happy to have Haile sitting where Bethanne was sitting. She had met the woman on a trip to Morocco and had definitely approved of her.

He had seen pictures. She was a pretty woman. But not striking as Bethanne was. And he doubted she'd have shown much personality around his mother.

What would be his mother's reaction when he told her about Haile's fleeing? Nothing would bring her more happiness than to see one of her sons married—especially to a woman she liked. The fact he was the eldest—by seven minutes—made it seem as if the destiny of his family rested on his shoulders. One day he would have to marry—to father the next generation. He pushed aside the thought. As soon as the deal with al Benqura was finalized, he'd tell his mother Bethanne hadn't turned out to be the one for him after all. Maybe he'd even ask her help in finding him a suitable bride. Being a grandmother would delight her, he was sure.

"Tell me about North Dakota," he invited. "The only time I see snow is when we ski in Switzerland."

He was charmed by her storytelling skills. She made her experiences seem amusing while also revealing her reactions to different situations. She was skilled at entertaining and in giving him what he wanted—a devoted companion intent on meeting his needs. He hoped his mother saw her in that light. For a little while he could imagine what life would be like married to Bethanne. Never boring, of that he was sure.

She was having way too much fun, Bethanne thought at one point. This man was being polite in asking questions so she could talk, but she didn't need to give them her life's history—though Rashid did seem to be enjoying her rendition of her brief stint as an Air Force pilot. His mother looked rather horrified.

Glancing around, she could hardly believe she was sitting in an elegant penthouse overlooking the capital city. The furnishings were amazing. She wished her stepfather could see them. And surrounding the penthouse was a spacious terrace that had banks of pots with fragrant flowers. The doors were opened to allow the breeze to enter. It was delightful.

"You have a beautiful home," she said to her hostess. She had to find common ground or this dinner would end awkwardly.

Madame al Harum inclined her head regally. "I decorated it for my husband. He loved to retreat from the world and find a place of beauty." She glanced at her son. "It's important that two people have much in common to make a happy marriage."

Bethanne also looked at Rashid. His mother wasn't buying their supposed commitment at all. Would he tell her now?

"Similar likes and dislikes, certainly," Rashid said. "But there is something to be said about learning about each other as the years go by, and have enough differences to be interesting."

His mother gave Bethanne a sour look and then nodded to her son. "That is important as well."

The rest of the meal processed without much comment. Bethanne was glad this was only a charade. She would not like being married into a family where the mother didn't like her. Or was it only because of her disappointment Haile hadn't come?

They did not stay long after dinner finished.

The ride back to the villa was completed in almost total silence. Bethanne knew Rashid had to be regretting his impetuous suggestion about their charade. Perhaps he'd end it tonight. The thought depressed her.

To her surprise, Rashid did not simply leave her at the door.

"It's early yet. If you are not tired, perhaps a few minutes on the veranda," he suggested.

"That would be nice. So do we change the charade now that we both know your mother doesn't like me?"

"My mother does not dictate my life. She is annoyed I didn't bring Haile tonight. She was instrumental in making that arrangement."

"It's more than that. She doesn't like me. Not just because I'm not Haile, but because of who I am," Bethanne said. She didn't need everyone in the world to like her, but she was a bit hurt Rashid's mother found her wanting.

"It's of no account," he said.

Of course not. This wasn't real. It was make-believe—until he had his huge deal signed and sealed. Then she'd be on the next plane to Texas and his life would resume its normal course. Gossip would be quelled. He'd get his way and his mother would be very relieved.

"Her home was lovely," she said, looking for conversation. "Did you grow up there?"

"There and here and other places."

He looked out at the garden, visible now by the

discreet lighting illuminating paths and special plants. He could hear the soft sound of the sea, noticeably different from faint traffic noise. "My flat today is not as pretty as this estate. It's downtown, not far from Mother's. I like living there yet I had almost forgotten how enjoyable this place is."

"Well, I appreciate being allowed to stay here. It's so much better than a hotel."

"I'm sure my grandmother would have been delighted to have visitors enjoy her home. She spent several months a year here. But had other property, as well."

Well, duh, Bethanne thought. His family probably had two dozen residences among them. She wondered idly if there were enough bedrooms among all the residences for him to sleep in a different one each night of the month. What must that feel like?

She had a sudden longing for her small apartment, with its familiar furnishings and photos. It might be fun to consider being Cinderella, but at the end of it all, wasn't she happier in her own home?

As Bethanne prepared for bed some time later, she thought about the evening. It would not have been better for Rashid's mother to welcome her into the family. She was not truly involved. And if the woman had liked her, she would have been disappointed when the charade was exposed.

Talking with Rashid on the veranda had given her a glimpse of what life married to him could be like. Only—there was no good-night kiss. She sighed softly. Was she going to be disappointed with no kiss before returning home? Yes. Yet she wasn't bold enough to kiss him.

Before turning off the lights, she opened the French doors to let the sea breeze sweep in. The light curtains billowed. The scents and fragrances from the garden were a delight. She slipped between cool sheets and lay down.

An hour later Bethanne was still wide awake. She'd tried lying on one side then the other, then flat on her back. Nothing worked. If she had a book or magazine to read, it might lead to sleep. She considered the situation, then sighed and got up. She had not brought a robe, thinking she'd be alone in a hotel room and not need one. Quietly she dressed in her slacks and shirt. Bare feet would be okay, she was sure. It was unlikely she'd run into anyone. It was after eleven. Surely all the staff had retired for the night.

She opened the door and stuck her head out, struck suddenly with the romantic-comedy picture that flashed into her mind. People sneaking from one room to another, peering into the hall to make sure the coast was clear. She planned nothing of the sort and stepped boldly out. She walked down the stairs, surprised when she reached the foyer to see a light coming from the library.

Silently she walked to the doorway. When she was within hearing distance she heard a phone. It was answered before the second ring.

The words were in Arabic, but she recognized Rashid's voice. She thought he had left long ago. When he'd bid her good-night, he said he had to pick up something from the library.

He was still here, and the phone call wasn't going well—not if the terse tone was anything to go by. She hesitated at the doorway, not wishing to interrupt, but still wanting something to read. She'd come this far; she'd wait for the conclusion of the call and then step in to find a book.

The conversation didn't take as long as she'd expected before a harsh word was sounded, then a string of them. She wondered what was going on. He sounded angry. Sudden silence ended the call.

When the silence had lasted several minutes, she took a breath and stepped closer, knocking slightly on the door frame. She saw him standing by open French doors. His back was ramrod straight. His body seemed to radiate strong emotion in contrast to the stillness with which he held himself.

He spun around, glaring at her for a second. Then he quickly adjusted his expression to reveal nothing. "Something wrong?" he asked.

"I was going to ask you the same thing. I thought you left a while ago."

"I did. Then I remembered a file I had left and returned for it. I was about to leave when I got a phone call on my mobile phone." He still held it in his hand.

"I heard. Not that I understood a word, but it didn't sound like a very friendly call."

"It was from al Benqura. He found out about Haile. She contacted him. He was angry with me for not letting him know."

"How awkward that would have been."

Rashid sighed and walked back to the desk, leaning against it and nodding. "Awkward for him. He's threatening to end the deal. I told him in no uncertain terms that would not be acceptable unless he never wanted dealings with anyone in Quishari again."

Bethanne could empathize with the father whose daughter had run away and put him in a difficult situation. She watched as Rashid gradually relaxed. He was quick to anger, but also quick to regain his equilibrium. She saw when his curiosity was piqued by her arrival.

"What are you doing here?" His gaze dropped to her bare feet. His lips curved in a slight smile.

"I came for a book to read. I can't seem to sleep. You said you had some English books—I thought I'd get one of those."

He nodded and gestured to the shelving on the left. "English books on that wall. My grandmother used to entertain several friends from Great Britain. She has an assortment. The mysteries are on the lower shelves."

She crossed, conscious of his regard, and began to scan the titles. Finding a couple that sounded promising, she drew them from the shelf. Had Rashid read them? Could they discuss them after she finished?

Deciding to take both, she hugged them to her chest as she turned to face him.

"Now what?" she asked.

"You read them and fall asleep?" he asked.

"I mean with our charade. Did the phone call help or change things?"

"We continue. Whichever way the winds blow, we will adapt."

CHAPTER THREE

"I DON'T mean to intrude. But if you need someone
to talk to, I could listen." She wished she'd had
someone to listen to her when her father's disappearance became known. Her mother had long ago
divorced herself from Hank Pendarvis—both
legally and emotionally. She and Bethanne's stepfather had a loving and happy marriage from which
Bethanne had often felt excluded. Plus, they never
had a kind word to say about her father. Bethanne
wished she could have him give her one of his bear
hugs again. Did Haile's father feel that way?

"Did he hear from Haile?" she asked.

"He did. And is furious with her and with me."

"You're the injured party—why is he angry
with you?"

"He believes I should have told him immediately. He could have taken steps. He overrates his
power. By the time I found out, Haile had had
hours to flee Morocco. She and her lover were

married in Marseilles that very day. My telling him would not have prevented that."

"Will he tell others? Your minister?"

"Not if he wants this deal to go through."

He pushed away from the desk. "I have my folder. I won't keep you up any longer."

He looked at her slacks and T-shirt.

"Was sleeping attire not included in the clothes I ordered?"

"Yes, but no robe. I didn't know whom I might see if I came down for books."

"I shall remedy that in the morning."

"Please, I'm fine. Next time I'll take a book up with me. You've been more than generous. I don't need anything else."

"I thought all women loved beautiful things."

"I expect we do. But we don't have to own everything we see. Good night, Rashid."

Reaching her room a minute later, she softly closed the door and flung herself on the bed, the books falling on the mattress beside her. She had not expected to see him again tonight. He'd looked tired and somewhat discouraged. Not the best way to end a day. She hoped the deal would be signed soon. There was nothing else she could do but go along and hope in some small part she'd contribute to a satisfactory conclusion to their negotiations.

Trying to settle into a fictitious mystery when she had a real-life scenario in her own life was difficult. Murder was not involved in her case, but finding clues was. She tried to glean ideas from the book, but her mind turned time and time again to Rashid.

She knew he believed Hank to be a thief, but wouldn't he still want answers? Letting the book fall onto her chest, she gazed at the dark night beyond the billowing curtains. The man at the airport had said the son had no idea why her father took the plane. Didn't he want to know? She couldn't picture Rashid ignoring the situation. He'd push until he got answers.

Just before she fell asleep, she pictured herself with Rashid finding her father and finding the reason for the apparent theft. It could be explained away. Then Rashid would look at her with admiration and sweep her into his arms for a kiss….

She stopped herself—she had to stop fantasizing about his kisses!

Once again Minnah woke Bethanne the next morning, bringing a breakfast tray. The hot chocolate was as rich and satisfying as the previous day. The croissants were warm and buttery, melting in her mouth.

She debated going for a swim, but decided she had best set to searching for her father. She wanted to prove to Rashid his belief was misplaced.

"Pardon, I almost forgot," Minnah said after she opened the French doors and curtains to allow the sunshine to flood the room. "It is a letter from His Excellency. I will return for the tray in a while." She handed Bethanne an ivory-colored envelope with her name written in a bold script.

She opened it and read the brief note, her heart revving up. It had taken ages to fall asleep and then her dreams about Rashid had been exciting and most certainly not ones she wanted to share with anyone. The best favor she could do herself would be to remember always that this was merely make-believe.

A car will be at your disposal today. The driver will be waiting when you are ready to take you where you wish. He speaks English, and can translate if you wish to stop to shop or have coffee.

Disappointment warred with relief at the missive. What had she expected? A love note? An offer to spend the day with her?

The bold handwriting continued: *Saturday I have a polo match, I would like you to attend. Perhaps you'd care to see the horses before the game. If there is not a suitable dress for you to wear, let the maid know and she'll relay the information and something appropriate will be ordered.*

Bethanne was almost giddy with excitement. Trying not to act like a schoolgirl with a major crush, she took a deep breath. Of course someone being in a position of special guest would want to attend the polo match. Mentally she reviewed the new clothes. She wasn't entirely certain what was suitable for a polo match, but didn't think any of the lovely dresses were the right kind.

Still, the thought of his buying more clothes caused a pang. He didn't need to spend so much on this charade.

"Get real," she said aloud. "He can afford it and the clothes can go to some worthy cause when I leave."

Pushing the thought of leaving away, she quickly finished breakfast, showered and dressed in a light tan linen skirt and soft yellow cotton blouse. She planned to take advantage of the driver the sheikh offered to see some of the sights of old town this morning. She couldn't wait to see the ancient buildings, walk where generations past had walked. And maybe find out more about her father.

Then, if time permitted, she'd take advantage of the beauty of the Persian Gulf and laze on the beach until Rashid came after work.

Bethanne was pleased to see the driver at her disposal was the same one she'd asked about her father. She greeted him and told him of her desire to see the old city, and where Hank had lived.

When they arrived, he pulled into the curb and stopped.

"I cannot take the car any farther. The road

becomes too narrow. Down there two blocks." He handed her a sheet of paper with Arabic writing. "I wrote his name and when he lived there and where. Show it to people for information about Hank. Many speak some English. If not, come get me to translate. I will wait with the car."

"Thank you."

"You will not get a good reception," he warned.

"Why not?" That thought had never crossed her mind.

"The old sheikh was well liked. It was not a good thing to steal his plane. Some speculate the pilot's betrayal caused the heart attack that killed him. The man had flown the sheikh for years. His treachery cut deep."

Bethanne recognized she was fighting an uphill battle to clear her father's name. He would not have treated his employer that way—she knew it. His letters and phone calls had been full of admiration and respect for his employer. But how to prove that, and find out what really happened?

When she climbed out of the car, she was instantly in a foreign world. The tall sandstone walls were built closer to each other than most American buildings. Rising fifteen to twenty feet in height, they seemed to encase the street. Archways, windows and doors opened directly onto the narrow sidewalks, most already shuttered against the day's rising heat.

Bethanne was almost giddy with delight. She'd longed to visit Quishari ever since her father had first spoken about it. He had loved it and she knew she would as well. Savoring every moment, she slowly walked along, imagining she heard the echo of a thousand years. The heat shimmered against the terra cotta–colored walls. Here and there bright colors popped from curtains blowing from windows, or painted shutters closed against the heat.

She got her bearings and headed in the direction indicated in the drawing. Where the street intersected another, she peered down the cross streets, seeing more of the same. Archways had decorative Arabic writings. Recessed doorways intrigued, beckoned. For the most part, however, the reddish-brown of sandstone was the same. How did anyone find their own place when they all looked alike? she wondered.

Reaching a square, she was pleased with the wide-open area, filled with colorful awnings sheltering stalls with everything imaginable for sale. There were booths of brass, of glass, of luscious and colorful material and polished wood carvings. Some stalls sold vegetables, others fruit or flowers. Women and children filled the aisles. The sounds of excited chattering rose and fell as she looked around. On the far side, tables at two outside cafés crowded the sidewalk. Men in traditional Arab dishdashahs with white gitrahs covering their hair sat drinking the strong coffee. Others wore European attire. Several women dressed all in black stood near the corner talking, their string bags ladened with fresh produce from the stands in the square. The air was almost festive as shoppers haggled for the best bargain and children ran and played.

Bethanne watched in awe. She was actually here. Looking around, she noticed she was garnering quite a bit of attention. Obviously a curiosity to the daily routine. She approached one of the women and showed her the paper. The woman began talking in Arabic and pointing to a building only a few steps away. Bethanne thanked her, hoped she was pointing out the apartment where her father had lived. She quickly crossed there. No one responded to her knock.

Turning, she explored the square, stopping to ask in several of the stalls if anyone had known Hank Pendarvis, showing the paper the driver had prepared. No success until she came to one of the small sidewalk cafés on the far side of the square. A waiter spoke broken English and indicated Hank had been a frequent customer, years ago. He had met with a friend often in the afternoons. The other man still came sometimes. She tried to find out more, but he had told her all he knew. She had to make do with that. If she got the chance, she'd return another time, to see if her father's friend was there.

She asked if she could leave a note. When presented with a small piece of paper, she wrote only she was trying to find out information about Hank Pendarvis and would return in three days.

She dare not at this point mention her tenuous relationship to the sheikh. She did not want anyone trying to reach her at the villa. Until she knew more, she had to keep her secret.

Bethanne returned to the car then instructed the driver to take her to the best store in the city. She wanted to search for the perfect outfit to wear to a polo match. She did not need Rashid buying every stitch she wore.

When Bethanne returned to the villa late in the afternoon, the driver must have had some way to notify Fatima. The older woman met her in the lobby, her face disapproving, her tone annoyed as she said something Bethanne didn't understand. Probably chastising her for leaving her chaperone behind.

To her surprise, Rashid al Harum came from the library.

"Ah, the eternal pastime of women—shopping," he said, studying the two bags with the shop's name on the side.

"Your stores had some fabulous sales," she said.

"Wait until you see the dress I bought for the polo match. I hope it's suitable—the saleswoman said it was." Conscious of the servants, she smiled brightly and hurried over to him, opening the bag a bit so he could peek in.

He did so and smiled. Glancing at the staff, he stood aside.

"Perhaps you'd join me in the salon."

"Happy to," she said.

He spoke to Fatima and the woman came to take Bethanne's bags, then retreated.

"Is anything wrong?" Bethanne asked once the two of them were alone in the salon.

"Not at all. I have some spare time and came to see if you wanted to have lunch together. I have not forgotten you wanted to see some of my country. Where did you go this morning?"

"To a place in the old town. I walked around a square there, saw a small market. Then went shopping for the dress."

"I'd be delighted to show you more of the old town, and some of the countryside north of the city, if you'd like."

"Yes. I would. I probably won't get the chance to visit Quishari again after I leave." Especially if she didn't find her father, or convince Rashid he was innocent.

"And I remember you like exploring new places," he commented, studying her for a moment.

"I'll run upstairs and freshen up. I can be ready to leave in ten minutes."

"There's no rush."

She smiled again and dashed up to her room. She should have been better prepared for Rashid, but had not expected him to disregard work to spend time with her. She was delighted, and hoped they'd find mutual interests for conversation. She could, of course, simply stare at him all day—but that would look odd.

Rashid walked to the opened French doors. He gazed out at the gardens, but his thoughts centered on his American visitor. Bethanne fascinated him. Her profession was unusual for a woman. Yet whenever she was around him, she appeared very feminine. He liked looking at her with her fair skin, blue eyes and soft blond hair. Her casual manner could lead some to believe she was flighty—but he'd checked her record and it was spotless. He also found her enthusiasm refreshing after his own rather cynical outlook on life. Was that an American trait? Or her individual personality?

Rashid knew several American businessmen. Had dined with them and their wives over the years. Most of them cultivated the same aloof cosmopolitan air that was so lacking in Bethanne. Maybe it was that difference that had him intrigued.

His mother had called again that morning, bemoaning the fact Bethanne was visiting and that Haile had not come. When he'd told her he was just as well out of the deal, she'd appeared shocked. Questioning him further, she'd become angry when he'd said he wasn't sure the arrangement had been suitable in the long run. He didn't come out and tell her of firm plans with Bethanne, but let her believe there was a possibility.

He almost laughed when his mother had tentatively suggested Bethanne wasn't suitable and he should let her help him find the right bride. He knew he and Bethanne didn't make a suitable pair. Yet, if he thought about it, she would probably have beautiful children. She was young, healthy, obviously intelligent.

He stopped. It sounded as if he were seriously considering a relationship with her. He was not. His family would never overlook what her father had done. And after the aborted affair with Marguerite, he didn't fully trust women. He would do better to focus on finalizing the details of the agreement with al Benqura.

His mother had reminded him she expected a different guest, and so would others.

"Until they see Bethanne. Then they'd know why she's visiting," he'd said, hoping to fob her off. It would certainly give a shot in the arm to the gossip circulating. And, he hoped, throw off any hint of scandal the minister might try to expose. Animosity ran deep between them. Rashid would not give him anything to fuel their feud.

He'd already invited Bethanne to the polo match. Perhaps a dinner date or two, escorting her to a reception, would give gossips something else to talk about. It would not be a hardship. And al Benqura was in a hurry to finish the deal, as Rashid had suspected. Once the papers were signed, Bethanne would be leaving. Life would return to normal and no one except he and she would know the full circumstances of the charade. The thought was disquieting. Maybe he wouldn't be in so much of a hurry to finalize everything.

Bethanne took care when freshening up. She brushed her hair until it shone. Tying it back so it wouldn't get in her face, she refreshed her makeup. She felt like she was on holiday—lazing around, visiting old town, now seeing more of the country. Spending time with a gorgeous man. What was not to like about Quishari?

She was practical enough to know she wasn't some femme fatale; she'd never wow the sheikh like some Arabian beauty would. Haile had had that sultry look with the fine features, wide choco-late-brown eyes and beautiful dark hair so many Arab women had. Next to them, she felt like a washed-out watercolor.

Leaving her room, she started down the stairs.

"Prompt as ever," he said from the bottom.

She glanced down at him, gripping the banister tightly in startled surprise. She could take in how fabulous he looked in a dark suit, white shirt and blue-and-silver tie. His black hair gleamed beneath the chandelier. His deep brown eyes were fixed on her. Taking a breath, she smiled and tried to glide down the stairs. Was this how Cinderella felt going to the ball? She didn't want midnight to come.

"You look lovely," he said.

Bethanne smiled at him. "Thank you, kind sir."

Once seated in the limo, Rashid gave directions to the driver. Bethanne settled back to enjoy being with him.

"So if I'm to watch a polo match on Saturday, maybe I should learn a bit of the finer points of the game," she said as they pulled away from the villa. "What should I watch for?"

Rashid gave her an overview of the game. Bethanne couldn't wait to see Rashid on one of the horses he spoke about. She knew he'd looked fabulous. She had to remind herself more than once on the ride—sheikhs didn't get involved with women from Galveston, Texas.

When they arrived at the restaurant, Bethanne was impressed. It was on the shore of the Gulf, with tall windows which gave an excellent view to the beautiful water. Their table was next to one of the windows, tinted to keep the glare out, making Bethanne feel as if she were sitting on the sand.

"This is fabulous," she murmured, captivated by the view.

"The food is good, as well," he said, sitting in the chair opposite.

The maître d' placed the menus before them with a flourish.

After one glance, Bethanne closed hers and looked back out the window. "Please order for me. I'm afraid I can't read Arabic."

"Do you like fish?"

"Love it."

"Then I'll order the same filet for us both and you'll see what delicious fish we get from the Gulf."

After their order had been taken, Bethanne looked at him. "Do you ever go snorkeling or scuba diving?"

"From time to time," he said. "Do you?"

She nodded. "It's almost mandatory if one grows up in Galveston. I've had some great vacations in the Florida Keys, snorkeling and exploring the colorful sea floor."

"We will have to try that before you go," he said politely.

She studied him for a moment. "I can go by

myself, you know. You don't have to take time away from your busy work schedule. It's not as if—"

His raised eyebrow had her stopping abruptly. "What?"

"We do not know who can hear our conversation," he cautioned.

She glanced around. No one appeared to be paying the slightest bit of attention to them, but she knew it would only take a few words to cause the charade to collapse and that would undoubtedly cause Rashid a lot of trouble.

"So how goes the deal?" she asked, leaning a bit closer and lowering her voice.

"We should sign soon, if certain parties don't cause a glitch."

"The father?" she asked, feeling as if she were speaking in code.

"No, he'll come round. It's some of our own internal people who are against the proposed agreement who could still throw a wrench into the works."

"And your mother?"

Rashid leaned closer, covering one of her hands with his, lowering his voice. "My mother has no interest in politics or business. She only wants her sons married. Our personal lives have no interest to anyone, unless it causes a breach between me and al Benqura. That's what we are guarding against."

Bethanne knew to others in the restaurant, it must look as if he were whispering sweet nothings. Her hand tingled with his touch. For a moment she wished she dared turn it over and clasp his. The Quishari culture was more conservative than Americans and overt displays of affection were uncommon in public. Still, he had made the overture.

"Do not be concerned with my mother. She will not cause a problem."

"I wished she liked me," she murmured.

"Why? You'll hardly see her before you leave. She will be at the polo match and perhaps one or two events we attend, but her manners are excellent, as I expect yours to be."

Bethanne bristled. "I do know how to make nice in public," she said.

Amusement danced in his eyes. "I'm sure you do."

Their first course arrived and Bethanne was pleased to end the conversation and concentrate on eating and enjoying the view.

"This is delicious," she said after her first bite. The fish was tender and flavorful. The vegetables were perfect.

He nodded. "I hoped you would like it."

Conversation was sporadic while they ate. Bethanne didn't want to disturb the mellow mood she was in as she enjoyed the food. She glanced at Rashid once in a while, but for the most part kept looking at the sea.

When the sugared walnuts appeared for dessert, she smiled in delight. "I didn't know restaurants served these," she said, taking one and popping it into her mouth.

"I ordered them specially for you," he said.

"You did?" Amazing. She'd never had anyone pay such attention to details and then act on their knowledge. "Thank you very much. I love these."

She savored another then asked, "So what happened to your brother? Did he get the fire out?"

"He did. He heads a company that specializes in putting out oil fires as well as acting as consultants for wells around the world."

"Sounds dangerous."

"Putting out the fires can be, but the rest is consulting work."

"Isn't he part of the family business?"

"He is, but more a silent partner in the day-to-day operations. He prefers not to be stuck in an office, as he puts it."

She studied him, taking another walnut and savoring it as she put it in her mouth. "I don't see you as *stuck* in an office. I expect you love pitting your mind against others."

He smiled slightly. "One way to put it, I suppose. I find it satisfying to make deals to benefit the company. Pitting my wits against others in the field and continuing to expand the company beyond what my father did."

"How did your father die?" It was a bold question, given what she'd learned this morning, but she would never have a better opportunity.

"Heart attack. He was only sixty-three…far too young to die."

"I hope heart problems don't run in your family." Nothing said about what caused it. Maybe the timing was coincidental to the disappearance of her father and the plane. She hoped so. It was bad enough they thought her father a thief. Surely they didn't blame him for the old sheikh's death.

"No. He had rheumatic fever as a child and developed problems from that. The rest of us, including two of his older brothers, are fine."

More than fine, she thought, looking away lest she gave him insight into her thought process. Really, Bethanne, she admonished, you've seen other gorgeous men before. Just not so up close and interested in her—even if it was only pretend.

"Ready to leave? We can take the walnuts with us. I want Teaz to drive us up the coast. There are some beautiful spots along the way. And some ruins from ancient times."

Settled in the luxurious limousine a few moments later, Bethanne knew she could get used to such treatment in no time. And she could gain a bazillion pounds if she kept eating the sweets. Just one or two more and she'd stop. Until later.

Rashid gave a running commentary as they drove along one of the major highways of Quishari. With the Persian Gulf on the right and huge family estates on the left, there was a sameness that gradually changed as they went farther from the city.

Soon they were surrounded by the desert, stretching from the sea to as far to the west as she could see.

"The ruins are best viewed walking through them," he said when Teaz stopped the car. The place was lonely, sandy and windswept, only outlines of the buildings that had once comprised a thriving village.

"Lonely," Bethanne said, staring west. Nothing but miles of empty land. And the memory of people now gone.

"Once it was a lively trading port. You can see a few of the pilings for the piers in the water. It's estimated these are more than two thousand years old."

"Makes America seem like a toddler. Most of our history goes back four hundred years—once the Europeans settled in. I'd like to see this from the air. Tell me more."

By the time the sun was sinking lower in the sky,

they'd gone north almost to the border and turned to head for the villa. Bethanne enjoyed every moment. It was obvious that Rashid loved his country and enjoyed sharing his devotion with his guest. She learned more about the history of the area in their ride than she'd ever learned in school or from her father. Rashid had appeared surprised at the knowledge she did have.

"Tomorrow we can take the plane up again. Fly over the ruins and maybe west. There are a few oases that are large enough to support small communities."

"Did your family gather at the villa for holidays?" she asked.

"For some of them. Other times we met at my father's home. But the family loved the villa. In the summer, my parents often spent several weeks visiting my grandmother and enjoying the sea. My brother and I loved those times."

Rashid escorted her to the door when they arrived.

The butler met them, speaking rapidly to Rashid.

"We seem to have company," Rashid said to her in English. "My brother."

"Oh. Do you want me to go on upstairs?"

"No, come meet Khalid."

When they entered the salon, a man sitting on one of the chairs reading the newspaper rose. For a split second, Bethanne stared. He looked just like Rashid. Twins!

Then he turned to face them and the image was disturbed by the slash of burned skin going from just beneath his right eye, down to the collar of his shirt in a disfiguring swath. Bethanne caught her breath, trying not to imagine the pain and suffering that had resulted from such a burn.

"Bethanne, this is Khalid."

"How do you do. Rashid didn't tell me you two were twins."

Khalid nodded but stayed where he was, his eyes alert and suspicious.

"He told me about your plan to fool the world. Stupid idea," Khalid said.

She blinked at the hostility, then glanced at Rashid, who shrugged. "So you say. If it holds off the wolves until the deal is signed, I'm good with it. What brings you here?"

"I wanted to meet her," Khalid said.

Bethanne walked over and sat down. "Now you have. Questions?" She had spent her fair share dealing with obstreperous officers in the past. And some cranky clients. She could handle this.

"Do not cross the line," Rashid warned his brother.

"What do you expect from this?" Khalid said, ignoring his twin.

"A signed acceptance of the jet aircraft I delivered and a few days exploring a country I have long wanted to see," Bethanne responded quickly.

Rashid watched his brother ask more questions than he should have. He was looking for a gold digger and that was not Rashid's assessment of Bethanne. She was more concerned with clearing her father's name than getting clothes or money from him. Not that Rashid had any intentions of providing his visitor anything more than was needed to attend the events where he'd show her off. Khalid was worried for naught.

"Did you get that oil fire out?" she asked at a pause in the interrogation.

Khalid nodded. "How do you know about that?"

"My dear friend Rashid tells me everything," she said sweetly.

Rashid laughed aloud. "Subtlety is not your strong suit. Leave her alone. I'm happy with the arrangement we have. No need to look for trouble where there is none."

Khalid studied her. Bethanne met his gaze with a considering one of her own.

"We are dining in this evening—would you care to join us?" Rashid asked.

He decided in that instance to stay for dinner. Maybe a few hours in Bethanne's company would end his brother's suspicions and gain his own cooperation in the situation.

CHAPTER FOUR

PROMPTLY at eight the next morning, Bethanne descended the stairs, dressed in her uniform. She was looking forward to another ride over Quishari. She and Rashid had discussed the trip last night. It would give one of his pilots a chance at the controls. She knew he would love the plane.

And she would spend more hours in Rashid's company. She was treasuring each, knowing the memory of their time would be all she'd have in the future. But for now, she relished every moment.

Fatima sat on one of the elegant chairs in the foyer. She rose when Bethanne reached the tiled floor. Saying something in Arabic, she smiled politely. Bethanne hadn't a clue what she said, but smiled in return.

The limo was in front and whisked them both away. Obviously today was a day that needed a chaperone. Was she going on the plane with them as well?

Bethanne had braided her hair in a single plait down the back to keep it out of the way. Her uniform was a far cry from the silk dresses she'd been wearing. Still, this was business. It would have been highly inappropriate for her to wear one of the dresses when flying the plane.

The jet gleamed in the sunlight when they arrived. Ground crewmen stood nearby, but no one stood next to the plane. Once she and Fatima got out of the limo, the translator broke away from the group and headed their way.

"His Excellency and Alexes are already in the plane," he said with a slight bow.

Bethanne's heart skipped a beat and then began to race.

"I'll start the ground checklist," she said, ignoring her clamoring need to see Rashid again. She had her tasks to perform to carry everyone safely. "Ask Fatima if she wishes to accompany me or board now?"

A quick interchange, then he said, "She will remain by the stairs until you are ready to enter."

Bethanne took her time checking the aircraft then nodded to Fatima and climbed the steps to the plane. After the bright sunshine, it took a couple of seconds for her eyes to adjust. She saw an older man talking with Rashid in the back of the cabin. Starting back toward them, Bethanne watched as they studied the communication panel.

Rashid saw her and introduced the pilot. "We are looking at the various aspects of the aircraft. This one has more features than the one I've been using."

"But the one that was lost had some of these same capabilities," the pilot murmured, still looking at the dials and knobs.

The plane that was lost—was that the one her father had flown? The pilot was someone who might have known Hank. She hoped they had some time together on today's flight so she could ask him.

"If you are ready to depart, Alexes would like to sit in the cockpit to observe and then fly it once you give the go-ahead."

"I'm sure you'll be ready in no time," she said to the pilot. "For all the technology this baby carries, she's quick to respond and simple to fly."

The man didn't look convinced. Bethanne wondered if he was unsure of her own skills, or those of the plane.

"Fatima will accompany us," Rashid said. He handed Bethanne a topographical map. "I thought we could first fly over the ruins from yesterday, and then head west, toward one of the oases I spoke of."

"Sounds great. Did you already file the flight plan?"

"Alexes did."

"Then let's go."

The pilot bowed slightly to the sheikh and followed Bethanne into the cockpit. He slid into the copilot's seat and began scanning the dials and switches.

Bethanne smoothly taxied and took off, taking the route the pilot had filed with the ground control. She talked to the pilot the entire time about what she was doing and how the plane responded. His English was excellent and he quickly grasped the intricacies of the new jet.

When they reached their cruising altitude, she banked easily and headed north as the flight plan outlined. The sea was sparkling in the sunshine. The shoreline, irregular below them, gleamed. The vegetation edging the beach contrasted with the white sand and blue waters.

Even as she conversed with the other pilot, Bethanne scanned the land below, wondering if her father had flown this exact route. Her recall of the topographical map showed when they turned inland she would be flying almost directly west. Was that a routine flight for the old sheikh?

Rashid al Harum opened the cockpit door and looked in. "What do you think, Alexes?" he asked, resting one hand on the back of Bethanne's seat.

The pilot responded in Arabic and when Rashid spoke in the same language, the man looked abashed.

"My pardon. I told His Excellency that the plane handles like a dream. If I may take over for a while?"

Bethanne nodded and lifted her hands.

"Ahh, it does respond like a dream," Alexes said a moment later, approval in his voice.

"Below are the ruins," Rashid said, looking over her shoulder.

Bethanne looked out of the window, seeing the outlines of the structures they'd viewed yesterday. She kept her eyes on the ground when Alexes banked slightly so she could see the old piers marching out in the water. The crystal clarity of the Persian Gulf enabled her to clearly see each one. Her imagination was sparked by the picture below. Who had lived there? How had their lives been spent? What would they think of people soaring over them in planes they probably never even dreamed about?

Slowly the plane turned and the ruins were behind them. Below was only endless sand with hardy plants which could survive the harsh conditions. The scene became monotonous in the brown hues.

Bethanne looked over her shoulder at the sheikh. "How long to the oasis?" she asked.

"We'll be there in time to have lunch before returning. Once you're reassured Alexes knows what he's doing, perhaps you'd join me in the main compartment. Try out that sofa again."

She nodded, her heart skipping a beat. She didn't need to try out the sofa; she knew it was the height of luxury. She would love to spend a bit more time with Rashid, however. And demonstrate to the other pilot she trusted him with the plane.

The pilot seemed competent. He was murmuring softly, as if in love with the jet. She knew the feeling. It was her favorite model to fly. Still, she didn't leap at the chance to go back to the cabin. She had to focus on her primary responsibility, which was completing delivery of the aircraft—not spending time with the sheikh. She reviewed the various features of the cockpit, quoted fuel ratios, aeronautic facts and figures and answered all Alexes's questions.

When she was satisfied he could handle things, she turned over the controls and rose to head to the back. Fatima was dozing in one of the chairs near the rear.

Rashid looked up from a paper he was reading and watched as she crossed the small space and sat beside him on the long sofa.

"Alexes handling things well?" he asked.

"Of course. He said it was similar to another Starcraft plane he used to fly as backup. What happened to that one?"

"It was the one your father took—they both vanished," he said, putting aside his paper.

"It's hard to hide an airplane."

Just then the plane shuddered and began to dive.

Bethanne took a split second to act. She was on her feet and heading for the cockpit when it veered suddenly to the right. She would have slammed into the side if Rashid had not caught her and pulled her along.

Opening the cockpit door a second later, she saw Alexes slumped over the controls. The earth rushed toward them at an alarming rate.

Rashid acted instantly, reaching to draw Alexes back. Bethanne slid into her seat and began to pull the plane from the dive. Rashid struggled to get Alexes out of the seat, but the man was unconscious and a dead weight. He called for Fatima and she hurried forward to help him, trying to guide the unconscious pilot's legs away from the controls as the sheikh pulled him from the copilot's seat. Once clear, she helped the sheikh carry him to the sofa while Bethanne regained control of the plane.

In only seconds the jet had resumed a normal flight pattern and once she verified the altitude, she resumed their approved flight track. Glancing around, she was relieved there were no other planes in sight.

"How is he?" she called back. The door separating the cockpit from the cabin had been propped open.

"Still unconscious…most likely a heart attack," Rashid called, loosening Alexes's collar.

"Oxygen is by the first-aid kit in the galley," she

yelled back. She contacted ground control. Citing an emergency, she was directed to the nearest airport, in Quraim Wadi Samil, a few miles to the south of their original route.

Glancing over her shoulder, Bethanne could glimpse most of the cabin. Fatima held the portable oxygen tank while Rashid was still bent over the pilot. She shivered, hoping he was all right. What had happened?

In seconds Alexes's eyes flickered. He spoke in Arabic. Bethanne didn't understand him, but applauded Rashid's calm reply. In moments the sheikh had the older man take some aspirin and elevated his legs and feet. His color was pale, his speech slurred slightly.

"Might be a stroke," he called. "We'll head back immediately."

"They've directed me to an airport in Quraim Wadi Samil. It's closer and an ambulance will be standing by," she responded. She looked back again. "How's he doing?"

"Breathing hard. His color isn't good. How much longer?"

Contacting ground control, she requested emergency clearance for the airport and requested information on flight time remaining.

It came immediately. With new coordinates she altered course. In less than ten minutes she saw the small airport. In another ten, they were on the ground and the requested ambulance was already on its way to the hospital with Alexes. The sheikh conferred with the medical personnel before they left, then turned back to the two women standing at the bottom of the stairs.

"You handled that emergency well," Rashid said, his eyes rested on her.

"I was really scared to death. The plane responded well, however, and here we are. It's what I'm trained to do. What did the emergency medical technician say? Will he be all right?"

"Too early to tell. We'll follow to the hospital and see what we find out." He looked at the older woman and said something to her. She smiled and nodded, happiness shining from her face.

"What did you tell her?" Bethanne asked.

"That she was an asset in saving his life. It was providence that she was here and had Haile not left, things might have turned out differently."

"Helps with her guilt over Haile's defection, I'm sure," Bethanne said.

A cab drove up as he was speaking. The driver stopped near the plane and quickly got out, speaking to Rashid.

"Our transportation," he said.

"That was fast."

"I had one of the medical personnel radio for a cab. It'll take us to the hospital and I can decide our next move after I see how Alexes is doing."

"Will the plane be okay here?" Bethanne asked. They were on the far end of the airport tarmac. There were no personnel around and no fencing or other protection for the plane. Still, it was a small airport and so far off the beaten track, Bethanne couldn't imagine anyone wanting to harm the aircraft.

"It will be fine."

The cab was a standard sedan. Comfortable, but a far cry from the limo she'd been using. Oh, oh, she warned herself, don't be expecting that kind of luxury in the future.

When they arrived at the hospital, Alexes had already been cleared through the emergency room and was in a private room, with a nurse in constant attendance. Bethanne sat in the waiting room with Fatima while Rashid dealt with the paperwork. When he returned, she stood.

"Is he going to be all right?" she asked.

"Too early to tell, the doctor said." He looked worried. "I called the office to notify his family. If they wish to come here to be with him, I'll arrange for transportation."

Bethanne glanced around at the small facility. "Is this place equipped to deal with his situation?" she asked softly.

"It is not the latest in medical technology, but fortunately the doctors on staff are proficient. He will get good care here. Once he's stabilized, we can fly him back to Alkaahdar."

"And in the meantime?"

"We'll stay. Until we know something for certain."

He spoke to Fatima, who nodded.

"We'll find a hotel and check in. Then lunch. It's past one. Then you two can rest until we learn more about Alexes."

When they met for lunch on the small veranda of the hotel on the square, Bethanne wished she had something to wear besides her uniform. It still looked fresh and would have to do, but the warmth of the day had her wishing for one of the summer dresses in the closet at the villa. Something more feminine than a navy shirt and khaki pants.

Rashid sat at one of the tables. She joined him and he rose as she approached.

"Fatima decided to have lunch in her room. She wishes to lie down afterward," he said as he held the chair for Bethanne. "I think the excitement is catching up with her."

"I hope the situation didn't give her a fear of flying," she said.

"We're safe—that's what counts. I ordered already—a light lunch since it is so late. We'll eat here tonight if we don't have definite word about Alexes before then."

Bethanne nodded. She hoped the other pilot would recover quickly, and be ready to fly again soon. For a moment she wondered what she'd do if she ever had to stop flying. She loved it so much, it would be a drastic change for her life.

The entire situation spooked her a bit. If Alexes had been flying solo, he could have crashed and no one would likely know why. Is that what happened to her father? A crash in some lonely location that no one had found?

"I hope he's going to be okay." She felt an immediate affinity to the older pilot. She hoped he recovered from whatever hit him and could continue flying.

Once they were served, Rashid asked if her room was to her liking.

"It's clean and neat and overlooks the square. Charming, actually."

"Not like the villa."

"Nice in its own way," she replied. "This changes your plans, doesn't it? You didn't expect to be away from the office all day."

"I can be reached by phone if there is an emergency. The staff is capable of handling things. Shall we explore the town after lunch?"

"I would love to."

When they started out, Rashid insisted on buying her a wide-brimmed hat to shelter her head from the sun.

"You aren't wearing one," she said as they left the gift shop.

"I'm used to the sun. Your skin is much fairer than mine and I don't want it burned."

She smiled, feeling cherished. No one had looked out for her in a long, long time.

They walked around the square, looking into the shops, but when asked if she wanted to enter any, she declined. She wanted to see as much of the town as she could. The old buildings had ornate decorative carvings and bas-reliefs that intrigued her. The cobblestone streets showed wear but were still functioning centuries after they'd first been laid down.

"Tell me about this place. It's old, feels steeped in history. Is it a true representation of old Quishari?"

Rashid gave her a brief history of the town, telling her it had been on the trade routes, a favorite resting place because of the plentiful water.

As the afternoon grew warmer, she could feel heat radiating from the walls as they passed. Turning a corner and exploring some of the side streets put them in line with the breeze and it was pleasant.

"The air feels drier than the coast," she commented.

"Quite. There's a danger of dehydration. We'll stop soon and have something to drink."

Stopping after three o'clock for cold drinks at a small sidewalk café, she was glad the tables had umbrellas. Even with the hat, she was hot beneath the sun. Yet she relished the sights. She loved the sense of timelessness. This town had been here for a thousand years and would likely be around another thousand. If only the walls could talk.

"Will we be able to walk out on the desert a little?" she asked.

"We can ask the driver to take us as far out as you wish to go."

"Just enough to get the feel for it. It's amazing to me anyone can live in the desert."

"The old tribes knew the water spots which were crucial for survival. Caravans and nomads once roamed known trails. Now the routes are known to fewer and fewer people."

When they returned to the hotel, Rashid summoned the same cab. He spoke with the driver and before she knew it, she was sitting in the backseat with Rashid as the man drove crazily toward the west.

"So we ditch the town and take off," she murmured, feeling the delightful cool air from the air conditioner.

"For a while. It's best to see the desert with those interested, not those who wish they were elsewhere."

She laughed and settled down to enjoy the drive.

To the right were rows of oil wells, the steady rising and fall of the pumpjacks timeless.

"I've seen those pumps in California," she commented. "In one place they are even painted to look like whimsical animals," she said, watching the monotonous up-and-down action of the machines.

"These kind of pumps are used all over the world. I had not thought about decorating them. They're functional, that's all."

"Is this an oil field that belongs to your company?"

"It is."

"Do you come here often?"

"No. Only once before, actually." He was silent for a moment, then said softly, "It was my father's special project. The wells don't produce as much as in other areas, but he insisted on keeping the field going, and on checking on it himself. I came with him once. It held special attraction for him, not so much for me. As long as there are no problems, I don't need to visit. Khalid comes occasionally."

"Must be nice for the local economy."

"One reason my father kept it going, I think. The discovery of oil helped revive the town and he felt an obligation to keep it going."

"And you do as well."

He shrugged. "I try. My father was a great man. I'm doing my best to do what I think would make him proud."

"Keep an open mind about mine," she said.

He looked at her, eyes narrowed. "What further is there to discuss?"

"We don't know what happened. But I know my father. And he was an honorable man. He would not have stolen your father's plane."

"My father was also an honorable man. The betrayal of his pilot and the disappearance of the plane caused such stress and anxiety he suffered a heart attack, which killed him. It isn't only the betrayal but the end result I find abhorrent."

Bethanne stared out across the desert as if she could search around and find a clue as to what happened to her father. She had only her belief in her dad to sustain her. "I have faith in my father just as you do in yours," she said slowly.

"It is not something we are going to agree on," he said.

"Tell me about being a twin," she said, turning to look at Rashid. It was a definite change of subject, but she wanted the afternoon to be special—not have them at odds because of the past. "I don't even have a sibling, much less a twin. It is true, you're so close you can read each other's mind?"

"Hardly. I can sense things when we are together—like if he's angry and hiding it. But we are two individuals. Growing up was fun. We delighted in playing tricks on our parents and tutors, switching identities, that sort of thing."

"Tell me," she invited.

He spoke of when he and Khalid were boys, visits to the villa to see their grandmother, trips to Europe and other countries around the Mediterranean Sea.

To Bethanne, it sounded glorious. So different from her childhood in Texas. She laughed at some of the antics he described, and felt a bit of sadness for their homesickness when sent to school in England for eight years when Rashid told her how much they'd missed their country.

When he spoke to the driver, he stopped. Rashid looked at Bethanne. "When we get out, look in all directions. Nothing but desert."

She did so, stepping away from the car, seeking all she could from her senses. The air was dry, hot. The breeze was soft against her skin, carrying the scent of plants she didn't know. In the distance the land shimmered in heat waves, and she thought she saw water.

"A mirage," she breathed softly.

"There?" Rashid stood next to her at the rear of the cab, bending down so his head was next to hers so he could see what she saw. He pointed to the distant image and she nodded. "It does look like water, but we would never find it."

"I know. I have only seen one other mirage. This is fascinating. And quiet. If we don't speak, I think I can hear my heartbeat in the silence."

He didn't reply and for several long moments Bethanne absorbed everything, from the awesome, stark beauty of the desert to the heat from Rashid's body next to hers, his scent mingling with that on the wind. She never wanted to forget this special moment.

Turning, she was surprised how close he stood. "Thank you for bringing me," she said.

To her surprise, he put his palm beneath her chin and raised her face to his. "You constantly surprise me," he said before kissing her.

His lips were warm against hers, moving slowly as if savoring the touch. He pressed for a response and Bethanne gave it to him, sighing softly and stepping closer. His lips opened hers and his tongue teased her. She responded with her own and was drowned in sensation. Forgotten was the world; she was wrapped up in emotions and feelings and the exquisite touch of his mouth against hers. Only the wind was witness, only the sand reflected the heat of passion.

All too soon he ended the kiss and gazed down at her as she slowly opened her eyes. His dark gaze mesmerized. Her heart pounded, her blood sang through her body. If she could capture only one moment of her entire life to never forget, it would be this one.

"We should head back," he said.

The spell shattered. She stepped back and

turned, trying to regain her composure so he would never know how much the kiss meant.

"I'm ready. Thank you for bringing me here. It is a special spot." And would forever remain so.

The drive back to Quraim Wadi Samil was silent. Bethanne hugged the sensation of his kiss to herself as the desert scenery whizzed by. Before long the roof lines of the buildings could be seen. They drew closer by the moment. As she and Rashid drew further apart. It had been a whim, an alignment of circumstances—the scare in the plane, the worry about the pilot, being away from home. It meant nothing beyond they were glad to be alive.

She wished it had meant something.

Dinner that evening was again on the terrace of the small hotel. Fatima joined them and the sheikh kept the conversation neutral, translating back and forth between the two women. Bethanne wasn't sure if she were glad Fatima was present or not. It kept things on an even keel, preventing her from reading more into the afternoon's outing than warranted. But it also meant she had to share the precious time with Rashid. And of course the topic of conversation remained focused on Alexes. The doctor had been cautiously optimistic.

Rashid had obtained the report upon their return to the hotel. It looked as if it was a small stroke.

"But he'll fully recover?" Bethanne asked when Rashid told Fatima.

"That's what the tests are assessing. I hope so. But I don't know if he'll ever fly again."

Bethanne nodded. "Or at least not as a solo pilot," she said. "If he were copilot, there'd be someone else in case of another emergency." Her heart hurt for the man. Flying was a way of life; how sad if it ended prematurely.

Rashid nodded. "However, I do not want my family or employees put in any danger if unnecessary. Alexes has served us well for many years. He will not be abandoned."

Sending up a quick prayer for his recovery, Bethanne asked if he would be released before they returned to Alkaahdar.

"Unlikely. We will return in the morning. He'll need care for several days."

Fatima spoke.

"She wonders when she will return home," Rashid said to Bethanne.

"She doesn't need to stay on my account," she replied.

"I believe my mother is more comfortable with her as your chaperone. Otherwise, you might have to stay with my mother."

Bethanne stared at him in dismay. "You can't be serious."

"If we are to continue the pretense, we need to

be authentic. I would not have a woman in a home I owned without a proper chaperone—not if I were serious about making her my wife."

"That's totally old-fashioned."

"We are an old culture. We have certain standards and procedures that have served us well for generations. One is the sacredness of the marriage bond. And the high standards we hold for women we make our wives."

"So you might have a fling with someone in another country, but once in your own, it's old-world values all the way?"

He nodded, amusement showing at her indignation.

"I protect whom I'm interested in. There would be no gossip or scandal. The full authority of the al Harum family would be behind the woman I showed interest in—as it would for Khalid's chosen bride."

"Is he also getting married?"

"Not that I know of. He's not the older son."

Bethanne thought it over for a moment. In an odd way, it was interesting. Old-fashioned and a bit chauvinistic, but romantic at the same time. A woman who truly caught Rashid al Harum's interest and affection would be cherished, cosseted and treated like royalty at every turn.

Lucky girl!

* * *

The next morning Bethanne piloted the plane back to Alkaahdar. Rashid sat in the copilot's seat. Alexes had been declared out of danger, but the doctor in charge wanted him to remain a bit longer for observation to assess his reaction to medications. He would be transported home in another company plane in a few days' time.

As she flew back, Bethanne was lost in thought as she studied the landscape, so different viewed from the air than on the ground. There were endless miles of sand beneath them, no signs of life. Yet she'd felt the vibrancy of the desert when they'd stopped yesterday.

In a short time she saw the high-rises of the city on the horizon.

"I can't imagine living down there without the modern conveniences," she said.

"My brother likes the challenge. He goes to the desert a lot. I'm like you. I prefer modern conveniences—especially air-conditioning."

"Funny that twins would be so different."

"More a difference in circumstances. When Khalid was burned so badly, he withdrew. I know the woman he thought to marry was horrified and did not stand by him. I thought he was better out of that arrangement, but it was still a bitter pill to swallow. It was after that he began seeking solitude in the desert."

"Can't the burned skin be fixed with plastic surgery?"

"He had some operations, decided against any more. He says he's satisfied."

Bethanne knew even with the badly burned slash of skin, Khalid was as dynamic and appealing as his brother. "Too bad."

"It could have been worse. He could have died."

Once they landed at the airport, the familiar limousine slid into place near the plane.

"I have work to do. Teaz will take you to the villa. I'll see you for dinner around seven?" Rashid said.

"I'll look forward to it," she said, disappointed they wouldn't spend this day together. "I'll double-check things on the plane before leaving."

Since Rashid would be tied up until later, she'd revisit the café in the square near where her father once lived to see if his friend had shown up. The longer she was around Rashid, the more she wanted to clear her father's name. It grew in importance as her feelings for the sheikh grew.

CHAPTER FIVE

SATURDAY Bethanne rose early. Today was the polo match, followed by a dinner dance in the evening. She hoped the dress she'd brought for the actual match was suitable. The light blue cotton had appealed to her the moment she'd first seen it. It was slightly more casual than the dresses Rashid had bought. Suitable for outdoors and easily cleaned if something spilled on it. She hoped she'd chosen well. The sparkle in her eyes and the blush of color on her cheeks showed how excited she was with the excursion.

The maid knocked on the door before nine and told her Rashid was waiting.

Grabbing her small purse and the wide-brimmed hat Rashid has bought in Quraim Wadi Samil, she hurried down to greet him.

He was waiting in the foyer, dressed in jodhpurs and a white shirt opened at the collar. He watched as she ran lightly down the stairs while she could hardly take her eyes off him. He looked fabulous.

"I'm ready," she said as she stepped onto the tile floor.

"A good trait in a woman, always being on time."

"Comes from pilot training, I expect," she said as they went outside.

A small sports car stood where the limousine normally parked.

"I will drive," Rashid said, escorting her to the passenger's side.

Bethanne loved riding in a convertible—especially beside Rashid.

Within twenty minutes, they had reached the polo field. The bustle of activity reminded Bethanne of horse races in Texas. Lots of people walking around, studying horses, reviewing printed programs, laughing and talking. Clothing varied from designer originals to the jodhpurs and white shirts that Rashid wore. Once in a while she spotted a man in more traditional robes, but for the most part she could be in England or France, or Texas.

Rashid parked near a stable and Bethanne went with him to one of the stalls where a groom already had a beautiful Arabian saddled.

"This is Morning Star," Rashid said with affection, patting the arched neck of the horse. His glossy chestnut coat gleamed. His mane and tail had been brushed until they looked silky soft.

"He's beautiful," she said, reaching out to pet him as well.

"He is one of four I have. Come, we'll look at the rest, all great animals. But Morning Star is the one I ride most often."

Bethanne loved the entire atmosphere of the event. She was introduced to other players. She petted a dozen or more beautiful horses. She watched as the grooms prepared horses for the event.

Khalid was also riding and they visited him shortly before Rashid escorted her to the viewing stands. His welcome wasn't exactly warm, but better than his mother's was likely to be, Bethanne thought.

"My mother is already in the royal box," Rashid said as they began to climb the stairs.

Bethanne's heart dropped. She had not known she'd be spending time with Madame al Harum. It was enough to put a damper on her enthusiasm. Still, with any luck, the woman would be so busy rooting for her sons, she would ignore the unwelcomed woman her one son was entertaining.

There were several guests in the al Harum box, and Rashid made sure everyone was introduced to Bethanne before he left.

"See you later," he said, with a special caress on her cheek.

She played the part of adoring girlfriend and told him to win for her.

Smiling at the others, she took a seat left for her on the front row and focused on the playing field and not the chatter around her. Not that she could understand it. Just before the match began, Madame al Harum sat in the seat next to her.

The game was exciting and Bethanne was glad Rashid had gone over the main points so she had a glimmer of an idea how it was played. Often she saw a blur of horses and riders when the players vied for the ball. Other times Rashid would break free and hit the ball down the field. Or Khalid. His horse was a dark bay. That wasn't the only way she could tell the men apart, but it helped. She seemed tuned in to Rashid and kept her eyes on him for most of the game.

When the match ended, Rashid's team had won by two points. The people in the box cheered and Bethanne joined right in.

"Come, we will meet them for celebration, then return home to change for tonight's fete," Madame al Harum said, touching Bethanne on the shoulder. The older woman walked proudly to the area where the winners were celebrating.

When Rashid saw them, he broke away and crossed swiftly to them, enveloping Bethanne in a hug. She hugged him right back, enthusiasm breaking out.

"It was wonderful! You looked like you were part of the horse. And that one long drive…I thought the ball would never stop."

"Well done, Rashid," his mother said, watching in disapproval the animation on Bethanne's face.

Khalid came over, hugging his mother and standing with his arm around her shoulders as he greeted Bethanne again.

"Great match," she said with a smile.

He nodded.

"Don't you ever worry you'll get hit by the maillot?"

"It's happened. Glad you enjoyed it. Your first match?" he asked.

"Yes. I hope not my last," she said. Rashid had mimicked his brother with his arm around Bethanne's shoulders. She tried not to be self-conscious, but she knew his mother did not approve. She didn't care. She would not care. It's not as if they'd made a lifelong commitment to each other. The older woman would find out soon enough.

"Come to the dinner tonight," Madame al Harum said to Khalid.

"Not tonight. I have other plans." He gave her a kiss on her cheek, sketched a salute to Rashid and Bethanne and left, weaving his way through the crowd.

His mother watched with sad eyes.

"He never comes," she said.

"Let him find his own way, Mother," Rashid said gently.

After Rashid checked with the groom on the state of his horse, he escorted Bethanne to the sports car.

"So how often do you play? When do you find time to practice? Do you ever have games away from Alkaahdar?" she asked, fascinated by the sport.

He answered her questions as he skillfully drove through the city traffic, giving Bethanne a fascinating insight to more of his life.

"I'll pick you up at six-thirty," he said when they arrived at the villa. "Dinner starts at seven. And the party will last until late."

"I'll be ready," she said.

Before she could get out of the car, however, he stopped her. "You did well today."

"I will do fine tonight as well," she replied gravely. "I'll be most adoring, now that you won the match."

He laughed at her sassy remark and watched as she entered the house.

Bethanne dressed with care for the dinner. She wore an ivory-white dress from the ones Rashid had bought. The one-shoulder gown fell in a gentle drape down to the floor, moving when she walked, caressing her skin with the softness of pure silk. Minnah came to ask if she could assist and Bethanne asked her to do her hair up in a fancy style.

The quiet woman nodded and set to work when Bethanne sat in front of the vanity.

"Could you also teach me some Arabic?" Bethanne asked.

"Like what?"

"Pleased to meet you. I am enjoying visiting your country. Just a few phrases?"

"It would be my pleasure," the maid said.

For the moments it took the maid to arrange her hair, she also taught Bethanne several phrases. With a skill for mimicking sounds, Bethanne hoped she was getting the correct intonation to the sounds she heard.

Minnah beamed with pleasure a few moments later. Bethanne gazed at herself in the mirror, very pleased with the simple, yet sophisticated style the maid had achieved.

"Thank you," she said in Arabic.

Minnah bowed slightly and smiled. "You pick up the words quickly."

"I'll be repeating them from now until we begin dinner," she said in English.

"His Excellency will be pleased with the effort you have made starting to learn our language. It is good for you to speak Arabic."

Bethanne didn't abuse her of the idea that she

was being considered for Rashid's wife. Nothing like servants' gossip to spread like wildfire. That should suit him.

Bethanne was waiting in the salon when Rashid arrived. He wore a tuxedo. She loved the different facets of the man. From suave businessman to casual polo player to elegant sophisticate. She couldn't decide which appealed more.

"Ever prompt," he repeated when he stepped into the salon. "And you look lovely."

"Thank you," she said in Arabic, almost laughing at his look of surprise.

He said several words in that language which had her actually laughing aloud and holding up a hand.

"Please, I only learned a very few—such as please and thank you, nice to meet you and I am enjoying my visit."

"Very well done," he said.

His obvious approval warmed her.

"The dress is lovely, but missing something," he said.

She looked down. "I have a wrap on the chair," she said, moving to gather it.

"I was thinking of jewelry," he said, stepping closer. From his pocket he pulled out a beautiful necklace of sapphires and diamonds on a white gold chain.

Bethanne caught her breath. "It's beautiful." She took a step back. "But I can't wear that. What

if it came undone and was lost?" She couldn't
replace a fine piece of jewelry like that for years.

"It will not come undone and the stones match
your eyes. It will complete the dress."

She looked at the necklace and then at Rashid.

"My intended bride would not come as a pauper
to the wedding," he said.

Of course. It was for show. For a moment she
was swamped with disappointment. What had she
expected—that he'd really give her a lovely piece
of jewelry like that?

"Very well, but it's on you if it gets lost."

She stepped forward and held out her hand, but
he brushed it aside and reached around her neck
to fasten it himself. She stared at his throat, her
heart hammering in her chest. The touch of his
warm fingers on her neck sent shivers down her
spine. She could scarcely breathe.

Bethanne turned when he'd finished, seeking a
mirror to see how it looked. There were none in
the salon. "I want to see," she said.

"In the foyer, then we should leave."

Standing a moment later in front of the long
mirror in the foyer, she gazed at her reflection. She
looked totally different. It wasn't only the expen-
sive clothing and jewelry, the sophisticated hairstyle. There was a glow about her, a special look
in her eyes. She sought Rashid's in the reflection.
He looked at her steadily.

"Thank you. I feel like Cinderella before the ball."

"It does not end at midnight," he said. "Shall we?"

The limo carried them the short distance to the luxury hotel where the dinner was being held. The huge portico accommodated half a dozen cars at a time and Bethanne had a chance to observe the other women getting out of cars and limousines who were wearing designer creations and enough jewelry to open a mega store.

Once inside, Bethanne was delighted with the sparkling chandeliers overhead that threw rainbows of color around the lavish room. Tables were set with starched white linen clothes, ornate silverware and fine crystal glassware. The room was large enough to accommodate hundreds, yet the space was not crowded.

Rashid placed her hand in the crook of his arm, pressing her arm against his side as they walked in. He greeted friends, introducing Bethanne to each. She smiled and gave her newly learned Arabic greeting. Many of the people seemed pleased, and then disappointed she hadn't yet learned more. They encouraged her to continue learning.

An older man stopped their progression. He spoke to Rashid, but his gaze never left Bethanne.

Rashid answered then spoke in English.

"Bethanne, may I present Ibrahim ibn Saali, minister of finance for Quishari. He is a great polo fan. I've told him you are my special guest."

"Come to visit Quishari?" the minister asked.

Bethanne smiled brightly. "Indeed, and I'm charmed by what I've seen." She leaned slightly against Rashid, hoping she looked like a woman in love in the minister's eyes.

"I thought another was coming," the minister said.

She looked suitably surprised, then glanced at Rashid. "There had better not be another expected."

He shook his head, his hand covering hers on his arm. "Not in this lifetime," he said. To the minister he nodded once. "We are expected at my mother's table."

"Nice to have met you," Bethanne said in Arabic.

The older man merely nodded and stepped aside.

She could feel his gaze as they crossed to the table.

"He's the one, isn't he?" she asked.

"Indeed. But your acting skills were perfect." He glanced down at her and smiled. "If we keep him satisfied, the deal is as good as done."

When they reached their table, Madame al Harum was already seated. Next to her was an elderly man. He rose when Bethanne arrived and greeted her solemnly. Both expressed surprise at her Arabic response. For a moment she wondered if the older woman would thaw a bit. That thought was short-lived when Madame al Harum virtually ignored Bethanne and indicated that Rashid should sit next to her.

Despite not understanding the language, Bethanne enjoyed herself. The polo club was celebrating their victory and she could clap and cheer with them all. Several speakers were obviously from the club. Rashid leaned closer to give capsulated recaps of the speeches. At one point the speaker on the platform said something that had everyone turning to look at Rashid. He rose and bowed slightly to thunderous applause.

When he sat down and the speaker resumed, she leaned closer.

"What did he say?"

"Just thanks for funding the matches."

"Ah, so you're the sponsor?"

"One of several."

She knew he was wealthy, but to fund a sports team cost serious money. She was so out of her element. No matter how much she was growing attracted to her host, she had to remember in the great scheme of things, she was a lowly employee of a company selling him the jet she'd delivered. He was a wealthy man, gorgeous to boot. He had no need to look to the likes of her when any woman in the world would love to be in her position. How could Haile have chosen someone else over Rashid?

When the after-dinner speeches were finally finished, a small musical ensemble set up and began playing dance music. Some of the older guests gathered their things to leave, but the younger ones began to drift to the dance floor.

Rashid held out his hand to Bethanne. "Will you dance with me?" he asked.

She nodded and rose.

He was conscious of the stares and some of the conversation that erupted when they reached the dance floor. Her blond hair and blue eyes stood out in this group of mostly dark-haired women. He enjoyed taking her into his arms for the slow dance. She was taller than most women he had dated and it was a novelty to not have to lean over to hear if she spoke. Or to kiss her.

He'd thought a lot about that kiss in Quraim Wadi Samil as they moved with the music. He tightened his hold slightly in remembrance. One kiss had him fantasizing days afterward. He'd kissed his share of women. He'd even thought he loved Marguerite. But Bethanne had him in a quandary. He knew this was an interlude that would end as soon as the contract with al Benqura was signed. Yet he found reasons to seek her out and spend time with her. He loved to hear her talk. She wasn't one to mince words, or be totally agreeable. He knew too many people who sought favor above friendship.

And while he tried to ignore the physical attraction, he couldn't do it. He longed to press her against him, kiss her, make love to her. Her skin was as soft as down. Her sparkling eyes held wit and humor and made him think of the blue of the Gulf on a sunny day. He wanted to thread his fingers through that silky blond hair and stroke it, feeling the softness, the warmth from Bethanne.

Comparing her to other women was unfair—to others. Unlike Marguerite, she was unpretentious and genuine. She did not show an innate desire to garner as much money as she could in a short time. He detected no subterfuge; had heard no hints about keeping the necklace she wore. He smiled slightly when he thought of her worry if it came undone. He would never expect her to repay the cost of the jewelry. When he'd asked his assistant to find something with blue stones, an array had been brought to the office. These sapphires had matched her eyes. He'd chosen it immediately.

How had he known they would match her eyes? He could not even remember what color Marguerite's eyes were. Glancing down, he studied his partner as they circled the room. She looked enchanted. And enchanting. Her gaze skimmed around the room, a slight smile showing her enjoyment. As if she could feel his attention, she looked up.

The blue startled him with its intensity. Her smile made him want to slip away from the crowd to a private place and kiss her again.

"Enjoying yourself?" he said, to hear her speak.

"Very much. This is even better than my senior prom, which was the last formal dance I attended, I think. Some of the gowns are spectacular. I'm trying to remember everything so I never forget."

"There will be others," he said, taking for granted the setting and the people—many of whom he'd known all his life. His polo team members had been friends for years.

"For you. Once you sign that contract, I'm heading back to Texas."

"Or you could stay a little longer," he suggested, wishing to find a way to keep her longer.

From the jump she gave, he'd surprised her with his suggestion.

"I may delay signing the papers until well after the deal is finalized," he said, half in jest. Far from being angry at Haile, he now thanked her for her defection. Otherwise he would not have known Bethanne. What a shame if he'd merely thanked her for delivering the jet and never seen her again.

"Now why would you do that?" she asked, leaning back a bit to smile up at him with a saucy grin.

It took all of Rashid's willpower to resist the temptation to kiss her right there on the ballroom floor. She was flirting with him. It had been years since someone had done that in fun. He knew she had no ulterior motives.

"Alexes might never fly again. Perhaps you could become my personal pilot." He hadn't thought about that before, but it would be a perfect solution. She'd remain in Quishari and he could see her whenever he wanted.

"My home is in Texas," she said slowly. "I don't speak the language here. I have family and friends in Galveston. I don't think it would work."

At least she sounded regretful.

"Think about it before deciding," he said.

"Would there be more dances like this?" she teased.

He laughed and spun her around. "Yes, as many as you wish to attend. I don't go often, except the ones with the polo team. But that could change. I receive dozens of invitations."

"I would imagine attending them all would prove tiring. And it would dim some of the splendor if you saw this kind of thing all the time. What makes it special is being rare."

"A wise woman."

The music ended. In a moment another song began. Rashid held her hand during the short break, rubbing his thumb lightly over the soft skin. The couple next to them smiled but said nothing, for which he was grateful. Even more grateful when the music began again and he could draw her back into his arms again. It had been a long time since he'd enjoyed spending time with anyone beyond his family.

The evening flew by. Bethanne focused on the offhand invitation to stay. She wasn't sure if he were serious or not. It was tempting. Maybe too much of a good thing. What would happen if she actually fell in love with the sheikh and he only wanted her as a pilot because Alexes was incapacitated? She gazed off, picturing him with other women—beautiful women with pots of money. He'd ask her to fly them to Cairo or even Rome on holiday. She'd be dutiful and resentful. She didn't want to fly him and some other woman anywhere. She wanted him for herself.

Startled at her thoughts, she glanced at him quickly, and found his gaze fixed on hers.

"If you are ready to leave, we can return to the villa," he said.

"I've had a lovely time, but it is getting late." Her heart pounded with the newly admitted discovery. She was in love with Rashid.

"Too late for a walk along the beach?"

To walk along the Persian Gulf in the moonlight—who could pass up such an opportunity?

"Never too late for that."

On the ride to the villa, he continued to hold her hand. Bethanne told herself it was merely a continuation of the evening. But she felt special. Would it ever be possible for a sheikh to fall for a woman from Texas? With no special attributes except the ability to fly planes? Undoubtedly when he chose a bride, he'd want a sophisticated woman who was as at home in the capital city as she would be anywhere in the world.

When they reached the villa, he helped her from the limo then bypassed the front door to head for the gardens. The pathways were discreetly lighted by soft lamps at foot level. Selective spotlights shone on a few of the topiary plants; the ambient glow felt magical. Fragrances blended delightfully with the salty tang of the sea. She heard the wavelets as they walked along.

"Should we change?" she asked, concerned for the lovely gown.

"More fun this way."

An unexpected side of Rashid. Every time she thought she had a grasp on his personality, he surprised her.

When they reached the beach, they sat on the chairs to take off their shoes. Rashid rolled his pant legs up and held out his hand for her when she rose. They ran to the water. Bethanne pulled her skirt to above her knees in an attempt to keep the beautiful silk from getting wet, holding it with one hand.

The water was warm. The moon was low on the horizon, painting a strip of white on the calm sea. Stars sprinkled the dark skies. In the distance a soft glow showed where the capital city lay. As if in one accord, they turned and began walking north.

"I can't believe you live in the city when you have this house," Bethanne said. "I'd walk along the beach every chance I got if I lived here."

"You seem to like simple pleasures," he said. Unlike other women he knew who loved new clothes, jewelry and being seen in all the right places.

"What's better? Maybe flying."

"Tell me why you like that so much."

"I'm not sure I can put it into words. There's a special feeling soaring high into the sky. The power of the plane at my command. The view of the earth, seeing the curvature, seeing the land as it is and not as man has rearranged it. I never tire of it."

"I see flying as an expedient way to get from one place to another in the shortest time."

"Then you need to fly in the cockpit more and give work a rest."

He laughed. "I would not be where I am today if I didn't pay attention to business."

"There's such a thing as balance."

"So you suggest I take more time off?"

"Take time to relax. Even in your time off you're busy. Do you ever just lie on the beach and listen to the waves?"

"No."

She danced in the water. "I do when I'm home. Galveston has some beautiful beaches and I like to just veg out and do nothing but stare at the water and let the rhythm of the surf relax me."

"Not often, I bet." She was too full of energy to be content to sit and do nothing for long.

"I guess not. That's why when I do, it's special."

He stopped and turned to face her. "You're special, Bethanne Sanders." He put his free hand around the back of her neck and drew her slowly closer, leaning over to kiss her.

The night was magical, the setting perfection, the woman with him fascinating and intriguing. The temporary nature gave an urgency to their time together. Too short to waste.

She kissed him back, slinging one arm around his neck, her other hand still holding her skirt.

For a long time Rashid forgot about responsibilities, about duties and about the pretense of their relationship. There was only Bethanne and the feel of her in his arms.

Both were breathing hard when he ended the kiss. They were alone on the beach, quite a distance from the villa. He was tempted to sweep her in his arms and find a secluded spot and make love all night long.

"We should return," he said. Duty over desire, hard to harness.

"Yes." She let go of his hand, gathered her skirt in both hands and began walking briskly back to the villa.

"Wait." He hurried to catch her. "Are you okay?" He tried to examine her expression in the faint light but she kept her head averted.

"I'm fine." She did not stop walking.

"Then the kiss upset you."

She stopped at that and turned to glare at him. "It did not upset me. What upsets me is that I don't know the rules of this game. We're pretending. But that kiss seemed real. You are solicitous in public playing the perfect gentleman who is showing someone around. It's all fake. Why the kisses?"

Rashid paused. "Because I can't resist," he answered, daring to reveal his feelings. It had been a long time since he'd let emotion make inroads. Would he regret the confession?

She blinked at that. "What?" It almost squeaked out.

"Why should that surprise you? I find you beautiful, fun, interesting, different. I want to be with you, touch you." He reached out his hand and trailed his fingertips down her bare arm, struck again by the warm softness of her skin. "I want to kiss you."

He could see her indecision. Finally she nodded once. "Okay, but unless we are really going somewhere with this relationship, no more than kisses."

Her words jerked him from the reverie he had of the two of them spending time together. He was not going anywhere with any relationship. He had tried love and failed. He had tried arranged marriage—and that didn't look like it was in the cards, either. Was it too much to ask just to enjoy being together for a while—as long as they both wanted?

"Then I'll just have to settle for kisses," he said, drawing her back into his embrace.

Bethanne awoke the next morning feeling grumpy and tired when Minnah entered with the usual breakfast fare. She refused to let her crankiness show and almost screamed with impatience while the maid fussed around before leaving. Bethanne had not had a good night's sleep and it was all Rashid's fault. She'd been a long time falling asleep thinking of the kisses at the beach. And the words he had not spoken—that their relationship had a future. That hurt the most.

She sipped her chocolate and wondered what she was doing. Always one to face facts, she simply could not let herself imagine she was falling for the sheikh. She needed to visit the places she wanted to, search for her father and remind herself constantly that Rashid's interests did not coincide with hers.

If she told herself a dozen times an hour, maybe she'd listen. But her heart beat faster just thinking of Rashid and the kisses they'd stolen in the night. His scent was permanently affixed in her mind, his dark eyes so compelling when he looked directly at her she could feel herself returning his regard, wishing there were only the two of them. She had run her hands through his hair, pulled him close and shown her feelings while all he had wanted were a few kisses.

She frowned. Time to rise above the attraction that seemed to grow by leaps and bounds and forget any flighty feelings of love. She had her own quest that being here afforded. Today she'd return to the square to see if the man her father had met had returned. Yesterday the waiter who had spoken to her that first day wasn't there. The one working had not understood English. Maybe the other would be back today.

She'd focus on her search for her father and get over Rashid before she saw him again!

Arriving at the square around ten, she went straight to the sidewalk café, searching for the waiter she'd spoken with before. Thankfully he was there. He came out of the interior to greet her.

"I have a note for you," he said with great pride. With a flourish, he withdrew it from his apron pocket and handed it to her. "I knew you would return," he said.

"Thank you. I'll sit over here and have coffee, please." She sat down at a side table and opened the folded paper.

"Hank was a friend of mine. A fellow American. I will stop by the café each day this week in hopes of seeing you." It was signed, Walt Hampstead.

Another American. That made it simple; at least she and he would speak the same language. She would have needed Teaz to translate if Hank's friend had been a native of Quishari.

"What time did the man come?" she asked the waiter when he delivered her coffee.

"Before lunch each day. He will be here soon." Setting the small cup and carafe on the table, he walked away.

Bethanne sipped the hot beverage while she waited until Walt showed up. She had a feeling things were speeding up and she needed to get any information she could before it was too late.

Sometime later a middle-aged man stopped at her table. She'd been writing a letter to a friend at home and looked up when he cast a shadow over the paper.

"Are you Hank's friend?" he asked. "No, that's not right. You're his daughter, Bethanne."

"Walt?" she asked, feeling emotion welling up inside her.

He nodded. Pulling out another chair, he sat down at the table. "He spoke of you often. I saw a picture once. You were younger. I'm Walt Hampstead. Pleased to finally meet you."

"You knew my father? He mentioned a professor at the university, but not by name. Is that you?"

He nodded. The waiter appeared and Walt gave an order for coffee.

"What happened to him? He's dead, isn't he?" Bethanne asked, hoping Walt would deny it all and tell her where Hank was.

But Walt nodded sadly. "I'm afraid so. I haven't heard from him in almost three years. He was a good friend. Not many Americans live in Alkaahdar. We'd meet and hash over how things were going at home. Expats sharing tales of home to fend off homesickness. And he'd tell me the amazing stories about his daughter."

"Have you lived here long?" Bethanne asked, trying to remember all she'd read and heard about his professor friend. She knew her father had liked the man, but always called him the prof.

"Yes, actually, longer than Hank. I teach English as a foreign language at one of the universities. I married a Quishari woman and we have made our home here."

"Tell me what you know about my father. It's

been years since I've heard from him. Time just got away. I've been busy and I thought he was as well. But I can only find out the al Harum family thinks he stole a plane. He wouldn't have!"

The waiter returned with Walt's coffee. Once he'd left, Walt began to speak. "He told me two days before he left that he had a top-secret assignment, then laughed. Just like the movies, he said. I asked him what he was talking about, but he said he was sworn to secrecy, but maybe he'd give me some hints when he returned. He seemed in high spirits and I thought I'd hear from him soon after that. Only I never saw him again."

"I've heard he stole a plane and then vanished," Bethanne said, disheartened. This man had known and liked her father, but knew no more than she did on what had happened to him.

"There were stories going around. Then the head of Bashiri Oil died unexpectedly and the news was full of that and the stories of his twin sons. I never knew the official result of that secret mission," Walt said. He looked pensive for a moment. "Hank was a true friend. It was good to have someone from home to talk over things with. I miss him."

He sipped his coffee. "He flew the plane for the old sheikh, and often told me about where they went, what the different cities were like. Hank loved seeing the world and knew the job he had was great for that. He flew the sheikh to Europe, Egypt, even once to India. Most of the flights were around the Persian Gulf, though."

"Did the secret mission have something to do with the sheikh?"

"That I don't know. I could speculate it was because he worked almost exclusively for the man. But being a secret, I never heard any more. Your father did not steal a plane. He was too honorable for that."

Bethanne felt a wave of gratitude toward Walt for his comment. "I want to find out exactly what happened and let others know he wouldn't do such a thing." Especially let Rashid know. Every time he looked at her he had to remember his belief her father had caused the death of his. It was so unfair!

"Don't know how you'll find out. Do you speak the language?" he asked.

"No, except for pleased to meet you."

"This country is still very much a man's world. I bet they were surprised to discover you're a pilot," he said.

"At first. What happened to my dad's things?" she asked.

"I don't know. I went by his apartment once I realized he was probably dead. It had already been rented and the young woman who answered the door said it had been immaculately cleaned before she moved in. I guess the sheikh's people packed up. I don't know if they threw his things away or stored them."

"My mother tried to find out what happened to him—as his onetime wife. But no one told her anything. I guess if they had any of his things, they would have sent them to her." Bethanne gazed across the square, seeing the buildings her father would have seen every day. She missed him with a tangible pain.

"He spoke of you a lot. You were a bright spot in his life. He talked about when you'd come to visit and what you two would see."

"We discussed it more than once. I longed to see Quishari, but not like this. It's a beautiful country and I've enjoyed everything I've seen. But I had hoped to see it with my dad."

Walt scribbled on a page of his notebook and tore it out. "Here's my phone number and address. Call me if you need anything. Or wish to visit. My wife would be delighted to meet you. She liked Hank, too. He came to dinner occasionally. Her English is not as fluent as it could be, so she enjoyed listening to our conversations and hearing English spoken by natives."

"Thank you." She took the paper and put it in her purse. "I don't know how you could contact me if you remember anything. I am staying at the sea villa of Sheikh Rashid al Harum. But I have no idea what the address is, or the phone number."

"Do you like him? Hank really respected his father."

"I do like him." Understatement, she thought. But she certainly didn't know this man well enough to even hint at more.

Walt rose. "I'll contact the sheikh if I think of anything else you might wish to know. Nice to have met Hank's daughter. He'd be proud of you. Do consider coming to meet my wife."

Bethanne rose as well and shook hands. "Thanks for coming each day until I was here."

Walt walked away, then stopped and turned. "I do have a photograph of him with me at home. Call me when you can come again and I'll bring it for you to see."

Bethanne nodded. Disappointment filled her and she smiled, blinking away tears. She had so hoped her father's friend would know more. What could a secret mission have been? One filled with danger that ended up costing him his life? How could the old sheikh have demanded that? Did Rashid know?

CHAPTER SIX

BETHANNE rode back to the villa wondering how she could find out more about that secret mission. The only one who had probably known was the old sheikh and he was dead. Would his wife have known anything? If she had, Bethanne would be the last person she'd tell.

Yet everyone seemed to think the plane was stolen. Even so, Hank would have had to file a flight plan. Someone must have known something more about the plane. But she wasn't sure if it were even possible to get a copy in Quishari, much less at this late date.

She could ask Rashid.

Mulling over the possibility of being rebuffed, she weighed it with the possibility of annoying Rashid. But she hadn't a clue where else to go.

When she reached the villa, Fatima was in the foyer, her suitcase beside her. Minnah was there as well and smiled when she saw Bethanne.

"Fatima leaves for the airport. She is returning home," the maid said in English.

Bethanne nodded. "Please tell her I'm sorry for the inconvenience of remaining here when she must have wished to return home immediately."

Minnah relayed the comment, then listened to a rapid burst of speech from Fatima.

"It is she who is grateful for you and whatever arrangement you made with the sheikh that she does not fear returning home. Her charge put her in a very awkward situation and if not for the compassion of the sheikh, she'd not wish to return home. She spoke with her family and there is no retribution awaiting."

"I should hope not," Bethanne said. "She couldn't help—" She paused. Hopefully Fatima had been circumspect in her complaints. Remembering the charade, she finished. "She couldn't help the situation. Tell her I wish her a pleasant journey home."

Once Fatima left, Bethanne went into the library again, wandering around, studying the various books on the shelves. She stopped at the desk and looked at the computer, considering. Turning it on, she sat down and began to search the Internet on any information she could get about Quishari and flight plans and Rashid's father.

Losing track of time, she was surprised when

Minnah knocked on the opened door. "Miss, you haven't come for lunch. It is on the terrace. Are you not hungry?"

Bethanne nodded, reluctant to leave her search, but suddenly feeling ravenous.

She was glad she took the break a few moments later when Rashid arrived. She felt almost guilty using the computer to find out more about his father. If her need hadn't been so strong, she would not have done more than a cursory look to learn a bit more about him. Rashid loved his father and wanted to be like him.

She loved her father, and wanted to clear his name.

"Late lunch," Rashid said, drawing out a chair and sitting at the small table.

"I had coffee at a square in the old town mid-morning, so wasn't ready to eat until now," she explained. "What are you doing here? Is the workday over?" She knew he devoted many hours to business; was something special going on to have him leave so early?

"I thought we could take the jet up again, fly over the wells to the south and see how things are going. Khalid said the well that was burning has been capped. I'd still like to see how much damage was done. There's an airport nearby and I'll have a car waiting so we can drive to the docks, and then go to the derricks themselves."

"I'm at your command," she said, taking another drink of the iced lemonade she enjoyed so much. This was unexpected, but she relished a chance to see more of what he dealt with daily. She was soaking up as much as she could about Rashid. Down the years, she'd have plenty of memories.

"No rush. Finish your lunch. Where in old town did you go?" he asked.

Bethanne looked at her salad, hoping hearing about her morning wouldn't make him angry. "I went for coffee at the square near where my dad lived. I met another American—a friend of Hank's," she said.

"Anyone I know?" he asked.

"A professor of English at the university. Walt Hampstead. He was pleased to see me. My dad had spoken of me to him. He said he's lived here for more than twenty years. Even married a local girl and they have two children."

Rashid appeared unconcerned by the revelation. "Did you visit the shops?"

"No, I enjoyed the architecture and got a feel for the place. The older section really draws me. I love it. If we are going soon, I'll run up and change."

When they reached the airport an hour later, Bethanne went to the air traffic control office to file a flight plan. The service was quick. As she was turning to leave, she asked if there were archived flight plans for the past five years. The clerk was instantly curious as to why she wanted to know. She shrugged it off as mere curiosity and left. The reports would be in Arabic undoubtedly. No help there—unless Walt could translate them for her.

Rashid had remained with the plane and she did her visual inspection before boarding. He was already in the cockpit and for a moment, the intensity of her wish that things had been different floored her. What would it have been like if she and he had met under different circumstances? If he did not think her father a thief and he was seriously interested in her? That they were going off for a day of fun, just the two of them.

She couldn't help her own excitement at seeing him. Try as she might, it was difficult to remember it was all a charade. Especially after his kisses.

Once soaring over the Persian Gulf, she leveled out the plane and watched the earth below. There were large container ships on the sea, white beaches lining the shore. As they approached the oil rigs several hundred yards offshore, she circled slowly. The fire was out. There was a huge oil tanker anchored on the seaward side of one of the high platforms.

"Taking in oil?" she asked, pointing to the ship.

"Yes. Then it goes to a refinery. That's one of our ships. Another branch of the company,"

Rashid said. "My uncle runs that. Set us down and we'll head out to the rigs."

They landed on the runway that ran beside the sea. After Bethanne taxied the plane to a sheltered area as directed, she shut down the engines. A dark car drove over and a man jumped out of the driver's side. In only moments they were driving toward the docks.

The launch that took them to the rigs was small and rode low on the water. Bethanne studied the huge platforms that rose on pilings from the sea floor. When they arrived, they had to climb a hundred steps to get to the main platform. The noise surprised her as machinery hummed and clanked as it pumped the crude from beneath the sea.

Khalid was there and strode over to greet them. His manner was reserved and more formal than Rashid's. A difference in the twins. Even though they looked alike, they didn't behave alike.

A moment later Rashid excused himself, saying he had to confer with Khalid on a private matter.

Bethanne walked away, toward the activity near the ship. There were lots of men working in a choreographed way that showed they all knew their respective jobs well.

After watching for a while, she saw a man walk over to say something to her.

"Sorry, I only speak English," she said.

"I speak it," he replied with a heavy accent. "You fly jet that landed at airport?"

"Yes," she replied.

"I used to work planes for the old sheikh." He shrugged. "After he die, I come to oil—" He gestured around them. "Sheikh Rashid don't travel like father did."

"The old sheikh traveled a lot?" she asked, suddenly wondering if this man had known her father.

"More than son." He looked at the activity, studying it a moment as if assessing the efficiency.

"Did you know Hank Pendarvis?" she asked.

He looked back at her and nodded.

"Someone asked me to look him up if I got to Quishari. I think maybe he died several years ago."

The man nodded. "Bad time. Caused old sheikh's death."

"What happened?"

"Flight in west, something special." He paused a moment as if searching for the English word. "Sandstorm crash plane. All die."

"I heard he stole the plane, took an illegal flight." Her heart pounded. This man said her father had crashed. She knew something kept him from contacting her. Still, maybe all hadn't died. Maybe it was even a different plane.

"No. Job for old sheikh."

Bethanne's interest became intense. "Did you tell anyone? Why does everyone believe he stole a plane?"

"Those need to know do."

"Where did he crash?"

"West."

"Who knows about this?"

He shrugged.

Either he knew no more or wasn't going to give her specifics.

"And he is buried out west, too?"

He shrugged. He peered at her closely, searching her face and eyes. "In a town called Quraim Wadi Samil."

Bethanne gave an involuntary start of surprise. "We were just there," she said.

The man shrugged. "Perhaps you go again."

"Why didn't you tell someone at the time? Sheikh al Harum believes he stole the plane."

"No, I tell the sheikh." He looked at where Rashid stood talking with the other men.

A helicopter approached, its blades whipping the air around the platform. It set down near the far edge.

Someone on the platform called the man and he waved. "I go." He loped across the platform and climbed aboard the helicopter with two other workers.

Bethanne stared at the helicopter until it was out

of sight. It had not remained on the rig for more than a few minutes. Where was it taking the maintenance worker? She had to have answers. According to him, he had told Rashid.

That didn't make sense. If Rashid knew, why not tell her? He didn't pull punches accusing her father of being a thief, why not say if he were dead? If Rashid knew about the sandstorm and the plane crash, why not tell her?

"Makes you wonder, doesn't it?" a male voice asked to her right.

Turning, she saw Khalid had joined her, staring at the damaged oil rig.

"What?"

"Why men put themselves in danger just to pump oil from beneath the sea," he said.

"Was anyone injured in the fire?"

"One man was killed. Another burned."

"I'm sorry."

"As were we. Mohammad was a good man."

"You were burned once, yet you still fight the fires."

"I do not want fire to win. Why are you here?"

"Rashid brought me."

"I mean, why still in Quishari. You delivered the plane. You did not deliver Haile. Yet you stay."

"Ask your brother."

"I did. He said to stop rumors flying that would damage the negotiations with Benqura. I say forget it. Rashid has little to offer for you to stay—unless you hope to cash in somewhere down the line. A story for a tabloid? A bit of blackmail for your silence?"

She turned to him, affronted at his comment. "I have no intentions of blackmail or talking to a tabloid. Maybe I feel a bit responsible I didn't make sure Haile was on board when we took off. What's not to like about a few days in this lovely country? The villa is exquisite. The staff makes me welcomed. Your brother has shown me places I would not otherwise have seen. I would not repay such hospitality with anything you suggest. I stay because he asked me to." She wasn't going to dwell on the attraction she felt any time she was near Rashid. That was her secret alone.

Khalid studied her for a moment, his eyes assessing. "Maybe. But I don't buy it. Not from an American woman in this day. There has to be something for you in it."

"You're cynical. Maybe I'm enjoying a mini vacation."

"Yet you still fly."

She laughed. "That's for fun."

Rashid walked over. "Khalid." He acknowledged his brother. Rashid looked at Bethanne and then Khalid. "Problems?"

"Just questioning your guest as to why she's here. Watch your back, brother."

"I know what I'm doing," Rashid said with a steely note.

"Maybe it's time for me to leave," she said.

Rashid shook his head, his gaze still locked with his brother.

"No one helps out a stranger by pretending so much without something in return," Khalid warned.

Obviously Rashid had not shared all he knew about Bethanne to Khalid. She wanted to confront him about the information she'd learned from the older man. But not with Khalid standing there. How soon could she get back to Quraim Wadi Samil?

Rashid reached out to take her hand, pulling her closer to his side. "Give me an update on the estimated repair time, if you would. Then we'll be going." He was making a definite statement for his twin.

Khalid shrugged and began speaking in rapid Arabic. Bethanne could feel the tension from Rashid as his hand held hers. She let her mind wander since she couldn't understand a word. Why had Rashid asked her to stay—actually almost coerced her? The longer she knew him, the more attached she became. For a few moments, she'd let herself imagine he'd fall in love with her. He'd be as attracted to her as she was to him. Which could lead to happiness beyond belief.

But the reality was more like heartache the size of Texas. She wondered if she dare hint that her feelings were engaged. He'd given her no indication he wanted anything more than a buffer with the minister to buy him some time. And he had not told her the truth about her father.

Yet those kisses had been magical. Had he felt any of the pull she had? With all the women he could date with a snap of his fingers, the fact he spent so much time with her had to mean more than just subterfuge for the minister's sake. Or not. He was so focused on work.

"Is there anything else you wish to see?" Rashid asked her. Bethanne looked at him. Khalid was already some distance away, walking to a group of men near one of the large machines.

"A quick tour would be great. I'll probably never be on an oil rig again." Chafing with impatience to find out more about her father, she refrained from asking him while others could hear. And a quick tour might give her time to figure out how to formulate her question so he'd answer.

"I thought Hasid might have explained some things to you."

"Who?"

"The man you spoke with earlier."

"No." So much for waiting. "Rashid—he said my father's plane crashed near Quraim Wadi Samil. He said you knew."

Rashid stared at her, glancing briefly to the sky where the helicopter had flown. "I do not know what happened to your father. Why would he say that? He never told me. Why does he think that?"

She stared back. Had the other man lied? Why would he? Yet, she couldn't believe Rashid would lie about it. It didn't make sense.

"I'll speak to him. Maybe you misunderstood him. While he speaks some English, he is not fluent. He would have come forward when the plane was lost if he knew anything."

"He says he spoke to you."

"He did not."

She broke her gaze and looked across the water. What to believe? She wished she could return to Quraim Wadi Samil and search for the grave herself. What if he was there? Who could she trust? Who to believe?

The flight home was conducted in almost total silence. Bethanne was trying to figure out how to find out for sure if her father had crashed. Rashid seemed to have dismissed the other man's revelation without a care. Would he if it were true?

Or would he try to stop her if she suggested another visit to Quraim Wadi Samil?

After lunch at the villa, Rashid invited her to go swimming. Bethanne's first response was a yes!

She'd love to spend more time with him. But the situation with her father loomed between them.

"I'd like that. I'd also like to learn more about my father."

"Very well. Today we swim. I'll have someone contact Hasid and ask for details. I think you misunderstood him. We have no knowledge of where your father is, or the plane. Do you think a plane crash could be hidden?"

Put that way, she doubted it possible. Still, she had understood what the man said. There was no denying he said he spoke to Rashid.

There was nothing more to be done today. If she didn't get a satisfactory answer from Rashid's questioning, she'd see if she could get back to the oil rig and speak with him again.

The small boat Rashid drove to was larger than a runabout yet easily handled by one. The marina not far from the villa, it didn't take long to be on their way.

Once out on the water, Bethanne seated in the seat next to his, he turned south. The homes along the shore were varied, from tall and austere, to low with lush gardens and fountains sparkling in the sunlight. Some were set back from the water, some bordered the beach. The farther south they went, the more space grew between homes. Finally he nodded to the thick foliage. "Can you see the villa?"

She caught a glimpse of the roof and a tiny corner of the veranda.

"That's where we eat," she said. It looked smaller from this vantage point. She sighed in pleasure. "It's as pretty from the water as the view is from balcony."

"My grandmother loved beautiful things. This is only one of her homes. They all had gardens that gave her such pleasure."

"My grandmother loves roses. She's a longtime member of the rose society in Galveston and wins prizes for her blossoms year after year."

"Yet another thing we have in common," Rashid said, cutting the engine and letting the boat drift. "Care to swim?"

"I'd love it." She quickly shed the cover-up and reached into the pocket for a band to hold her hair back. Tying it into a ponytail, she waited while Rashid went into the small cabin to change. "Ready when you are," she called.

Rashid stepped out a moment later, clad only in swim trunks. Bethanne almost caught her breath at the masculine beauty. His shoulders were broad; that she already knew. His chest was muscular and toned, not a spare ounce of flesh anywhere. His skin was bronzed by the sun. Masculine perfection. She could sit and stare at the man for hours.

She just hoped she didn't look liked a stunned

star-struck groupie. Get your mind on swimming and nothing else, she admonished herself.

Rashid tossed two towels on one of the seats and brought a small ladder from one of the storage compartments. Hooking it to the side, he stood aside, gesturing with one hand.

"After you."

She took a breath, passed close enough to feel the radiant heat from his body, before taking a quick vault over the side. The water closed over her head a moment later, cooling her off in an instant. She felt the percussion of his hitting the water, then rose, blinking in the bright sunshine.

"It's heavenly," she said, turning to swim slowly parallel to the beach. She didn't want to get too far from the boat. The water felt like soft silk against her skin. Its temperature enough to cool, yet warm enough to caress. After a few minutes of swimming, Bethanne stopped and began to tread water. Rashid was right beside her.

"This is fabulous," she said, shaking water from her face, and spraying him with the water from her ponytail.

He laughed and splashed her. In only seconds a full-fledge water fight was under way. Finally Bethanne cried to stop. She was laughing so hard she was swallowing water.

She began to cough and Rashid was there in

an instant, supporting her in the water, pounding on her back.

"I'm okay," she gasped a minute later. "I shouldn't be laughing when I'm being deluged by tidal waves."

"I haven't played like that in a long time," Rashid said as they began slowly swimming back toward the boat.

"You should. I think you work too hard."

"Ah, maybe it's the company I'm keeping. Makes it more fun."

She glowed with the compliment. From a rocky beginning, it looked as if things were changing.

"I could say the same. I've enjoyed being here."

"It won't be much longer."

She felt her heart drop. "How close are you to completing your deal?" she asked, almost fearing the answer.

"Close enough to expect to sign the papers this week."

Bethanne felt the disappointment like an anchor in her chest. She actually faltered a moment in swimming. What had she expected—that it would take years to sign the contracts?

"I hope you won't dash off the instant the ink hits the paper," Rashid said.

They reached the boat. He steadied the ladder while she climbed. Once she was on board, he swiftly followed.

"I need to return to Texas," she said slowly. She could stay a few days, maybe, yet to what end? She could go sightseeing on her own, but it wouldn't be the same as with Rashid. And he had to believe her father had taken the plane, no matter what the man on the platform had said. He'd mentioned it often enough. Had she misunderstood Hasid?

"I could stay for a little longer." Was that breathless voice hers? Those foolish dreams lingering?

"Because?" he pressed.

"Because I want to."

Rashid smiled in satisfaction, then pulled her gently into his arms to kiss her.

His warm body pressed against hers as the boat bobbed on the sea, his arms holding her so she didn't lose her balance. Her own arms soon went around his neck as she savored every inch of contact. She was in love with the most exciting man she'd ever known. And he hadn't a clue.

They dined together on the veranda. As twilight fell, Bethanne felt as if she couldn't hold so much happiness. The conversation was lively and fun. She wondered who else saw this side of the man.

"How come you aren't married?" she asked at one point, wondering why some smart woman hadn't latched on to him years ago.

The atmosphere changed in an instant. His

demeanor hardened. "The woman I planned to marry ran off, remember?"

"Come on, you're too dynamic and sexy to not have your share of women interested. How did no one capture your fancy?"

He was silent for so long Bethanne wondered what she'd said to cause the change. Wasn't it all right to question his single state?

"I was engaged a long time ago," he said slowly.

Oh, oh, she hadn't seen that coming. "What happened?" No matter what, it couldn't have a happy ending. She was bubbling with so much happiness, she wanted him to share. Now her stupid comment had changed the evening. She wished she could recapture her words.

"She loved my money."

"Ouch."

"I should have seen it coming." He looked at her. "All her conversation centered on things and trips. I was the gold at the end of her rainbow."

"She might have loved you as well?" she offered.

He shook his head. "When my father bought her off, she left like a fire exploding at the rigs. I haven't heard from her since."

Bethanne didn't know what to say. Her heart hurt for the pain of betrayal he must have felt.

"How about you? You're not married," he said a moment later.

"I'm footloose and fancy free. I don't see settling down when there is the entire world to see. Working with Starcraft, I get the chance to explore places I haven't been." Besides, I have never fallen in love before, she thought, watching him. And I don't expect to find another like you.

"You don't see yourself settling down, making a family?" he asked.

"If I meet the right guy, I guess I would," she said. "If he loved me in return." For too long she'd considered herself like her father—too interested in the wide world to settle for one spot. Now that she met Rashid, she sure didn't feel that way. She'd traveled to every continent on the globe. Made friends in various places. Yet nothing drew her like Rashid. Maybe that was the difference falling in love made.

Rashid nodded, wondering why he cared if she settled down or not. He was not interested in marriage. He'd agreed to the scheme with Haile as a business move. Her defection saved him. He would be grateful to her on two counts—keeping him single, and introducing Bethanne into his life.

She was different from women he knew. That was the novelty of being around her. Soon the novelty would fade and he'd move on. He didn't want to think like a cynic, but he had no expectations of falling in love. He wanted Bethanne, liked being with her. But surely there was more to love than that.

She was a refreshing break from the routine of his life. One he didn't want to end too soon. It didn't hurt that she was so pretty. He enjoyed watching her. Or taking her to events. She looked relaxed and pleased with life in the blue dress she wore. He would love to adorn her with jewels, but she'd carefully returned the sapphire necklace once they returned to the villa after the polo dinner. He'd offered for her to keep the necklace, but she'd refused.

He should have told Khalid that. Maybe knowing Bethanne better, he'd realize his assessment was off. She wanted nothing personal from this charade. She was almost too good to be true. But he'd seen no sign of avarice in her.

He stared out across the garden, wondering about Hasid's comments to her. The old man couldn't know more about Hank than he did. Hank had worked for his father. In the morning he'd have his assistant find out more about the wild story the man had told Bethanne.

"I need to fly to Morocco on Friday to sign the contract."

She sipped her coffee before nodding. "Then I'll ask for a few more days of vacation so I can stay a bit longer," she replied.

He was pleased she agreed to stay. Maybe he'd take time from work and spend it all with Bethanne before she left for good.

The thought of her departure weighed heavily. Yet he knew better than she that there was no long-term future for them together. His family would never accept the daughter of a thief—moreover the one whose actions contributed to his father's death. She didn't speak his language. He didn't want a wife. And he would not dishonor her by having an affair. Time together, memories made, then goodbye.

His gaze shifted to her as she sipped the hot tea. She loved flying. And he couldn't see asking her to stop. It was a novelty to have her fly his plane. Maybe he could hire her to fly for him—his private pilot. That way she'd always be around. And when he needed to travel, Bethanne would travel with him.

"After Morocco we could fly on to Paris, if you like," he said. He knew women around the world loved Paris.

"That would be nice."

"You don't sound as excited as I thought you'd be."

"I haven't seen Paris with you. That would make it special," she said slowly. "I enjoyed our excursion into the western part of your country. Maybe another trip there?"

"Quraim Wadi Samil? It's hardly a hot spot. Not a place we would have gone had Alexes not needed immediate medical attention."

She faced him. "It hardly matters where we go, if we're together, don't you think?"

He wanted her as he had wanted no other woman. Not even Marguerite. But caution held him back.

"It doesn't matter, as long as we're together," he said, already regretting the day they would say goodbye.

CHAPTER SEVEN

RASHID answered the phone the next morning when his assistant told him it was Khalid.

"So the deal is done. You've both signed?" his brother asked without amenities.

"I'm flying to Morocco on Friday to sign with Benqura. Then it is done. And a better deal than expected, thanks to his daughter's flight. He needs to save face and I've assured him I will handle things on this end."

"And how to explain to the minister that your special friend Bethanne left?"

"I don't have to explain anytime soon."

"Because?"

"I've asked her to stay. I may offer her a pilot's job. Alexes will not be able to fly again. Another stroke could happen at any time."

"There are other pilots who work for us."

"I choose who will fly my planes."

"Fly your planes and warm your bed."

"Hardly that. Bethanne and I are not involved to that extent," Rashid said coldly. Not for lack of desire on his part. Bethanne was special, and he would treat her so. For as long as it suited him. And her.

"She wants something. Mark my words."

"And what does it take to prove you wrong— her friendship and loyalty for fifty years?" He knew what Bethanne wanted. It was impossible to give it to her. Beyond that, she cared for nothing he had to offer.

"That's a start."

Rashid laughed. "Give it up, Khalid. She is not like the others."

A groan sounded. "You are too far gone. All women are alike."

"Cynic. Is that why you called—just to warn me again about her?"

"No, I'm going to open Grandmother's other house. I can't decide whether to live there or sell it. So I thought if I stayed there a few weeks, I'd know what I want to do. It's strange to go there without her."

"She wanted you to have it, Khalid. She loved that house because it was her father's that he gave to her when she married."

"My flat suits me. I'm not in it long enough to feel closed in."

"Give it a fair chance. You don't have to rush into selling."

When Rashid hung up, he thought about his

brother. Life had treated them so differently. Both had the same advantages until the fire had destroyed part of his brother. It wasn't only the scar. There were wounds that went deeper. Were the al Harum men doomed to stay single? Not leave heirs on the earth?

How would he fare if he took that step? What if he considered marriage with someone like Bethanne? Their children would be beautiful. She'd be full of surprises for a long time. Would they agree on how to focus their lives, or always want something different?

Not liking the way his thoughts were going, he picked up a report and refused to think about her for the rest of the morning.

Easier said than done, he admitted a few moments later. He didn't believe Khalid. His brother had not been around Bethanne long enough to know her. Yet that shadow of doubt wouldn't fade. Marguerite had seemed devoted, until offered a sum of money. Would Bethanne prove as shallow?

Restless, he checked his calendar. There was nothing pressing. Telling his assistant he was going to take the rest of the day off, he headed for the villa. He wanted to see her, spend time with her. Assuage the doubt and prove once and for all she was different.

Prove to Khalid that Bethanne was unique.

* * *

When Rashid reached the villa it was to find Bethanne had gone out.

"Where?" he asked the maid. Maybe he should have kept Fatima to watch her.

But Bethanne wasn't a prisoner. She was free to go where she wished.

"She received a note and then asked if Teaz could drive her to the city," Minnah said. "I don't know when she will return."

Rashid nodded and went into the study. Using his mobile phone, he called the driver.

"Where are you?" he asked when Teaz answered.

Hearing they were in old town, Rashid arranged for Teaz to stay there until he arrived. He'd enjoy showing Bethanne some of the history of the capital city. She'd enjoyed Quraim Wadi Samil; he was sure she'd enjoy the architecture of the Romula district.

When Rashid pulled in behind his limo, driving his own small sports car, Teaz climbed out and came to open his door.

"Where is she?"

"I stop here. She walks to the square," Teaz said.

"You're dismissed. I'll bring her back to the villa."

The chauffeur bowed and returned to the limo.

Rashid walked toward the square. It brought back memories. Hank Pendarvis had lived in this area of town. He remembered that. His father had thought so highly of him. His assistant had not yet contacted Hasid. What if there was some truth to the old man's story? Could Hank have crashed? It still did not explain why he stole the plane.

When Rashid reached the square he paused for a moment, searching. Her blond head was quickly found. She sat at a table with an older man. From the way they were talking, Rashid knew they weren't strangers. Who was he?

The spurt of jealousy that hit him surprised him. He didn't want to admit he had stronger feelings for her. But seeing her laugh at something her companion said jarred him. He wanted her laughter and her smiles. He wanted her.

Walking around the square, his gaze never left them. They were so caught up in their conversation, neither looked up until he stopped at the table.

Bethanne's eyes widened when she saw him. For a moment anger burned. He realized he was used to seeing a spurt of happiness when he came near. Now she looked startled—guilty? He kept his anger under control. The first rule—find out the facts before acting. Nothing so far condemned her.

"Hi, Rashid. I didn't expect to see you here," she said with a quick glance at her companion.

"Probably not." He looked at the other man.

"This is Walt Hampstead. He teaches English at the university," Bethanne said quickly. "Walt, this is my host, Sheikh Rashid al Harum."

Host? They were pretending more than that. To everyone.

The man rose and extended his hand. "Sheikh al Harum. It's a pleasure to meet you."

Rashid shook hands and then looked at Bethanne. "The man who knew your father?"

She nodded. "Do join us. We were talking about mutual friends." She gathered the photographs displayed in front of her and stacked them, handing them back to Walt. He put them in an envelope before Rashid could see them.

"I was showing her pictures of my family. It's good to talk to Hank's daughter. I don't see many Americans in Quishari, you know," he said easily, tapping the envelope against his leg.

"You have lived here long?" Rashid asked.

"Almost twenty years. Married a local girl. We have two children—teenagers now." He glanced at Bethanne. "I hope to see you again soon. Thanks for the update."

Bethanne smiled and nodded, her glance flicking to Rashid.

"I did not mean to run you off," he said.

"I need to be going. Classes soon." Walt nodded once and quickly walked across the square and down one of the side roads.

Rashid pulled out a chair and sat. The waiter hurried over and asked if he wanted anything.

"I'll have a coffee," he said, leaning back. His curiosity rose. "What was really going on?"

Bethanne looked at him, her eyes wide. "He knew my father. He doesn't believe my father stole a plane, either."

When his coffee was delivered, he took a sip of the hot beverage. Bethanne fidgeted with her own coffee cup, now nearly empty.

"What are you doing here?" she asked at last.

"I thought I'd take you up on your offer to take some time off. I expected to find you at the villa."

"I still want to see as much as Alkaahdar as I can. Wander around town. This is a nice café."

"We can wander around old town if you like. I sent Teaz away. I drove."

"Lovely. The architecture is similar to that in Quraim Wadi Samil, don't you think?"

"It's from the same age."

They finished their coffee and started out. The stalls selling food were crowded. The others had vendors calling out, enticing people with special sales. Bethanne smiled and walked at his side. When they reached a cross street, he waited to see what she'd do. She appeared to be studying the architecture as if she were genuinely interested. Rashid watched her. He was still bothered by the encounter with the other man. She was tenacious in searching for Hank. She was not one to give up quickly. He wondered how she'd found the man who had known Hank.

A woman came from an apartment building. Rashid stepped aside to allow her to pass on the narrow sidewalk. When she saw Rashid's gesture, she smiled as she walked past—stopping suddenly when she saw Bethanne.

"Were you coming to see me?" she said in Arabic.

"No. Should I be?" Rashid asked, wondering who she was.

"The woman was here in the street a few days ago searching for the man who had the flat before me. She was told I knew nothing about him. I thought maybe you were coming to seek more information. I have nothing else to add."

Bethanne watched, her eyes darting from Rashid to the woman back to him.

He looked at her.

"You were looking for more information about your father?" he asked in English.

Bethanne nodded. "I was hoping he'd left something behind that might tell me where he'd gone and why. She wasn't home last time I was here. But Walt said he came by when he hadn't seen my dad for a while and was told the apartment had been cleared before being rented again. The man on the oil rig told me he crashed. Walt said he spoke of a secret assignment, a special flight. There had to be more to it than he appropriated a plane and I want to know what. I want to know the truth. I want you to admit the truth."

He stared at her. "I would tell you if I knew more. Do you think I like knowing your father was a thief? Especially after years of service with my family? What else might he have stolen? What other harm might he have done?"

"None. He was not like that. He loved working here. We often spoke about his finding his ideal job. He planned to show me the country, introduce me to his friends. He went on some secret mission for your father. If you don't know what it is, come with me to find out what it was."

"Come with you where?"

"Quraim Wadi Samil. Isn't that where the answers lie?"

"There are no answers."

"Only questions? Like why people think he is a thief? I need to find out what happened to him."

"Everyone wants something—Khalid was right. I thought we had something developing between us. But you only see me as a way to prove the unprovable."

"We might have something growing between us. Just because the reasons I agreed to stay haven't changed doesn't mean my feelings aren't genuine or aren't involved. I…love you, Rashid."

"No!"

"If I do?"

"Impossible." He glared at her. "Please give me some credit. Women say words like that hoping to bend men to their will."

"We're talking two different things here, Rashid. First I want to prove to you my dad is not what you think. And second, why wouldn't I fall for someone like you? You're—"

"Enough! We have an agreement, nothing beyond the charade until the negotiations are complete and the contract signed. What do you hope…that I'll fall for you? Maybe see you as my wife? I would not dishonor my family by marrying a woman whose father was a thief. Who caused the death of my father."

Rashid resumed walking, at a quicker pace. He clamped down on his emotions. Khalid had been right; he should have sent her back the first day. How dare she say she loved him? He knew better— he was a means to an end. Find out about her father. Hadn't they tried that three years ago? The sooner he got her to the villa, the sooner he could be rid of her.

Except for the flight to Morocco, he thought. Should he consider using another pilot?

"Wait." She hurried to catch up. "Rashid, this doesn't change anything."

"It changes everything. Here's my car. Get in."

Ignoring his manners, he strode to the driver's side and got in just as she jumped in the passenger's side.

Starting the engine, he pulled away from the curb at a pace faster than safe. For a moment anger ruled. Then he deliberately slowed down. He would not take his anger out on others.

How dare she suggest she was in love with him? They had not known each other long enough for emotions to grow. It was a ploy, just as Khalid suggested. He was furious for letting his own emotions grow concerning her. He'd been so confident he could enjoy her company and then say farewell. She turned out to be like all others.

"What did Hampstead tell you?" he bit out.

"That the last time he saw Hank, my dad spoke about a secret mission. Walt thought he was pumped up about it, like a thriller or something. He wouldn't tell Walt any more than that. But Walt thought it more a lark than a dangerous mission. He was obviously wrong since it seems likely my dad ended up dead. The man at the derrick said Hank's buried in Quraim Wadi Samil. It would be worth checking out. Did you question him?"

"My assistant is handling that." And it sounded like Rashid needed to make sure it was done immediately. "The reason he was pumped up was probably considering stealing a multimillion-dollar jet plane."

Bethanne refused to respond.

Rashid stopped in front of the villa a short time later. She scurried out of the car before he could come around to her door. Running up the shallow steps, she turned and looked at him. "I shall leave the villa, of course. I understand you wouldn't want me here. I'll call a taxi to take me to a hotel."

"Stay here until we leave."

"We?" she asked.

"I still need to fly to Morocco tomorrow."

"And Quraim Wadi Samil?"

"Once we return, you'll have to find your own way there."

She glared at him. "Don't worry, I shall!" She turned to enter the villa.

Rashid stood standing beside his car. The door closed. She was gone.

For endless minutes he stood staring at the door, feeling numb. One moment she says she loves him. The next she's talking about leaving. The images of them together over the last few days danced in his mind. He could almost hear her laughter, see the sparkle in her eyes. For the first time since Marguerite he'd let himself consider— No, he was not going there.

He clenched a fist and hit the top of the car. He'd been thinking of ways to keep her in

Quishari, and she'd been playing him. At least she had no idea he'd been halfway falling in love with her.

It was a small solace.

Bethanne reached her bedroom and shut the door. Sinking on her bed, she blinked her eyes. She would not cry. But the heartbreak she'd feared was closing in. Rashid had been so annoyed. Why? It wasn't as if he hadn't known from the beginning she was searching for her father. She should not have confessed her feelings. He hadn't wanted any emotional entanglements. He was probably laughing all the way back to the city about her claim. Her throat ached with keeping back the tears.

His reaction was unexpected. How could he feel so strongly about his own family and not recognize the same bond she had for hers?

She loved him. She hadn't meant to tell him, not without some indication he might be feeling something for her. But she had blurted it out. And he threw it back in her face. She did not want to go to Morocco or ever be around him again. How embarrassing that would be. Oh, if only she could go back in time a few hours and change everything.

She jumped up and began to pace the spacious area between her bed and the French doors. Rubbing her chest, she tried to erase the ache that was growing in her heart. She had warned herself repeatedly. But no matter—she'd fallen in love with a man who had never given any hint he returned her feelings. If he thought she was as dishonorable as he thought her father, he never would. Despite the kisses they'd shared.

Her father had been an honorable man. She resented the fact people thought he'd stolen a valuable plane and disappeared. She wanted the world to know the truth.

And she wanted Rashid to fall in love with her—daughter of a thief or not.

She might as well wish for the moon.

Minnah came into the room some time later with a message the sheikh had moved up the departure for Morocco to the next morning. They would depart at six.

Bethanne accepted her visit to Quishari was over. She'd fly the sheikh to sign his important contract, return to Quishari and be on the next commercial flight to the United States.

Packing, she took only those clothes she'd brought. She fingered the beautiful dresses that hung in the closet. She had felt like a princess wearing them. Who would wear them next? Would he donate to a charity or dump in the trash?

Taking advantage of her last afternoon, she went to the beach. Walking eased some of her distress.

She was still trying to figure out a way to get to Quraim Wadi Samil when she looked up and saw Rashid.

Her traitorous heart gave a leap of happiness when she saw him, even though his face was grave. When would she get over this feeling of delight in his presence?

"Is something wrong?" she asked when he got closer.

"My mother is having a small dinner party tonight and insists we attend." The muscles in his cheeks clenched with anger.

Bethanne hadn't expected that. She searched his face for a clue he also wanted to attend. He glared at her. No hope there.

"Surely you can tell her about the charade. She wouldn't expect us to attend after finding out about that," she said.

"The minister and his wife will be there. The contracts are not yet signed. I will do nothing to jeopardize this deal. Not having come this far."

"Of course. The deal. No matter what."

"Nothing's changed. Except my perception of your cooperation. If you do anything tonight to enlighten anyone, you'll be sorry."

"Gee, what will you do? Send me back to the U.S.? Banish me from the country I'm leaving anyway?" An imp of mischief goaded her. She wanted him to want her. As she'd thought his

kisses had indicated. So be it that he had not fallen
in love with her as she had with him. She would
not go off like some quiet, docile child. He was a
wonderful man. Her love was not returned, but it
didn't make it wrong, just sad that the one man
she'd found she'd want to build a life with had no
similar feelings for her.

"Don't push me, Bethanne."

"You have something I want. I have something
you want. Let's make a deal."

"You have nothing I want."

"My silence. My continued acting like a love-
struck woman clinging to your every word—especially if the minister is present."

He looked out to the sea.

"And in return, I want a plane ride to Quraim
Wadi Samil. We swap."

He was silent for so long she knew he was going
to refuse. She had no other leverage. She would
have to find the grave herself—if in fact it was there.

"Deal."

His answer surprised her. Before he could
change his mind, she held out her hand, but when
he turned back, it was to grab her shoulders and
draw her close enough to kiss. It wasn't a sweet
kiss, but one full of anger. His mouth pressed hard
against hers. His fingers gripped tightly. She
scarcely caught a breath before he released her a
second later. No matter, her heart pounded.

"Consider the deal sealed," he said and turned to head toward the villa.

"I'll pick you up at six-thirty," he called over his shoulder.

She brushed her fingertips across her lips. Tears filled her eyes. She wanted kisses, but not punishing ones. Could she ever forget the passionate ones they'd shared? She was afraid she never would. All men in the future would come short when compared with Sheikh Rashid al Harum.

"I hope your deal brings you joy. Nothing else seems to," she said to the empty beach.

Bethanne took extra care getting ready for her farewell performance, as she termed it. She had Minnah style her hair and selected the prettiest of the gowns hanging in the closet. It was a deep burgundy, long and sleek. Her makeup was donned for impact, making her eyes look larger and mysterious. She matched the gown color with lipstick and studied the dramatic effect in the mirror.

"Eat your heart out, Rashid," she whispered.

She went downstairs to await her escort. When he arrived, she met him at the door. "I'm ready," she said, walking past, head held high. She planned to deliver exactly what he wanted: a woman infatuated with him—when in public.

Teaz stood at the back door of the limo. Once

she was seated, Rashid joined her on the bench seat. The ride was conducted in total silence.

Once at his mother's, Rashid morphed into a charming host. He greeted the other guests, introducing Bethanne to those she hadn't met before. She was gracious and friendly. She was never going to give him a single reason to think of her as less than professional in all her dealings. Her greeting to Madame al Harum was warm, as she felt suitable to a prospective mother-in-law. The older woman did not thaw at her overtures. Bethanne merely smiled. She would never please her. And tonight she had no reason to even pretend.

She greeted the minister again. Tonight she met his wife. The woman did not speak English, so Rashid translated. When they moved on, she breathed a sigh of relief. So far so good.

Conversation was a mixture of Arabic, French and English. She had a nice chat with a young diplomatic couple, on their way to a post in Egypt. The minister of finance was no more friendly than he'd been at the polo event. She wondered if he were perpetually grumpy. She wished Walt had been invited. It would have been nice to have one friendly face in the group.

Dinner was traditional Arabic fare—from an avocado appetizer to the delicious lamb to the sweets at the conclusion. Bethanne enjoyed every bite. She especially liked the sugared walnuts that

Rashid insisted be brought for her enjoyment. She smiled her appreciation, wishing he'd meant the gesture for more than show to the people present. To the rest of them, she was sure they looked like a couple who enjoyed each other's company. Maybe were in love.

Only the two of them knew the lie behind the facade. It was bittersweet to have him so attentive, when she knew by the look in his eyes how false it was. She met him gaze for gaze, tilting her chin up to convey she had no qualms of standing up for herself. Or defending her stance. He'd asked her to stay to foil the attempts of the opposition to bring an end to negotiations. She'd done just that. He had not asked for more. It was her own foolish heart that betrayed her—not him.

The company moved to the salon and terrace after dinner. Soft music played in the background. The view from the terrace was beautiful; the entire city of Alkaahdar spread out before them, lighted in the darkness. In the distance, the Persian Gulf, where a lone ship gleamed with lights as it slid silently along on the horizon.

She would miss this place, she realized. In the short time she'd been here, she'd fallen in love with Quishari and one very special person. Her father had loved this country and she felt the same.

She realized she was alone on the terrace when Madame al Harum came to stand beside her.

"You are leaving," she said.

"Yes. We fly to Morocco tomorrow. When we return to Quishari, I will fly home."

"It is good."

"I'm sure you think so. What if Rashid loved me? Do you think a broken heart is good?" she asked.

"He would never be so foolish to marry someone so unsuitable. It's obvious you have fallen for him, but my son knows his duty. He will marry to suit his family. It is the duty of children to honor their parents."

"It is a bit old-fashioned," Bethanne said gently. "We honor our parents, but don't marry to please them."

"We are a traditional country. We have the modern conveniences necessary to enjoy life, but our values are time-honored. My son does not need you."

Bethanne nodded, the thought piercing. "You are right. I'm leaving and you will be happier for it, right?"

The older woman stared at her for a long time, then looked out toward the sea. "I will be content. It is what I want."

Bethanne longed to ask her if she missed her husband. Hadn't they been love? If not when first married, had love come? No matter what the custom, it had to be awkward to marry if not in love. Yet the union had produced two dynamic men. Had she longed for a daughter? For grand-children?

Bethanne had once thought she'd never marry. She'd been fooling herself. If Rashid asked her, she'd say yes in a heartbeat. Her declarations of independence had been made before falling in love. The world changed when that happened.

Even if the ending wasn't happy.

"Mother, one of your guests is leaving," Rashid said from the doorway.

She turned and smiled politely at Bethanne. "If I do not see you again, have a pleasant flight home."

"Goodbye, Madame," Bethanne replied.

Rashid stepped onto the terrace. "Are you ready to leave?"

"Anytime. Your mother can't wait for me to be gone. I'm glad this pretense will end soon. I'm thinking it never should have begun."

But then she would not have spent but ten minutes with Rashid while he signed the papers for the new jet. She'd have missed these days which, despite the circumstances, would remain some of the happiest of her life.

"The past can never be changed," Rashid said.

The future could. But she refused to cling to false hope.

* * *

Bethanne arrived at the airport before the sheikh the next morning. She checked with the ground crew and had visually inspected the aircraft before he arrived. Her flight bag was already stowed. Teaz loaded a small suitcase for Rashid and then drove away. Rashid brought a briefcase and was soon seated on the sofa, papers already pulled out to review.

"The weather outlook is good the entire way," she said. "We'll have a refueling stop in Cairo."

He nodded and Bethanne went to the cockpit to begin her preflight checklist. They were soon airborne. She watched as the land moved beneath her. She was not familiar enough with it to recognize landmarks. Somewhere below them soon would be the oasis in the desert where her father lay. She was not going home without stopping there. Maybe she'd ask Khalid to find out from Hasid where exactly her father was buried. If he knew she were leaving, he might be amenable to helping her.

As the hours slipped by, the topography changed. The hills and valleys gave way to mountains. Crossing over a while later, the blue of the Mediterranean Sea could be seen in the distance.

It was late afternoon Morocco time when she approached the runway of Menara Airport, serving Marrakech.

It had been a long day. They'd refueled in Cairo

where Bethanne had stretched her legs for a while. The flight had not brought the usual delight. She dwelled on the vanished hope the two of them might come to mean more to each other. It was also a bit lonely without someone to share the cockpit with. She would love to talk about the beauty of the earth below or the freedom flying usually gave her.

Rashid remained in the cabin. He'd declined to get off in Cairo. She had hoped for some kind of truce, but he obviously wasn't of the same mind.

She followed the directions from the tower and pulled the jet to a stop near a private hangar on the edge of the vast airport. Cutting the engines, she leaned back in her seat and closed her eyes for a moment. She was tired—not just from the long flight but from the emotional toll of the last two days.

Garnering what energy she could, she finished her checklist, signed it and left the clipboard on the copilot's seat. Going to the door, she opened it and stood aside, waiting for Rashid to leave.

He carried his briefcase and headed down the stairs, where there was already a chauffeured limousine for his use. She wondered how all the details of such precision were conveyed. She knew his staff was efficient, but this seemed almost miraculous.

When the uniformed chauffeur saw him into the back of the car, he came to the plane to retrieve the sheikh's suitcase. He nodded briefly to Bethanne, but didn't say a word. She stood back and watched as the limo pulled away.

If she had not told him about her feelings, or if he had believed her, she would be going with him, meeting the man whose daughter caused the charade. There was no need to keep up the pretense here where no one from his country could see. Once the contracts were signed, it would no longer matter.

She sighed and turned to check the cabin. It was as neat and tidy as if she'd flown it empty.

A maintenance worker came aboard, saying something in Arabic.

She replied in English. He shook his head, so she tried French. That he understood and explained he'd come to clean the interior. She told him to go ahead, but she'd wait until he was done. In fact, Bethanne wasn't sure what she would do. Stay with the plane was her inclination. She had no hotel reservations, hadn't a clue how to get a cab to this isolated area of the airport, didn't know how to find a place to stay since she couldn't speak the language. She could sleep on the sofa. Food and beverages stocked the refrigerator.

"And as the ranking crew member present on the plane, what I say goes," she murmured. When the maintenance worker left, she activated the door, retracting the steps and closing it. Cocooned in the aircraft, she hunted up a magazine and went to flop down on the sofa. In less than ten minutes she was asleep.

Rashid registered at the hotel, paid for a second room for Bethanne's use and sent the limo driver back to get her. It was petty to leave her like that, but he was still angry—more with himself than her. She had things to do when a plane landed, so the timing would probably be perfect.

He checked out his suite, found it satisfactory. Truth be told it could have been a hovel and he wouldn't have cared. Leaving it behind, he went to find a decent restaurant for an early dinner and to finalize his strategy for tomorrow's meeting.

When Rashid returned to the hotel, it was after ten. He'd had a leisurely meal, then gone to a small coffeehouse to work on the final details of the deal he and al Benqura would sign the next day. Walking back to the hotel, he enjoyed the atmosphere of Marrakech. He'd visited as a younger man on holiday one summer. The walk brought back memories.

He crossed the lobby heading for the elevators when the desk clerk called him.

"Yes?"

"Message for you, sir," he said.

Rashid went to the counter and took the folded paper. Scanning it as he started for the elevators, he stopped.

"When was this delivered?" he asked, turning back.

"A bit before six. It's written on the back."

He murmured an expletive. The note explained Bethanne had not been at the plane when the chauffeur arrived. The door was closed and no one had seen her since the arrival. Crossing to the house phone discreetly located in a quiet corner, Rashid dialed the number on the note. The car service was closed for the day. Crushing the paper in his hand, he went outside and asked the doorman to hail a cab.

CHAPTER EIGHT

WHERE could she have gone? She didn't know anyone in Marrakech. Not that he knew of. Of course she had a life apart from the few days she'd spent in Quishari. Maybe she had a host of friends here.

But she'd said nothing about that when they'd first discussed the flight.

The cabdriver was reluctant to go to the section of the airport Rashid directed. An extra handful of coins changed his mind. The hangar had a light on inside, scarcely enough illumination to see the door. The jet was parked nearby, where it had been that afternoon. It was dark inside. The door was closed. How had she managed that from the ground?

A lone guard came out of a small office, alert with hand poised on a gun worn at his side.

"Sir? This is private property," he said when Rashid got out of the cab.

"This is my jet. I am Sheikh Rashid al Harum. I arrived this afternoon."

"What are you doing here now, sir?" the man asked, still suspicious.

"I'm looking for my pilot."

The man looked surprised. He glanced around. "There's no one here but me. The maintenance workers come back in the morning. I haven't seen a pilot."

"I need to know where she went," Rashid said.

"She? The pilot is a woman?" the man exclaimed in surprise.

"Yes. Who do you call if there is a problem?"

"What problem?"

"Like a missing pilot," Rashid said, leaning closer. The guard took a step back.

"I will call."

Rashid followed him to the small office. In a few moments he was talking to one of the men who worked the special planes. He had not serviced the private jet but knew who had. He'd call him to find out if he knew where the pilot was.

Rashid had his answer in less than five minutes.

"Open the door," he instructed the guard, walking back to the jet.

"I do not know how," he said, following along.

Rashid cupped his hands and yelled for Bethanne. He heard only the background noise from the busy part of the airport. This was futile. The jet was insulated; she couldn't hear a call.

"Bring a ramp."

"A ramp?"

Rashid was getting frustrated with the echoing by the guard.

"Yes, I want to open that door from the outside. I'm not tall enough standing on the tarmac." He was losing his patience trying to determine if Bethanne was indeed on board the jet.

Beckoning the cabdriver, the three men pushed a ramp in place, ramming it into the side of the jet as they tried to line it up next to the door, so as not to interfere with the steps coming down if he was successful in opening it.

He started up the steps but before he reached the top platform, the door to the jet opened, the stairs slowly unfolding. Bethanne stood in the opening.

"Rashid, what in the world are you doing?"

"Trying to find you. I sent the limo back for you but the fool driver didn't see you so left. What are you doing here?"

"I was asleep." She frowned as she looked at the ramp and the two men at the foot of it. "Your crashing into the side of the plane woke me. I hope you haven't scratched or dented it."

"Doesn't matter. It's my plane. Come on. The taxi is waiting."

"Come on where?" she asked warily.

"I booked you a room at the hotel I'm using."

He walked back down the ramp and thanked

the two men who had helped him, giving each of them a folded bill. From the look of surprise on one and gratification on the other, he was satisfied they'd been amply rewarded for their help.

Bethanne still stood in the doorway, indecision evident in her expression.

Rashid hoped he wouldn't have to use stronger measures to get her to the cab. But he was not leaving her to spend the night in the jet. Unless he stayed with her.

She ducked back inside and a moment later tossed her bag over the railing of the movable ramp. Stepping over herself, she reached back and initiated the mechanism that closed the jet's door. When the plane was secure, she picked up her bag and walked slowly down the stairs.

"I'm guarding the plane," the guard said when she reached the tarmac. "No one will get on it tonight."

She looked at Rashid with a question in her eyes.

He translated for her and she smiled at the guard, saying in her newly learned Arabic, "Thank you."

Rashid took her bag and handed it to the cab-driver. Taking her hand, he helped her into the back of the cab and climbed in next to her.

"You can't have thought I would leave you to fend for yourself in a country where you don't speak the language," he said gruffly as the driver started the engine and they pulled away from the maintenance hangar.

"You're angry at me. Why not?"

He looked at her. "Bethanne, anger or not, I wouldn't do such a thing."

She nodded. He was not reassured.

"It is quite a few hours after you left," she said.

"I went to dinner. When I returned to the hotel, I learned you had not checked in. It's taken me all this time to find you."

"I appreciate it, but I was fine in the jet. It has all the conveniences of home."

When they arrived at the hotel, Rashid accompanied her to her room. Once he'd checked it out, he went to the door. "I'm in suite 1735. Call me if you need anything."

"Thank you for the room. What time do we leave tomorrow?"

"My meeting with al Benqura is at ten. I expect to be finished before noon. Perhaps you'd care to explore Marrakech before we leave."

"I'll do that in the morning, and be at the plane by noon," she said, standing near the window.

As if putting as much distance between them, he thought. "I meant, explore together. I was here about twelve years ago. I wouldn't mind seeing some of the souks and the Medina again."

"With me?" Her surprise was exaggerated.

He debated arguing with her, but decided against it.

"I'll meet you here at the hotel at noon." He left before she could protest.

Bethanne watched the door shut behind Rashid. She didn't know what to make of his coming to find her. She would have been okay all night on the jet. She'd slept in worse places. And she did not want to feel special because of the determination he'd displayed in locating her. But it touched her heart. She blinked back tears. She'd so love to have him always look after her. To know she was special to him in a unique way.

Taking a quick shower, she went to bed. It was more comfortable than the sofa for a night's sleep, she thought as she drifted off.

The next morning she ordered room service. She sat at the table next to the window, wishing she had a balcony and a sea breeze. Which would be hard to do in Marrakech, which was located far from the sea. She gazed out her window at the newer buildings, anticipating the afternoon tour of the old section, the Medina.

Bethanne went down to the lobby shortly before noon. She sat on one of the plush sofas and people-watched. It was a favorite activity. She wished she spoke the languages she heard. There were a variety, from Arabic to French to German and Spanish.

She saw Rashid the instant he entered through

the revolving doors. He strode directly toward the elevators and she wondered if she should call him or let him deposit the briefcase and then let him know she was here. As if she had spoken, however, he looked directly at her. He walked over.

"So did you get it signed?" she asked as she stood.

"I did." The quiet satisfaction showed her more than anything that he was pleased with the deal.

"Good."

His eyes stared into hers. For a second, Bethanne felt the surroundings fade. There was only Rashid in her sight. Then sanity returned and she blinked, looking away.

"I know you want to ditch the briefcase. I'll wait here."

"I can send it up to the room," he said. "Ready to go?"

"Yes."

He gave the briefcase to the bell captain with instructions to deliver to his suite. Then he offered his arm to Bethanne. The gesture surprised her. It was almost as if he were continuing their pretense.

She glanced down at the uniform she wore and slowly shook her head.

He reached for her hand and drew it through the crook of her arm.

"I'm hardly dressed like a woman going out with someone," she said.

"You look fine. Al Benqura has invited us to dine with him tonight. I said I had to make sure you wanted to do so."

"Do you want to?" she asked, surprised by the invitation.

"It would be a nice gesture to wind up the negotiations and the signed deal. But if you say no, I'll decline."

"I have nothing to wear."

He laughed sardonically. "Classic woman's response."

Bethanne looked at him. "Am I missing something? You were so angry the other day I thought you'd have a fit. Now you're like Mr. Nice Guy. What's going on?"

He didn't reply until they were in the back of the limousine she'd seen yesterday.

"I'm afraid I let the pretense go further than it should," he said cryptically. "You did your part. There was never anything more I could have expected. So today is about exploring Marrakech and seeing the sights. Tomorrow we'll return to Quishari and you'll be free to return home."

"So today we celebrate success," she said, disappointed at his explanation. She wanted more. She wanted him to say he couldn't let her go. That he'd fallen in love with her as she had with him. That he believed in her no matter what.

Only, today was merely a reward for a pretense

well done. Some of the sparkle and anticipation dimmed.

Still—if today was all she had, she'd take it. Make more memories to treasure down through the years. Maybe she could pretend for just a few hours that they still enjoyed the camaraderie they had before. They were both away from home, no one to see or hear. She would be herself and hope he'd at least come to realize she had not lied or been dishonorable in any way. She wanted him to remember her well even if he couldn't love her.

First Rashid had the driver crisscross through town, pointing out places of interest, telling her a little about when he'd visited before.

They stopped at a hotel with a renowned restaurant on top where they had lunch. Then it was to the old fortified section of town, the Medina. Because of the crowd, Rashid took her hand firmly in his as they walked along the narrow streets. The souk was also crowded with vendors and tourists and shoppers. The wares were far more varied than the ones at the square in Rumola near where her father had lived. Bethanne stopped to look at brass and some of the beautiful rugs. She ran her hands over the bolts of silks and linens for sale. Whenever Rashid suggested she buy something, she merely smiled and shook her head.

Late in the afternoon they ended up in the large square of Djemaa el Fna.

"This is said to be the largest open-air market in north Africa," Rashid said.

There were stalls selling orange juice and water. Food and flowers. Acrobats performed on colorful mats. A snake charmer caught her eye and she watched for several moments as he mesmerized crowds with his ability. The atmosphere was festive.

"Is it a holiday or something?" she asked.

"No, it's always like this. It was when I was here last."

They walked around, ending up in a sidewalk café on a side street that was just a bit less noisy and hectic. Ordering cold drinks, they sat in companionable silence for several moments.

"Thank you," she said.

"For?"

"For today."

For a moment she feared she'd shattered the mood, but he quickly looked away and she wasn't sure she'd seen a flash of anger in his eyes.

"Today has been enjoyable. Tonight we dine with al Benqura."

"I still don't have a dress," she said, sipping her iced drink.

"One will be at the hotel when we return."

She gazed across the amazing square. "It must be nice."

"What?"

"To wave your hand and have things taken care of. You live a charmed life, Rashid."

He stared at her for a long moment. "No, Bethanne. You see only the surface. I live a life like others, maybe not the majority of the world, but others of my station. We have heartaches and disappointments like any other men."

"Like what?"

He hesitated, took a sip of his own drink and then put the glass down.

"I thought I was in love when I was in my early twenties. Marguerite was beautiful, sophisticated and fun to be with. We shared so much—or so I thought. I told you before that my father bought her off. That taught me forever that love is an illusion. I cannot depend on it."

"Wrong. You may have loved her. She didn't love you. But that doesn't negate love. You are the better person for having loved her. I know it must have hurt when she left. But would you trade those feelings for money? Would you pretend to care for someone and be only out for money?"

"People can pretend and be out for other things."

She nodded. "Or maybe they don't pretend. Maybe things become real. Love is not rationed. It is available for all. And I don't believe there is only one love in all the world for each of us. I think we have the possibility of falling in love with the wrong person as well as the right person."

"So how does one know who is the right person?"

She shrugged. "I can't say. It's just there." She knew Rashid was her right person. She wished she was his.

"Never in love?" he asked.

"Only once. For me it was the right person," she replied slowly.

"What happened?"

"He doesn't love me back," she said, her gaze on her glass. "But I wouldn't trade a moment of being together. I can't make someone love me. I will always have memories of happy hours spent together. And just maybe, because I loved once, I will love again and be happy."

After a long silent moment, he said slowly, "I wish that for you."

She nodded, blinking lest the tears that threatened spilled over. She'd told the truth. She loved him and would have happily spent the rest of her life with Rashid. But if that was not meant to be, she hoped some day in the future she'd find another man to love.

Though she wondered if it would ever be the same.

True to his word, a lovely dress awaited her when they returned to the hotel. It was white, shot through with gold. A golden necklace and golden slippers were part of the package. She felt like a princess in the lovely clothes. No matter what, she'd go with her head held high. She really wanted to meet the father of the woman Rashid might have married. Would there be any mention of that tonight?

The dinner surprised her. She expected only another couple or two, but there were thirty couples. The dinner was a lavish affair with servants scurrying to carry in the dishes, remove dirty plates and make sure everything went smoothly.

Because she could not speak Arabic, Bethanne sat next to Rashid. But she noticed other couples were separated to mingle with the other guests.

"I'm content to eat and watch. You don't have to translate everything for me," she said softly after about ten minutes of his commenting on what others said.

"You'll be left out."

She looked at him in exasperation. "Rashid, I would never fit in here. I'm delighted to taste some more dishes and watch the other women in their finery. But I don't expect to become friends with anyone. Enjoy yourself. Truly, I'm happy enough."

Sheikh al Benqura was not like Bethanne's image. To her he looked like a father who had been disappointed in his only child. His gray hair was worn a bit long. His wife looked sad—especially every time her gaze landed on Rashid. Bethanne knew they had both wanted the marriage. Still, they were doing their best now to smooth things over. Rashid had told them he and Bethanne had a special friendship. It was true to a certain degree, but not to the level they suspected. Clever use of words, she thought.

After dinner, they stayed for only a short time, claiming an early departure time in the morning as a reason to be the first to leave.

"That went better than I expected," Rashid said as they settled in the limo for the ride back to the hotel.

"Did it?"

"Yes. You played the part perfectly. Madame al Benqura wished me happiness in our marriage."

"Which you denied."

"Of course, but in such a way she didn't believe me. I wonder why."

"Because she's also embarrassed by her daughter's running off. And I think she believed your heart might be involved. So she would be relieved if you were involved with someone else. No matter how unsuitable."

"You are not unsuitable," he replied.

Bethanne didn't respond. He still thought her the daughter of a thief. She was tired and wanted to go to bed. Tomorrow they'd return to Quishari and the goodbyes that waited.

"You are a kind man, Rashid. It was good of you to save face for them. It will make the working relations run more smoothly in the future."

The next morning they took off early, leaving Marrakech just awakening in the dawn. Once again the plane was refueled in Cairo. Then began the final leg of the trip. It was growing dark as they flew over the Quishari western border. Before long scattered lights speckled the landscape below them. The skies were full of stars, so much clearer at this elevation. Bethanne loved flying at night. There was something special about rocketing through the darkness with only the stars as a guide.

She checked her coordinates and contemplated her next move. If Rashid wasn't going to help, she'd have to do it herself.

Rashid rested his head on the sofa cushions. He was tired. The dealing with his new associate had been long and more difficult because of Haile's actions. To pretend things were fine when they weren't went against his grain. He was all for openness and honesty—where it didn't hurt anyone. Having Bethanne along, pretending he was involved with her, had given his host a way to save face. The deal was too important to end up contentious because of a willful woman's actions. But the strain of being with her and yet not wore on him.

The airplane shifted slightly. Rashid opened his eyes. Glancing at his watch, he saw it was too early to be landing in Alkaahdar. Yet it definitely felt as if the plane was descending. Was there a problem?

He rose and walked to the cockpit just as Bethanne spoke into the microphone, "Fasten up."

"Is there a problem?" he asked.

She shook her head, concentrating on the task at hand. "You need to sit down and fasten your seat belt," she said.

"Why are we descending?"

"We're landing."

He slipped into the copilot's seat and looked out. The blackness below went on for miles, with only a speck of light here and there and a small glow in front of them. Ahead was an array of lights—a runway.

"Where are we?"

"Buckle up, Rashid. We're going to land in about five minutes and if it's bumpy, you don't want to be tossed around."

He snapped on the belt and reached out to take her arm.

"Where are we?"

"Airborne over Quishari, soon landing in Quraim Wadi Samil."

"No."

"Oh, yes," she said softly.

He heard the determination in her tone. Unless he knew how to take control of the plane, there was nothing he could do.

"I'll call your office and have you fired."

"Go for it." She flicked him a glance. "I came to Quishari with two purposes. To deliver the plane and to find my father. I'm not going home when I'm so close. Now, I would like to concentrate on the landing, so kindly keep quiet."

Rashid was struck by the novelty of having someone telling him to shut up. Did she know who he was?

Of course she did, and was not a bit intimidated by the fact. She claimed to love him. Yet she had not repeated that statement once he'd shown her he couldn't be persuaded. Had it been a gambit?

With a resignation that the truth was probably she had tried that to get his cooperation, he settled back and watched her bring the jet in with a perfect landing.

It was not so late the airport wasn't still functioning. But late enough they were probably the last plane to land this evening. Quraim Wadi Samil didn't qualify as a hot spot in the world of travel.

She taxied where directed and shut down the engines.

"We're here," she said.

"Do you plan to go to the cemetery in the dark?"

She shook her head. "I plan to find a room somewhere, sleep until morning and then go. After you get the location from your assistant. If you want me to, I'll take you to Alkaahdar before leaving for Texas."

"And if I call your home office to have you dismissed?"

"As I said, go for it. I may never get this chance again. I need to know for absolute certain." She rose and went to get her small suitcase and open the door. Walking down the steps, she turned toward the terminal.

Rashid was tempted to call her bluff. She had openly defied him. He sat down in the seat and considered his options.

He knew why she had landed here. If it had been his father, wouldn't he do all he could to find out the truth? To learn what happened?

He reached in his pocket for the cell phone and called his assistant at home. It was late, but he needed answers now.

Rashid checked into the hotel they'd used when last in Quraim Wadi Samil. He verified Bethanne was already there before heading up to his room. He had a lot of thinking to do.

The next morning, he waited in the lobby until she came down. Crossing to her, he took her arm and pulled her aside.

"I've ordered a car to take us to the cemetery near the older part of town. I know where your father is buried."

She looked at him in astonishment. "You're kidding. Have you always known?"

"I learned of it last night. Come, we have time before the car comes to have breakfast. Have you eaten?"

She shook her head.

They sat in the sunshine in the small courtyard off the main restaurant adjacent to the hotel. Once their orders had been given and the waiter left, Rashid began.

"I called my assistant last night. He had talked with Hasid. Then I called Khalid."

"Khalid?" Bethanne said, puzzled.

"He is the sheikh Hasid spoke with, not me."

Of course, both the twins were sheikhs. Hasid had nodded toward where Rashid and Khalid had been speaking. In his mind he probably thought she knew who he meant.

"And?"

Rashid looked around, as if assuring himself they would not be overheard.

"I owe you an apology, Bethanne. Your father's friend was correct. Hank was doing a special favor for my father—a secret assignment, as said. He came here to Quraim Wadi Samil to pick up someone special. The flight was cut short with a freak sandstorm shortly after they departed the airport. They were blown off course, or flew wide trying to avoid the sand. But the plane crashed. Everyone on board died."

Bethanne stared at him. Rashid tried to gauge her feelings, but her expression was wooden. "What was the secret?"

He didn't want to tell her. He didn't want to believe it, but his brother had made it clear it was the truth. After accusing her father—he owed her the truth.

"A daughter my father had with a woman not his wife. He wanted to see her before sending her to finishing school in Switzerland. Hearing of her death triggered his heart attack and he died. Khalid has known, and chose not to reveal it to anyone. Until I forced it out of him last night."

She still didn't say anything.

"My apologies for accusing your father. Had I known the truth from the beginning, I would never have said such a thing."

"So you know where he's buried?" she asked.

"I have directions."

She nodded and then stared around the courtyard as if she didn't know where she was.

"I'm sorry, Bethanne."

She nodded again. "Does your mother know?" she asked.

"No. Khalid's rationale was no one needed to

know. He never expected Hank's daughter to show up. When I told him who you were, he finally agreed to tell me everything. He was protecting my mother."

"And you," she said slowly.

He nodded. "It's hard to discover the honorable man I revered my entire life had cheated on his wife and had another child. One, moreover, he spent a great deal of time with. I thought his reasons for keeping the oil fields operational and under such close observation was he wanted the best for the people of Quraim Wadi Samil. Turns out it was a cover for visiting his mistress and child."

"Now I'm the one who's sorry. That has to be hard to learn at this late date."

"I can deal with it. It's my mother who continues to need protecting. Fortunately he was circumspect and few people knew of the situation. Now that the daughter is dead, and my father, the story is unlikely to come out."

The waiter reappeared with their breakfast. Conversation ended while they ate. Rashid wished Bethanne would say something. But he couldn't have said what. She had a lot to forgive with his family. If he'd told Khalid sooner, would he have told Bethanne the truth immediately? Before he had a chance to know her, to grow to care for her?

* * *

After they finished eating, they summoned a hired car. Rashid gave directions to the cemetery and when they reached it instructed the driver to wait. The graveyard was dusty and brown. Few scraggly plants grew, no grass. The tombstones were lined up in rows. The main path cut the grounds in half.

Bethanne looked at the tombstones as they walked through one section. Her heart was heavy. Tears threatened. She had known for a long time her dad was dead. He would not have ignored her this long had he not been. But she had clung to hope as long as she didn't know for sure. Now that hope was gone.

As if he knew exactly where he was going, Rashid led her across a series of sections and stopped in front of a newer stone. Hank's name was in English. Other words were carved in Arabic. She hadn't a clue what they said.

"What does the inscription say?" she asked, staring at the foreign script.

"It says, 'Here rests a true friend, loyal to the end.'"

"Probably not the words that would be used if he were a thief," she murmured. She wished the words had been in English.

"Hi, Dad. I found you," she said softly. She knelt on the ground, reached out and touched the stone. It was already warm from the sun. Memories flashed through her mind. She loved her father. Felt curiously happy to find him, even though he had died three years ago. She had known it all along, just denied it. He would not have ignored her for so long had he been on earth. The cards and letters had came sporadically, but the phone calls had been as regular as the sunrise.

She wouldn't have been a pilot if he hadn't fostered the love of flying in her. She wouldn't have seen as much of the world as she had. And he wouldn't be lying here now at age fifty-two if he hadn't been who he was. Wild and free, only touching down when he had to. Otherwise the skies were his home.

Would she end up like he had? Alone, far from her native land? Having lived life the way she wanted?

She glanced at Rashid. One thing she wanted she wasn't going to get.

"How did you know right where he was buried?" she asked.

Rashid was silent for a moment, staring at the headstone. "Khalid told me. And where our half sister lies. I want to see that stone as well. I didn't know I had a sister until last night."

"The mechanics at the airport said Hank stole the plane and vanished. That the sheikh's son didn't know anything. Hasid said he'd told you."

"No. I didn't know. But Khalid did. He was the one who discovered what happened when they didn't arrive as planned. She was to go to college in Europe and my father wanted to see her before she left."

"How was he planning to do that without your mother's knowledge?"

"I have no idea. But she doesn't know. She would be so hurt. She herself always wanted a daughter."

Bethanne looked at the graves marching away from her father.

"And where is her place?"

"Come, Khalid told me. It was he who arranged the stones. He who took care of everything, careful to keep our father's name out of it."

Bethanne rose and touched the stone again. She would in all likelihood never be here again. She'd found her father, only to have to say softly, "Goodbye, Dad."

Rashid led the way down several rows. Soon they stood before a stone engraved completely in Arabic.

"The place next to it is saved for her mother. She loved my father and he loved her. When they met—when he came to start the oil fields—he was already married with two sons. According to Khalid, the arranged marriage with my mother was important in a business sense. Yet he wanted to end it. My mother would not without causing a scandal and pulling out the money that would have sunk the business back then. In the end he stayed married to her. He told Khalid this as he was dying. He visited Quraim Wadi Samil as often as he could, enjoying his daughter and spending time with the woman he loved. He swore to Khalid our mother never knew.

"The plane crash and his daughter's death caused his own heart attack and death. Khalid never made the facts known. It would do nothing for those who died. He said he'd rather have the living content with life as they knew it. What point to shatter that?"

"I'm so sorry, Rashid," she said simply. She had no idea of the circumstances. Yet she was glad he had not known and not told her. She was glad her father had been helping someone when he died. It sounded more like him than being a thief.

"You once said truth always comes out. This is one I hope doesn't," he said.

"I understand. Thank you for telling me. And restoring my faith in my father. I never believed what you thought."

"Ironic, isn't it?" he said.

"What?"

"Hank was a loyal employee of our company and a loyal friend to my father. A man trusted to carry his most precious daughter. A man of integrity. It was a tragedy to end as it did."

She looked around the cemetery, imprinting it

on her mind. She'd remember the words on the stone. Remember he'd died trying to help a friend.

"Instead, it was my father who was less than honorable. I'm sorry, Bethanne, for doubting your father."

"I'm ready to leave now," she said, turning away lest he see the tears in her eyes. She'd never hug her robust father again. Never get a card or letter. Never be able to tell him how much he'd meant to her—even though they rarely saw each other. She knew he'd known, but the plans they'd made—for someday—would be carried out solo now. She had his memory and his love of flying. It would have to be enough.

"Thank you for bringing me. I will honor the secret. I would do nothing to hurt your mother," she said as they walked slowly back through the cemetery.

"Her behavior could be better toward you."

"She doesn't like me. That's okay. She doesn't need to." Bethanne stopped at the gate, the hired car only a few yards away.

"Truth always comes out. I'm glad you found out before I left. And told me. If I hadn't been able to wrangle the flight to deliver the plane, I would never have gotten to know you, and that would have been my loss. I'm grateful for all you've done for me. I wish you the best life has to offer, Rashid."

He studied her for a moment. This was the time for him to say something, if there was anything to say. He merely inclined his head.

"And you, Bethanne."

Bethanne summoned a smile and turned, walking swiftly to the car. There was nothing left to say.

When the jet landed in Alkaahdar, she finalized all the details for leaving the plane near the private hangar. Taking her bag, she saw Rashid had already disembarked. She carefully withdrew the beautiful dress from her case, along with the shoes and golden necklace. Putting them on the sofa, she was sure they wouldn't be overlooked. Glancing around once more, she smiled. This jet was the best Starcraft had to offer. She knew Rashid would get years of service from it. She'd think about him from time to time, imagining him flying high in the plane. And she'd remember the times they'd flown together.

"Bless this aircraft and all who fly it," she murmured before leaving.

When she reached the tarmac, she looked around for a conveyance to take her to the main terminal. She had a flight to Texas to catch.

CHAPTER NINE

"So the deal is signed," Khalid said.

"It is. We begin to implement next week," Rashid returned. He looked up from his desk. "What are you doing here?"

"Came to say goodbye for a while. I'm heading inland on another consultation job for a new field opening up. I'll be gone a few weeks, probably."

"The Hari fields?"

Khalid nodded, walking around the office. He touched one of the statues on the bookcase, then went to the window.

"Where's your pilot?"

"She's not my pilot."

Khalid turned at that. "You could have fooled me. You seemed as besotted with her as you were with Marguerite."

"Then that should have told you something."

"Only I don't think Miss Bethanne Sanders is anything like Marguerite."

"Don't bet the oil field on it," Rashid said.

Khalid raised an eyebrow in silent question.

Rashid hesitated, but Khalid was his twin.

"She wanted something from me after all."

"Money?"

He shrugged. Hesitating a moment, he looked up. "She said she loved me. Once."

Khalid stopped and stared at his twin.

"And that's a problem because?"

"She was trying to get info on Hank."

"That must have hit her hard, when she learned you thought he'd stolen the plane."

Sighing at the inevitability, Rashid related the entire story to his brother.

"I wanted you to remember our father with love. How honorable was it for him to have another family?" Khalid said. "I never expected anyone from Hank's family to show up. Was she hurt when she discovered his death?"

He shook his head. "I believe she'd known all along, just kept hoping. I'm the one in the wrong, accusing her father of theft when it was ours who acted dishonorably. Did you ever meet her? Our sister? What was she like?"

"I didn't know about her until after her death," Khalid said. "Father had pictures of her. He loved her mother and her. I have the photos. You can look at them if you wish."

"So there is love in the world," Rashid said.

"Which doesn't always bring happiness. Do you think any of them were happy?"

"Maybe the daughter, cherished by both her parents."

"At least he went after the love he wanted. Ever think you should have gone after Marguerite?"

Rashid shook his head. "But I'm thinking of going after Bethanne."

"Why not?" Khalid asked.

"You're suggesting that I should? I thought you didn't like her."

"I like her fine. I was worried she was after something else. But if she wanted closure about her father, that's different."

"She doesn't care about me—she only wanted to find out about her father."

"There were other ways to do that than pretend to be involved with you. To say she was in love."

"You thought she was after something and she was."

"Family. Not money. There's a big difference," Khalid said.

Rashid nodded. "She wished me a good life." He remembered how he'd fought to resist taking her into his arms when she'd said that. He had let her go without telling her he wanted her more than anything—even his next breath.

"She's gone?"

Rashid shook his head. "I still haven't signed

off on the new jet. She can't leave before then. That's as important to her as finding her father was."

"Then I suggest you decide if you want to end up like our father, or maybe grab for the gold ring first time round," Khalid said.

Rashid drove to the villa as soon as Khalid left. Entering, he called for Bethanne. Minnah came into the foyer.

"Excellency, she is not here. She took you to Morocco. Did she not fly you back?"

"She did, earlier this morning. She didn't return here?"

"No. I have not seen her."

He turned and went back to the car. Where would she be? He never knew what to expect with her. Was she still at the plane like in Marrakech? Rashid headed for the airport, feeling a sense of déjà vu.

A quick cursory inspection upon arrival showed the jet empty—except for the dress he'd bought her in Marrakech. She truly had wanted nothing from him except to find her father. A woman more unlike Marguerite he'd never find.

He pulled out his cell phone and called his office, setting every assistant he had with the task of finding Bethanne Sanders. He also instructed them to let him know the minute the Starcraft office opened in Texas. He had to find her and he was calling in all markers to do so.

Impatiently Rashid drove back to his office. He would find out more from there than running around town. Walking in, he began to fire questions at his assistant.

"Did you check the local hotels? How about car rental companies? Car hire companies. She has to be somewhere."

The assistant nodded. "We've been checking every place in the capital city, Excellency."

"I have a confirmation," one of the clerks said, looking worried.

"And?" Rashid snapped.

"She departed the airport at eleven on a flight to Rome."

Rashid couldn't believe she'd left.

He went into his office and closed the door.

Bethanne watched as the smoggy air of Rome seemed to encase the airliner as it descended into Leonardo Da Vinci Airport. She had several hours to wait for a connecting flight to New York. Time enough to visit a few of the highlights of the city. She couldn't muster much enthusiasm for that, however. Still, who knew if she'd ever be in Rome again? And it beat the other choice— sit and brood.

When they landed, she waited until more impatient passengers had deplaned, then followed. Finding a locker, she stowed her flight bag and went to find a cab to drive her around the city. Her flight did not depart until ten that evening. She had time to see some of Rome and get a fabulous dinner before heading for the United States.

Despite her best efforts, Bethanne couldn't help comparing what she saw in the city with the buildings and architecture she'd loved in Quishari. Both countries were old, both rich in history. She was fascinated by all she saw and wished she could share it with Rashid.

How long would it be until she no longer felt his loss like a part of her had been cut out? She knew she would survive, but wasn't sure she wanted to. She *ached* with longing to see him again. Touch him. Share a warm kiss. Go sailing or flying. Or just spend the evening on the veranda listening to the waves of the sea.

Hours later, after finishing her dinner, she took another taxi back to the airport. The city gleamed with lights, looking beautiful in the soft illumination. But Bethanne was blind to it all. It was all she could do to keep from bursting into tears.

She probably had no job. Would be hard-pressed to find another one as perfect as this one had been. She had walked away from the only man she'd ever loved, which had been the hardest thing she'd ever done. Harder than acknowledging finally that her beloved father was gone. Raw emotions had her so confused. She wanted to go home, crawl into bed and weep for a week.

Her future was uncertain, except for the ache in her heart. She pressed a hand against her chest, trying to ease the pain.

She'd found her father, but would have traded that for another few days with Rashid al Harum. Pretending they were falling in love.

Or not pretending, falling for real.

She retrieved her flight bag when she reached the airport. Shopping at one of the kiosks there, she couldn't find any books in English. She'd do better to sleep on the flight, but was too keyed up. Finding a couple of magazines she could look at, she headed for her gate.

"Bethanne."

Turning, she stared at Sheikh Rashid al Harum. Or a man who looked a lot like him. She shut her eyes tightly, then opened them. He still stood in front of her.

"Rashid?" she asked tentatively.

"You constantly surprise me. Makes for an interesting relationship."

"What are you doing here?"

"I'm flying to the United States on a flight that leaves at ten. You?"

She licked her lips. "I'm leaving on that flight, too. Why are you going to the United States?"

"To spend time with you, of course."

"Of course? There's no of course. You made your feelings perfectly well known to me."

"Perhaps we have a minor misunderstanding."

"Rashid, what's going on?"

"I didn't expect you to leave like that. I guess I expected more Yankee tenacity."

"What are you talking about? You practically ordered me to leave. I don't understand."

He glanced at his watch, stepped out of the way of a porter with a trolley of bags. Taking her arm, he pulled her to the side of the concourse. "It's not often I admit to making mistakes. I try not to make them to begin with. But I made a monumental one with you."

"Pretending to be involved?" That hurt.

"Not admitting when the pretense ended."

"When you signed the contract in Marrakech," she said.

"No, when it changed to love."

Bethanne's eyes widened. "If you're throwing that up to me—"

"What I'm trying to say is that I love you."

Rashid smiled at her look of astonishment, dropping his briefcase and pulling her into his embrace, kissing her on the mouth.

"Rashid!" she exclaimed when she pulled back. "This is a public place."

"So? I want the world to know I love you. What better place to start than here?"

"Here?"

"Everyone is greeting someone or bidding them farewell. Kisses are not out of the ordinary. Though I prefer our kisses to be in private. I don't wish to share."

"Did you say you loved me?" she asked.

"I did. I'll say it again. I love you, Bethanne Sanders. I fought against it. I didn't want to fall in love—my experience with that emotion has not been good. But foolish thought, that I can control emotions. You are all I have ever sought for in a partner. Beautiful, smart, talented in ways I can't compete, and interesting enough to keep me enthralled for decades."

She laughed, throwing her arms around his neck. "I am so unsuitable to be the wife of Arabian royalty. I'm much too casual in dress and manner to impress your associates. I want to fly whenever I can and I really don't think your mother is going to be at all happy with this. But I love you! I've been in the biggest funk ever since I left Alkaahdar. I thought I'd never see you again."

"I couldn't believe you left." He hugged her tightly, as if he'd never let her go. "So does this mean you will marry me? Live with me in Quishari? Spend our nights together, maybe even have a few kids to round things out? I love you, my dearest Bethanne. Will you marry me?"

She stared at him, faces so close she could not see anything around them. Her heart pounded. He'd asked her to marry him. Dare she risk it?

Dare she refuse?

"I would be so honored, but you must know what you're doing first."

"Oh, I know exactly what our life will be like. We'll live at the villa. My grandmother loved that house. We can raise our children to love the sea and the air. Will you insist on their learning to fly?"

"Perhaps not insist. But if they love it, we can't stand in their way. Are you serious? About everything? Marriage, children? You and me?"

"I love you. Why wouldn't I want to spend the rest of my life with you? I thought a lot about my father and his love and daughter in Quraim Wadi Samil. His happiness could not be complete because he never severed the legal bonds that kept him from staying with the woman he loved. I don't want to be dying and regret a single moment we spent apart."

"I never thought I'd get married. I wanted the life my father had—flying around the world. But he found his spot in Quishari. He lived there the longest of any place after he was an adult. And I know why. I love what I've discovered about Quishari. I think I would be happy living there. And flying wherever the mood takes us."

"I have just the plane for that."

The announcement for their flight was made.

He hugged her and then released her. "So, do we go on to the U.S. or back to Quishari?"

"Whichever you choose," she said.

"Ah, the perfect answer for a perfect wife-to-be." He dropped a quick kiss on her lips.

"This time. I'm not planning to become a yes person," she warned, warmth in her voice.

He laughed, clasping her hand in his and retrieving his briefcase. "I never expected that. I'll take it when I can get it. Let's go to Texas so I can meet your parents and tell them of our plans."

"My mother is going to be astonished." And, she bet her mother would be thrilled to know her daughter was marrying a sheikh.

"I believe my mother will be as well," he said wryly.

"I told you, I value truth. Your mother's honest. Maybe she'll come around one day, or maybe not. It will never change how I feel about you. I love you. I always will."

"That I'll hold you to." He lifted her hand to kiss it. "I will always love you," he vowed. "Come what may, we'll always have to look for clear skies and smooth flights."

"Always."

The future beckoned bright with happy promise.

MARRYING THE SCARRED SHEIKH

BY

BARBARA McMAHON

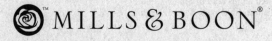

MILLS & BOON

First published in Great Britain 2010
Harlequin Mills & Boon Limited,
Eton House, 18-24 Paradise Road, Richmond, Surrey TW9 1SR

© Barbara McMahon 2010

ISBN: 978 0 263 87350 4

Printed and bound in Spain
by Litografia Rosés, S.A., Barcelona

Dear Reader

Twins as adults are different from twins as kids. Switching places and fooling people is undoubtedly fun as children. However, as twins mature, childish antics are put away. Still—from time to time they are undoubtedly mis-identified.

In Khalid's story, he is unlikely to be mistaken for his brother, due to a scar obtained when fighting oil fires. His choice of career is unlike his brother's as well. He likes to be in the desert, working in actual oil fields, vetting equipment and drilling procedures—or putting out dangerous conflagrations that most men never even consider facing.

It was one such fire that damaged his face and led him to believe no one would ever want to be close to him. So when he meets a stranger on the beach after midnight, he's struck with the novelty of being accepted solely for what he says, not for how he looks.

If you had loved and lost the one man you thought was for you, would you search for another? Or even be open to the possibility if one showed up unexpectedly? Ella considers any thought of marriage pointless. She's already loved a wonderful man and, after his death, plans her future alone. Running into a stranger on the beach is exciting—so long as they keep their meetings brief.

It's when they come face to face in the harsh light of day each realises things are going to change in a big way.

All the best

Barbara

To Kelly-Anne, Jeff, Justin, Dylan and Bridgette:
Family is always best. Love from me.

CHAPTER ONE

ELLA PONTI walked along the shore. The night was dark. The only illumination came from the stars overhead. No moon tonight. The wavelets gurgled as they spent themselves on the sand. Alexander had loved walking in the dark and she felt a closer tie than any other time.

He'd been dead for over a year. The crushing pain of his death had eased, as others had told her it would. Only a lingering ache where her heart was reminded her constantly that she would never see him again.

Sighing, she looked to the sky. The stars sparkled and shimmered through the heat of the night. Turning slowly, she looked at the black expanse that was the Persian Gulf. Nothing was visible. Some nights she saw ships sailing silently through the night, their lights gliding slowly across the horizon. Nothing there tonight. Turning toward home, she began walking, splashing lightly through the warm water at land's edge.

What a contrast this land was, she mused as she enjoyed the silence. Here at the seashore it was as beautiful as any Mediterranean resort; lush plants grew in abundance. She loved the leafy palms, the broad-leaf ferns and the flowers were nothing short of breathtaking. Each house around the estate she lived on seemed to flourish with a horticulturist's delight.

She enjoyed sitting out in the afternoons in the shady nooks of the garden, smelling the blend of fragrances that perfumed the air. While only a short distance from the capital city of Alkaahdar, it felt like worlds away from the soaring skyscrapers of the modern city.

She would go to bed when she reached her place. It was already after midnight. She liked to work late, as she had tonight, then wind down by a walk on the deserted beach—alone with only the sand, sky and sea.

With few homes along this stretch of beach, only those who knew the place well knew where to turn away from the water to follow winding paths through lush foliage that led home. Ella knew exactly where to turn even in the dark.

From a distance, as she walked along, she saw a silhouette of another person. A man, standing at the edge of the water. He was almost in front of where her path opened to the beach. In all the months she'd lived here, she'd never seen another soul after dark.

Slowing her pace, she tried to figure out who he might be. Another person who had trouble sleeping through the night? A stranger exploring the beach? Or someone intent on nefarious activities?

Ella almost laughed at her imagination. The homes along this stretch of beach belonged to the fabulously wealthy of Quishari. There were guards and patrols and all sorts of deterrents to crime. Which was why she always felt safe enough to walk alone after dark. Had that changed? She had only nodding acquaintances with her neighbors. Ella kept to herself. Still, one of the servants at the main house would have told her if there were danger.

She could cut diagonally from where she was to where the path left the beach, avoid the stranger entirely. But her curiosity rose. She continued along splashing in the water. The flowing skirt she wore that hit her midcalf was already wet along the hem. The light material moved with the slight breeze, shifting and swaying as she walked.

"Is it safe for a woman to walk alone at night?" the man asked when she was close enough to hear his voice.

"Unless you mean me harm, it is," she replied. Resolutely, she continued walking toward him.

"I mean no harm to you or anyone. Just curious. Live around here?" he asked.

As she walked closer, she estimated his height to be several inches over six feet. Taller than Alexander had been. The darkness made it impossible to see any features; even his eyes were hidden as he tilted his head down to look at her. No glimmer of light reflected from them. The traditional white robes he wore were highlighted by the starlight, but beyond that, he was a man of shadow.

"I live nearby," she replied. "But you do not. I don't know you."

"No. I'm here on a visit. I think." He looked back out to sea. "Quite a contrast from where I've been for the last few weeks."

She turned to look at the sea, keeping a safe twelve feet or so of space between them.

"Rough waters?"

"Desert. I wanted to see the sea as soon as I got here. I've been traveling for almost twenty-four hours straight, am dead tired, but wanted to feel the cool breeze. I considered going for a swim."

"Not the safest thing to do alone, especially after dark. If you got into trouble, who would see or hear?" Though Ella had gone swimming alone after dark. That had been back shortly after Alexander's death when she hadn't thought she cared if something happened or not. Now she knew life was so precious she would not wish harm on herself or anyone.

"You're here," he said whimsically.

"So I am. And if you run into trouble, do you think I could rescue you?"

"Or at least go for help." With that, he shed the robe, kicked off the shoes he wore.

Startled, Ella watched. Was he stripping down to nothing to go for a swim?

It was too dark to know, but in a moment, he plunged into the cool waters of the Gulf and began swimming. She had trouble following him with her eyes; only the sounds of his powerful arms cleaving the water could be heard.

"So I'm the designated life guard," she murmured, sitting down on the sand. It was still warm from the afternoon sun. Sugar-white and fine, at night it nurtured by its warmth, soft to touch. She picked up a fistful letting it run between her fingers. Idly she watched where she knew him to be. She hoped he would enjoy his swim and not need any help from anyone. She hadn't a clue who he was. For tonight, it was enough he had not had to swim alone. Tomorrow, maybe she'd meet him or maybe not.

Ella lost track of time, staring out to sea. So he came from the desert. She had ventured into the vast expanse that made up more of Quishari than any other topography. Its beauty was haunting. A harsh land, unforgiving in many instances, but also hiding delights, like small flowers that bloomed for such a short time after a rare rainstorm. Or the undulating ground a mixture of dirt and sand that reminded her of water. The colors were muted, until lit by the spectacular sunsets that favored the land. Once she'd seen an oasis, lost and lonely in the vast expanse of the desert. But her fervent imagination found it magical. Water in the midst of such arid harshness.

She wished she could capture that in her own work. Show the world there was more to the desert than endless acres of nothing. She began considering plans for such a collection. Maybe she'd try it after finishing her current project. Tomorrow was the day she tried the new technique. She had the shape in mind of the bowl she wanted to make. Now she had to see if she could pull it off. Colors would be tricky, but she wanted them to swirl in glass, ethereal, hinting and tantalizing.

She felt relaxed as the moment ticked by. It was pleasant in the warmth of the night, with the soft sound of the sea at her feet and the splashing in the distance. Would the man ever get tired?

Finally she heard him approach. Then he seemed to rise up out of the water when he stood in the gradual slope. She rose and stepped back as he went directly to where his robes lay and scooped them up.

"You still here?" he asked.

"As designated life guard. Enjoy your swim?"

"Yes, life giving after the heat of the desert." He dried himself with the robes, then shrugged into them.

She turned. "Good night."

"Thanks for keeping watch."

"I don't know that I would have been any help had you gotten into trouble," she said, turning and half walking backward to continue along the shore.

"Shall I walk you home? It would be easy enough for me to do." He stood where he was, not threatening.

"No." She did draw the line there. She knew nothing about the man. It was one thing to run into a stranger on the beach, something else again to let him know where she lived—alone.

"I might be here tomorrow," he said.

"I might be, as well," she replied, then quickly walked away. She went farther down the beach and then cut into a neighbor's yard. She didn't want to telegraph her location. Hopefully he couldn't see enough in the darkness to know which path she'd taken. She walked softly on the edge of the neighbor's estate and soon reached the edge of the property she rented. Seconds later she was home.

Khalid watched until he could no longer see her. He had no idea who the woman was or why she was out after midnight on a deserted beach. He was dripping. Taking a last look at the sea, or the dark void where it was, with only a glimmer of reflected starlight here and there, he turned and went back to the house his grandmother had left him last summer. Her death had hit him hard. She'd been such a source of strength. She'd listened to his problems, always supportive of his solutions. And she had chided him often enough to get out into society. He drew the line there. Still, he cherished her wisdom and her sense of fun. He would always miss her.

He thought about the woman on the beach. He could only guess she wasn't all that old from the sound of her voice. But aside from estimating her height to be about five feet two inches or so, he didn't know a thing about her. The darkness had hidden more than it revealed. Was she old or young? Slender, he thought, but the dress she wore moved in the breeze, not revealing many details.

Which was probably a good thing. He had no business being interested in anyone. He knew the scars that ran down his side were hideous. More than one person had displayed shock and repulsion when seeing them. Like his fiancée. Damara had not been able to cope at all and had fled the first day the bandages had been removed and she'd seen him in the hospital after the fire.

His brother, Rashid, had told him more than

once he was better off without her if she couldn't stick after a tragedy. But it didn't help the hole he'd felt had been shot through his heart when the woman he'd planned to marry had taken off like he was a horrible monster.

He'd seen similar reactions ever since. He knew he was better off working with men in environments too harsh for women to venture into. Those same men accepted him on his merits, not his looks.

He had his life just as he wanted it now. Except—he had to decide what to do with the house his grandmother left him. It had been a year. He had put off any decisions until the fresh ache of her dying had subsided. But a house should not sit empty.

He walked swiftly across the sand to the start of the wide path that led straight to the house. It was a home suited for families. Close to the beach, it was large with beautiful landscaping, a guest-house and plenty of privacy. The lawns should have children running around as he and his brother had done. As his father and uncles had done.

The flowers should be plucked and displayed in the home. And the house itself should ring with love and laughter as it had when he and Rashid had been boys visiting their father's parents.

But the house had been empty and silent for a year. And would remain that way unless he sold it. It would be hard to part with the house so cherished by him and his family. Especially with the memories of his beloved grandmother filling every room. But he had no need for it. His flat in Alkaahdar suited him. There when he needed it, waiting while he was away.

As he brushed against an overgrown shrub, his senses were assaulted by the scents of the garden. Star jasmine dominated the night. Other, more subtle fragrances sweetened the still air. So different from the dry, acrid air of the desert. Instantly he was transported back to when he and Rashid had run and played. His father had been alive then, and of course his grandmother. Who knew the odd quirks of fate, or that he'd end up forever on the outside looking in at happy couples and laughing families. That elusive happiness of families denied him.

Not that he had major regrets. He had done what he thought right. He had saved lives. A scar was a small price to pay.

He entered the house through the door he'd left open from the veranda. Bed sounded really good. He'd been traveling far too long. Once he awoke, he could see what needed to be done to get the house ready for sale.

Ella woke late the next morning. She'd had a hard time falling asleep after meeting the stranger on the beach. She lay in bed wondering who he was and why he'd been traveling so long. Most people stopped when they were tired. No matter, she would probably never see him again. Though, she thought as she rose, just maybe she'd take another walk after midnight tonight. He said he'd be there. Her interest was definitely sparked.

But that was later. Today, she wanted to try to make the new glass piece that had been taking shape in her mind for days.

After a quick breakfast at the nook in the kitchen, Ella went to her studio. As always when entering, she remembered the wonderful woman who had sponsored her chance at developing her skill as a glassblower and who had offered to help her sell her pieces when they were ready. She missed her. She pursued her passion two-fold now—for herself and for her benefactor.

In only moments, she was totally absorbed in the challenge of blending colors and shapes in the bowl she was creating.

It was only when her back screamed in pain that Ella arched it and glanced at the clock. It was late afternoon—she'd been working for seven hours straight. Examining the piece she'd produced, she nodded in satisfaction. It wasn't brilliant by any means, but it had captured the ethereal feel she wanted. For a first attempt at this technique, it passed. A couple more stages to complete before the glass bowl was ready for a gallery or for sale. A good day's work.

She rubbed her back and wished there was some way she could pace herself. But once caught up in the creative process, it was hard to stop. Especially with glass. Once it was at the molten stage, she had to work swiftly to form the pieces before it cooled. Now it needed to go into the annealer that would slowly cool it so no cracks formed. This was often the tricky part. Especially when she had used different glass and different color mediums that cooled at different rates.

It would end up as it ended up. She tried to keep to that philosophy so she didn't angst over every piece.

Once the bowl was in the oven, she went back to her kitchen, prepared a light meal and carried it to the small terrace on the shady side of the house. The air was cooling down, but it was still almost uncomfortably warm. She nibbled her fruit as she gazed at the flowers that grew so profusely. Where else in the world would she be so comfortable while working on her art? This house was truly a refuge for her. The one place she felt safe and comfortable and almost happy. She'd made it a home for one.

Thinking about the flat she'd given up after Alexander's death, she knew she had traded their happy home for her own. It had taken her a while to realize it, but now she felt a part of the estate. She knew every flower in the garden, every hidden nook that offered shade in the day. And she could walk the paths at night without a light. It was as if the cottage and estate had welcomed her with comforting arms and drawn her in.

So not like the home of her childhood, that was for sure. She shied away from thinking about the last months there. She would focus on the present—or even the future, but not the past.

Taking a deep breath, she held it for a moment, listening. Was that a car? She wasn't expecting any friends. No one else knew where she was. Who would be coming to the empty estate? The gardener's day was later in the week. For a moment she didn't move. The car sounded as if it were going away. Soon the sound faded completely. Only then did Ella relax.

After she ate, she rose and walked around the cottage. Nothing seemed disturbed. How odd that the car sounded so near. Had the sound been amplified from the road, or had it been in the drive for some reason?

The late-afternoon sun was hot. She debated taking a quick swim, but reconsidered. She wanted to walk along the beach tonight to see if the stranger returned. For the first time in over a year, she was curious about something—someone. Not many people shared her love of the

night. Did he? Or had last night been only an ab-
erration because of his long trip? Where in the
desert had he been? She'd like to visit an oasis or
drive a few hours into the desert, lose sight of any
signs of man and just relish the solitude and stark
beauty that would surround her.

She needed a car for that. Sighing softly, she
considered renting a vehicle for such an expedition. Maybe one day in the fall.

Ella could scarcely wait until midnight. Very
unusual, her impatience to see if the man was there
again. For a year she'd felt like she was wrapped
in plastic, seeing, but not really connected with the
rest of the world. Yet a chance encounter in the
dark had ignited her curiosity. She knew nothing
about him, except he liked the sea and wasn't
afraid to swim after dark. Was he old or young?
Did he live nearby or was he sneaking through the
estates to gain access to the private beach?

Would he be there tonight?

Promptly at the stroke of twelve, Ella left her
home to walk quickly through the path to the
beach. Quickly scanning from left to right, she felt
a bump of disappointment. He was not there.
Sighing softly for her foolishness, she walked to
the water's edge and turned to retrace last night's
steps.

"I wondered if you would appear," the familiar

voice said behind her. She turned and saw him walking swiftly toward her. His longer legs cut the distance in a short time. No robes tonight, just dark trousers and a white shirt.

"I often walk at midnight," she said, not wishing him to suspect she'd come tonight especially to see if he were here.

"As do I, but mainly due to the heat of the day."

"And because you don't sleep?" she asked.

He fell into step with her.

"That can be a problem," he said. "For you, too?"

"Sometimes." Now that he was here, she felt awkward and shy. Her heart beat a bit faster and she wondered at the exhilaration that swept through her. "Did you catch up on your sleep after your trip?"

"Got a few hours in."

"Holidays are meant for sleeping in late and lazing around," she said, trying to figure out exactly how to ask questions that wouldn't sound as if she were prying.

"If I were on holiday, which I'm not, I still require little sleep."

"Oh, from what you said…" She closed her mouth.

"I did come off a job at an oil field west of here. But I'm here on business. Personal business, I guess you'd say."

"Oh." What kind of business? How long would it take? Would she see him again after tonight? Not that she could see him exactly. But it was nice to share the walk with someone, if only for one night.

"I have some thinking to do and a decision to make," he added a moment later.

"Mmm." She splashed through the water. There was a slight breeze tonight from the sea which made the air seem cooler than normal. It felt refreshing after the heat of her workshop.

"You speak Arabic, but you're not from here, are you?" he asked.

She looked up and shook her head. Not that he could likely see the gesture. "I've studied for years, I can understand it well. Do I not speak it well?"

"Yes, but there is still a slight accent. Where are you from?"

"Italy. But not for a while. I live here now."

"With family?"

She hesitated. Once again safety concerns reared up. "Do you think I need a chaperone?" she asked, shying away from his question.

"I have no idea. How old are you?"

"Old enough." She stopped and turned, looking up at him, wishing she could see him clearly. "I am a widow. I am long past the stage of needing someone to watch out for me."

"You don't sound old enough to be a widow."

"Sometimes I feel a hundred years old." No one should lose her husband when only twenty-eight. But, as she had been told before, life was not always fair.

"I'm sorry for your loss," he said softly.

She began walking again, not wanting to remember. She tried to concentrate on each foot stepping on the wet sand. Listen to the sea to her right which kissed the shore with wavelets. Feel the energy radiating from the man beside her. So now he'd think she was an older woman, widowed and alone. How old was he? She had no idea, but he sounded like a dynamic man in his prime.

"Thank you." She never knew how to respond to the comment. He hadn't known her husband. He hadn't loved him as she had. No one would ever feel the loss as she did. Still, it was nice he made the comment. Had he ever lost a loved one?

They walked in silence for a few moments. Then she asked, "So what did you do at the oil field?"

"I consult on the pumps and rigs. My company has a retainer with Bashiri Oil among others to assist when new fields are discovered. And to put out fires when they erupt."

"You put out oil fires?" She was astonished. She had seen the pictures of oil wells burning. Flames shot a hundred feet or more in the air. The intense heat melted and twisted metal even yards from the fire. She found it hard to work with the heat in her own studio with appropriate protective gear. How could anyone extinguish an oil well fire? "Is there any job more dangerous on earth?"

He laughed softly. "I imagine there are. It's tricky sometimes, but someone has to do it."

"And how did you get interested in putting out conflagrations? Wasn't being a regular fireman enough?"

"I'm fascinated by the entire process of oil extraction. From discovering reserves, to drilling and capping. And part of the entire scenario is the possibility of fire. Most are accidents. Some are deliberately set. But the important thing is to get them extinguished as quickly as possible. That's why we do consultation work with new sites and review existing sites for safety measures. Anything to keep a well from catching fire is a good thing. It's an interest I've always had. And since I could choose my profession, I chose this one."

"I just can't imagine. Isn't it hot? Actually it must be exceedingly hot. Is there a word beyond hot?"

He laughed again. She liked the sound of it. She smiled in reaction, not at all miffed that he was laughing at her questions.

"Oh, it's hot. Even with the special suits we wear."

He explained briefly how they dealt with fire.

Ella listened, fascinated in a horrified way. "You could get killed doing that," she exclaimed at one point.

"Haven't yet," he said.

She detected the subtle difference in his voice. He was no longer laughing. Had someone been injured or killed fighting one of those fires? Probably. The entire process sounded extremely dangerous.

"They don't erupt often," he said.

"I hope there is never another oil fire in the world," she said fervently. "No wonder you wanted to go swimming last night. I'd want to live *in* the sea if I ever survived one of those."

"That is an appeal. But I'd get restless staying here all the time. Something always draws me back to the oil fields. A need to keep the rigs safe. And a sense of need to return burning wells to productivity. Duty, passion. I'm not totally sure myself."

"So it's the kind of thing you'd do even if you didn't need to work?"

He laughed again. "Exactly."

She stopped. "This is as far as I usually go," she said.

"Ben al Saliqi lives here, or he used to," Khalid said, turning slowly to see the house from the beach. Only the peaks of the roof were visible above the trees that lined the estate, a soft glow from the lamps in the windows illuminating the garden.

"How do you know that?" she asked. There was hardly any identifying features in the dark.

He turned back to her. "I spent many summers here. At my grandmother's house," he said. "I know every family on the beach—except yours."

"Ohmygod, you're one of the al Harum men, aren't you? I'm your tenant, Ella Ponti."

CHAPTER TWO

"MY TENANT?" Khalid said.

"I rent the guesthouse on your grandmother's estate. She was my patron—or something. I miss her so much. I'm so sorry she died."

"She rented out the guesthouse? I had no idea."

"I have a lease. You can check it. She insisted on drawing one up. Said it would be better for us both to get the business part out of the way and enjoy each other's company. She was wonderful. I'm so sorry she died when she did. I miss her."

"I miss her, as well. I didn't know about this," Khalid said.

"Well, I don't know why you don't. Haven't you been running the estate? I mean, the gardener comes every week, the maids at the house keep it clean and ready."

"This is the first I've visited since her death. The servants know how to do their job. They don't need an overseer on site."

"It's the first visit in a long while. You didn't visit her the last few months she lived here. She talked about her grandsons. Which are you, Rashid or Khalid?"

"Khalid."

"Ah, the restless one."

"Restless?"

"She said you hadn't found your place yet. You were seeking, traveling to the interior, along the coast, everywhere, looking for your place."

"Indeed. And Rashid?"

"He's the consumed one—trying to improve the business beyond what his father and uncles did. She worried about you both. Afraid—" Ella stopped suddenly. She was not going to tell him all his grandmother had said. It was not her business if neither man ever married and had children. Or her place to tell him of the longing the older woman had had to hold a new generation. Which never happened and now never would.

"Afraid of what?" he asked.

"Nothing. I have to go back now." She began walking quickly toward home. How was she to know the mysterious stranger on the beach was her new landlord? She almost laughed. He might hold the lease, but he was nothing like a landlord. He hadn't even visited the estate in more than a year. She knew, because she'd never seen him there and she'd live here for over a year and had heard from his grandmother how much she wished to see him beyond fleeting visits in the capital city.

He easily caught up with her. Reaching out to take her arm, he stopped her and swung her around.

"Tell me."

"Good grief, it's not that big a deal. She was afraid neither of her grandsons would marry and have children. She was convinced both of you were too caught up in your own lives to look around for someone to marry. She wanted to hold a great-grandchild. Now she never can."

"She told you this? A stranger."

Ella nodded. "Yes. We became friends and had a lot of time to visit and talk. She came to the guest cottage often, interested in what I was doing." And had been a rock to lean against when Ella was grieving the most. Her gentle wisdom had helped so much in those first few months. Her love had helped in healing. And the rental cottage had been a welcomed refuge. One guarded by the old money and security of the al Harum family. Ella had found a true home in the cottage and was forever grateful to Alia al Harum for providing the perfect spot for her.

Sheikh Khalid al Harum came from that same old money. She hadn't known exactly what he did but it certainly wasn't for money. No wonder his grandmother had complained. It was a lucky thing he was still alive.

"And what were you doing?" he asked, still holding her arm.

"Working. You could call her a patron of the arts."

"You're a painter?"

"No, glassblower. Could you let me go?"

Ella felt his hold ease. His hand dropped to his side. She stepped back and then headed for home. So much for the excitement of meeting the stranger. She could have just waited until she heard him at the main house and gone over to introduce herself.

Now she wanted to get home and close the door. This was the grandson who was always roaming. Was he thinking of using the house when in the capital city?

"Oh." She stopped and turned. Khalid bumped into her. She hadn't known he was right behind her. His hands caught her so she didn't fall.

"Are you planning to sell the estate?" she asked.

"It's something I'm considering."

"Your grandmother wanted you to have it. She'd be so hurt if you just sold it away."

"I'm not selling it away. It's too big for one man. And I'm not in Alkaahdar often. When I am, I have a flat that suits me."

"Think of the future. You could marry and

have a huge family someday. You'll need a big house like that one. And the location is perfect—right on the Gulf."

"I'm not planning to ever marry. Obviously my grandmother didn't tell you all about me or you'd know the thought of marriage is ludicrous. So why would I want a big house to rattle around in?"

Ella tried to remember all her sponsor had said about her grandsons. Not betraying any confidences, not going into detail about their lives, she still had given Ella a good feel for the men's personalities. And a strong sense that neither man was likely to make her a great-grandmother. The longing she'd experienced for the days passed when they'd been children and had loved to come to her home had touched Ella's heart. Alia had hoped to recapture those happy times with their children.

"Don't make hasty decisions," she said. Alia had died thinking this beloved grandson would live in her home. Ella hated the thought he could casually discard it when it had meant so much to the older woman.

"My grandmother died last July. It's now the end of May. I don't consider that a hasty move."

Ella didn't know what tack to use. If he wanted to sell, the house was his to do so with as he wanted. But she felt sad for the woman who had died thinking Khalid would find happiness in the house she'd loved.

"Come, I'll walk you back. You didn't use the path last night that leads to the house or guest-house," he said.

"I didn't know who you were. I didn't want to indicate where I lived," she said, walking back. The night seemed darker and colder. She wanted to be home. So much for looking forward to the evening walk. Now she wished she'd stayed in the cottage and gone to bed.

"Wise. You don't know who might be out on the beach so late at night."

"I've been taking care of myself for a long time. I know this beach well." She was withdrawing. There was something liberating about walking with a stranger, talking, sharing. But something else again once actually knowing the person. She'd be dealing with him in the near future. She didn't know this man. And until she did, she was not giving out any personal information.

A blip of panic settled in. If he sold the estate, where would she go? She had made a home here. Thought she'd be living in the cottage for years to come. She had to review the lease. Did it address the possibility of the estate being sold? She knew Madame al Harum had never considered that likelihood.

As soon as she reached the path, she walked even faster. "Good night," she said. She wasn't even sure what to call him. Sheikh al Harum sounded right, or did she use his first name, as well, to differentiate him from his brother who also was a sheikh? She was not used to dealing with such lofty families.

When she reached her house, she flipped on the lights and headed for the desk. Her expenses were minimum: food, electricity and her nominal rent. It wasn't as if the al Harum family needed her money. But she had needed to pay her way. She was not a charity case. It wasn't a question of money; it was a question of belonging. Of carrying out her dreams. Madame al Harum had understood. Ella doubted the sheikh would.

She read the Arabic script, finding it harder to understand than newspapers. She could converse well, read newspapers comfortably. But this was proving more difficult than she expected. Why hadn't she asked for a copy translated into Italian?

Throwing it down in disgust, she paced the room for a long time. If she had to leave, where would she go? She studied the cream-colored walls, the soft draperies that made the room so welcoming. Just beyond the dark windows was a view of the gardens. She loved every inch of the cottage and grounds. Where else would she find a home?

The next morning Ella was finishing her breakfast when one of the maids from the main house knocked on the door. It was Jalilah, one who had also served Alia al Harum for so many years.

"His Excellency would like to see you," she said. "I'm to escort you to the main house."

So now he summoned her—probably to discuss her leaving. "Wait until I change." She'd donned worn jeans and an oversize shirt to work around the studio. Not the sort of apparel one wore to meet with a sheikh. Especially if doing battle to keep her home.

Quickly she donned a dress that flattered her dark looks. It was a bit big; she'd lost weight over the last few months. Still, the rose color brought a tinge of pink to her cheeks.

Her dark eyes looked sad—as they had ever since losing Alexander. She would never again be the laughing girl who had grown up thinking everything good about people. Now she knew heartache and betrayal. She was wiser, but at a price.

Running a brush through her hair, she turned to face the future. Was there a clause in the lease that would nullify her claim if the estate was sold? As they walked across the gardens, she tried to remember every detail about the terms Madame al Harum had discussed.

She entered the house and immediately remembered her one-time hostess. Nothing had changed since the last time she'd visited. It was cool and pleasant. The same pictures hung on the walls.

Her first vase from her new studio still held a place of honor on the small table in the foyer, holding a cascading array of blossoms. She'd been so happy it had been loved.

The maid went straight to the study. Ella paused at the doorway for a moment, her eyes widening in shock as she got a good look at Sheikh Khalid al Harum. He looked up at her, catching the startled horror in her expression. His own features hardened slightly and she felt embarrassed she'd reacted as she had. No one had told her he'd been horribly burned. The distorted and puckered skin on his right cheek, down his neck and obviously beneath his shirt, disfigured what were otherwise the features of a gorgeous man. She'd been right about his age—he looked to be in his prime, maybe early thirties. And he was tall as she noted when he rose to face her.

"You wanted to see me?" she said, stepping inside. She held his gaze, determined not to comment on the burn, or show how sympathetic she felt at the pain he must have endured. She'd had enough burns herself in working with molten glass to know the pain. Never as big a patch as he had. What was a fabulously wealthy man like he had to be risking his life to fight oil fires?

Her heart beat faster. Despite the burn scar, he was the best-looking guy she'd ever seen. Even including Alexander. She frowned. She was not comparing the two. There was no need. The sheikh was merely her new landlord. The flurry of attraction was a fluke. He could mean nothing to her.

"Please." He gestured to a chair opposite the desk. "You're considerably younger than I thought. Are you really a widow?"

She nodded as she slipped onto the edge of the chair. "My husband died April a year ago. What did you wish to see me about?"

He sat and picked up a copy of the lease. "This. The lease for the guesthouse you signed with my grandmother."

She nodded. It was what she expected. He held her future in his hands. Why didn't she have a good feeling about this?

"How did you coerce her to making this?" he asked, frowning at the papers.

Ella blinked. "I did not coerce her into doing anything. How dare you suggest such a thing!" She leaned forward, debating whether to leave or not at his disparaging remark. "She offered me a place to live and work and then came up with the lease herself so I wouldn't have to worry about living arrangements until I got a following."

"A following?"

"I told you, I blow glass. I need to make enough pieces to sell to earn her livelihood. Until that time, she was—I guess you'd say like a patroness—a sponsor if you would. I rented the studio to make my glass pieces and she helped out by making the rent so low. Did you read the clause where she gets a percentage of my sales when I start making money?"

"And if you never sell anything? Seems you got a very cushy deal here. But my grandmother's gone now. This is my estate and if I chose to sell it, I'm within my rights. I don't know how you got her to sign such a lopsided lease but I'm not her. You need to leave. Vacate the guest quarters so I can renovate if necessary to sell."

Ella stared at him. "Where does it say I have to leave before the end of the five years?" she asked, stalling for time, trying to think about what she could do. Panic flared again. It has seemed too good to be true that she'd have a place to live and work while building an inventory. But as the months had gone on, she'd become complaisant with her home. She couldn't possibly find another place right away—and she didn't have the money to build another studio. And not enough glass pieces ready to sell to raise the money. She was an unknown. The plans she and his grandmother had discussed had been for the future—not the present.

"I do not want you as a tenant. What amount do you want to leave?"

She didn't get his meaning at first, then anger

flared. "Nothing. I wish to stay." She felt the full force of his gaze when he stared at her. She would not be intimidated. This was her *home*. He might see it as merely property, but it was more to her. Raising her chin slightly, she continued. "You'll see on the last page once I begin to sell, she gets ten percent of all sales. Or she would have. I guess you do, now." She didn't like the idea of having a long-term connection with this man. He obviously couldn't care less about her or her future. Madame al Harum had loved her work, had encouraged her so much. She appreciated what Ella did and would have reveled in her success—if it came.

Sheikh Khalid al Harum saw her as an impediment to selling the estate.

Tough.

"I can make it very worth your while," he said softly.

She kept her gaze locked with his. "No."

"You don't know how much," he said.

"Doesn't matter. I have the lease, I have the house for another four years. That will be enough time to make it or not. If not, I'll find something else to do." And she'd keep her precious home until the last moment.

"Or find a rich husband to support you. The estate is luxurious. You would hate to leave it. But if I give you enough money, you'll be able to support yourself in similar luxury for a time."

She rose and leaned on the desk, her eyes narrowed as she stared into his.

"I'm not leaving. The lease gives me a right to stay. Deal with it."

She turned and left, ignoring her shaky knees, her pounding heart. She didn't want his money. She wanted to stay exactly where she was. Remain until those looking for her gave up. Until she could build her own future the way she wanted. Until she could prove her art was worth something and that people would pay to own pieces.

Khalid listened to the sound of her hurried foot-steps, then the closing of the front door. She refused to leave. He glanced at the lease again. As far as he could tell, it was iron tight. But he'd have the company attorneys review. There had to be a way. He did not want to sit on the house for another four years and he suspected no one would buy the place with a tenant in residence. What had his grandmother been thinking?

He leaned back in his chair and looked at the chair his unwanted tenant had used. Ella Ponti, widow. She looked like she was in her midtwenties. How had her husband died? She was far too young to be a widow, living alone. Yet the sadness that had shone in her eyes until the fire of anger replaced it, showed him she truly mourned her loss. And he felt a twinge of regret to be bringing a change to her life.

Yet he couldn't reconcile her being in the cottage. Had his grandmother been taken in? Was Ella nothing more than a gold digger looking for an easy way in life? Latch on to an old woman and talk her into practically giving her the cottage.

He was on the fence about selling. He remembered his grandmother in every room. All the visits they'd shared over the years. Glancing around the study, he hated to let it go. But he would never live in such a big house. Which left selling the estate as the best option.

He should have visited his grandmother more often. He missed her. They'd had dinners together in Alkaahdar when he was in town. Sometimes he escorted her to receptions or parties. But long weekends at the estate doing nothing were in the past. And in retrospect she'd asked after him and what was going on in his life more than he'd asked after hers. Regrets were hard to live with.

Though if she'd seen Ella's reactions, maybe she would have stopped chiding him that he made too much of the scar. Ella's initial reaction had been an echo of his one-time fiancée's own look of horror. He knew it disgusted women. That was one reason he spent most of his time on the oil fields or in the desert. He saw the scar himself every morning when he shaved. He knew what it looked like.

Shaking himself out of the momentary reverie,

he picked up the phone to call the headquarters of Bashiri Oil. The sooner he found a way to get rid of his unwanted tenant, the better.

Ella stormed home. She did not want to be bought out. Why had Khalid al Harum come to the estate at this time? He'd never visited in all the months she'd live here, why now? She had her life just as she wanted it and he was going to mess it up.

And how dare he offer her money to move? She was not going anywhere. She needed this tranquil setting. She'd gradually gotten over the fierce intensity of her grief. She owed it to Alia al Harum. The older woman had such faith in her talent and her ability to be able to command top money for her creations. She had strongly encouraged Ella to prove it to herself. And she would for the memory of the woman who had helped her so much.

And no restless grandson was going to drive her away.

She shrugged off the dress and tossed it on the bed. So much for dressing up for him. He only wanted her gone. She pulled on her jeans and oversize shirt. Tying her hair back as she walked, she went to the studio. The glass bowl she'd created yesterday still had hours of graduated cooling to complete before she could take it from the oven. She was impatient to know if it would be as beautiful as she imagined. And flawless with no cracks from irregular cooling, or mixing different types and textures of glass that cooled at different rates. Fingers crossed. Patience was definitely needed for glasswork.

In the meantime, she picked up her sketchbook and went to sit by the window. She could do an entire series in the same technique if the bowl came out perfect. She stared at the blank page. She was not seeing other glass artwork, but the face of Khalid al Harum. What a contrast—gorgeous man, hideous scar. His grandmother had never mentioned that. She'd talked of her grandchildren's lives, her worry they'd never find happiness and other memories of their childhood.

When had the fire happened? He could have been killed. She didn't know him, nor did she care to now that he'd tried to bribe her to leave. But still, how tragic to have been burned so severely. She looked at the couple of small scars on her arms and fingers from long-ago childhood scrapes. Fire was dangerous and damaging to delicate human skin. Every burn, no matter how small, hurt like crazy. She shivered trying to imagine a huge expanse of her body burned.

Had it happened recently? It didn't have that red look that came with recent healing. But with all the money the al Harums had, surely he could have had plastic surgery to mitigate the worst of the damage.

Impatient with her thoughts, she rose and paced the studio. She needed to be focused on the next idea, the next piece of art. She had to build a collection that would be worthy of an exhibit and then of exorbitant prices. Had Madame al Harum spoken to the gallery owners as she had said she would do when the time was right? Probably not. Why speak of something that was years away from happening.

"Great. It's bad enough he'll try to get me off the property. I truly have no place to go and no chance of getting a showing if I don't have someone to vouch for me," she said aloud. She could scream.

But it would do no good.

"Deal with it," she said to herself. She'd take the advice she'd given him and make sure she made every moment count. He might try to evict her, but until she was carried kicking and screaming from the studio, she'd work on her collection.

The day proved interminable. Every time she'd start thinking about Khalid al Harum, she'd force her mind to focus on designing pieces using the swirling of blues and reds. It would work for a few moments, then gradually something would drift in that had her thinking about him again.

She didn't like it one bit.

After dinner, she debated taking a walk on the beach. That usually cleared her mind. But after the last two nights, the last thing she wanted was to run into *him* again.

She sat on her terrace for a while, trying to relax. The more she tried to ignore his image, the more it seemed to dance in front of her. She was not going to be intimidated by him. Jumping to her feet, she headed down the path to the beach. She'd been walking along the shore for months. Just because he showed up was no reason to change her routine.

When she stepped on the sand, she looked both ways. No sign of anyone. Slowly she walked to the water, then turned south. If he did come out, chances he would head north as she had the last two nights. She'd be safe from his company.

It didn't take long for the walk to begin to soothe. She let go of cares and worries and tried to make herself one with the night.

"I took a guess," a voice came from her right.

Khalid rose from the sand and walked the few yards to where she was. "I thought you might go a different way tonight and I was right." The smug satisfaction in his tone made her want to hit him.

"Then I'll turn and go north," she said, stopping and facing him. She'd tried an earlier time and a different direction. Had he come out to the beach a while ago to wait for her? She ignored the fluttery feeling in her stomach. So he came out. It probably was only to harangue her again about leaving.

"I am not stopping you from going in either direction," he said. He stood next to her, almost too close. She stepped back as a wavelet washed over her feet. The cool water broke the spell.

"You are of course welcomed to walk wherever you wish," she said. She began to walk again along the edge of the water.

Khalid walked beside her.

The silence stretched out moment by moment. Ella had lost all sense of serenity. Her nerves were on full alert. She was extremely conscious of the man beside her. Her skin almost tingled. She could see him from the corner of her eye—tall, silhouetted against the dark sky. She didn't need this sense of awareness. This feeling of wanting to know more. The desire to defend herself to him and make him change his mind and want her to stay in the guesthouse until the lease expired.

She kept silent with effort, wondering if she could outlast him. It grew harder and harder to keep silent as they went along.

"I called an attorney," he said at last.

She didn't reply, waiting for the bad news. Was there an escape clause?

"You'll be happy to know the lease is airtight. You have the right to stay as long as you wish. The interesting part is, you have the right to terminate before the end but my grandmother—and now me—didn't have the same right."

She'd forgotten. Madame al Harum had insisted Ella might wish to leave before five years and didn't want her to feel compelled to remain. At the time Ella had not been able to imagine ever leaving. She still didn't want to think about it. Would four more years be enough time?

"So if you wished to leave, I'd still make it lucrative for you."

"I don't live here for the money," she said.

"Why do you live here? You're not from here. No family. No husband. What holds you to the guesthouse, to Alkaahdar?"

"A safe place to live," she said. "A beautiful setting in a beautiful country. I also have friends here. Quishari is my home."

"Safe? Is there danger elsewhere?" he countered, focusing in on that comment.

She stopped to look at him. She wanted to get this through to him once and for all. "Look, I came here at a very hard time in my life—just after my husband died. Your grandmother did more for me than anyone, including making sure I had a place to live, to work, sheltered from problems and a chance to grieve. I will forever be in her debt. One I can now never repay. It hit me hard when she died. I grieve for her, as well. Now I'm coming to a place of peace and don't wish to have my life disrupted because you want to get rid of a home she loved and left to you in hopes you'd use it. Do not involve me in your life. I have no interest in taking a gazillion dollars to leave. I have no interest in disrupting my life to suit yours. I want to be left alone to continue as I have been doing these last months. Is that clear enough for you?"

"Life changes. Nothing is as it was last year. My grandmother is dead. Yes, she left me the estate in hopes I would settle there. You saw me this morning. You know why I'll never marry. Why should I hold on to a house for sentimental reasons, visiting it once or twice a year when some other family could enjoy living in it daily? Do you think it is easy for me to sell? I have so many memories of my family visiting. I know I'll face pressure from others in the family to hold on to it. But it's more of a crime to let it sit vacant year after year. What good does that do?"

"Why will you never marry? Did the fire damage other parts of you?" she asked, startled by his comment.

"What?"

She'd surprised him with that question.

Oh, this was just great. Why had she opened her mouth? Now she had to clarify herself. "I mean, can you not father children or something?"

He burst out laughing.

Ella frowned. It had not been a funny question.

"So you're all right in that department, I guess," she said, narrowing her eyes. "So what's the problem?"

He leaned over, his face close enough to hers she felt the warmth of his breath. She could barely see his eyes in the dark. "As I said, you saw me this morning. What woman would get close enough for me to use those other parts?" he asked very softly.

She stared into his eyes, as dark as her own, hard to see in the dim light of the stars. "Are you stupid or do you think I am? You're gorgeous except for a slight disfiguration on one side. You sound articulate. I expect you are well educated and have pots of money. Why wouldn't someone fall for you? Your grandmother thought you should be married. Surely she'd have known if there was a major impediment."

"I do not wish to be married for my money. I have a temper that could scare anyone and, I assure you, looks count a lot when people are looking for mates. And my grandmother saw only her own happy marriage that she wished replicated for her grandsons."

"So again I say what's the problem?"

"Maybe you are stupid. This scar," he said, reaching for her hand and trailing her fingers down his cheek, pressing against the puckered skin.

He let her hand go and she left it against the side of his face. The skin was warm, though distorted. Lightly, she brushed her thumb against it, drifted to his lips which had escaped the flame. Her heart pounded, but she was mesmerized. His warmth seemed to touch her heart. She felt heart-break for his reasoning. He was consigning himself to a long, lonely life. She knew what that was like. Since Alexander's death, hadn't she resigned herself to the same?

But the circumstances were different. She had loved and lost. Khalid needed to feel someone's love, to know he was special. And to keep the dream his grandmother had so wanted for him.

Khalid was shocked. Her touch was soft, gentle, sweet. Her thumb traced a trail of fire and ice against his skin. No one had touched him since the doctors had removed the last of the bandages. When he released her, he expected her to snatch her hand away. It was still there. The touch was both unexpected and erotic. He could feel himself respond as he hadn't in years.

"Enough." He knocked her hand away and took a step back. "Tell me what it would take to get you to leave the guesthouse."

"Four years," she replied, and turned to resume her walk.

He watched as she walked away along the sea's edge. She was serious. At least at this moment. She didn't want money. She wanted time.

Why was she here? Was there anything in his

grandmother's things that explained why she'd befriended Ella Ponti and made that one-sided deal
with her? He hadn't gone through all her papers,
but that would be his next step first thing in the
morning.

He remained standing, watching. She didn't
care if he walked beside her or not. If this was her
regular routine, she'd been coming for nightly
walks for a year. She didn't need his company.

Why had he come out tonight? He usually kept
to himself. He couldn't remember the last time
he'd sought out a woman's company. Probably
because it would have been an exercise in futility.
Ella had seen him in broad daylight. Tonight it had
been like the last two: wrapped in darkness he
could almost forget the burn scar. She had treated
him the same all three nights.

Except for her touch tonight.

Shaking his head, he almost smiled. She
shocked him in more ways than one. Was the
reaction just that of a man too long without a
woman? It had to be. She had done nothing to encourage him. In fact, he couldn't remember
another woman standing up to him as she had,
both tonight and earlier this morning. Deal with it,
she'd said, dismissing his demand she leave as if
it were of no account.

Which legally it proved to be. Maybe he'd stop
pushing and learn a bit more about his unwanted

tenant before pursuing other avenues. She intrigued him. Why was she really here? Maybe it was time to find out more about Ella Ponti, young widow living so far from her native land.

CHAPTER THREE

MAYBE she had finally gotten through to him, she thought as she walked alone. He had not followed her. Good. Well, maybe there was a touch of disappointment, but not enough to wish he was with her.

She clenched her hand into a fist. His skin had been warm, she'd felt the strong line of his jaw, the chiseled outline of his lips. Not that she wanted to think about his lips—that led to thoughts of kisses and she had no intention of ever kissing anyone else. It almost felt like a betrayal of her love for Alexander. It wasn't. Her mind knew that, it would take her heart a bit longer to figure that out. She still mourned her lost love.

"Alexander," she whispered. It took a second for her to recall his dear face. She panicked. She couldn't forget him. She loved him still. He'd been the heart beating in her. But his image wavered and faded to be replaced by the face of Khalid al Harum.

"No!" she said firmly. She would dismiss the man from her thoughts and concentrate on something else, anything else.

Wildly, she looked around. Out to sea she spotted a ship, gliding along soundlessly in the distance. Was it a cruise ship? Were couples and families enjoying the calm waters of the Gulf? Would they be stopping in one of the countries lining the coast? Maybe buy pearls from the shops or enjoy the traditional Arab cuisine. Maybe couples would be dancing. For a moment she regretted she'd never dance again. She was young to have loved and lost. But that was the way life was sometimes.

She had her art.

Stopping at last, she gazed at the ship for a long moment, then glanced back up the beach. Khalid al Harum stood where she'd left him. Was he brooding? Or just awaiting her return. She studied his silhouette and then began walking toward him. She had to return home. It was late and she'd had enough turmoil to last awhile.

When she drew even she stopped. "Now what?"

"Now we wait four years," he replied.

That surprised her. Was he really going to stop pressuring her? Somehow she had not thought he'd give up that easily. Yet, maybe he was pragmatic. The lease was valid. She had the law on her side—even against a sheikh. Dare she let her guard down and believe him?

"Since we'll be neighbors for the time, might as well make the best of things," he said.

That had her on instant alert. He didn't strike her as someone who settled for making the best of any situation unless it suited his needs and demands.

"And how do we do that?"

"Be neighborly, of course." He walked beside her. "Surely you visited with my grandmother from time to time."

"Almost every day," she said. "She was delightful. And very encouraging about my work. Did you know you have one of my early pieces in your house?"

"What and where?"

"The shallow vase in the foyer. It's a starburst bowl. Your grandmother liked it and I gave it to her. I was thrilled when she displayed it in such a prominent place."

"Maybe I'll come by one day and see your work."

Ella wasn't sure she wanted him in her studio or her house. But she probably had to concede that much. If he truly stopped pushing her to leave, she could accept a visit or two.

"Let me know when," she said.

* * *

Khalid caught up on some e-mail the next morning and then called his brother. Rashid was the head of Bashiri Oil. Khalid was technically equal owner in the company, along with an uncle and some cousins, but Rashid ran the business. Which suited Khalid perfectly. He much preferred the oil fields to the offices in the high-rise building downtown.

"What's up?" Rashid asked when he heard his brother's voice. "Are you still in Hari?"

"No, I'm at Grandmother's estate. Did you know she rented out the guesthouse last year?"

"No. Who to?"

"An artist. Now I'm wondering why the secrecy. I didn't know, either." Another reason to find out more about Ella Ponti.

"Good grief, did he convince her to sponsor him or something? What hard-luck story did he spin?"

"Not a he, a she. And I'm not sure about the story, which is the reason for the call. Can you have someone there run a background check? Apparently Ella has an airtight lease to the premises and has no intention of leaving before the lease expires—in four more years."

"A five-year lease? Have someone here look at it."

"Already done. It's solid. And she's one determined woman. I offered her as big a bribe as I could and she still says no."

"So, look for dirt to get her out that way." Rashid suggested.

"No, I think I'll go along with it for a while. I just want to know more about her. I respect Grandmother's judgment. She obviously liked the woman. But she also knew her and I don't."

There was a silent moment before his brother spoke again. "Is she pretty?"

"What does that have to do with a background check? She's a widow."

"Oh. Sure, I'll have one of the men call you later and you can give him what you have to start with. Bethanne and I are dining with Mother tonight… care to join us?"

"I'll take a rain check. I'm going through Grandmother's things. I still can't believe she's gone. It's as if she stepped out for a little while. Only, she's never coming back."

"Planning to move there?"

"I was thinking of selling the place, until I found I have an unbudgeable tenant."

"Then good for the widow. None of us wants you to sell."

"It's not your place. You got the villa south of the city."

"Where I think Bethanne and I will live. You love the sea. Why not keep it?"

"It's a big house. You don't need it—you have

your own villa by the sea. Why let it sit idle for decades?"

"Get married and fill it up," his brother suggested.

"Give Mother my love and have someone call me soon," he said, sidestepping the suggestion. Rashid should know as well as he did that would never happen. But his brother had recently become engaged and now had changed his tune about staying single. He was not going to get a convert with Khalid.

Ella's words last night echoed. He shook his head. Easy to say the words in the dark. Harder to say when face-to-face with the scars.

He hung up the phone and looked again at the vase sitting on his desk. He'd taken it last night from the foyer to the study. It was lovely. Almost a perfect oval, it flared at the edges. From the center radiating outward was a yellow design that did look like a sunburst. Toward the edges the yellow thinned to gossamer threads. How had she done it? It was sturdy and solid yet looked fragile and enchanted. He knew his grandmother had loved it.

Seeing the vase gave validity to Ella's assertion she was an artist. Was she truly producing other works of art like this? Maybe his grandmother had seen the potential and arranged to keep her protégée close by while she created. She'd been friendly and helpful to others, but was an astute woman. She must have seen real talent to encourage Ella so much. So why not tell the rest of the family?

Khalid rose and headed next door. It was time he saw the artist in her studio, and assessed exactly what she was doing.

He walked to the guest cottage in only seconds. Though it was close, because of the lush garden between it and the main house there was a feeling of distance. He saw a new addition, obviously the studio. How much had his grandmother done for this tenant?

He stepped to the door, which stood wide-open. He could feel the heat roiling out from the space. He looked in. Ella was concentrating on her project and didn't notice him. For a long moment Khalid watched her. She wore a large leather apron and what looked like leather gloves that reached up to her elbows. She had dark glasses on and straddled a long wooden bench. At one end a metal sheet was affixed upon which she turned molten glass at the end of a long tube. As he watched, the glass began to take shape as she turned it against the metal. A few feet beyond was a furnace, the door open, pouring out heat.

Her dark hair was pulled back into a ponytail. He studied her. Even attired as she was, she looked

feminine and pretty. How had she become interested in this almost lost art? It took a lot of stamina
to work in such an adverse environment. It had to
be close to thirty-seven degrees in the room. Yet
she looked as cool as if she were sitting in the
salon of his grandmother's house.

Slowly ,she rotated the tube. She blew again
and the shape elongated. He was afraid to break
her concentration lest it cause her to damage the
glass globule.

She looked up and frowned, then turned back
to her work. "What do you want?" she asked,
before blowing gently into the tube again.

"To see where you worked." He stepped inside.
"It's hot in here."

"Duh, I'm working with fire."

He looked at the glowing molten glass. She
pushed it into the furnace. No wonder it was so
hot; everything inside the furnace glowed orange.

She pulled out the molten glass and worked on
it some more.

Khalid began to see the shape, a tall vase
perhaps. The color was hard to determine as it
was translucent and still glowed with heat.

He walked closer, his scar tissue reacting to the
heat. He crossed to the other side, so his undam-
aged cheek faced the heat. How did she stand it
so close for hours on end?

"Do you mind if I watch?"

"Not much I can do about it, is there?" she asked with asperity.

Khalid hid a smile. She was not giving an inch. Novel in his experience. Before he'd been burned, women had fawned over him. He and Rashid. He'd bet Ella wouldn't have, no matter what.

"Did my grandmother build this for you?"

"Mmm," she mumbled, her lips still around the tube.

"State of the art?"

"Mmm."

He looked around. Other equipment lined one wall, one looked like an oven. There were jars of crushed glass in various colors. On one table were several finished pieces. He walked over and looked at them. Picking up a vase, he noted the curving shape, almost hourglasslike. The color was pastel—when held up so the white wall served as a background, it looked pale green. When on the table, it grew darker in color contrasting with the wood.

He wondered how much all this cost and would his grandmother ever have made any money as a return on her investment. She must have thought highly of Ella to have expended so much on an aspiring artist.

He looked at the other pieces. He wasn't a connoisseur of art, but they were quite beautiful. It was obvious his grandmother had recognized her talent and had encouraged it.

When he glanced back at Ella, she was using a metal spatula to shape the piece even further. He watched as she flattened the bottom and then began molding the top to break away from the tube. Setting the piece on the flat bottom, she ran the spatula over the top, gradually curving down the edge. He watched her study it from a couple of angles, then slide it onto a paddle and carefully carry it to the oven. She opened the top doors and slid it in, closing the doors quickly and setting a dial.

Turning, she looked at him, taking off her dark glasses.

"So?" she said. Her skin glowed with a sheen of perspiration.

"Interesting. These are lovely," he said, gesturing to the collection behind him. Trying to take his eyes off her. She looked even more beautiful with that color in her cheeks.

"I hope so. That's the intent. Build an inventory and hit the deck running. Do you know any art dealers?" she asked hopefully.

Khalid shook his head. His family donated to the arts, but at the corporate level. He had no personal acquaintance with art dealers.

She sighed and untied her apron, sliding it off and onto the bench. "Me, neither. That was another thing your grandmother was going to do—introduce me to several gallery owners in

Europe. Guess I'll have to forge ahead on my own."

"Too bad you can't ride in on the al Harum name," he murmured.

Her eyes flared at that. Was he deliberately baiting her to see her reaction? He liked the fire in her eyes. It beat the hint of sadness he saw otherwise.

"I was not planning to ride in on anyone's name. I expect my work to stand on its own merits. Your grandmother was merely going to introduce me."

"Still, an introduction from her would have assured owners took a long look before saying yea or nay, and think long and hard about turning down a protégée of Alia al Harum. She spent a lot of money in some galleries on her visits to France and Italy."

"I don't plan on showing in Italy," she said hastily.

Khalid's suspicions shot up. She was from Italy—why not show in her home country? He'd given what information he had to a person at the oil company to research her background. Now he wanted more than ever to know what brought her to Quishari, and how she'd met his grandmother.

"Do you think you can sell enough to earn a living?" he asked.

"Your grandmother thought so. I believe her, so yes, I do. I don't expect to become hugely wealthy, but I have simple needs, and love doing this creative work, so should be content if I ever start selling."

"Have you sent items out for consideration?"

"No. I wanted to wait until I had inventory. If the pieces sell quickly, I want more in the pipeline and can only produce a few each month. I have a five-year plan."

He met her eyes. Sincerity shone in them. It seemed odd to have this pretty woman talk about five-year plans. But the longer he gazed at her, the more he wanted to help. Which was totally out of character for him. He broke the contact and gave a final glance around the studio. Heading for the door, he paused before leaving. "I say give it a test run, send out some of your best pieces and see if they'll sell. No sense wasting five years if nothing is worth anything."

Ella stared out into the garden long after Khalid had left. He made it sound so simple. But it wasn't. What if she didn't sell? What if her pieces were mundane and mediocre? She could live on hope for the next few years—or have reality slap her in the face and crush her. She was still too vulnerable to venture forth to see if her work had merit. Madame al Harum had been so supportive. Now she ran into a critic. She had to toughen up if she wanted to compete in the competitive art world. Could she do it?

She cleaned up, resisting the temptation to peer into the lower part of the annealer to check the progress of the piece she'd done yesterday. She hoped it would be spectacular. Maybe Khalid al Harum was right. She should not waste time creating glass pieces if they would never sell. The slight income from Alexander's insurance would not carry her forever. If she couldn't make a living with glass, she should find another means to earn her livelihood.

Only, she didn't want another means. She loved making glass.

Once she finished cleaning the studio, she grabbed her notebook and went to sit on the terrace. The arbor overhead sheltered it from the hot sun. She enjoyed sitting outside when planning. It was so much more pleasant than the hot studio. She opened the pages and began to study the pictures she'd taken of the different pieces she had already made. She had more than one hundred. Some were quite good, others were attempts at a new technique that hadn't panned out. Dare she select a few pieces to offer for sale?

What if no one bought them?

What if they skyrocketed her to fame?

She did not want to rock the boat. She liked life the way it was. Or the way it had been before Khalid al Harum had arrived.

Idly she wondered what it would take to get rid

of him. The only thing she could think of was moving out so he could sell the estate. She wasn't going to do that, so it looked as if she were stuck with him.

He was so different from his grandmother. Distracting, for one thing. She'd known instantly when he appeared in the doorway, but had ignored him as long as she could. Of course he had the right to visit his property, but his grandmother had always arranged times to come see what she was working on. There was something almost primordial about the man. He obviously was healthy and virile. She was so not interested in another relationship, yet her body seemed totally aware of his whenever he was near. It was disconcerting to say the least.

And distracting.

Ella stayed away from the beach that night. She listened to music while cataloging the pieces she thought might do for a first showing. She only had a couple of photos of the first batch of vases and bowls she'd made when she moved here. She needed to take more pictures, maybe showcase them in one of the salons in the main house. It was an idea she and Madame al Harum had discussed.

Good grief, she'd have to ask Khalid and she could imagine exactly what he'd say to her proposal. Or maybe she could sneak in when he wasn't there. Surely there was an oil field somewhere in the world that needed consulting. If he'd take off for a few days, she was sure Jalilah would let her in to photograph the pieces sitting in prominent display in the main salon. It would add a certain cachet to her catalog and maybe garner more interest when she was ready to go.

She went to bed that night full of ideas of how to best display the pieces she would put in her first catalog. The only question was if she dare ask Khalid for permission to use his salon for the photographs.

By the time morning arrived, Ella regretted her decision to forego her walk. She had slept badly, tossing and turning and picturing various scenarios when asking Khalid for his help. Maybe she should have been a bit more conciliatory when discussing her lease. She planned to stand fast on staying, but she could have handled it better.

Only she disliked subterfuge and manipulation; she refused to practice it in her own life.

After a hasty breakfast, she again dressed up a bit and headed for the villa. Walking through the gardens, she tried to quell her nerves. The worst he could do was refuse. The guesthouse had a small sitting area, not as lavish as the main dwelling. She could use that, but she longed for the more elegant salon as backdrop for her art.

Jalilah opened the door when she knocked.

"I'd like to see Sheikh al Harum," Ella said, hoping she looked far more composed than she felt.

"He has someone visiting. Wait here."

Ella stood in the foyer. Her vase was gone. She peered into the salon; it wasn't there, either. Had something happened to it? Or had Khalid removed it once he'd learned she made it? That made her feel bad.

"Come." The maid beckoned from the door to the study.

When Ella entered, she stopped in surprise. Two men looked at her. Except for their clothing, and the scar on Khalid's cheek, they were identical.

"Twins?" she said.

Khalid frowned. "Did you want something?"

"Introduce us," the other man said, crossing the room and offering his hand.

"My brother," Khalid said.

"Well, that's obvious." Ella extended her hand and smiled. "I'm Ella Ponti."

"I am Rashid al Harum. You're the tenant, I take it."

She nodded. "Unwanted to boot."

"Only because I want to sell," Khalid grumbled. "Rashid is trying to talk me out of it, too."

"Good for you. I told him your grandmother wanted him to have the house. She could have left it to a charity or something if she hadn't hoped he'd live here," she said.

"It's a too big for one man," Khalid said.

"So—"

He raised his hand. "We've been over that. What do you want?"

Rashid glanced at his twin. "Am I in the way?"

Ella shook her head, bemused to see her vase in the center of Khalid's desk.

"Not at all. I came to ask permission to photograph some of my work in the salon. Give it a proper showing—elegant and refined. The guest cottage just doesn't have the same ambiance."

"You want to take pictures of my house?" Khalid asked. "Out of the question."

"Not the house, just some of my special pieces sitting on a table or something which would display them and give an idea of how they would look in another home. The background would be slightly blurred, the focus would be on my work."

"Use the table in your workroom."

"That's elegant."

He frowned. "I don't see—"

"—any problem with it," Rashid finished before his twin could finish. "I was admiring your vase when you arrived. Khalid explained how you made it. I'd like to see more of your work. I bet Bethanne would, as well."

"She'd do anything you say," Khalid grumbled.

"Bethanne?" Ella asked.

"My fiancée. She's making some changes to

my villa in preparation of our marriage and moving in there."

"So the consumed one is getting married— wouldn't my grandmother love to know that?" Khalid asked.

"What are you talking about?" Rashid asked, glancing at his twin.

"Nothing, only something your grandmother said to me once. I'm happy for you and your fiancée. You might tell your brother how happy you are so he could go find someone to make a life with and leave me alone," Ella said hastily.

Rashid looked at her and then Khalid.

"Forget it. We've been over this before. I'm not marrying," Khalid growled.

Rashid looked thoughtful as he again looked back and forth between the two others in the room.

"I, uh, have to be leaving. I'll bring Bethanne by tomorrow if that suits you, Ella. She'd love to see the glass objects. Khalid, you have what you asked for. Let me know if you need more." He nodded to both and left, a small smile tugging at his lips.

Ella hated to see him go. He was much easier to be around than his brother.

"So I can use the salon?" she asked. Rashid had indicated yes, but it was still Khalid's place and his decision she needed.

"What if I say no?" he asked, leaning casually against the side of the desk.

"Then I'll pester you until you say yes," she replied daringly. "Maybe it'll help sell some of my work earlier than originally planned and I could move away sooner."

"How much sooner?"

"I don't know, five days?"

A gleam of amusement lit his eyes. "For such an early move, how can I refuse?"

"Thank you. I'll give credit in my brochure so everyone will know you helped."

"No. No credit, no publicity."

She started to protest but wisely agreed. "Okay. I'm cooling a couple of pieces now and once they are ready, I will begin taking pictures. I appreciate this."

"You weren't on the beach last night," he said.

He had been, obviously.

"I, uh, needed to get to sleep early. Big day today."

"Doing what?"

"Coming to ask you about the salon" sounded dumb. What else could she come up with?

He watched her. Ella fidgeted and looked around the room. "Just a big day. Why is my vase in here?"

"I was looking at it. I thought it was mine."

"I guess. I should have said why is the vase I made in here instead of the foyer."

"I wanted to look at it. I like it."

She blinked in surprise. "You do?"

Amusement lurked in his eyes again. "You sound surprised. Isn't it good?"

She nodded. "I just can't imagine you—"

"Having an eye for beauty?"

"I wasn't exactly going to say that."

"You haven't held back on anything else."

"You are very exasperating, do you know that?" she asked.

"Makes a change from other names I've been called."

If he drove the other people he knew as crazy as he did her, she wasn't surprised.

Khalid stood and moved around to sit at the desk.

"So, you'll be on the beach tonight?" he asked casually.

Ella shrugged. "Thanks for letting me use the salon for the photographs."

"One caveat," he said, glancing up.

She sighed. It had been too good to be true. "What?"

"I get to give final approval. I don't want certain prize possessions to be part of your sales catalog. No need to give anyone the idea that more than your glass is available."

"Done." She nodded and turned. At the door she stopped and looked at him over her shoulder. "I do expect to take a walk tonight as it happens."

She wasn't sure, but she suspected the expression on his face was as close to a smile as she'd seen.

CHAPTER FOUR

ELLA and Khalid fell into a tentative friendship. Each night she went for a walk along the beach. Most evenings Khalid was already on the sand, as if waiting for her. They fell into an easy conversation walking in the dark at the water's edge. Sometimes they spoke of what they'd done that day. Other times the walks were primarily silent. Ella noted he was quieter than other men she'd known. Was that his personality or a result of the accident? She gathered the courage to ask about it on the third evening after he said she could use the salon.

"How did you get burned?" she asked as they were turning to head for home. She hadn't wanted to cut the walk short if he got snippy about her question.

"We were capping a fire in Egypt. Just as the dynamite went off, another part of the well exploded. The shrapnel shredded part of my suit, instant burn. Hurt like hell."

"I can imagine. I've had enough burns to imagine how such a big area would be almost unbearable. Were you long in hospital?"

"A few months."

And in pain for much of that time, she was sure. "Did you get full mobility back?"

"Yes. And other parts were unaffected."

She smiled at his reminder of her attempt at being tactful when he said he wouldn't marry. A burned patch of skin wouldn't be enough to keep her from falling for a man. She suspected Khalid was too sensitive to the scar. There were many woman who would enjoy being with him.

"Good. What I don't get is why you do it?"

"Do what?"

"Put your life at risk. You don't even need to work, do you? Don't you have enough money to live without risking life and limb?"

He was quiet a moment, then said, "I don't have to work for money. I do want to do what I can to make oil production safe. Over the last fifty years or so many men have died because of faulty equipment or fires. Our company has reaped the benefit. But in doing that we have an obligation to make sure the men who have helped in our endeavors have as much safety guarding them as we can provide. If I can provide that, then it's for the good."

"An office job would be safer," she murmured.

"Rashid has that covered. I like being in the field. I like the desert, the challenge of capturing the liquid crude beneath the land, or the sea. I like knowing I'm pitting my skills and experience against the capricious nature of drilling—and coming out on top more than not."

"Still seems ridiculously dangerous. Get someone else to do it."

"It's my calling, you might say."

Ella was silent at that. It still seemed too dangerous for him—witness the burn that had changed his life. But she was not someone to argue against a calling. She felt that with her art.

She turned and he caught her hand, pulling her to a stop. She looked up at him. The moon was a sliver on the horizon, the light still dim, but she could see him silhouetted against the stars.

"What?"

"My mother is hosting a reception on Saturday. I need to make an appearance. I want you to go with me."

Ella shook her head. "I don't do receptions," she said. "Actually I don't go away from the estate much."

"Why?"

"Just don't," she murmured, turning to walk toward home.

He still held her hand and fell into step with her.

"Consider it payment for using the salon," he said.

"You already agreed to my using the salon. You can't add conditions now."

"Sure I can—it's my salon. You want to use it, consider this part of the payment. It's just a reception. Some people from the oil company, some from the government, some personal friends. We circulate, make my mother happy by being seen by everyone, then leave. No big deal."

"Get someone else."

He was silent for several steps.

"There is no one else," he said slowly.

"Why not?"

"I've been down that road, all right? I'm not going to set myself up again. Either it's you, or I don't go. My grandmother helped you out—your turn to pay back."

"Jeeze, talk about coercion. You're sure it'll only be people who live here in Quishari?"

"Yes. What would it matter if foreigners came? You're one yourself."

"I am trying to keep a low profile, that's why," she said, hating to reveal anything, but not wanting to find out her hiding place had been found.

"Why?"

"I have reasons."

"Are you hiding?" he asked incredulously.

"Not exactly."

"Exactly what, then?" He pulled her to a stop again. "I want to hear this."

"I'm in seclusion because of the death of my husband."

"That was over a year ago."

"There's a time limit on grieving? I hadn't heard that."

"There's no time limit, but by now the worst should be behind you and you should be going out and seeing friends. Maybe finding a new man in your life."

"I see my friends," she protested. "And I'm not going down that road again. You're a funny one to even suggest it."

"When do you see friends?"

"When they come to visit. I'm working now and it's not convenient to have people over. But when I'm not in the midst of something, they come for swimming in the sea and alfresco meals on my terrace. Did you think I was a hermit?"

"I hadn't thought about it. I never see these friends."

"You've lived here for what, almost a week? No one has come in that time. Stick around if you're so concerned about my social life."

"Mostly I'm concerned about your going with me to the reception this weekend."

"No."

"Yes. Or no salon photos."

Ella glared at him. It missed the mark. He couldn't see her that well. And she suspected her

puny attempts at putting him in the wrong wouldn't
work. He did own the estate. And she did need permission to use the salon. Rats, he was going to win
on this one. She did not want to go. She was content
in her cottage, with her work and with the solitude.

Only sometimes did it feel lonely.

Not once since Khalid had arrived.

Dangerous thoughts, those. She was fine.

"All right, we'll go, greet everyone and then
leave."

"Thank you."

They resumed the walk, but Ella pulled her
hand from his. They were friends, not lovers. No
need to hold hands.

But her hand had felt right in his larger one. She
missed the physical contact of others. She hadn't
been kissed in ages, held with passion in as long.
Why did her husband have to die?

"I'll pick you up at seven on Saturday," he said.

"Fine. And first thing tomorrow, I'm coming to
take photographs. I don't want to miss my chance
in case you come up with other conditions that I
can't meet."

He laughed.

Ella looked at him. She'd never even seen him
smile and now he was laughing in the darkness!
Was that the only time he laughed?

"I expect I need to wear something very
elegant," she mumbled, mentally reviewing the

gowns she'd worn at university events. There were a couple that might do. She hadn't thought about dressing up in a long time. A glimmer of excitement took hold. She had enjoyed meeting other people at the university, speaking about topics far removed from glass making. Would the reception be as much fun? She felt a frisson of anticipation to be going with Khalid. She always seemed more alive when around him.

"You'll look fine in anything you wear," he said easily.

Just like a man, she thought, still reviewing the gowns she owned.

The next morning Ella carefully took two of her pieces, wrapped securely in a travel case, and went to the main house. Ringing the doorbell, she was greeted by Jalilah.

"I've come to take pictures," she said.

"In the salon, His Excellency has told me. Come." The maid led the way and then bowed slightly before leaving.

Ella put the starburst bowl on one of the polished mahogany tables.

Khalid appeared in the doorway. He leaned against the jamb and watched.

"What do you want?" she asked, feeling her heartbeat increase. Fussing, she tried pictures from different angles. She could hardly focus the lens with him watching her.

"Just wanted to see how the photo shoot went."

"Don't you have work to do?"

"No."

She tried to ignore him, but it was impossible. She lifted the camera and framed the bowl. She snapped the picture just as the doorbell sounded. She looked at Khalid. "Company?" she asked. Maybe someone who would take him away from the salon.

He looked into the foyer and nodded. "Rashid and Bethanne. Good timing. They can help."

"Help what?"

"You get the best pictures. You want to appeal to the largest number of buyers, right?"

"Of course." The sooner she started earning money, the sooner she might move.

"Hello," Rashid said, coming into the room with a tall blond woman. "Ella, this is my fiancée, Bethanne Sanders. Bethanne, this is Ella Ponti. Now, can you two talk?" he asked in Arabic.

"I also speak Italian and French and English," Ella said, crossing the room to greet the pair.

Switching to English, Rashid said, "Good, Ella speaks English."

"I'm so delighted to meet you," Bethanne said, offering her hand.

Ella shook it and smiled. "I'm happy to meet

you. My English is not so good, so excuse me if I get things mixed."

"At least we can communicate. And you speak Arabic. I'm learning from a professor at the university. That's not easy."

"And the maid," Rashid said softly.

Bethanne laughed. "Her, too."

"Would that be Professor Hampstead?" Ella asked.

"Yes, do you know him?" Bethanne asked with a pleased smile.

"My husband worked at the university in language studies. I know the professor and his wife quite well. He's an excellent teacher."

"We came to see your work," Rashid said. "I see you've started on the pictures."

"Photographing some pieces for a preliminary catalog. I'd like to see if I can move up my timetable for a showing. Once I have enough pictures, I can make a small catalog and circulate it."

"Why are you taking pictures here?" Bethanne asked, walking over to look at the bowl. "Oh, this is exquisite. You made this? How amazing!" She leaned over and touched the edge lightly but made no move to pick it up.

"I think the ambiance of the other furnishings here will show it off better. I want the background to be blurry, with only the glass piece in clear focus, but to give the feel that it would fit in any elegant salon."

"And Khalid was all for the project, obviously," Rashid said with a glance at his twin.

"Obviously—she's here, isn't she?" Khalid said. "You two can help with the project. Give us an unbiased perspective and select the best pictures."

"I'd like to see the other pieces you've made," Bethanne said.

"I'm happy to show you. Shall we go now?"

"Finish the pictures of these, then when you go to your studio, you can bring some more over," Khalid suggested.

The next couple of hours were spent with everyone giving opinions about the best angle for pictures and which of the different art pieces Ella had created should be included. Rashid said he'd see if his mother had some recommendations on art galleries who would help.

Ella felt as if things were spinning out of control. She and Alia al Harum had discussed the plans, but they'd been for years down the road. Now so much was happening at once.

Khalid looked over at her at one point and said, "Enough. We will return to the main house and have lunch on the terrace. Bethanne, you haven't told Ella what you do. I think she'll be interested."

Ella threw him a grateful smile. "I'll just tidy up a bit and join you."

Rashid and Bethanne headed out, but Khalid remained behind for a moment.

"They only wanted to help," he said.

"I'm glad they did."

"But you're feeling overwhelmed. You set the pace. This is your work, your future. Don't let anyone roll over you."

"Good advice. Remember that next time you want your way," she said, sitting down on her bench, touched he'd picked up on her mild panic and dealt with it. She hadn't expected such sensitivity from the man.

"You are coming for lunch?"

"Yes. I just need a few minutes to myself."

"I'll come back for you if you don't show up in twenty minutes."

"Did anyone tell you you're a bit bossy?" she asked.

"Twenty minutes," he said, and left.

Ella took less than the twenty minutes. After a quick splash of cool water against her face, she brushed her hair and lay down for ten minutes. Then hurried to the main house. Khalid and the others were on the terrace and she walked straight there without going through the house.

Lunch was delicious and fun. It was a bit of a struggle to remember to speak English during the meal, but she was confident she held her own in the conversation that ranged from Bethanne's career as a pilot to Rashid's recent trip to Texas to the reception on Saturday night.

"Are you coming?" Rashid asked his brother at one point.

"Yes," Khalid said.

Rashid and Bethanne exchanged surprised looks. "Great."

"I'm bringing Ella," Khalid continued.

Both guests turned to stare at her. She smiled brightly. Was this such an amazing thing? Surely Khalid had brought other women to receptions before.

"Condition of using the salon for the pictures," she murmured.

"Of course," Rashid said with another quick glance at his fiancée.

"Great. Maybe you could go shopping with me before then," Bethanne said. "I'm not sure I have anything suitable to wear."

Ella hesitated. She hadn't been shopping except for groceries since her husband's funeral. Dare she go? Surely it would be okay for one afternoon. It wasn't as if anyone was hanging around the main streets of the city looking for her.

"I don't know if I would be much help." She felt Khalid's gaze on her and glanced his way.

"Help or not, don't women love to buy beautiful dresses?"

"I don't need one. I have several," Ella said.

"Come help me find several," Bethanne urged.

Rashid watched the interaction and then looked at his brother. He narrowed his eyes when Khalid never looked away from Ella.

"Okay, I'll go tomorrow afternoon," Ella said fast, as if afraid she'd change her mind.

When lunch finished, Ella thanked her host and fled for her cottage. She'd had more activity today than any time since Alexander had died. And she'd agreed to go shopping—out along the main district of Alkaahdar. Surely after all this time it would be safe. She had a right to her own life. And to live it on her terms.

That night she debated going for a walk. She was getting too used to them. Enjoying them too much. What happened when Khalid moved on? When he went to another oil field to consult on well equipment, or had to go fight a fire. That thought scared her. He was trained; obviously an expert in the field. He knew what to do. It was dangerous, but as he'd explained, except for that one accident, he'd come through unscathed many times.

But that one could have killed him. Didn't he realize that? Or another one similar that might rip the helmet and protection totally off. She shivered thinking about it.

She went for her walk, hoping he'd be there. It

was better than imaging awful things that could happen.

He sat on the sand near the garden.

"It's warm," he said when she appeared, letting some sand drift from his hand.

"Sometimes I sit on the beach in the night, relishing the heat held from the day."

"Sand makes glass," he commented.

"Yes. I've heard that lightning strikes on beaches produces glass—irregular in shape and not usually functional. I'd like to see some." She sat beside him. "I like the fact I'll know your brother and Bethanne at the reception."

"And me."

"Yes, and you. We aren't staying long, right."

"I said not long. Why are you nervous? You've been to university receptions—this would be sort of the same, just a different group of people. You'll be bored out of your mind with all the talk about oil."

She smiled at his grumbling. "Is that the normal topic?"

"With a heavy presence of Bashiri executives it usually is. The minister of finance is not in charity with us right now. Rashid closed a deal he didn't like. But I'm sure a few million for pet projects will sweeten his disposition."

Ella didn't want to talk about money or family. She jumped up. "I'm going to walk."

He rose effortlessly beside her and kept pace.

"Tell me more about the oil fields you've been to," she said, looking for a way to keep her thoughts at bay. She liked listening to Khalid talk. Might as well give him something to talk about.

The next afternoon Ella had a good time shopping. Once inside boutiques, she didn't glance outside. While in the car she had seen no one that appeared to be paying the two of them any attention. Bethanne was fun to shop with. She looked beautiful in the elegant cool colors that went so well with her blond hair. Twice, salesclerks offered jewel-tone dresses and Bethanne had suggested Ella try them on. Of course the sizes were wrong. Ella was slight, almost petite, not nearly as tall as the American. She was tempted, but conscious of her limited funds, cheerfully refused. She had dresses that would suit. She wasn't going to spend a week's worth of groceries on a dress she'd wear for about an hour.

Bethanne decided on a lovely blue that mimicked the color of her eyes.

"Done. Let's get some coffee. And candied walnuts. They're my favorites," she said when she received the dress in a box.

Having the chauffeur stow the dress in the limo's trunk, Bethanne asked him to take them to an outside café. When they found a coffee house with outside seating on a side street, she had him wait while she and Ella went for coffee.

"This was fun," Bethanne said. "I hope we can become friends. I will be marrying Rashid in a few months and don't know but a handful of people in Quishari. And most of them don't speak English. So until I master this language, I'm left out of conversations."

"I would like another friend. Tell me about Texas. I've never been to the United States."

"Where have you been that you learned so many different languages? And that's not even your career, like the professor's is."

"I went to school in Switzerland for a few years and in England."

"And the Arabic?"

"That I learned because Alexander was learning it and planned to come to an Arabian country to work."

"Alexander was your husband?" Bethanne asked gently.

Ella nodded. "We knew each other from when we were small. I loved him it seems all my life."

"I'm sorry for your loss," Bethanne said.

"Me, too." Ella didn't want to think about it. Every time she grew sad and angry. It had happened. Nothing could change the past. She had to go on. Today she was with a new friend. And beginning to look forward to the reception on Saturday.

* * *

Ella worked through the next two days culling her collection, deciding which pieces to display and which to hold in reserve.

She tried on the dresses she'd worn to university events, dismayed to find she had lost more weight than she'd thought. They all were loose. Finally she decided on a dark blue long gown that shimmered in the light and almost looked black. If she wore her hair loose, and the pearls she received when she was eighteen, she'd do. It wasn't as if it were a real date or anything. But she wanted to look nice for Khalid's sake. If he broke his normal habit of non-attendance, it behooved her to look her best.

Saturday evening, Ella prepared for the reception with care. She had some trepidation about venturing forth into such a large gathering, but felt safe enough since the guests would most likely all be from Quishari. Her hair was longer than she usually wore. The waves gleamed in the light. She hoped she would pass muster as a guest of a sheikh. Her heart tripped faster when she thought of spending the evening with his family and friends. And some of the leaders of the country. She planned to stay right by Khalid's side and remind him how soon they would leave.

Promptly at seven he knocked on the door of the cottage. She picked up a small purse with her keys and went to greet him.

"You look lovely," he said when she opened the door.

She thought he looked fantastic. A man should always wear a tux, she decided.

"I could say the same. Wow, you clean up good."

"Ready?"

"Yes." She pulled the door shut behind her. To her surprise, Khalid had a small sports car waiting. She had expected a limousine as Rashid used. She liked the smaller car; less intimidating. More intimate.

"If we were going for a spin in the afternoon, I'd put the top down. But not tonight."

"Thank you. I spent hours on my hair."

"Literally?"

She laughed, feeling almost carefree for the first time in months. "No, I just washed and brushed it."

He reached over and took some strands in his fingers. "It feels soft and silky. I wondered if it would."

She caught her breath. His touch was scarcely felt, yet her insides were roiling. She looked out the windshield, trying to calm her nerves. It was Khalid, cranky neighbor, reluctant landlord. She tried to quell the racing of her heart.

When they arrived at the reception, Ella was surprised to find it held in a large hotel. "I thought your mother would have it at her home," she commented when he helped her from the car. A valet drove the sports car away.

"Too many people, too much fuss. She prefers to have it taken care of here."

"Mmm." Ella looked around. She hadn't been to such an elegant event in years. Suddenly she felt like a teen again, proud to be going to the grown-up's affair. Excited. She could do this, had done so many times before. But she preferred smaller gatherings, friends to share good times. Like she and—

No, she was not going there. Tonight was about Khalid. She owed him for his reluctant help. So she'd do her best to be the perfect date for a man of his influence and power.

"Khalid, I'm so glad you came. Rashid said you would—but your track record isn't the best." A beautiful woman came up and embraced him. She smiled at him, patted his good cheek then turned to look at Ella.

"Salimeia, may I present Ella Ponti. Salimeia is my cousin," Khalid said, looking somewhat self-conscious.

Ella couldn't imagine he felt that way. She was aware of his self-confidence—almost arrogance when around her. She watched as he gave a quick glance around the gathering.

An older woman, dressed in a very fashionable gown came over, her eyes fixed on Khalid.

"I am so glad you came," she said, reaching out to grab his hands in hers.

"Mother, may I present Ella Ponti. Ella, my mother, Sabria al Harum."

"Madame, my pleasure," Ella said with formal deference.

"How do you do?" Khalid's mother looked at him in question, practically ignoring Ella.

"I'm glad he came, too. Mo is here. I'll find him and tell him you're here," his cousin said. She smiled and walked away.

"Ella is my tenant," he clarified.

She looked horrified. "Tenant? You are renting her the house your grandmother left you?"

"No, she has the cottage on the estate and has lived there for a year. Didn't you know about her, either?"

Ella expected the woman to shoo her out the door. She was not the warm, friendly woman her mother-in-law had been.

Sabria al Harum thought for a moment. "The artist Alia was helping?" she guessed.

Ella nodded once. She felt like some charity case the way the woman said it.

"I did not know she had her living on the premises." She said it as if Ella was a kind of infestation.

"I do live there and have an airtight lease that gives me the right to stay for another four years,"

Ella said with an imp of mischief. She did not like haughty people.

"Nonsense. Khalid, have our attorneys check it out." His mother sounded as if any inconvenience could be handled by someone else.

Ella hid a smile as she looked at Khalid.

"Already done, Mother. Ella's right, she has the right to live there for another four years."

Other guests were arriving. Khalid took Ella's arm and gently moved her around his mother. "We'll talk later," he said. "You have other guests to greet."

"Gee, is she always so welcoming?" Ella said softly, only for his ears.

"No. She is very conscious of the position our family holds in the country. Perhaps because she came to the family as an adult, not raised as we were. Come, I see someone I think you'll enjoy meeting."

She went willingly, growing more conscious of the wave of comments that were softly exchanged as they passed. She caught one woman staring at Khalid, then looking at Ella. Giving in to impulse, she reached out to take his arm. It automatically bent, so she could have her hand in the crook of the elbow. He pressed her against his side. She moved closer, head raised.

Khalid introduced her to a friend and his wife. They chatted for a few moments, Khalid mentioning Ella's art. Both were interested.

"My uncle has a gallery in the city. Do send me your catalog so I can send it to him," the wife said.

"I would love to. Thank you." Ella replied.

They mingled through the crowd. Once the complete circuit of the ballroom had almost been made, she tugged on Khalid. He leaned closer to hear her over the noise. "Once we've made the circle, we leave, right?"

"If you're ready."

"Ah, Khalid, I heard you came tonight." A florid faced, overweight man stepped in front of them. "Tell your brother to stop sending our business outside of the country. There are others who could have handled the deal he just consummated with the Moroccans." He looked at Ella. "Hello, I don't believe we've met."

"Ella, the finance minister, Ibrahim bin Saali. This is Ella Ponti."

The minister took her hand and held it longer than needed. "A new lovely face to grace our gatherings. Tell me, Miss Ponti, are you from Quishari?"

She tugged her hand free and stepped closer to Khalid. "I've lived here for years. I love this city."

"As do I. Perhaps we can see some of the beauty of the city together sometime," he said suavely.

Ella smiled politely. "Perhaps."

"Excuse us," Khalid said, placing his hand at the small of her back and gently nudging her.

They walked away.

"That was rude," she said quietly in English.

"He was hitting on you."

"He's too old. He was merely being polite."

"He does not think he's too old and polite is not something we think of when we think of Ibrahim."

She laughed. "I don't plan to take him up on his offer, so you're safe."

Khalid looked at her. "Safe?"

She looked back, and their eyes locked for a moment. She looked away first. "Never mind. It was just a comment."

Khalid nodded, scanning the room. "I think we've done our duty tonight. Shall we leave?"

"Yes."

He escorted her out and signaled the valet for his car. When it arrived, he waited until Ella was in before going to the driver's side. "Home?"

"Where else?" she asked.

"I know a small, out-of-the-way tavern that has good music."

"I love good music," she said.

He drove swiftly through the night. What had possessed him to invite her to stay out longer? She had attended the reception, he got some points with his mother, though she hadn't seemed that excited to meet Ella. They could be home in ten minutes.

Instead he was prolonging the evening. He'd never known anyone as interesting to be around as his passenger. She intrigued him. Not afraid to stand up to his bossiness, she nevertheless defended Ibrahim's boorish behavior. He smiled. Never could stand the man. He had been afraid for a moment Ella might be tempted by Ibrahim's power and position. Not his Ella.

He had to give her credit. No one there had guessed she'd come as part of a bargain. No one made comments about how such a pretty woman was wasting her time with him.

The tavern was crowded, as it always was on Saturday nights. It was one place few people recognized him. He could be more like anyone else here, unlike the more formal events his mother hosted. There were several men he knew and waved to when they called to him. Shepherding Ella to the back, they found an empty table and sat, knees touching.

Ella looked around and then at Khalid. "I hear talk and laughter, but no music."

He nodded. "It starts around eleven. We're a bit early. Want something to eat or drink?"

"A snack would be good. We hardly got a chance to sample the delicacies your mother had available."

"Want to go back?"

"No. This suits me better."

"Why is that?" he asked. He knew why he preferred the dim light of the tavern, the easy camaraderie of the patrons. The periodic escape from
responsibilities and position. But why did she
think it was better?

"I don't know anyone."

"That doesn't make sense. Wouldn't it be better
to know friends when going to a place like this?"

She shrugged. "Not at this time."

"Did you have a favorite spot you and your
husband liked to frequent?" he asked. He wanted
to know more about her. Even if he had to hear
about the man who must have been such a
paragon she would never find anyone to replace
him.

She nodded. "But I don't go there anymore. It's
not the same."

"Where do you and your friends go?" he asked.

"Nowhere." She looked at him.

Her eyes were bright and her face seemed to
light up the dark area they sat in.

"This is the first I've been out since my
husband's death. Friends come to visit me, but I
haven't been exactly in a party mood. But this isn't
like a real date or anything, is it? Just paying you
back for letting me use the salon for my pictures."

"Exactly. You wouldn't want to go on a real

date with me. I know about that from my ex-
fiancée."

"What are you talking about?"

"This." He gestured to the scar on the side of his
face.

"Don't be dumb, Khalid. That has nothing to
do with it. I still feel married to Alexander and
am faithful."

Khalid nodded and looked away, feeling her
words like a physical blow. Even if they got
beyond the scar, she would never be interested in
him. She loved a dead man. He wished they'd
gone straight home. She could be with her
memories, and he could get back to the reality of
his life. Only her words had seemed so wrong.

CHAPTER FIVE

HE LOOKED back at her. "You're not serious? You are not married—that ended when your husband died. And you are far too young and pretty to stay single the rest of your life."

She blinked in surprise. "I'm not that young."

"I'd guess twenty-five at the most," he said.

"Add four years. Do you really think I look twenty-five?" She smiled in obvious pleasure.

Khalid felt as if she'd kicked him in the heart. "At most, I said. Even twenty-nine is too young to remain a widow the rest of your life. You could be talking another sixty years."

"I'll never find anyone to love like I did Alexander," she said, looking around the room. For a moment he glimpsed the sorrow that seemed so much a part of her. He much preferred when she looked happy.

"My grandmother said that after her husband died. But she was in her late sixties at the time.

They'd had a good marriage. Raised a family, enjoyed grandchildren."

"I had a great marriage," she said.

"You could again."

She looked back. "You're a fine one to talk. Where's your wife and family?"

"Come on, Ella, who would marry me?"

"No one, with that attitude. How many women have you asked out in the last year?"

"If I don't count you, none."

"So how do you even know, then."

"The woman I was planning to spend my life with told me in no uncertain terms what a hardship that would be. Why would I set myself up for more of the same?"

The waiter came and asked for drink orders. Khalid ordered a bowl of nuts in addition.

"She was an idiot," Ella said, leaning closer after the man left.

"Who?"

"Your ex-fiancée. Did she expect life to be all roses and sunshine?"

"Apparently." He felt bemused at her defense. "Shouldn't it be?"

"It would be nice if it worked that way. I don't think it does. Everyone has problems. Some are on the inside, others outside."

"We know where mine is," he said.

She shocked him again when she got up and

switched chairs to sit on his right side. "I've noticed, you know," she said, glaring at him in defiance.

"Noticed what?" He was growing uncomfortable. He tried to shelter others from the ugly slash of burned skin.

"That you always try to have me on your left. Are you afraid I'll go off in shock or something if I catch sight of the scar?"

"No, not you."

"What does that mean?"

"Just, no, not you. You wouldn't do that, even if you wanted to. I'd say your parents raised you very well."

"Leave my parents out of any discussion," she said bitterly.

"Touch a nerve?"

She shrugged. "They and I are not exactly on good terms. They didn't want me to marry Alexander."

"And why was that?"

"None of your business."

The waiter returned with the beverages and plate of nuts. Ella scooped up a few and popped them into her mouth.

"Mmm, good." She took a sip of the cold drink and looked at the small stage.

"I think your musicians are arriving."

So his tenant was at odds with her parents. He

hadn't considered she had parents living, or he would have expected her to return home after her husband's death. Now that he knew they were alive, it seemed strange that she was still in Quishari and not at their place. His curiosity rose another notch. He would nudge the researcher at the oil company to complete the background check on his tenant.

Khalid spent more time watching Ella as the evening went on than the musicians. She seemed to be enjoying the music and the tavern. He enjoyed watching her. They stayed until after one before driving home.

"Planning to take a walk on the beach tonight?" he asked.

"Why not?" she asked. "I'm still buoyed up by that last set. Weren't they good?"

"I have enjoyed going there for years. We'll have to go again sometime."

"Mmm, maybe."

He didn't expect her to jump at the chance. But he would have liked a better response.

"Meet you at the beach in ten minutes," she said when she got out of the car.

"No walking straight through?" he asked.

"I don't know about you, but I don't want to get saltwater and sand on this gown. And I'd think it wouldn't be recommended for tuxedos, either."

Khalid changed into comfortable trousers and

a loose shirt and arrived at the beach seconds ahead of Ella.

They started north. The moon was fuller tonight and spread a silvery light over everything. Without much thought, he reached for her hand, lacing their fingers together. She didn't comment, nor pull away. Taking a deep breath, he felt alive as he hadn't in a long while.

"I appreciate your going with me tonight. My mother is always after me to attend those things for the sake of the family," he said.

"She would have been happier without me accompanying you," Ella said.

"She doesn't like anyone who shows an interest in her sons. Unless it's the woman she's picked out. Did you know Rashid almost had an arranged marriage?"

"No, what happened?"

"His supposed fiancée was to be flown in on the plane Bethanne delivered. Only she never left Morocco. When he fell for Bethanne, Mother was furious. I think they are getting along better now, but I wouldn't say Mother opened her arms to Bethanne."

"I bet your grandmother would have loved her."

"She would have loved knowing Rashid was getting married."

For a moment Khalid felt a tinge of envy for his brother. He had found a woman he adored and who seemed to love him equally. They planned a life in Quishari at the other home their grand-mother had left and had twice in his hearing mentioned children. He'd be an uncle before the first year was out, he'd bet.

"Bethanne doesn't strike me as someone who cares a lot about what others think of her," Ella said.

"I'm sure Mother will come around once she sees how happy Rashid is. And once she's a grand-mother."

Ella fell silent. They walked for several minutes. Khalid wondered what she was thinking. Had she wanted to be a mother? Would her life be vastly different if she had a small child to raise? She should get married again.

She was right—that was easy enough for him to say. They were a pair, neither wanting marriage for different reasons. Maybe one day another man would come along for her to marry. Once she was out, showing off her creations, she'd run into men from all over the world.

Khalid refused to examine why he didn't like that idea.

"Ready to head back?" she asked.

He nodded, but felt curiously reluctant to end the evening. He liked being with Ella.

The return walk was also in silence, but not without awareness. Khalid could breathe the sweet scent she wore, enjoy the softness of her hands, scarred here and there by burns from her work. She wore a skirt again. He didn't think he'd seen her in pants except when working at her studio. It made her seem all the more feminine. He didn't want the evening to end. Tomorrow would bring back the barriers and status of tenant and landlord. He had no more reasons to seek her out or take her out again. But he wanted to.

"I can get home from here," she said when they reached the path.

"I'll walk that short distance." He was not ready to say good-night.

When they reached the cottage, she tugged her hand free. "Good night. I enjoyed the tavern. And am glad I got to meet your mother even if she wasn't as glad to meet me."

He reached for her, holding her by her shoulders and drawing her closer. "I'm glad you went with me."

"We're even now, right?" Her voice sounded breathless. He could see her dimly in the light from the moon, her eyes wide, her mouth parted slightly.

With a soft groan, he leaned over and kissed her. He felt her start of surprise. He expected her to draw away in a huff. Instead, after a moment, she leaned against him and returned his kiss. Their mouths opened and tongues danced. Her arms hugged him closer and his embraced her. For a long moment they kissed, learning, tasting, touching, feeling.

She was sweet, soft, enticing. He could have stood all night on the doorstep, kissing Ella.

But she pushed away a moment later.

"Good night, Khalid," she said, darting into the house and shutting the door.

"Good night," he said to the wooden door.

This was not going to be their last date, no matter what Ella thought.

Ella leaned against the door, breathing hard. She closed her eyes. She'd kissed Sheikh Khalid al Harum! Oh, and what a kiss. Unlike anything she'd ever had before.

"No!" she said, pushing away and walking back to the kitchen. She wanted water, and a clear head. She loved Alexander. He was barely gone a year and she was caught up in the sensuousness of another man. How loyal was that? How could she have responded so strongly. Good grief, he'd probably think she was some sex-starved widow out to snare the first man who came along.

How could she have kissed him?

She took a long drink of water, her mind warring with her body. The kiss had been fantastic. Every cell in her tingled with awareness and yearning. She wanted more.

"No!" she said again. She had her life just as she wanted it. She did not need to become the slightest bit involved with a man who wanted her to leave so he could sell a family home.

On the other hand, maybe she should do just that. Put an end to time with Khalid by moving away.

She went to her bedroom and dressed for bed, thoughts jumbled as she brushed her teeth. She had a good place here, safe and perfect for making new pieces of art. She wasn't going anywhere. She just had to wait a little while; he'd get tired of being here and be off on some other oil field consultation and she'd be left alone. She just had to hold out until then. No more night walks. No more kisses.

Though as she fell asleep, she brushed her lips with her fingertips, remembering their first kiss.

The next morning Ella went to her studio, ready to work. She had to focus on her plans for the future and forget a kiss that threatened to turn her world upside down.

Easier said than done. Her dreams last night had been positively erotic. Her first thought this morning was that kiss. And now she was growing warm merely thinking about Khalid and his talented mouth. Why had he showed up? Why not go consult at some oil field and leave her in peace.

Try as she might, as the morning wore on, she

couldn't get last night off her mind. Finally putting a small dish into the annealer to cool down, she decided to go see Khalid and make sure he knew she was not interested in getting involved.

She cleaned up, had a light lunch and then went to broach him at his home.

When she rang the bell, Jalilah opened the door, looking flustered. "Come in, things are hectic. His Excellency is leaving in a few minutes."

"Leaving?" This was perfect. He was leaving even earlier than she planned. He'd probably been as horrified by their kiss as she had been. He'd leave and if he ever came back, they'd have gotten over whatever awareness shimmered between them and they could resume the tenant-landlord relationship.

"A fire. He and his team are gathering at the airport in an hour."

Fear shot through Ella. He was going to another fire. For a moment she remembered Alexander, bloodied and burned from the car crash. He'd been coming after her. He hadn't deserved to die so young. She didn't like that memory any more than the one that flashed into her mind of Khalid burned beyond recognition. Nothing as unforgiving as flames.

She walked swiftly to the study, where Khalid was speaking on the phone. Entering, she crossed to the desk.

"See you then," he said, his eyes on her. "Got to go now."

"You can't go put out a fire," she said.

He rose and came around the desk. Lightly brushing the back of his fingers against her cheek, he asked, "Why not. It's what I do."

"It's too dangerous. Don't you have others who can handle that?"

"Others work with me on these projects. It's another one at a well Bashiri Oil has down on the southern coast. It blew a few months ago and it's burning again. Something's wrong with the pump or operators. Once this is capped, I plan to find out why it keeps igniting."

"It's dangerous."

"A bit. Are you all right? You have circles beneath your eyes."

She brushed his hand away. "I'm fine. It's you I'm worried about. What if something goes wrong? You don't have to do this. Send someone else."

"Something has gone wrong—a well is on fire. My team and I will put it out and do our best to make sure it doesn't happen again. I have to do this. It's what I do."

"It's too dangerous."

"I like the danger. Besides, what does it matter who does it as long as it gets put out? If not me, another man would be in danger. Maybe one who has a wife and children waiting at home."

She couldn't reach him. He would go off and probably get injured again. Or worse.

"Don't go," she said, reaching out to clutch his arms. She could feel his strength beneath the material, feel the determination.

"I have to—it's what I do."

"Find another job, something safer."

"Not today," he said, and leaned over to brush his lips against hers. "Come on, you can walk me out."

She stepped back, fear rising even more. What if something happened to him? She'd planned to tell him to stay away, but not like this.

When they reached the foyer, she noticed the duffel bags and heavy boots. He lifted them easily and nodded to Jalilah to open the door. A moment later they were stowed into the back of the small sports car. Ella followed him like a puppy, wishing she had the words to stop him. The seconds flew by. She could not slow time, much less stop it. But if she could, she would. Until she could talk him out of this plan. What if something happened to him?

"See you in a few days," he said easily.

"I hope so," she replied. But what if she didn't? What if she never saw him again? The feelings that thought triggered staggered her. She didn't want to care. That way lay heartache when tragedy struck.

She rounded the car and stood by him as he opened the driver's door. "Come back safely," she said, reaching up to kiss him. All thoughts of putting distance between them vanished. She couldn't let him go off without showing just a hint of what she felt. She would not think of all that could go wrong, but concentrate on all that could go right.

He let go the car door and kissed her back, cupping her face gently in his hands. His lips were warm but in only a moment she felt cold when he pulled away.

"I'll be back when the job's done," he said, climbing into the car. "Stay out of trouble," he said, and pulled away.

She watched for a moment, then with an ominous sense of foreboding, returned to her cottage. She felt as if she was in a daze. Fear warred with common sense. He knew what he was doing. Granted it was dangerous. But he'd done it before. And he did not have a death wish. He would take all necessary precautions.

Changing into work clothes, she went to the studio. She could always lose herself in art.

But not, it appeared, today. She tried to blow a traditional bowl, but the glass wasn't cooperating. Or her technique was off. Or it was just a bad day. Or she couldn't concentrate for thinking of Khalid. Glancing at her watch, she wondered where he was. She should have asked questions, found out where the fire was. How long he thought he'd be gone.

After two hours of trying to get one small project done, she gave up. Her thoughts were too consumed with Khalid. If he'd left the airport an hour ago, he could already be in harm's way. She paced her small studio, wondering how she could find out information about the fire. She did not have a television. She tried a radio, but the only programs she found were music.

Finally she went to the main house. When the maid answered the door, Ella asked to use the phone. She had done so a couple of times when Madame al Harum had lived here, so Jalilah was used to the request. Ella hoped Khalid had not given instructions to the contrary.

Jalilah showed her into the study and left. Ella stayed in the doorway for a moment. Everything inside instantly reminded her of Khalid. How odd. She'd visited Madame al Harum in this room many more times than she had her grandson. But he'd stamped his impression on the room in her mind forever.

She went to the phone. Who could she call but his brother. She hunted around for the phone number of Bashiri Oil and when she found it on a letterhead, she tried the number. It took her almost ten minutes to get to Rashid's assistant.

"I'm calling for Sheikh Rashid al Harum," she said for about the twentieth time.

"Who is calling?"

"Ella Ponti. I'm his brother's tenant in the house his grandmother once owned," she repeated.

"One moment, please."

On hold again, Ella held on to her composure. What would she do if Rashid wasn't there? Or wouldn't take her call? She had no idea how to reach Bethanne, who might be an ally.

"Al Harum." Rashid's voice came across the line sounding like Khalid's. She closed her eyes for a second, wishing it were Khalid.

"It's Ella Ponti. Khalid left this morning to put out a fire. Do you know anything about that?"

"I do. It's on one of the wells in the southern part of the country. Why?"

"I, uh…" She didn't know how to answer that. "I wanted to make sure he's all right," she said, wondering if Rashid would think her daft to be asking after his brother with such a short acquaintance.

"So far. The team arrived a short time ago. They assess the situation then plan their attack. It could be a day or two before they actually cap it."

Two days he could be in danger and she wouldn't know? This was so not the answer she wanted.

"Um, could you have someone keep me updated?" she asked tentatively. She didn't know if Sheikh al Harum would be bothered, but she had to ask. Surely there was some clerk there who could call her once something happened.

"I worry about him, too," Rashid said gently. "I'll let you know the minute I hear anything."

"Thank you. I'm using his phone. I don't have one. Jalilah can get me." She hung up, a bit reassured. She didn't want to question her need to make sure he was safe. She'd feel the same about anyone she knew who had such a dangerous job.

Ella sat in the desk chair for several moments. She studied the room, wondering what Khalid thought about when he sat here. She suspected he missed his grandmother more than he might have expected. The older woman had spoken so lovingly about her grandsons. Their family sounded close.

Except perhaps their mother. Or was her hesitancy welcoming women into the fold mere self-protection. It would be too bad to have someone pretend affection if they were only after money. How would she become convinced? Nothing had convinced her parents Alexander had not been after their money. They hadn't seemed to care that their only daughter was very happy in her marriage. The constant attempts to end the union had only alienated them. Ella hoped Madame al Harum never resorted to such tactics, but accepted Rashid's choice and wished him happiness.

She stood up and went back to her place. She didn't want to think about her parents, or Alexander, or anything in the past. She didn't want to worry about a man she hardly knew. And she didn't want to worry about the future. For today she'd try to just make it through without turmoil and complications, fear and dread.

Shortly after lunch there was a knock at the door. When Ella opened it, she was surprised to see Bethanne.

"Hi, I thought you might wish for some company," she said.

"Come in. I'm glad for company. I couldn't work today."

"I wouldn't be able to, either, if Rashid was doing something foolishly dangerous."

When they were on the terrace with ice-cold beverages, Ella smiled at her new friend. "What you said earlier, about Rashid being in a dangerous position—ever happen?"

"Not that I know about. And I would be sick with worry if he went off to put out an oil well fire."

"You and he are close, as it should be since you will be marrying him. Khalid is my landlord."

Bethanne laughed. "Right. And Madame al Harum and I are best friends."

Ella wrinkled her nose slightly. "I don't think she thinks in terms of friends."

"Well, not with the women who might marry her sons."

"I heard she helped arrange a marriage, but it didn't take place."

"Good thing for me. Rashid was going along with it for business reasons. Honestly, who wants to get married for business reasons? I'm glad he caught on."

"And the other woman?"

"She ran off with a lover and I have no idea what happened after that. But she obviously had more sense than my future husband. Much as I adore him, I do wonder what he was thinking considering an arranged marriage. I can't imagine all that passion— Oops, never mind."

Ella looked away, hiding a smile. She remembered passion with Alexander when their marriage was new. The image of Khalid kissing her sprang to mind. Her heart raced. She experienced even more passion that night. She did not want to think about it, but couldn't erase the image, nor the yearning for another kiss. Would that pass before he returned?

She had not helped her stance by kissing him goodbye. She should have wished him well and kept her distance.

"If they don't get the well capped today, they'll try tomorrow," Bethanne said, sipping her drink. "And if that doesn't work, Rashid wants to go there. If we do, want to fly with us? I took the crew down. They spent the entire flight going over schematics of the oil rig. It's in the water, you know. You'd think with the entire Persian Gulf at their feet it would be easy enough to put out a fire."

Ella laughed, but inside she stayed worried.

Bethanne was wonderful company and the two them spent the afternoon with laughter. Ella was glad she'd come to visit. Except for a very few friends from the university, she didn't have many people she saw often. She had wanted it that way when Alexander first died. Now she could see the advantage of going out more with her friends. It took her mind off other things. Like if Khalid was safe or not.

The next morning she took an early walk along the beach. She never tired of the changing sea, some days incredibly blue other days steely-gray. She loved the solitude and beauty. During the day other people used the beach and she waved to a family she knew by sight. Watching the children as they played in the water gave her a pang. She and Alexander never had children. They thought they had years to start a family. They had wanted to spend time together as a couple before embarking on the next stage of family life.

His death cut everything short. She wished she'd had a baby with him. Would a child have brought her more comfort? Or more pain as every day she saw her husband in its face? She'd never know.

When she returned to the cottage, she saw a black car parked in front of the main house. Staying partially hidden behind the shrubs, she watched for a moment. It was not Khalid's sleek sports car. Was Madame al Harum visiting? Surely she knew her son was gone. Unless—had something happened. She could scarcely breathe. If Khalid had been injured, would Rashid send someone to tell her?

A moment later a man came from the house and got into the car, swiftly driving away.

Ella caught her breath at the recognition. She pulled back and waited until the car was gone before moving. In only seconds she was home, the door firmly locked behind her. How had they found her? She paced the living room. Obviously the maid had not given out where she lived or he would have camped on her doorstep. But it was only a matter of time now before he returned. Maybe he wanted to speak to the sheikh. Good grief, Khalid didn't know not to give out the information. His grandmother had been a staunch ally, but Khalid was looking for a way to get her to leave early. Had he any clue? Could she convince him not to divulge her whereabouts if her brother came calling again?

He had no reason to keep her home a secret. In fact, she could see it as his benefit to give out the information and stand aside while he tried to get her to return home.

Pacing did little but burn up energy, which seemed to pour through her as she fretted about this turn of events. She had grown comfortable here. She liked living here, liked her life as she'd made it since Alexander's death. She was not going home, no matter what. But she did not want the pressure Antonio would assert. Should she leave before Khalid returned? If he didn't know where she was, he couldn't give the location away.

But she didn't want to leave. Not until she knew if he was all right. What if the fire damaged more than equipment? Men could die trying to put out an oil fire. She so did not need any of this. She'd worked hard the last year to get her life under control.

Drawing a deep breath, she went to her desk and pulled out a sheet of paper. She'd make a list of her choices, calmly, rationally. She'd see what she could do to escape this situation—

Escape. That's what she wanted. Could Bethanne help? She could fly her to a secret location and never tell anyone.

Only, would she? And how much would it cost to hire the plane? Maybe she should have sold some of her work to give herself more capital.

She had enough for her needs if she was careful. But a huge chunk spent on a plane trip could wreak the financial stability she had. Did she have the luxury of time? She could find a bus to take her somewhere in the interior. But not her equipment. Not her studio.

She couldn't leave that behind. It was her only way to make the glass art that she hoped was her future.

Jumping up, she began to walk around, gazing out the window, touching a piece of glass here and there that she'd made. What was she going to do?

There was a knock on the door. Ella froze. Had he found her already? Slowly she crossed the room and peeked out of the small glass in the door. It was Jalilah.

Ella opened the door.

"Hello," the maid said. "I came to tell you someone was at the house earlier, asking after you. He said the sheikh had sent inquiries to Italy. I remember Madame's comments when you first came here to live. She wanted you to have all the privacy you wanted. I told the man the sheikh was away from home and did not know when he would return."

"Thank you!" Ella breathed a sigh of relief. She had a respite. No fear of discovery today.

But—Khalid had sent inquiries to Italy? Why?

Jalilah bowed slightly and left.

Had Khalid sought to find other ways to get her to leave? Anger rose. How dare he put out inquiries? Who did he think he was? And more importantly, who did he think she was? He couldn't take her word?

After a hasty lunch Ella could barely eat, she went to the studio, trying to assess how much it would take to move her ovens, bench and all the accoutrements she had for glassblowing. More than a quick plane ride west.

Maybe she could leave for a short while, let her brother grow tired of looking for her again and when he left, she'd return. Only, what if Khalid then told him when she returned. She'd never be safe.

She heard a car and went to the window, peering out at the glimpse of the driveway she had. It was Khalid's car. He was home.

Without thinking, she stormed over to the main house. The door was shut, so she knocked, her anger at his actions growing with every breath.

Jalilah opened the door, but before she could say a word of greeting, Ella stepped inside.

"Where is he?" she demanded.

"In the study," the maid said, looking startled.

Ella almost ran to the study door. Khalid was standing behind the desk, leafing through messages. He hadn't shaved in a couple of days, the dark beard made him look almost like a pirate—especially when viewed with the slash of scar tissue. His clothes were dirty and she could smell the smoke from where she stood. None of it mattered.

"What have you done to my life?" she asked.

CHAPTER SIX

HE LOOKED up. "Hello, Ella."

"I mean it. What gives you the right to meddle in things that don't concern you? You have ruined everything!"

"What are you talking about?" he asked.

"You sent inquiries to Italy, right?"

He lifted a note. "Garibaldi?"

"If you wanted to know something, why not ask me? I told you all you needed to know. I told you more than I've told anyone else."

"Who is Antonio Garibaldi?" he asked, studying the note a moment, then looking at her. His eyes narrowed as he took in her anger.

"He's my brother. And the reason my husband is dead. I do not wish to have anything to do with him. How could you have contacted them? How could you have led them right to me? I've tried so hard to stay below the radar and with one careless inquiry you lead them right to me. I can't believe this!"

"Wait a second. I don't know what you're talking about. Your family didn't know you were living here?"

"If I had wanted them to know, I would have told them."

"How did your brother cause your husband's death? Didn't you say it was a car crash? Was your brother in the other car?"

"No. He practically kidnapped me. He lured me to the airport with the intent of getting me on the private jet he'd hired. Only someone told Alexander. He was coming to get me before Antonio could take me out of the country. He crashed on the way to the airport. The police, thankfully, stepped in and stopped our departure." She looked away, remembering. "So I could identify Alexander's body."

She burst into tears.

Khalid looked at her dumbfounded. In only a second he was around the desk and holding her as she sobbed against his chest.

"He had a class. He should have been safely inside, teaching, instead he was trying to come to my rescue," she said between sobs. She clutched a fistful of his shirt, her face pressed against the material, her tears soaking the cotton. She scarcely noticed the smoke. "He would still be alive today if Antonio hadn't forced me. *Alexander*." She cried harder.

* * *

Khalid held her close, her pain went straight to his heart. He'd felt the anguish of losing a woman he thought he would build his life with. But his anger soon overcame any heartache. This woman was still devastated by the loss of her husband. What would it be like to mean so much to someone? He thought about his brother and the woman he was going to marry. Bethanne loved him; there was no doubt to anyone who saw them together. She'd be as devastated if something happened to Rashid.

Khalid knew that kind of attachment, that kind of love, was rare and special. Her husband had been dead for more than a year. Ella should have moved on. But the strength of her sobs told him she still mourned with an intensity that was amazing. The emotions told of a strong bond, a love that was deeply felt.

He had never known that kind of love. And never would.

Finally she began to subside. He didn't know what to do but hold her. He'd caused this outburst by his demand to know more. Had the man at Bashiri Oil been clumsy in his research? Or was the family on alert for information about their daughter? Was her brother's involvement the cause of the estrangement, or did it go deeper? Khalid wanted answers to all the questions swirling around in his mind.

But now, his first priority was to make things right with Ella.

Slowly he felt her hands ease on the clutching of his shirt. A moment later she pushed against his chest. He let her go, catching her face in his palms and brushing away the lingering tears with his thumbs. Her skin was warm and flushed. He registered the softness and the vulnerability she had with her sorrowful eyes, red and puffy.

"I did not know making an inquiry would cause all this," he said. "You are safe here. I will not let anyone kidnap you. Tell me what happened."

She pushed away and stepped back. "I'm not telling you anything. You tell my brother when he contacts you again that you have no idea where I'm living. Make him go away. Make sure he never finds me."

"You think he'll come again?" Khalid asked.

"Of course. He's tenacious."

"Why should he come for you?"

"My family wants me home. I want to stay here. If you can't guarantee I can stay, I'll have to disappear and won't tell you where I go."

Two weeks ago Khalid would have jumped at the offer. He wanted his tenant gone so he could put the estate up for sale. But two weeks changed a lot. He wasn't as anxious to sell as he had once been. He liked living near the sea. He liked the after dark walks along the shore. He did not want his tenant to leave and not give a forwarding address.

More importantly, he wanted to know the full story of what was going on. How could she be so afraid of her family?

"How old are you?" he asked, stepping back to give her more space.

"Twenty-nine. You know that. What does that have to do with anything?"

"As far as I understand the laws in most countries, that makes you an adult, capable of making your own decisions on where to live."

"You'd think so," she said bitterly, brushing the last of the tears from her face. She walked to the window and peered out, but Khalid didn't think she saw the colorful blossoms.

She rubbed her chest, as if pressing against pain. "Alexander and I were childhood sweethearts. My parents thought we'd outgrow that foolishness. Their words. They had a marriage in mind for me that would probably rival what your mother had for Rashid. Combining two old Italian families, and merging two fortunes that would only grow even larger over the years."

Khalid frowned. He made a mental note to get in touch with the man at the company who had been doing the research for him. What had he discovered?

"So you and Alexander married against parental wishes. It happens."

"When they discovered where we were living, Antonio came and said I had to return home. There would be an annulment and the arranged marriage would go forth. I laughed at him, but he was stronger than I was and soon I was in a car heading for the airport. The rest you know. I managed to dodge him at the police station and then hid until I thought he'd left Quishari. Mutual friends contacted your grandmother who offered me a place to live. I'm forever grateful to her. I miss her a lot. She really liked my work, and I think she liked me. But more importantly—she gave me a safe haven. I'll never forget that."

"I'm sure she did," Khalid said, stunned to learn this. Had his actions threatened the haven Ella clung to? He would have to take steps to remedy the situation.

Ella turned and looked at him.

"If my actions caused this, I will fix it," he said.

"If? Of course they did. No one has ever come here before. Why did you have to ask about me. I told you about me."

"I wanted to know more. My grandmother never mentioned you. My family doesn't know about you. What you told me was limited."

"You're my landlord—you know all you need

to know about me. I pay my rent on time and I have a lease. I don't trash the place. End of story."

"I want more."

"Well, we don't always get what we want in life," she snapped.

Khalid stared at her, seeing an unhappy, sad woman. One to whom he'd brought more pain and suffering. It didn't come easy, but he had to apologize. "I'm sorry."

She shrugged. "Sorry doesn't change anything."

"It lets you know I didn't deliberately cause you this grief. I said I'd fix it and I shall."

"How? Erase my brother's memory? Put up guards so no one can get on the estate? Wouldn't that also mean no one goes off, either? I had things going just fine until you showed up."

"Sit down and we'll get to the bottom of this." He went around the desk and called Bashiri Oil. In less than a minute he was speaking to the researcher in the office who had been asked to find out more about Ella Ponti. He listened for a solid five minutes, his expression impassive as the man recited what he'd discovered, ending with…

"One of her brothers was in the office yesterday, trying his best to get more information. We know better than to give that kind of information. He accosted people in the halls and in the parking area. Finally we had security remove him from the premises. But I'd watch out—he's looking for his sister and seems most determined."

"I, also, can be determined," Khalid said softly.

"True, Excellency. And I'd put my money on you."

Khalid ended the call.

"It appears the inquiries I had made did cause your brother to return to Quishari. He is staying at the Imperial Hotel. He has made a pest of himself at the company headquarters, questioning everyone trying to locate you. Why is it so important that you marry the man your parents picked out? Surely that was years ago. You said you'd been married for four years, and Alexander has been dead for one. What is so compelling?"

"To further the dynasty, of course. And ensure the money doesn't go outside the family or the family business—wine. I have a trust, that I can't access for another couple of years. But my father was convinced Alexander wanted only my money. He was wrong. Alexander loved me. We lived modestly on his income from the university. We were so happy."

Tears filled her eyes again, and Khalid quickly sought a way to divert them. He was not at all capable of dealing with a woman's tears. He wished he'd never thought to find out more about the woman his grandmother had rented the cottage to.

"I'll go see your brother and make sure he leaves you alone."

She blinked away the tears, hope shining from her eyes.

"You will?"

Khalid nodded, loath to involve himself in her family dynamics, but he felt responsible for causing the problem. "I'll shower, change and go to the hotel myself."

Ella thought about it for a moment, then nodded once. "Fine, then. You take care of it." She turned and went to the door, pausing a moment and looking back at him. "I'm glad you got home safely. The fire out?"

"Yes."

"Did you find out what caused it?"

"I believe so. We have taken steps to make sure there won't be another one at that rig."

"Good." She left.

Khalid rubbed the back of his neck. He had better get changed and to the hotel before her brother annoyed even more people. Or came back and found Ella.

Ella kept her house locked up all day. She knew her brother. He would not likely be sidetracked from his goal just on Khalid's say-so. Not that she would buck the power of the sheikh. He could probably buy and sell her brother without batting an eye. And it was his country. His family was most prominent. Antonio would find no allies in Quishari. Served him right. She couldn't forget the last time she'd seen him. If he had never come last year, Alexander would be alive today.

As the afternoon waned, Ella wondered if Khalid had truly gone to see her brother. She had not seen him return. What if he'd changed his mind? Upon further consideration, he had to know this would be the perfect way to rid himself of the tenant he didn't want. The more Ella thought about it, the more certain she was that was what happened. It could not take Khalid hours to go tell Antonio to go home.

Restless, she set off for her walk when it was barely dark. She doubted she'd sleep tonight. In fact, she might best be served by packing essentials and contacting Bethanne to ask for a ride someplace. At this point, Ella would take anyplace away from Alkaahdar.

She walked farther than normal, still keyed up. When she came to a more populated area, she sat near the water. There were others still on the beach. A small party had a fire near the water, and were sitting around it, laughing and talking. She watched from the distance. How long had it been since she felt so carefree and happy?

When that party began breaking up, Ella realized how late it was—and she still had a very long walk home. She rose and walked along the water, the moon a bright disk in the sky. She was resigned to having to leave. There didn't seem to be any choice unless she wanted her family to take over her life. And that she vowed would never happen. She was not some pawn for her father's use. She liked being on her own. Loved living in Quishari. She'd have to find a way.

She slowed when she drew closer to the estate. Would Khalid be on the beach? She wasn't up to dealing with him tonight. She'd made a fool of herself crying in his study. She didn't want to deal with any more emotion. She was content with her decisions and her walk. A good night's sleep was all she wanted now. Tomorrow she'd begin packing and slip away before Antonio found her. She'd contact her friend Marissa to come after she was gone to pack up her glass art. Once she was settled somewhere, she'd see about resuming the glass-blowing.

Khalid saw Ella slip through the garden on her way to the cottage. He had tried her place earlier, but she was already gone. Now she was back. It was late, however. He needed to tell her how the meeting with her brother had gone, but maybe it would be best handled in the morning.

He sat in the dark on the veranda, watching her go to her home. A moment later the lights came on in one room, then another. Before a half hour passed, the cottage was dark again. He hoped she had a good night's sleep, to better face tomorrow. He knew she would not be pleased with what he had to tell her.

The next day it rained. The dreary day seemed perfect to Ella as she packed her clothes in one large suitcase. She put her cosmetics in a smaller suitcase and stripped the bed, dumping the sheets into the washer behind the kitchen. She'd leave the place as immaculate as it had been when she moved in. The only part she couldn't do much with would be her studio. She hoped Khalid would permit her friend to come to clear away her things. If not, so be it. It wouldn't be the first time she'd started over. She was better equipped now than she had been a year ago.

The knock on the door put her on instant alert. She would not open to Antonio no matter what. Slowly she approached the door, looking through the glass, relieved to see it was Khalid.

Opening the door a crack, she stood, blocking the view into the living room. "Yes?" she said.

"I need to talk with you," he said. Today he wore a white shirt opened at the throat. His dark pants were obviously part of a suit. Was he going somewhere for business later?

"About?"

"Your brother, what do you think?"

"You saw him?"

"I did. Are you going to let me in or are we going to talk like this?"

She hesitated. "Is it going to take long? Either you got rid of him or you didn't."

He pushed against the door and she gave in, stepping back to allow him to enter.

She shut the door behind him and crossed to the small sofa, sitting on the edge. He took a chair near the sofa.

Wiping suddenly damp palms against her skirt, she waited with what patience she could muster.

"I saw your brother at the hotel. He is very anxious to talk with you. Seems there's a problem with your family that you only can help with."

"Sure, marry the man they picked out."

Khalid nodded. "Apparently there have been some financial setbacks and your family needs an influx of cash that the wedding settlement would bring."

She frowned. "What setbacks? The wine business is doing well. We've owned the land for generations, so there's no danger from that aspect. I don't understand."

Khalid shrugged. "Apparently your younger brother has a gambling habit. He's squandered money gambling, incurring steep debts which your father paid for. That didn't stop him. Unless they get another influx of cash, and soon, they will have to sell some of the land. It's mortgaged. They've been stringing creditors along, but it's all coming due soon and they are desperate."

"Giacomo has a gambling problem?" It was the first she'd heard about it. She frowned. For a moment she pictured her charming brother when she had last seen him. He had still been at university, wild and carefree and charming every girl in sight. They'd had fun as children. What had gone wrong?

"While I'm sorry to hear that, I don't see myself as sacrificial lamb to his problem. Let my father get him to marry some wealthy woman and get the cash that way." She could see her patriarchal father assuming she would be the sacrifice to restore the family fortunes.

"Both your brothers are already married."

Ella was startled at the news. She realized cutting herself off from the family when she married Alexander had meant she wasn't kept up-to-date on their activities. When had her brothers married? Recently? Obviously during the years she and Alexander had lived in Quishari.

"Apparently Antonio feels it is your duty to the family to help in this dire circumstance," Khalid said dryly.

"He's echoing my father. I have no desire to help them out. And I certainly am not going to be forced into marrying some man for his money to bail Giacomo out of a tight place." Antonio had always looked out for her and Giacomo. Looks as if he was still looking out for their younger brother. What about her?

Khalid nodded. "I knew you would feel that way."

"Does he know I live here?" she asked.

Khalid shook his head. "He could end up coming here to see me again and discover you around. But I did not tell him where you lived."

"I'm leaving."

He looked surprised at that.

"Going where?"

"I don't know yet. But I'm not telling anyone. That way they can't find me again."

"Would it be so bad to be in touch with your family? I can't imagine being cut off from Rashid."

"That's different. Your mother isn't trying to marry you off to the woman she wants. Just listen to what Antonio said—I'm to come home and marry some man for his fortune. You don't want to be married for money, why would you support that?"

"You know I wouldn't. Would it hurt to listen to what he has to say?"

"I'm not going back to Italy."

He shook his head. "I'm not suggesting that.

Parents can't arrange marriages for their off-springs."

"Your mother tried with Rashid."

"And it came to nought. I don't see her doing anything now but eventually accepting Bethanne will be his wife."

"She tried it, that's the point. She may try with you."

"I doubt it. She doesn't like the scars any more than another woman would."

"Honestly, I can't believe you harp on that. So you have a scar. Try plastic surgery if you don't like it. In truth, it makes you look more interesting than some rich playboy sheikh who rides by on his looks."

"Playboy sheikh?" he said.

Ella leaned forward. "This is about my problem, not yours."

"Of course." The amusement in his eyes told her he was not taking this as seriously as she was. Why should he? He had power, prestige, money. She had nothing—not even a family to support her.

"So did Antonio leave?" she asked.

"Not yet. He wants to see you. Hear from you that everything is fine."

"And try to kidnap me again to take me home."

"No. I, uh, made it clear he could not do that."

"How?"

Khalid looked uncomfortable. "Actually by the

time the meeting was drawing to an end, I was a bit exasperated with your brother."

Ella laughed shortly. "I can imagine. He's like a bulldog when he's after something. So what did you tell him?"

"That you and I were engaged."

Ella stared at him for a long moment, certain she had misheard him. "Excuse me?" she said finally, not believing what echoed in her mind.

"It seemed like a good idea at the time."

"You told my brother we were engaged? You don't even like me. We are not engaged. Not even friends, from what I can tell. Why in the world would you say such a thing?"

"To get him to back down."

"I don't believe this. You're a sheikh in this kingdom. You could order people to escort him to the country borders and kick him out. You could get his visa denied, declare him persona non grata. You could have—"

"Well, I didn't do any of that."

She blinked. "So Antonio thinks we're engaged."

Khalid nodded.

"And that's it? He's going home now?"

"After he's met you and is satisfied you are happy with this arrangement."

For a moment Ella felt a wave of affection for her brother. She didn't always agree with him, but for him to make sure she was happy sounded like the brother she remembered with love. However—

"No."

"No what?"

"I'm not taking that chance. I don't want to see Antonio. I don't want him to know where I live." She looked at him with incredulity. "You don't think they expect you to give the family money if I were really going to marry you, do you? He's probably just as happy with you as candidate as whomever they had picked out in Italy."

"I mentioned that I have a few thousand qateries put away for the future."

"Utterly stupid," she said, jumping to her feet. "I cannot believe you said that. You go back and tell him you were joking or something."

Khalid rose, as well, and came over to her. "Ella, think for a moment. This gets you off the hook. We'll meet him for dinner or something. Show we are devoted to each other. And that you have no intention of returning to Italy. Then he'll be satisfied and take off in the morning. You'll be safely ensconced here and that's an end to it. Once your family finds another way to deal with the debt, you can write and say the engagement ended."

She considered the plan. It sounded dishonest. But it also sounded like it might work. If she could convince Antonio she was committed to Khalid.

Glancing out the window, she wondered if she could look as if she loved the man to distraction when her heart was buried with Alexander.

Yet, he knew her. He could believe she'd fallen in love. He'd often teased her for being a romantic. And her family would welcome Khalid like they never had Alexander. This time they had no reason to suspect he was interested in her money. Next to him, she was almost a pauper.

"Do you think it'll work?" she asked, grasping the idea with faint hope.

"What could go wrong?" he asked. "You'll convince your brother you're deliriously happy. He'll go home and you'll go back to making glass art."

"What do you get out of this?" she asked cynically.

"No more tears?" he said.

She flushed. "Sorry about that."

"No, I didn't mean to make light of it. Just make sure you don't have another meltdown. I'll be gone again soon so you'll have the place to yourself again, like before."

"So you're not planning to sell?"

"Maybe not for a while. I find I'm enjoying living by the water."

"Okay. We'll try your plan. But if he doesn't leave, or tries anything, I'm taking off."

* * *

Khalid arranged dinner at a restaurant near the hotel. He picked Ella up at seven and in less than twenty minutes they arrived at the restaurant. She saw her brother waiting for them once they entered.

"Ella," he said in Italian, coming to kiss both cheeks.

"Antonio," she replied. It had been almost a year since she'd seen him. He looked the same. She smiled and hugged him tightly. No matter what—he was still her older brother.

He shook hands with Khalid. Soon all three were seated in a table near the window that looked over a garden.

"We've been worried about you," Antonio said.

"I'm fine."

"More than fine. Engaged to be married again." He gave her a hard look.

She looked at him. "And?"

"It will come as a surprise to our parents."

"As learning about Giacomo's gambling problem surprised me."

Antonio flicked a glance at Khalid and shrugged. "A way will be found to get the money. Family needs to support each other, don't you think?"

When the waiter came for the order, conversation was suspended for a moment. "Khalid doesn't speak Italian. He speaks English or French, so you choose," Ella said in English.

"English is not so good for me. But for, um, good feelings between us, I speak it," Antonio said.

"Ella tells me your family has been in the wine-making business for generations," Khalid said. "You are a part of that operation?"

Antonio nodded. "I sell wine. Giacomo helps father with the vineyard and the make. My father wants Ella to come home. She goes a long time."

"Maybe in a while. She cannot come now," Khalid said flatly.

Antonio looked surprised that anyone would tell him no. Ella hid a smile and took a moment to glance around the restaurant. The tables were given plenty of space to insure a quiet atmosphere and offer a degree of privacy for the customers. Her eye caught a glimpse of the minister of finance just as he spotted her.

"Uh-oh," she said softly in Arabic. "The minister is here."

Antonio frowned. "If we speak English, all speak," he said.

"Sorry, I forgot," she replied, looking at Khalid for guidance.

A moment later the minister was at their table.

"Ah, the lovely Madame Ponti," he said with a smile, reaching out to capture her hand and kiss the back. "Rashid, I didn't expect to see you with Madame Ponti," he said with a quick glance at Khalid.

Khalid stood, towering over the older man, exposing the scar when he faced him. "Minister," he said.

"Ah, my mistake. Khalid. No need to get up. I'm on my way out and saw you dining." He smiled affably at Antonio. "Another guest?"

"Ella's brother." Good manners dictated an introduction which Khalid made swiftly. Explaining Antonio was Italian and didn't speak Arabic.

"English?" he asked.

Antonio nodded.

"Welcome to Quishari," the minister said with a heavy accent.

"Happy to be here. We are celebrating good news—Ella's engagement."

CHAPTER SEVEN

ELLA was struck dumb. She wished she could stuff a sock in her brother's mouth. Her horrified gaze must have shown, as Khalid reached out and touched her shoulder.

"Congratulate us, Minister. You are the first outside the family to know," he said easily.

His grip tightened and she tried to smile. What a disaster this was turning out to be. Khalid must be furious. That's what they got for trying to put something over on Antonio.

"My felicitations. I have to say I am not surprised after seeing you at your mother's event the other evening."

Khalid nodded, releasing his hold on Ella's shoulder as if convinced she would not jump up and flee—which she strongly felt like.

"Don't let me keep you from dinner," the minister said as the waiter approached with their meals on a tray.

When he left, Ella gave a sigh of relief. Maybe Khalid could catch him later and explain. She needed to concentrate on getting her brother on the next plane to Italy.

"Mother and father will want to meet your fiancé," Antonio said as they began to eat. "You two should visit soon. I can wait here a few days and return with you."

"Unfortunately I am unable to get away for a while and Ella must work on her art," Khalid said.

"Art?" Her brother looked puzzled.

"You have not seen the beautiful glass pieces she makes?" Khalid asked in surprise.

"Oh, those." Antonio gave a shrug. "I've seen bowls and such. Nice enough."

Ella knew better than to take offense at her brother's casual dismissal of her work. He had thought it an odd hobby when she'd been younger. But she'd come a long way since those early attempts. Not that she needed to show him. If Khalid was successful in getting him to leave, she'd be grateful. If not, then maybe Plan B would work better—get Bethanne to fly her somewhere far away and tell no one.

The meal seemed interminable. Ella wanted to scream at her brother to leave her alone. She couldn't forget his part in Alexander's death. If he had not tried to take her home last year, Alexander would still be alive.

Everything was different. When they finished eating, Khalid escorted them to the curb where the limo was waiting. Ushering them both inside, he gave instructions for Antonio's hotel and settled back.

"We will drop you at your hotel and in the morning I will arrange for the limousine to pick you up to take you to the airport. Ella will contact your parents when it is convenient to visit."

Never underestimate the power of money, status and arrogant male, she thought as she watched her brother struggle with something that would assert his own position. But one look from the dark eyes of the sheikh had Antonio subsiding quietly.

"As you wish. My father will be delighted to learn his daughter is engaged to one of the leading families in Quishari. I hope you both can visit soon."

The ride home from the hotel was in silence. Ella didn't know whether to be grateful to Khalid or annoyed at his outlandish handling of the situation. If the minister hadn't learned of the bogus engagement, they could have muddled through without any bother.

"What if the minister says something?" she asked.

"Who's he going to tell? We are not that important in his scheme of things. You worry about things too much," he said, studying the scenery as they were driven home.

"At least I didn't go off half-cocked and say we were engaged. Too bad he speaks English. The language barrier could have prevented it. I doubt he speaks Italian."

Khalid looked at her. "Your brother will return home, tell your parents you are safe and go on with his life. Once things settle down, you can tell them things didn't work out."

She laughed nervously. "I doubt things will settle down. They will push for marriage."

"Tell them I am not ready."

"Oh, Khalid, if they really need money for Giacomo, then my guess is the next step is get me safely married to you and hit me up for some money. If you were poor as Alexander was, they would never be satisfied with a marriage between us."

"You're an adult. Just tell them no."

"Antonio tried to force me from the country last time. Just say no doesn't work with my family."

"He won't try you in the future, not as long as you live in Quishari."

"Then I may never leave," she said, still worried about the entire scenario.

Khalid had the limousine stop by Ella's cottage and dismissed the man. He escorted her to her door.

"Thanks for dinner, and for standing up for me," she said, opening it.

"That's what fiancés are for," he said, brushing back her hair and kissing her lightly on the lips.

He turned and walked to the villa, wishing he had stayed for a longer good-night kiss. He had hidden it from Ella, but he was worried the minister could stir up trouble that would be hard to suppress.

When he entered the study a few moment later, the answering machine was flashing. He pressed the button.

"What's this I hear about your engagement? You couldn't tell me before the minister?" Rashid's voice came across loud and clear—with a hint of amusement. "Or did he get it wrong? Call me."

Khalid sighed and sank onto the chair. Dialing his brother, he wondered if he could finesse this somehow. It was hard sometimes to have a twin who knew him so well.

"Hello."

"Rashid, it's Khalid."

"Ah, the newly engaged man. I didn't have a clue."

"It's not what you think?"

"So what is it?"

Khalid explained and heard Rashid's laughter. "Sounds almost like Bethanne and me. We pretended she was my intended to close the deal I was working on when the woman I expected didn't show up. Watch it, brother—fake engagements have a way of turning real."

"Not this time. In fact, I wasn't going to tell anyone beyond Ella's brother. Once he was back Italy, she'd be left alone."

"Now you have the minister calling me and undoubtedly Mother to congratulate us on your engagement. And I know from experience, Mother isn't going to be happy."

"She should be glad anyone would even consider marrying me with this face."

"Not if it isn't someone she picked out—which I'm coming to believe means someone she can boss around. Bethanne isn't exactly docile. So what's the plan?"

"I haven't a clue. It would have gone smoothly if the minister hadn't come over. Her brother would have left and things would have returned to normal."

"Whatever that is these days." Rashid was quiet for a moment, then said, "Any chance…"

"What, that she'd want to marry me? Get real. First off, I'm not planning to marry. Your kids will carry on the line. And second, she's still hung up on her dead husband. And I see no signs of that abating. She was crying over him today."

"Fine, you've played the role of hero, rescuing her from her brother. Would that make her feel she owes you? Maybe vacate the cottage so you can sell the place sooner?"

"I wouldn't use that to get her gone."

Rashid was silent.

"Anyway, things will work out."

"Call me if you need me," Rashid said.

When he hung up, Khalid contemplated finding a job ten thousand miles away and staying as long as he could. Who would think inheriting a beautiful estate could end up making him so confused.

The phone rang again.

When he answered, he sighed hearing his mother's greeting.

"I just had an interesting call," she began.

"I know." For a split second he considered telling her the truth. But that fled when he thought of her calling to set the minister straight. He would not like having been lied to.

"Is it true? Honestly, if I had thought you were planning to marry, which you have stated many time you are not, I know several nice women who would have suited much better than a widow of dubious background."

"I know her background."

"I don't. Where is she from? Are you certain she wants to marry you to build a life together, or is she in it to keep the cottage? Once her career takes off, will she leave for greener fields?"

"Who knows what the future holds," he said.

"Your father used to say that all the time. Honestly, men. I suppose I have to have another party to introduce her formally to everyone like I did with Bethanne."

"Hold off on that, Mother."

"Why?"

His mother was sharp; anything out of a normal progression would raise doubts. And he didn't want Ella talked about, or word to reach her family that the engagement wasn't going strong.

"You just had a party...we can wait a few weeks." Maybe by then something would occur to him that would get him out of the situation. He'd thought it the perfect answer to getting rid of Ella's brother. The first time in recent months he did anything spontaneous and it grew more complicated by the moment. Give him a raging oil fire any day.

"Nonsense. I'll call your aunt. She'll be thrilled to hear you are getting married and want to help. We had given up on you, you know."

Hold that thought, he wanted to say. But for the time being, he'd go along with her idea. He wondered if Ella would. Or if she'd put an end to it the minute her brother took off in the morning. She hadn't welcomed the idea when he first told her.

He went to change into casual clothes and headed for the beach. He didn't know if she'd join him on a walk tonight. He could gauge her reaction by her manner if she did show up.

When he reached the beach, there was no sign of her. He'd wait a bit. It wasn't that late.

Sitting on the still warm sand, he watched the moonlight dance on the water. The soft night breeze caressed. The silence was peaceful, tranquil. Why did men make things so complicated. A quiet night surrounded by nature—that's what he needed. That's what he liked about the desert. The solitude and stillness.

He heard her walking through the garden. Satisfaction filled him. She was coming again. Despite their differences, he felt closer to her in the dark than he did anyone except Rashid. Theirs was an odd friendship; one that probably wouldn't last through the years, but perfect for now.

"I wondered if you'd want to go walk," she said, walking over and sitting beside him. "You were right, you know. I overreacted, but this was a perfect scheme to get rid of Antonio. You know, of course, that had this been real, the minute we married, he'd be hitting you up for money."

"It crossed my mind," Khalid said. Antonio didn't know him well—nor ever would. But giving money away to people who wasted it was not something he did. Though he could understand family solidarity. Wonder if there were a different way to handle the situation.

He rose and reached out his hand to help her up. With one accord, they left their shoes and began walking to the water. Once on hard-packed sand, they turned north.

Khalid liked the end of the evening this way. Ella was comfortable to be around. With the darkness to cloak the scar, he had no hesitation in having her with him. She didn't have to see the horrible deformity and he didn't have to endure the looks of horror so often seen in people when they were around him. Not that he'd caught even a glimpse of that with Ella after that first day. She seemed to see right through the scar to the man beneath.

"At least we don't have to worry about that. I'm still working on a catalog and will see if I can get a showing earlier than originally planned. Once I have a way to earn a living, I'll be out of your way."

"There is one complication," he said.

"What?"

"My mother thinks we are engaged and is planning a party to announce it to the world."

"What? You've got to be kidding? How did your mother find out?" She stopped walking and stared at him.

"She called me tonight. The minister wasted no time. He has it in for Rashid and I expect is trying to gain an ally with mother in getting insider info or something."

Ella shook her head. "I can imagine how delighted she is to think we're engaged. Did you set her straight?"

"No."

"Why not?"

He refused to examine the reason. He felt protective toward Ella. He didn't want anything to mar her happiness—especially her family. It seemed she'd had enough grief to last a lifetime.

"Seemed better not to."

"Well, tell her in the morning."

"Or, let her think that for a while. What does it hurt?"

Ella thought about it for a moment. "Maybe no one," she said reluctantly.

"If people think you are engaged to me, it'll give you a bit of a step up when going to galleries."

"I wouldn't pretend for that reason."

"But you would to keep your family out of your life."

"I didn't know my younger brother had a gambling problem. He was the cutest little boy. So charming."

He took her hand and tugged her along and resumed walking. "I know. Family pressure can be unrelenting, however. If they think you are already out of reach, they have to look elsewhere for financial help. Personally I'd kick the man out and tell him to make a go of it on his own."

"You talk a hard line, but I bet you would try to work something out if it were Rashid," she said.

Khalid knew that to be true.

"I'm not sure it's fair to you," she continued.

"Why not? I'm the one who started the entire convoluted mess."

"I know, which I think is totally off the wall. But no one who knew us would believe we could fall in love and plan to marry."

"Because of the scar," he bit out.

She whacked him on his arm with her free hand. "Will you stop! That has nothing to do with anything. I'm still grieving for my husband. I don't want to ever go through something like that again. It's safer to go through life alone, making friends, having a great career, but not putting my heart on the line again. It hurts too much when it's shattered."

"Safer but lonely, isn't it?"

Ella glanced at him. Was he lonely? On the surface he had it all: good looks, money, family behind him. The downside would be the job he did. Yet because of the scarring on his face, he pulled away from social events, hadn't had a friend come to visit since he'd been in the main house. And to hear him talk, he was shunned by others.

She'd seen some looks at the reception, fascinated horror. Her regret was he had to deal with rude, obnoxious people who didn't seem to have the manners necessary to deal with real life.

"Come on," she said, pulling her hand free. "I'll race you to that piece of driftwood." With that, Ella took off at a run for the large log that had washed up on shore during the last storm. She knew she couldn't beat Khalid; he'd win by a long margin. But maybe it would get them out of gloomy thoughts. She felt she'd been on a roller coaster all day. It was time to regain her equilibrium and have some fun.

She'd taken him by surprise, she could tell as he hesitated a moment before starting to run. She had enough of a head start she thought for a few seconds she might win. Then Khalid raced past her, making it look easy and effortless.

Ella was gasping for breath when she reached the log. He was a bit winded, which helped her own self-respect.

"Do you often race at night?" he asked.

"No one can see me and I can race the wind. It's better than racing you, for I can convince myself I win."

He laughed and picked her up by her waist and twirled them both around. "I win tonight," he said, and lowered her gently to the ground, drawing her closer until they were touching from chest to knees. He leaned over and kissed her sweetly.

Ella closed her eyes, blocking out the brilliant

blanket of stars in the sky. Hearing only her own racing heartbeat and the soft sighing of the spent waves. Soon even they were lost to sound as the blood roared through her veins, heating every inch of her. She gave herself up to the wonderful feelings that coursed through her. His mouth was magic. His lips like nectar. His strong body made her feel safe and secure, and wildly desirable.

Time lost all meaning. For endless minutes, Ella was wrapped in sensation. She could have halted time and lived forever in this one moment. It was exquisite.

Then reality intruded. Slowly the kiss eased and soon Khalid had put several inches between them. She stepped forward not wanting to end the contact. His hands rested on her shoulders and gently pushed her away.

"We need to get back before things get out of hand," he said.

She cringed and turned, glad for the darkness to hide her embarrassment. How could she so wantonly throw herself at him when he made it perfectly clear he was not interested in her that way. His gesture with the fake engagement was merely a means to offer some protection to her. If her brother had never shown up, never threatened her, Khalid would never in a million years have pretended that they were involved.

And that was fine by her.

She increased her pace.

"Are we racing back?" he asked, easily keeping pace.

"No." She slowed, but longed to break into another run and beat him home, shut the door and pull the shades. She was an adult. She could handle this—it was only for the length of time to get to her cottage. Then she'd do her best from now on to stay away from Khalid al Harum!

That vow lasted until the next day. Ella spent the early hours working on a small bowl that would be the first of a set, each slightly larger than the previous. She concentrated and was pleased to note she could ignore everything else and focus on the work at hand.

It was past time for lunch when she stopped to get something to eat. In the midst of a project, she became caught up in the process. But once it was safely in the annealer, thoughts of last night surfaced.

Jalilah knocked on the door before Ella had a chance to fix something to eat.

"His Excellency would like to see you," she said.

"I'm getting ready to eat," Ella said. "Tell him I'll be over later."

Jalilah looked shocked. "I think he wants you now," she said.

"Well, he can't always have what he wants," Ella said. "Thanks for delivering his message. Tell him what I said. Maybe around three." She closed the door.

Who did he think he was, expecting her to drop everything just because he summoned her? He had delusions if he thought she'd drop everything to run to him.

In fact, she might not go at all.

Except her curiosity was roused. What did he want?

She prepared a light lunch and ate on her small veranda. The hot sun was blocked by the grape-covered arbor. The breeze was hot, blowing from the land and not the sea. She wouldn't stay outside long.

Sipping the last of her iced tea, Ella heard the banging on the front door. Sighing, she rose. It didn't take a psychic to know who was there. Dumping her dishes in the sink on her way to the front of the cottage, she wondered if she dare ignore him.

Opening the door, she glared at him instead. "What do you want?"

"To talk to you," he said easily, stepping inside.

She moved to allow him. It was that or be run over. He was quite a bit larger than she was.

Closing the door, she turned and put her hands on her hips. "About what?"

"My mother is hosting another party. This time to formally announce our engagement. We need to go."

"Are you crazy? This has gone on long enough. Tell her the truth."

"Not yet. You need to make sure your family turns elsewhere for relief from your brother's gambling. It's only one evening. You'll meet people, smile and look as if you like me."

"I'm not sure I do," she said, narrowing her eyes. "This gets more complicated by the moment."

"We need to invite some of your friends to make it seem real."

She crossed her arms over her chest. This was unexpected. "I'm not involving my friends. Besides, no one would believe it. They all know how much I loved Alexander. And do you really think they'd believe you'd fall for me?"

"So pretend."

"We don't have to pretend anymore. Antonio's gone and it was for his benefit, right?"

He was silent for a moment.

"Right?" she repeated.

"He did not leave as we thought."

"Why not?" She frowned. What was her brother doing? He wasn't waiting for the wedding, for heaven's sake, was he?

"Now how would I know what your brother

thinks…I just met him. But the limo showed up at the hotel in time to get him to the airport for the first flight to Rome and he said he'd changed his plans and would be remaining in Quishari a bit longer."

"Great." She walked across the room and turned, walked back, trying to think of how to get out of the mess the men in her life had caused.

"I'll go away," she said.

"After the announcement," he replied.

She looked at him. He was calm. There was a hint of amusement in his eyes. Which made her all the more annoyed. "This is not a joke."

"No, but it's almost turning into a farce. I thought telling him would shut him up. Do you think I want the world to think I got engaged again and then a second fiancée breaks the engagement?"

She had not thought about that at all.

"Then you break it," she said.

"That'll look good."

"Well, one of us has to end it, so you decide. In the meantime, I do not want to go to your mother's. I do not want the entire city to think we are engaged. I do not—"

He raised a hand to stop her.

"Then you come up with something."

"I wouldn't have to if you hadn't told my brother."

"You could have told him the truth at dinner last night."

She bit her lip. She did not want to return to Italy. She would not be pressured day and night by parents trying to talk her into a marriage with some wealthy Italian to shore up her brother's losses. The days when daughters were sacrificed for the good of the family were long past. If only her father would accept that.

"Okay, so we pretend until Antonio leaves. Can we hurry him on his way?" she asked, already envisioning her mother's tearful pleas; Giacomo's little boy lost entreaties; Antonio begging her to think of the family reputation. She loved her family, but she wasn't responsible for them all.

"He's your brother. I could never hurry Rashid. The more I'd push, the more he'd resist."

She nodded. "Okay, so brothers are universal. Somehow we have to get him to leave me alone."

"So we'll convince him tonight that it's an arrangement meant to be and maybe he'll leave."

"Or hit you up for a loan."

Khalid frowned. "Do you really think that's the reason for the delay?"

"I don't know." Maybe her brother just wanted to make sure she was happy. Yet he'd been right there when her parents had railed against her for marrying Alexander and never said a word in her behalf. She had no intention of letting any of her family dictate her life.

"What time do we go to your mother's?"

"I'll pick you up at seven."

"How dressy?"

"About like last time. Do you need a new dress?"

She looked at him oddly. "I have enough clothes, thank you. What—do you expect everyone to hit you up for money?"

"No. But women always seem to need new clothes. I can help out if you need it."

"I do not." She studied him for a moment. Thinking about her own family, she knew there were some shirttail relatives who had asked her father for handouts. He'd refused and when she was a child, she wondered why he didn't share. Once she was older, she realized some people always have their hands out.

For a moment she wished she had brought some of her clothes from home. She and her mother had shopped at the most fashionable couturiers in Rome. She'd left them behind when joining her husband in Quishari. The dresses for receptions were more conservative. She wished at least one would make Khalid proud to be escorting her.

Then she remembered the red dress she'd bought from a shop near campus. Her friend Samantha had urged her to buy it. She'd never worn it. It was too daring for a professor's wife. But for tonight, it might just be the thing. Sophisticated and elegant, it was far more cosmopolitan than anything else she now owned. She smiled almost daringly at Khalid. If he insisted they continue, she'd show him more than he bargained for.

He studied her for a moment, a hint of wariness creeping into his expression.

"Until tonight," he said.

She nodded, opening the door wide and watching him as he started to leave.

"I don't think I trust your expression," he said.

She feigned a look of total innocence. "I'm sure I have no idea what you're talking about, darling."

He tapped her chin with his forefinger. "Behave."

She laughed and shooed him out the door. Tonight might prove fun. She was not out to impress anyone, nor kowtow to them. Madame al Harum would be horrified. The minister might wish he'd kept his mouth shut. And her brother would learn not to mess with his sister's life anymore.

Ella was ready before the appointed time. She'd tapped Jalilah's expertise in doing up her hair. She remembered the maid had a talent for that which her former employer had used. The dress was

daring in comparison to the gowns Ella had worn
to the university functions. The thin crimson straps
showed brilliantly against her skin, the fitted
bodice hugged every curve down to where the
skirt flared slightly below the knees. The satiny
material gleamed in the light, shifting highlights
as she walked. She had her one set of pearls she
again wore. The dress really cried out for
diamonds or rubies, but Ella had neither. The high
heel shoes gave her several inches in height, which
would add to her confidence. She was ready to
face the world on her terms.

Khalid arrived at seven. He stared at her for a
moment, which had Ella feeling almost giddy with
delight. She knew she'd surprised him.

"You look beautiful," he said softly.

She felt a glow begin deep inside. She felt beautiful. The dress was a dream, but the color in her
cheeks came from being near Khalid. She knew
she would do him proud at the reception, and give
others something to think about. All too soon this
pretend engagement would end, but until midnight struck, she'd enjoy herself to the fullest. And
make sure he did, as well. He deserved lots for
helping her out without question.

"Thank you. So do you," she said with a flirta-
tious smile.

He gave a harsh laugh. "Don't carry the
pretense too far," he said. "This is a dumb idea."

"It was yours," she reminded him.

He laughed again, in amusement this time. "Don't remind me. I say we ditch the reception and go off on our own. You look too beautiful to be stuck in a room full of my mother's friends."

"You're not thinking. What would your mother say. She went to all the trouble to celebrate what she thinks is a happy occasion. You can't disappoint her."

"You got it right first time—it's hard to think around you the way you look right now."

Ella smiled, delighted he was so obviously taken with how she looked. The dress was really something and she didn't ever remember feeling so sexy or feminine. The hot look in Khalid's eyes spiked her own temperature. Maybe his idea of not going out had merit.

"Let's go wow them all. And when we've put in our appearance, we'll dash back here and take a walk on the beach. Much more fun that the ordeal ahead." Filled with confidence from his reaction, she could hold her own with his mother and anyone else who showed up.

CHAPTER EIGHT

WHEN they arrived at his mother's apartment building, Ella was impressed. It looked like a palace. They were admitted by the uniformed doorman and quickly whisked to the top floor by a private elevator.

"The family home, no hotel," she murmured.

"Only a few intimate friends, like maybe a hundred. You never gave me a list of your friends, so I had one of my assistants contact the university and find out who your friends were. Told them it was a surprise."

Ella gave a loud sigh. "You just can't leave things alone, can you? Did you drive everyone insane while growing up?"

"Hey, I had Rashid to help me then."

"But not now?"

"He knows, but he is the only one besides you and me. Unless he told Bethanne. I forget there is a new intimate confidant with my brother.

That'll be interesting—learning how to deal with that aspect."

Entering the large flat that overlooked Alkaahdar, Ella was struck by the large salon, ceilings at least twelve feet high. A wall of windows opened to a large terrace. The room held dozens of people yet did not appear crowded. Classical artwork hung on the walls. The chandelier sparkled with a thousand facets. The furniture looked more Western than Arabian, chosen for elegance and style.

"Khalid, you should have been here before the first guests," his mother chided, coming to greet them. She looked at Ella, her eyes widening slightly. "You look different tonight," she said taking in the lovely dress and the sophisticated hairstyle.

Ella inclined her head slightly. "I've been told I clean up good," she said cheekily.

Sabria al Harum didn't know how to respond.

Khalid gave his mother a kiss on her cheek. "We're here, that's the important thing. I can't believe you managed such a crowd on less than a day's notice.

"Everyone here wishes you well, son," she said, eyeing Ella as if she wasn't sure how to react to her.

Ella slipped her arm through Khalid's and leaned closer. "We are honored you did this for us on such short notice, aren't we, darling?" she said, smiling up at him.

"Indeed we are, *darling*," he said back, his eyes promising retribution.

"Mingle, let people congratulation you," Sabria said. She gave Ella an uncertain look.

Rashid crossed the room with Bethanne. He grinned at Khalid and Ella. "Congratulations, Brother," he said, then leaned in and gave Ella a kiss on the cheek. "Keep him in check," he said.

"I couldn't believe it when Rashid told me," Bethanne said, glancing around. She hugged Ella, and said in English. "I think it's fabulous."

Ella giggled a little. "Outlandish, I thought," she replied, one arm still looped with Khalid's.

Antonio came over, bowing stiffly.

"I thought you went home," Ella said when he stopped beside them.

"There were one or two things to deal with before I left. I spoke to our parents. They wish you both happiness in your marriage," he said. "If I had left, I would have missed this."

"And wouldn't that have been too bad," she murmured in Arabic.

"Come," Khalid said, "let me introduce you to some friends."

As they stepped away from the entry, they were surrounded by people who were mostly strangers to Ella. However one or two familiar faces had her smiling in delight to see again, though inside she felt guilty to be deceiving everyone.

Conscious she needed to convince her brother nothing would deter her from marrying Khalid, she stayed within touching distance all evening, reaching out sometimes to touch his arm as if to ground herself. Once when she did, he clasped her hand, lacing their fingers together and holding it all the while he carried on a conversation with a friend.

The finance minister saw Khalid with Ella and broke away from the small group he was talking with and came over to them.

"Your mother must be so pleased, both her sons are taking the next step to insure the family continues."

"There's more to marriage than having children," Khalid said dryly.

"Ah, but nothing like small ones around to keep you young."

"Do you have children?" Ella asked.

"Not yet."

"Yet you and your wife have been married for many years," Khalid said.

For a moment the minister looked uncomfortable, then he changed the subject. "So are you and your brother marrying at the same time? Or as Rashid is the elder, will you defer to him?"

"Our plans are not yet firm," Khalid responded.

"Excuse us, please, I see some friends of Ella's have arrived." Khalid moved them toward the door where two couples were standing, looking around in bewilderment.

"How do you know they are my friends?" she asked recognizing her friends.

"They look out of place. They obviously don't know anyone else here."

Greetings were soon exchanged. Though Ella's university friends were startled by the scar on Khalid's face, they quickly hid it and greeted him as warmly as they did her.

"I had no idea," Jannine said. "Though we haven't seen much of you this last year. I guess a lot has happened that I don't know about."

"It has been a hectic and busy year," Ella said vaguely. If this had been a true engagement, she would have shared the news with her friends immediately. She knew they'd wish only happiness for her.

"So, how are you doing with your glassmaking?" Joseph asked. He looked at Khalid. "You've seen her work, of course."

"Yes. Exquisite. She's planning a showing before too much longer. I predict a spectacular future for our artist."

"Do tell us all," Monique said.

Ella was pleased her friends had come on such short notice and silently vowed to keep in touch better. They'd been part of her life for several years and were each interesting people. She talked about the tentative plans for getting into a gallery someplace. They listened attentively, only now and again darting a glance at Khalid.

A moment later, he touched Ella's shoulder.

"Someone I must speak to. I'll leave you with your friends." He left and she watched as he crossed over to an elderly man. Turning back to her friends, she found all eyes on her.

"He's one of the richest men in the country, you know," Jannine said. "How in the world did you land him?"

"Good grief, Jannine, is that how you refer to me? I feel like a large-mouth bass," her husband said.

Everyone laughed.

"Okay, maybe that was not quite what I meant."

"So did you mean how did Ella attract him? She's pretty, young and talented. What's not to like?" Monique said.

"You all are twisting my words and you know it. Tell all, Ella."

She glossed over details mentioning simply that she had been renting a cottage on a family estate and they met that way. The rest they knew. "Tell me what's going on at the university. I've been so out of touch."

Joseph began telling her about professors and students she might remember. She enjoyed catching up on the news, but felt distant, as if that part of her life was over and she was no longer connected as she once had been. It felt a bit lonely.

Glancing around at one point, she saw Khalid and Rashid both talking with the elderly man. They were in profile, left sides showing. Stunning men, she thought. Then Khalid turned and caught her eye. Once again the ruined side of his face showed. She swallowed a pang of regret for the damage and smiled. That was easily overlooked when his dark eyes focused on her. Then she felt as if everything else faded away and left only the two of them in a world of their own.

"She's got it bad," Jannine said, laughing.

"What?" Ella asked, turning back to her friend.

"He's gone five minutes and you're already looking for him. How long until the wedding?"

"I'm not sure. We haven't made plans yet."

Antonio came over at that point. Ella made introductions and the group began talking in English, a common language for them all.

"This is a night of firsts," Jannine said. "I didn't even know Ella had family. She never spoke of you."

Her husband nudged her.

"Oh, sorry. Was that not the thing to say?"

Antonio looked at her. "You never spoke of us? Ella, we are your family."

"Who wouldn't accept my husband," she replied.

As the others looked on, she wished she could march her brother away and find Khalid. She was tired of the pretense, tired of trying to smile all the time when she wanted to rail against Antonio for getting her into this mess.

"But you like al Harum better, scar notwithstanding" Joseph muttered in Arabic.

Ella narrowed her eyes. "Khalid is a wonderful man. He puts out oil fires. Do you know how dangerous that is? He was injured trying to stop a conflagration. There are very few people in the world who can do something like that. And did you ever stop to think how much pain and agony he went through with such severe burns?"

Khalid put his hand on her shoulder. "Defending me?"

"There's no need," she said, glaring at Joseph.

Antonio watched, glancing between Joseph, Ella and Khalid.

"No offence meant, Ella," Joseph said.

"None taken," Khalid said. "Please, help yourselves to refreshments. I want to borrow Ella a moment to introduce her to an old friend."

He took her hand in his and they moved toward the man she'd seen before. Rashid and Bethanne were talking with him.

"He was a friend of my grandparents, Hauk bin

Arissi. Unfortunately he is thrilled with our engagement. It is awkward, to say the least. I do not like deceiving people."

"You should have thought of that."

"Or left you to your brother?"

Before Ella could respond, they were beside Hauk bin Arissi. Introductions were made.

"Ah, Khalid, you and your brother have once again surprised me. The antics you used to do. Your grandmother would be so happy today— both her precious grandsons embarking on a lifelong partnership with such beautiful women."

"You are most kind," Ella said.

"Ah, and you my dear, already speak our language."

"I've lived in Alkaahdar for several years. Studied the language before that."

"You speak it well."

"Thank you. My reading is not as proficient."

He waved his hand dismissively. "Have Khalid read to you. The evenings my wife and I enjoyed reading from the classics. I do miss that."

She glanced at Khalid, a question in her eyes.

"We all miss her, Hauk."

"So how did you two meet. I've heard about Bethanne's piloting."

"She lives on Grandmother's estate, the one I inherited."

"So he inherited me," Ella said.

"Are you the artist? The glassmaker? Alia told me about your excellent work. I saw the vase you made for her. It looks like captured sunshine."

Ella smiled. "Thank you for telling me. I miss her so much."

Hauk studied her a moment, then looked at Khalid. "You, also, have found a treasure. See you treat her appropriately."

Khalid bowed slightly. Ella saw the amusement in his eyes. For a moment she wished this was real. That he would treasure her and treat her appropriately. The thought startled her. This was one evening to get through, not let their pretense slip. Soon things would go back to normal.

By the end of the evening, Khalid's temper was held by a thread. His mother was pushing for a wedding date, pushing to learn more, pushing period. The minister watched Ella more than Khalid thought wise. His wife had been unable to attend, and Khalid did not like the way he eyed Ella. Rashid teased him, which normally he'd accept in good stead. But tonight, it rubbed him wrong.

He and Ella spent most of the evening together, except when she was visiting with her friends. It was growing late when she came over to him and smiled sweetly at the couple he was talking with.

"Will you please excuse us?" she asked, drawing Khalid away.

With the same smile on her face, she leaned closer, to speak only to him.

"My feet hurt, my cheeks hurt, I'm getting very cranky so suggest we leave very soon."

He leaned forward, breathing in the scent of her perfume, something flowery that he had grown familiar with over the last few weeks.

"I was ready to leave about two hours ago."

"I could have gone then. We've been here long enough, right? Your mother can't complain."

"She will, but that's her way. Come, follow me."

He led the way down a corridor and in moments they were in the primary hallway of the building. In seconds they descended in the elevator and were outside.

Ella leaned her head back and drew in a deep breath. It was all he could do to resist leaning over and kissing her. But standing in front of the building with the doorman and valet parking attendants standing mere feet away wasn't conducive for such activities.

Ella was tired. The strain of pretending she was wildly happy with a new engagement, and the anxiety over her brother, was wearing on her. To make matters worse, she almost wished she and Khalid were engaged. He had been most attentive tonight, hovering over her like he couldn't stay away. He even seemed the tiniest bit jealous when he spoke to the finance minister. He was so good in his role he almost had her convinced.

What would it be like to be engaged to him? Fabulous. She knew that without a doubt. He would lavish attention on the woman he chose for wife. She sighed softly, wishing she could imagine herself as his wife. To share their lives, to have his support of her art would be beyond wonderful.

Suddenly she was jealous of the unknown woman who would one day see past his own barriers and find a way into his heart. She would be the one to receive his kisses and caresses. She would be the one to share nights of passion and days of happiness. Ella could see them living on the estate his grandmother had left him—with a half dozen children running around, laughing and shouting with glee.

"Are you all right?" Khalid asked.

Ella hoped he couldn't read minds. "Of course. Just tired."

"So no walk along the beach tonight?"

Did he enjoy their shared time as much as she did? Unlikely. He probably liked walking and didn't mind if she accompanied him. The darkness hid all things. Was that special for him?

"Not tonight." She'd have to decide how to handle this. Everything was complicated. She was drawing closer and closer to Khalid and while he seemed to enjoy her company, she wasn't sure he was seeing her as anything but the woman who leased his cottage. Who was an impediment to his selling the estate.

When they reached home, Ella dashed into the cottage even before Khalid got out of the car. She closed the door and hurried to her bedroom, already unfastening the necklace. She didn't want to be thinking about kisses and caresses and dark nights alone with the man. He tantalized her with things she had thought lost forever.

Her life with Alexander had been all she ever expected. And when he died, she thought a part of her had, as well. But could she find another life, one unexpected but fulfilling nevertheless? Khalid was so different from Alexander it was amazing to her she could think of him in such terms. Alexander had been kind, gentle, thoughtful. Khalid was exciting, provocative, dynamic and intense. Yet she felt more alive around him than any other time in life. Colors seemed more vivid. Experiences savored longer. Nebulous longing rose, solidifying into a desire to be with him.

She put the pearls on the dresser and peeked out of her curtains. She could only see a small corner of the main villa from this room. Nothing to show Khalid had gone to the study or his bedroom. Or, would he take a walk on the beach tonight without her. That first night he'd not known she was there. Did he often swim alone after dark?

Suddenly she felt daring. Taking off her dress, she slipped on her bathing suit. Just maybe she'd go swimming in the dark. So much the better if he were there, as well.

Pulling on a cover-up, she hurried to the beach. The moon was waning, but still cast enough light over the beach to see a pile of material near the water. Scanning the sea, she thought she saw him swimming several yards offshore. Smiling at the thought of reading his mind, she dropped her own things by his and plunged into the warm water. It felt energizing and buoyant. Swimming toward him, she saw when he first realized she was there.

Treading water, he waited for her to get closer.

"What are you doing here?" he asked.

"I didn't want a walk. But a swim sounded nice," she replied. When she drew closer, she also tread water. "Do you swim every night?"

"Not every night. But many. I like it."

"Always after dark."

"Easier that way."

"How far do the scars go?"

Khalid stared at her for a long moment, then motioned her closer. When she paddled nearer, he reached out and caught one hand, drawing her up to him. Tracing the ruined skin down his right side, he tried to gauge her reaction in the dim light. Most women would be horrified. The scarring went across part of his chest and his upper arm. It no longer pained him, except to look at.

She kicked closer and brushed against him. Instant heat. It had been a long time since he'd slept with a woman. He was already attracted to Ella, but her touch sent him over the edge. He pulled her into his arms and kissed her, kicking gently to keep them both above water. Then he forgot everything except the feel of her in his arms. Her silky skin was warm in the water. Her hair floated on the surface, tangling with one hand as he held her closer. Her kiss spiked desire for more—much more.

The water covering them both brought him back to sanity.

She broke away and laughed, shaking her head. Water flew from her hair, splashing against him.

"Romantic," she said, pushing up against him again, wrapping her arms around his neck. "Unless you drown us." Her lips were close, then she brushed against him, teasing, tantalizing. She trailed light kisses along his lips, across to his left cheek, then to his right one. He pulled away.

"Don't," she said softly, cupping his ruined cheek with her hand. "Khalid, you make me forget everything. Don't pull away and bring reality back. This is a night just for us." Again she kissed him and this time he didn't hold back. He relished the feel of her in his arms, the length of her petite body pressed against his, banishing the loneliness of the last few years. He felt more aware of every aspect of life than ever before. All because she kissed him.

They were both breathing hard when the kiss ended. Khalid wanted to sweep her ashore and make love to her on the sand. He even began swimming that way, but stopped when he realized she was swimming parallel to the shore.

"It's a glorious night for a swim," she called out, swimming away with each stroke.

He'd been fooling himself. He knew what women saw when they looked at him. The night hid the scars, but light would expose them for the awful things they were. He'd take what he could get and ignore the vague yearning for even more.

He swiftly caught up with her.

"I thought you said it was unsafe to swim after dark," he said, keeping pace with her.

"If one is alone, it is. I'm not alone, I have you."

Together they swam along the coast, only turning back when Khalid began to fear she would tire out before reaching their things. Ella seemed as full of energy at the end as when they started. And once their towels and clothes were in sight, she stopped and tread water again. Curious, he stopped, too, and was greeted with a wave of water. A tap on his shoulder as he shook his head to clear the water from his eyes was followed immediately by "You're it!"

Ella dove under the water and for a moment he didn't know which direction she'd gone. When she resurfaced some yards away, he struck out. She laughed and dove beneath the water again. This time she appeared near the shore. Khalid laughed and reversed direction. By the time he reached her, she was already standing and hurrying up the shallow shelf to reach the beach.

Snatching up her towel, she wrung out her hair and then dried herself, all the while moving back, watching him.

"Dangerous games you play, Ella," he said, walking steadily toward her.

"It was fun." She laughed, but kept backing away.

Khalid pursued, gaining ground with every step.

"It was. But you don't play fair. Why leave the water?"

"I'm tired. That was a long swim." She giggled and stepped back. "I'm leaving my cover-up behind," she said.

"Come and get it."

"I'm not that dumb."

"No one said you were dumb," he said, reaching out to catch her.

She laughed but came willingly into his arms. "Khalid, you are the dangerous one," she said just before he kissed her.

* * *

The next morning Khalid stood on the veranda on the side of the house nearest Ella's cottage, looking toward the sea. He'd had breakfast early, checked in with the office and debated taking a consulting job that had been offered or sending his second in command. The time away would give him some perspective. Last night replayed itself like an endless film. He should have pushed for more. But his respect for Ella wouldn't allow him to press for more than she wanted. And it appeared as if kisses were the limit of her willingness.

He should take the job.

"The maid said I'd find you here," Rashid said behind him.

Khalid turned. His casual clothes contrasted with the Western suit and tie that Rashid wore.

"And she was right. What's up?" he asked his brother.

"Just came by to see you." Rashid pulled a chair away from the small table and removed his suit jacket, hanging it across the back. Sitting, he looked at his brother, eyebrows raised in silent question.

Khalid came across and pulled out another chair, sitting opposite his twin.

"I heard from an oil company in Egypt. They want us to come vet their new well."

"Are you going?" Rashid asked.

Khalid shrugged. "Don't know."

"You usually jump at foreign assignments."

"I've been to Egypt before."

"More than once. Maybe your new fiancée is keeping you closer to home."

"I don't need that from you. You know the entire thing escalated out of hand. Damn, I was only trying to help out my tenant. I told you."

Rashid smiled at that. "Right. Somehow I guess I forgot."

"Like you ever would. Is that why you're here? To rehash the entire affair?"

"Ah, you've moved on to an affair now."

"No, I have not. I stepped in to try to keep her family from pressuring her. Once her brother leaves, end of story." He rose and paced to the edge of the stone floor, then turned back.

"What would you have done?" he asked.

"The same thing, I'm sure. Actually I came by to see if you were at all interested in her. She seemed devoted to you last night. Maybe this could develop into something good."

The scene in the water and on the sand flashed into mind. Khalid wasn't sharing that with his brother, twin bond or not. "An act." Had it all been an act? He hoped not.

"A suggestion only—" Rashid began.

"What?" Khalid felt his barriers rise.

"Give the relationship a chance. She's a nice

woman. Talented, pretty. She loved the country, gave up her family for her first husband. Is loyal."

"Makes her sound like a dog or something."

"I'm trying to get through to you that not everyone is Damara. She was shallow and superficial and at the first setback fled. In retrospect, you got a lucky break. What if you were married and she couldn't stay for the long haul."

"I'm sure she felt she caught the lucky break." He turned back to gaze at the sea, remembering the scene in the hospital—he so doped up because of the searing pain and the one person beside his twin he thought he could count on instead shredding their relationship. As he watched the water sparkle beneath the sun, that image was replaced with a scene from last night: Ella's splashing him and then laughing.

Ella kissing his damaged skin. Ella.

More than anything, he loved her laugh.

Scowling at his thoughts, he turned back to Rashid.

"I'm taking off. The job in Egypt will last a couple of weeks at least."

"Give my suggestion some thought."

"There's nothing like that between us. She needed help. I gave it. She's locked into the cottage legally—nothing I can do to get rid of her before the lease expires. We'll muddle through. Not everyone is like you. Enjoy what you have with Bethanne. Don't try to find a happy ending here."

Rashid rose, slung his jacket over his shoulder and looked at his brother. "Okay. I gave it a shot. Your life is yours. Just don't screw it up any more than you can help."

Khalid laughed. "Thanks for the vote of confidence."

Once Rashid left, he went to the study and called his office. "Make the arrangements…I'll leave this afternoon," he told his assistant.

Ella had expected to hear from Khalid, but he had not sent word for her to come to the main house, nor visited. She kept busy sorting the glass pieces, pleased to study some and find they were better quality than she remembered. Stepping back a bit helped her gain perspective. The piece might not have attained her vision for it, but it was still good.

She had early pieces grouped together. Later ones separated. Definitely an improvement in the later ones. Maybe she should have a seconds sale—knock off the prices of the earlier less-than-perfect pieces. But only after she had started selling.

The pictures she had taken in the house looked great. She'd see about contacting a printer to make them into a booklet.

As much as she tried to concentrate on work,

she was on tenterhooks for Khalid. Last night had been amazing. She'd hated to go home alone.

But this morning—nothing.

Finally she took a light lunch on her veranda. Maybe she should just go over and find out what he was doing. Or if he had gone into his office today. It was a workday after all. She'd gotten used to his being available whenever she wanted. How spoiled was that?

She refused to hang around like some lovelorn idiot. She had her own life. If it coincided with his once in a while, so much the better.

The day seemed to last forever. She cleaned her small cottage. Did a load of laundry, even cooked dinner which was not something she often did. Finally—it was dark. Normally she walked after eleven, but even though it was scarcely past nine, she couldn't wait.

She headed for the beach. No sign of Khalid. She knew she was early. Slowly she walked to the water's edge. She'd wait.

Which wasn't easy to do when every nerve clamored for him. She sat on the warm sand, the water lapping the beach a few feet from her toes. Picking up handfuls of sand, she let it slip between her fingers. Last night had been surreal. One part at the party Khalid's mother had given. The other—the real part—had been swimming in the warm sea. She smiled remembering how much fun she'd had. How much she liked being with Khalid.

Glancing over her shoulder, she wondered what time it was. How long before he came?

CHAPTER NINE

THE next morning Ella headed to her studio, firmly intending to push all thoughts of a certain sheikh from her mind. It did not take a two-by-four hitting her on the side of the head to get it. He had not shown at the beach last night. When she finally gave up and returned home, all lights in the main house were off. Had he gone out?

It didn't matter. He was merely her landlord. Nothing else. She would not let herself believe there was something special between them. If there was any special feelings, they were obviously one-sided—on her side.

Now she was going to focus on her career and leave all men out of the equation until she was firmly on the path to money. Next place she lived, she wanted to own. To be able to come and go when she pleased and not worry about someone trying to evict her because of their own agenda.

Firing up the oven, she chose the glass shards

carefully, then melted the different colors, picking them up one at a time on her wand. Slowly the glasses melded and when she began shaping the blob, she was pleased with the greens and blues and turquoise that began to show through. Taking her time, concentrating on the task at hand, Ella fashioned a large flat plate.

It was early afternoon when she was satisfied and put the art piece in her annealer. Stretching to work out the kinks in knotted muscles, she went to the cottage for lunch. For the first time in hours her mind flipped to Khalid. Where was he? Despite her vow to refrain from thinking about him, now she could think of nothing else.

She wished he'd stroll around the corner of the veranda on which she sat and smile that lopsided smile that crinkled the skin around his eyes and caused her to catch her breath. Saunter over and sit casually in the chair, his dark eyes sending shivers down her spine as she lost herself in them.

She was becoming too involved with the man. He'd made it clear he was not interested in any relationship—short or long-term—and she'd do best to remember that.

Yet when she remembered the fun they'd had playing in the water, the drugging kisses that had her clamoring for more, it was hard to believe. Didn't actions speak louder than words? His actions showed he liked her. She wanted to spend more time with him. It was the first time since Alexander's death she'd had such an interest in anyone. Khalid was special. She felt stirred up every time they were together. When apart, she longed to see him again. Even if he never did more than talk about his work, she relished the moments together.

Frowning, she sat back in her chair and gazed toward the sea. She had a small glimpse of it from this place on her veranda. Normally it soothed. Today, however, she was more worried than before. She could not be falling for the man. She could list a dozen reasons why that would be such a bad idea—starting with she could get her heart broken.

Yet, testing her feelings as she might test a toothache, she had to admit there were a lot of similarities to falling in love. She wanted to be with him. Felt alive in his presence. Knew he was very special. Yet she didn't believe he was perfect. He could be short-tempered at times. And his idea that no one would ever find him attractive because of the scar was dumb. Sure, it was disfiguring, but he was more than a swatch of skin on the right side of his face and neck.

When he spoke to her, she felt like she was the only person in the world. The flare of attraction wasn't dying down. His kisses spiked her senses like nothing else had. And his protective view was

intriguing. Her own family didn't feel that obligation, yet he'd stepped in without being asked to try
to thwart her brother's goal.

She leaned back in the chair, trying to relax. She
should just go along with things—pretend to be
engaged and see what happened. Only it was hard
to play that part when half the couple had
vanished.

Perhaps vanished was a bit strong, she argued. He
had not come to the beach last night nor stopped by
today. He had no need to. Except she wanted him
to.

She jumped up and cleared her dishes. After
rinsing them off, she changed into a cool sundress,
brushed her hair and headed for the main house.

Jalilah answered the door to her ring.

"Madame Ponti," she said politely.

"Is His Excellency in?" Ella asked.

"No. He has flown to Egypt."

"Egypt?" Ella hadn't expected that. "When will
he be home?"

"I cannot say. He took a large suitcase, so I
suspect a few days at least."

Ella thanked the maid and turned to return
home. Walking slowly through the garden, she
wondered why he hadn't told her. She almost went
back to see if he had responded to a fire. That
would cause every moment to be precious as he
packed and left and he might not think to let his

fake fiancée know of his plans. But the maid had said he had a large suitcase and might be gone awhile. No sense of urgency in her tone. Had he just left?

Ella debated calling Bethanne to ask if she knew what Khalid was doing, but decided she would not.

Still at the front of the main house, Ella turned when a car drove down the driveway. She recognized her brother even before he got out of the vehicle.

"Ella," he said.

"Antonio. What are you doing here?"

"I came to speak to Khalid al Harum. I've spoken with father and he entrusts me to handle things. Are you visiting, as well?"

"What things?" Did he not know she lived on the estate? If not, she didn't plan to tell him. She was more interested in what her father wanted Antonio to handle.

"Marriage settlements," Antonio said after a moment's hesitation.

"Dowery?" she asked, walking closer to her brother.

He looked uncomfortable. "Not exactly."

"Exactly what? I've moved away from home. I was married several years to another man. I can't imagine why there would be any talk of settlements unless you plan to see if Khalid would give something to get out of the mess Giacomo caused. Which I absolutely forbid."

"Forbid? You can't do that—it's between me and your future husband."

"If you even speak to him about that, I'll refuse to marry him," she said recklessly. She would not put Khalid in such a situation. She was embarrassed to even think of her family asking the man for money. It would be bad enough if they were madly in love and truly engaged. But this was humiliating. She would not let Antonio do it.

He studied her for a moment. "If you don't marry him, you can come home and marry someone else."

"I may never marry again," she said, stepping up to her brother and tapping his chest with her forefinger. "But I sure will never marry someone I don't love. Giacomo got himself into this mess, let him get himself out of it. I am not a pawn to be used like in feudal days. I can't believe even our father would consider such a thing."

"Your family needs you," Antonio said, capturing her hand and pushing it away. "The sheikh has more money than anyone we know. He wouldn't miss a few thousand euros. Let him help us."

"No! I mean it, if you talk to him about this, I'll vanish and it'll be years before you find me next time."

Her brother stared at her for a long moment.

"We need help, Ella," he said softly. "Where else can we go? We cannot make it known in Italy or the business will suffer. If we don't get an infusion of cash soon, it will come out. A company in dire straits loses business which could help it get out of trouble. Then take-overs are bandied about. The business has been in our family for generations, for centuries. Would you see all that gone?"

"No, of course not. Look for other ways. Mother's jewelry—"

"Most already copied in paste and the originals sold."

That surprised Ella. Things were worse than she envisioned.

"Is Giacomo still gambling?" Ella asked, horrified at the lengths her family had already gone. She felt herself softening to them. They had practically excommunicated her when she married Alexander. But they were still her family. The problem seemed larger than she'd realized from what Antonio said.

"No. But the fallout is lasting."

"Go home, Antonio. If I can, I'll send some money." It was too bad her trust fund was not available until she turned thirty. Maybe she could borrow against that. Or she could see about selling some of her artwork. Madame al Harum had thought it had merit. Would others?

He looked at the house.

"Khalid is not home. He had a business trip to Egypt. I don't know when he'll be back."

Antonio nodded. "Very well, then. Come visit, Ella. Your mother misses you."

"One day." It was hard to overlook the obstacles her parents had thrown in her way when she had married Alexander. But she knew her husband never wanted her to be parted from her family. He would not want her holding on to wrongs of the past.

She watched Antonio drive away and began to walk back to the cottage. Alexander would not have wanted her to be a widow all her life, either. He had loved life, loved her and would always want the best for her. Including another husband who could bring her happiness.

Wistfully, she wished Khalid had the same thoughts.

It was amazing the absence of one slightly standoffish man made. As the days went by, Ella gradually resumed her former routine. Working during the day, long walks after dark. Always alone. Only her enjoyment of being alone had been disturbed. She missed Khalid. Which only went to reinforce her belief she had to get on with her life and not grow attached to him.

The bright spot in the week was a visit by Bethanne. She was driving a new car Rashid had just bought for her and wanted to take Ella for a spin.

"It's no fun to have a brand-new convertible and have no one to share it with," she said as the two began driving away from the estate.

"And Rashid doesn't want to go?"

"He has one of his own. I'm sure he's not as enchanted with the convertible as I am. Isn't it great?" She drove to the coast highway and flew along the sea. Ella glanced at the speedometer once and then quickly looked away. Obviously the pilot in Bethanne had no qualms about flying low. Instead of worrying, Ella relaxed and enjoyed the ride. The blue of the Persian Gulf was on their right. The road was straight and smooth. The wind through her hair made her feel carefree and happy. With sudden insight, she realized she was happy. In this day, in this moment. Worries were gone. Plans and projects on hold. Nothing held her back. She could enjoy this time and not feel sad or guilty.

It had taken a long time, but she knew she was ready to embrace life again. To find all it had to offer and enjoy every speck of the journey—even the heartbreaks and hardships.

"You're quiet," Bethanne said with a smile. "What are you thinking?"

Ella told her and Bethanne nodded. "I know the feeling. But I have an excuse. I'm in love. The colors in the sea seem brighter because Rashid's in my life. The flowers more delicate and lovely, especially when I'm in the garden with him. But I bet coming out of grieving is like falling in love with life again. I'm so sorry for your loss, but time does heal wounds. I was so devastated when I learned my dad was really dead. I grieved both before and after I found out. Then I realized he had loved life. He had done exactly as he had wanted throughout and had no regrets at the end. That's what I want."

"No regrets?"

"No regrets and feeling I lived life to the fullest. Which means even more than I expected before I met Rashid. He's so fabulous."

Ella laughed. "So says a woman in love."

"I know, and I'm so proud of him I could burst, and happy he loves me as much." She flicked Ella a glance. "How is Khalid these days?"

She gazed at the sea. "I wouldn't know. He's on a business trip."

"Still in Egypt?" Bethanne asked.

Ella nodded. "I have no idea when he'll be back."

"I'll ask Rashid if you like."

She hesitated. She didn't want to make demands or have him think she had any expectations. But she did want to know how he was, what he was doing, when she'd get to see him again. Ella almost groaned. She had it bad.

"Please." Khalid need never know she'd asked after him. When he returned, she'd play it cool, not going for walks, not expecting him to spend time with her. But for now—she wanted any information she could get.

Trying to change the subject, Ella asked about how much flying Bethanne was doing these days and the subject of Khalid was dropped.

That evening Ella was summoned to the main house by the maid for a phone call. It was Bethanne.

"Rashid said Khalid is still in Egypt. He called him to see when he was coming home. Turns out he's thinking about visiting some of the oil fields in the interior of Quishari before coming home. Stalling do you think?"

"Why would he?" Ella said, her heart dropping at the news he would be gone even longer.

"I could fly you inland, if you like," Bethanne said.

Ella blinked.

"You know, you could get some great ideas from seeing some of the nomadic people and the colors they use in weaving cloth. And there is an austere beauty of the desert that I find enchanting at all times of the day, from cool sunrise to the spectacular sunsets."

"It's tempting."

"I'll ask my darling fiancé if we can go

tomorrow. That way, when Khalid shows up, you'll already be there."

Ella wanted to protest, but she closed her mouth before the words would spill out. She longed to be with him again. Here was a chance to see him in the kind of environments he worked. Not in fire suppression, but as a consultant to oil fields. She'd never seen an oil pump and had only the vaguest idea of how everything worked from discovery to gasoline in her car. It would be educational.

She laughed at her foolishness. She was going to see Khalid! "You're on. And tell Rashid thank you very much!"

The next morning Bethanne picked Ella up and drove them to the airport in her new car.

The gleaming jet sat in solitary splendor in a private section of the airport. Service personnel scrambled around, making sure the jet was ready to fly. Ella watched with fascination as Bethanne changed her personality into a competent pilot, double-checking all aspects of the plane before being satisfied. She invited Ella into the cockpit, and talked as she went through the preflight routine. In only moments they were airborne. Ella leaned forward to better see the landscape below them. The crowded developed land near the sea gradually grew less and less populated until they were flying over desert sand. In the distance, toward the west, she saw hills, valleys and mountains. The flight didn't take long, and went even faster fascinated as she was by the sights below.

She knew Bethanne had been half joking when talking about getting new ideas, but Ella already had a bunch of them crowding in her mind. She had brought her sketchbook, but it was in her bag. Her fingers itched to get down the ideas. She would love to capture the feeling of the burning sand, the starkness of the open land. The contrast with the sea and distant mountains.

"Nice, huh?" Bethanne said.

"Beautiful. It's so lush where I'm from in Italy. And I've lived in Alkaahdar since arriving. I had no idea the desert could be beautiful."

"It's not to all. But I love it. Rashid tells me if I wish, he will build us a villa by an oasis surrounded by endless desert. I'm still too new at everything in Quishari to wish to change a thing. But the thought tantalizes."

"I think I should like that, as well. As long as there was enough water at the oasis."

They circled the town of Quraim Wadi Samil on the edge of an oil field and then Bethanne landed.

Ella watched the pumps on the field with their steady rise and fall as they made their approach. She regretted losing them from view as they landed.

"That's where Khalid will be tomorrow," Bethanne said. "Rashid arranged for someone to pick us up and drive us to the hotel. Once I know Khalid's arrived, I'll return home."

"Stranding me here?" Ella said. She hadn't expected that.

"Hey, he's good for helping a damsel in distress."

Ella laughed, growing nervous. What if he was more annoyed than anxious to help? And she wasn't exactly stranded. She'd be able to take a bus back to the capital city, or even one of the daily commercial planes.

Bethanne arranged for them to go to the hotel that Khalid would use when he arrived. She and Ella checked in and agreed to meet for lunch, then take a short tour of the town.

By dinnertime, they'd both showered, changed and were sitting in the lobby.

Bethanne watched the double doors to the street while Ella sat with her back to them.

"He just walked in," Bethanne said, smiling. She looked at Ella. "Go say hi and ask him to join us for dinner. We'll want to hear all about Egypt."

Ella rose and turned, her heart kicking up a notch when she saw him. He wore a dark suit and white shirt with blue and silver tie. He looked fantastic. She took a breath and crossed the lobby, her eyes never leaving him. She saw when he turned slightly and saw her. For a moment she thought she saw welcome in his eyes. Then he closed down.

"Ella, is everything all right?" he asked, crossing the short distance to meet her.

"Everything is fine. Did you have a good trip to Egypt?"

Khalid's eyes narrowed slightly, then he looked beyond her and saw Bethanne. She raised one hand in a short wave and grinned.

Khalid looked back at Ella. He hadn't expected to see her. One reason he'd decided to stop off at Quraim Wadi Samil was to delay returning home. But she was standing right in front of him, her eyes dark and mysterious, shadowed with a hint of uncertainty. He clenched his fists at his sides to keep from reaching out and pulling her into a hug that he might not ever let go.

"We wondered if you'd like to join us for dinner," she said quickly. "Tell us about your trip."

"You didn't come all this way to have dinner and hear about my trip," he said.

"Actually I'm getting new ideas for more glass pieces. You should see the sketches I've done since I've arrived. I'm hoping to go to the oil fields tomorrow." She stopped abruptly.

"With whom?" he asked, feeling a flare of jealousy that someone would show her around.

"You?" she said.

Khalid relaxed a fraction. His voluntary exile

for the last week hadn't done anything to kill his desire for this woman. Now she was right here.

"I don't usually eat dinner in restaurants," he said slowly.

She nodded. "I know, eating alone is awkward in public places. But you'll have me and Bethanne so it'll be fun."

Fun? The stares of the other customers? The whispers that ran rampant as speculation abounded?

"I'm glad to see you again," she was saying. "I've missed you at night when I walk along the beach." Her eyes were shining with more happiness than he'd ever seen before. For another smile, he'd face the horror of others at the restaurant. He'd make sure he was seated by a wall, with the damaged side of his face away from other diners.

"I need to check in, then it will be my pleasure to escort two such lovely ladies to dinner."

She reached out and touched his arm, pulling her hand back quickly as if unsure of a welcome.

"We'll be waiting." With another smile, she turned and walked back to Bethanne.

Dinner did not prove to be the ordeal Khalid had expected. As if in one agreement, the seating went as he wanted. With fewer people having to see the scar, they were more ignored than he normally experienced. For the first time in years, he enjoyed dining out. The food was excellent. The conversation lively. The more he grew to know Bethanne, the more he understood his brother's love for the woman. Yet his eyes kept turning to Ella. She was feminine and sweet. He detected a difference but couldn't put his finger on it. Was she more confident? Had the sadness diminished around her eyes?

"So Rashid called and doesn't want me to wait until tomorrow to return home. I'm leaving right after dinner," Bethanne said.

Ella looked startled. Khalid watched her as she turned to the other woman. "I thought we'd stay a day so I can see everything here."

Bethanne looked at Khalid. "You can show her around, can't you? She wants to see an oil field. You could explain things. And show her the sunrise. I think the colors in the sky are amazing."

Khalid knew a setup when he saw one. But instead of arguing, he looked at Ella. Another day together suited him. "Fine. We'll watch the sunrise together, I'll take you to the oil fields."

"And see she gets home safely?" Bethanne said.

Amusement warred with irritation. He suspected this was not Ella's plan but one of his soon to be sister-in-law's. Yet why not give in with good grace. He had to admit he'd missed Ella while in Egypt. More than once he'd seen something he'd wanted to share with her. Had almost called her a couple of times.

Dangerous territory, but he was a man who lived with danger. He liked being with her. There was no harm in that. It was only if he let himself dream of a future that could never be that he risked more than he wanted to pay.

Ella couldn't fall asleep after returning to her room. She was too much a night person to go to bed early. Yet Khalid had made no suggestion about spending time with her in the evening. Bethanne had now taken off for Alkaahdar. Ella sat at the window, watching the dark sky display the sparkles of lights from a million stars. There was no beach to walk along. It was too late to wander around town alone. There was nothing to do but think and that she didn't want to do.

She drew out her sketchpad, but instead of sketching various pieces of glass she wanted to try, she drew quick vignettes of Khalid—walking along the beach, swimming in the sea, leaning against his desk.

She also sketched him in traditional Arab robes, like he'd worn the first night she'd met him. She'd love to see him attired like that again. Did he wear the robes in the desert? Slowing in her drawing, she let her imagination drift as she thought about an oasis like Bethanne had talked of. What would it be like to have a small house in the scant shade of the palms surrounding a small pool of clear water? She envisioned a rooftop veranda that would provide a 360-degree view when the heat of the day dissipated. Quiet. Silent except for the wind sweeping across the sand. Sometimes the sand hummed in harmony. Would they feel cocooned together in a world apart?

She filled several pages with sketches, then tossed the tablet aside. Restlessness was getting her nowhere. She had best go to bed and hope to fall asleep quickly. She'd spend tomorrow with Khalid.

He was waiting for her when she stepped into the lobby the next morning. She greeted him and joined him in the small restaurant attached to the hotel for breakfast. The croissants were hot, the jam her favorite—grape. The coffee was dark and aromatic. She sipped the rich beverage, trying not to stare. Khalid looked fabulous. His dark eyes met hers.

"Ready for the scenic tour?" he asked.

"Ready. I have a hat, sunscreen and a long-sleeved shirt to put on at midday to protect against the sun."

"I have hired a Jeep for our use, and stocked it with a cooler and plenty of cold water. Even lunch."

She smiled in anticipation. "Lovely, a picnic, just the two of us."

"I know a place you'll love," he said.

She would love anyplace he showed her. Looking away before she made a fool of herself, she finished her meal.

In no time they were in the open Jeep, weaving their way through the streets of the old town. The sandstone walls blended with the color of the desert. Bright spots of blues and red punctuated the monotonous walls. Soon the crowded streets fell behind. The homes were farther and farther apart until they were left behind and she and Khalid continued straight for the oil field she could see in the distance.

Fascinated by the acres of oil pumpers slowly rising and falling as they drew the oil from deep in the ground, she ignored what was behind her, trying to see what was ahead.

"Amazing. How did anyone know there was oil here?" she asked. There was nothing in the sparse desert to differentiate it from any other area.

"Geologists can find it anywhere. My father is the one who started this field. For Bashiri Oil, of course."

She looked around. "Was the town this big when the oil was discovered?"

"No. First the drilling and now the activity of the wells boosted the population considerably. It was a small, sleepy oasis way back when oil was first discovered. Inhabited by a few families who had lived here for generations. It was on the trade routes and the migration of nomadic people, so this was a resting place for caravans."

"Now it's another city, though small. With an airport."

Khalid laughed. "With an airport. Did Bethanne really bring you here to get ideas for your glass?"

"That was one reason," she said, staring straight ahead.

She caught a glimpse of him from the corner of her eye when he looked at her. "And another?"

"To see you."

He didn't respond, so Ella looked at him. "Surprised?"

"A bit."

"I think we need to get straight on what we're doing," she said.

He looked at her again, then back to the road. "We're going to see the wells, then have a picnic."

"About this fake engagement. I think Antonio has finally returned home. That should be the end of that matter. Interesting, don't you think, my parents are not against my being engaged to you a stranger, but objected to my marriage to Alexander whom they had known for years."

"Money is important to a lot of people. You are not one of them," he said.

"I think people are much more important. And experiences in life. I'm enjoying today. I have never gone very far into the desert. And I've never been to an oil field." She gave him a shy look, "Nor with a sheikh."

"Hey, I'm a man like any other."

Oh, no, she thought privately. *You are unlike anyone else in the world.* For a moment she wanted to reach over and touch him, grasp his hand and hold on and never let go. Her heart beat faster and colors seemed brighter. She loved him. Closing her eyes for a moment, she wondered when it had happened. How it could have happened. And what she could do to make sure he never knew.

Khalid was the perfect guide when they reached the oil field. He introduced her to the foreman and then gave her an abbreviated tour, explaining how the wells were drilled, capped and put into production. He even told her how something minor could go wrong and cause a fire. She had a healthy respect for the men who worked the fields, their lives in danger if any one of a myriad of things went wrong.

After their visit to the oil field, he drove them straight into the desert. It was just past noon. The sun glared overhead. The air was hot, the breeze from the moving car not doing much to cool. Ella had donned her hat and long-sleeved shirt and was sweltering. She was about to suggest they give up this expedition and return to the air-conditioned comfort of the hotel when she saw the faint suggestion of green in the distance. She stared at the spot gradually seeing the palms as they drove close. A cluster of trees offering a respite to the monotonous brown of the sand.

"The oasis?" she asked, pointing to the spot.

"Yes. A small wadi that holds enough water for a few humans or animals, it can't support a settlement. But there is plenty of water for the trees and shrubs that grow around it. And it provides a nice shady spot in a hot afternoon."

Ella studied the contrast of the golden-brown of the desert with the surprise of green from the trees. It gave her an idea for a new art piece. Could she do a palm, leaning slightly as if wishing to touch the earth? Maybe a small collage with blue glass at the base surrounded by a smoky golden glass with the palm rising.

Khalid stopped in the shade and turned off the engine. For a moment only silence reigned. Ella felt the heat encompass them, then a slight cooling from the shade. She turned and smiled at him.

"It's beautiful here. I know now why Bethanne says she'd like a home in the desert with water nearby. It would be lovely. I could live in such a place."

"Sometimes when things get too much, I come here for a few days." Khalid studied the water, the pond a scant four feet in diameter. The palms were spread out, their roots able to find enough moisture to support them even some distance from the pool.

"Surprisingly the water is cool," he said.

"In this heat?" she asked.

"Come."

He got out of the Jeep and waited for her at the front. When she joined him, he reached over to take her hand, leading her to the water's edge. They sat on the warm sand. Ella trailed her fingers in the water.

"It is cool!" she said in amazement. The water felt silky and refreshing. "How did you find this place?"

"Exploring when I was a kid. Rashid and I spent lots of time exploring while my dad spent time in the town. We learned later it was to visit a woman who had had a child by him."

Ella looked at him in surprise.

He looked back. "We never met her. She died, the daughter. My father's only daughter. He kept her hidden from my mother, understandably. She died in a plane crash that claimed Bethanne's father's life. My father died only days later—we think of a broken heart. Rashid and I haven't mentioned it around Mother."

"Does she know?"

"We don't know. But out of respect we have not brought it up. If she does, it must hurt her and if she doesn't, we don't want to have her learn about it at this late date."

Ella nodded, understanding. She wished her family was as loving and concerned for each other instead of always thinking of money and how to expand the vineyard or protect the family name.

"Your mother is lucky to have you two," she said wistfully. Would she ever have a child? A strong son who would look like his father? Or a beautiful little girl with dark eyes and a sparkle that telegraphed the mischief she might get into?

CHAPTER TEN

THE afternoon was pleasant in the shade. Khalid had brought blankets to spread on the sand. The picnic lunch was delicious. Ella ate with relish. The cool water from the pool completed the meal. Afterward, Khalid made sure the blankets were in the shade and lay down. Closing his eyes, he looked completely relaxed.

Ella watched him for a time, growing drowsy. Finally she lay down and closed her eyes. The quiet and peace of the oasis enveloped her and before long, she slept.

When she awoke, Khalid was nowhere to be seen. The Jeep was parked where he'd left it so she knew he hadn't gone far. She splashed cool water on her face and then rose, folding the blankets and putting them in the back of the Jeep.

"Khalid?" she called.

He appeared a moment later from behind a sand

dune. "Just checking things out," he said, walking back to the shady area.

"Sandstorms can wreak havoc in this area. That's what brought down the plane my father's daughter was on. Yet time and again, this oasis reappears. I was trying to figure out why. Ready to return to town?"

Ella nodded, feeling reluctant to end the afternoon. She looked around, imprinting every bit of the scene in her mind. It would forever be special—because of Khalid.

The sooner they were back among others, the sooner she could get her emotions under control. She really wanted to stay. To camp out under the stars. To share feelings and thoughts on the vastness of the desert and the beauty found despite the harshness.

To tell him he was loved.

That she could not do. She hurried to the Jeep and jumped in.

Quraim Wadi Samil seemed to shimmer in the late sunshine as heat waves distorted the air. They drove into the town and straight to the hotel. Ella felt wrung-out with the heat. She would relish the coolness of the hotel. She began to long for the cottage by the sea. At least there seemed to always be a breeze by the Gulf.

"Dinner at seven?" Khalid asked as they entered the lobby.

"That's perfect." It would give her time to shower and change and cool down.

Her room was spacious with little furnishings to clutter the space. She lay down for a few moments, wondering if there could be any future between her and Khalid. His fake engagement had been to help her out, made public by the minister. Since he already had it in for Khalid's family, they dare not end the engagement so soon without negative gossip. Yet the longer it lasted, the more people would expect to see them together, and expect plans for a wedding to be forthcoming.

She wished she was planning a wedding with Khalid. She would so love to spend the rest of her life with him. It would be very different from the life she had before. Khalid had a stronger intensity with life than she was used to. Was it because he flirted with death whenever dealing with oil fires?

The thought of him being injured again had her in a panic. Would he consider not doing that in the future?

As if they had a future.

Ella rose and went to take her shower. She had some serious thinking to do. She could not bear to fall more in love with the man and then have fate snatch him away. Maybe it was time to consider going back to Italy and finding a life she could live there. She'd already lost one man she loved. She could not go through that again.

At least if she left, she could always remember Khalid as he was today. And hope to never hear of his death. As long as he was living in the world, she could find contentment. Couldn't she?

Khalid met Ella at the elevator when she stepped off in the lobby at seven. He had been tempted to go to her room, but had mustered what patience he could to wait for her in a public place. She'd looked perfect that afternoon sleeping in the shade at the oasis. He'd wanted to touch her cheeks, faintly pink. Her hair looked silky and soft. He had touched her hair before and knew its texture.

He was playing a fool's game, tempting fate by spending time with her. What if he became attached? He knew what he could expect from life. He'd made his peace with being alone years ago. His work was interesting and challenging. Especially when fighting fires. He liked the men he worked with. Liked being consulted by Rashid from time to time.

But he couldn't change reality. A scarred and bitter man was not going to appeal to a pretty woman like Ella. He'd help her out because he disliked the way her brother was handling things. And her family sounded totally unlike his. Despite the scarring, his family rallied around when needed.

He moved away from the pillar where he'd been

leaning when she stepped out. Her look of expectancy touched him. When she spotted him, she smiled. Khalid felt it like a punch in the gut. It always made him feel whole again. She didn't seem freaked out by the scar. He still remembered the night she had cupped his cheeks, touching the damaged skin without revulsion. He'd never forget it.

"I thought I wouldn't want to eat again after that lavish lunch," she said as she hurried over to meet him. "But now that I've cooled down, I'm famished."

"Then let's hope they have enough food to fill you up."

She laughed. He almost groaned. Her laugher was like water sparkling and gurgling over rocks in the high country. Light and airy and pleasing. He wished he could hear it all his life.

"So tomorrow we return home?" she asked as they walked to the restaurant.

"Yes. We'll summon a plane if you like."

"I'd love to see the country between here and the coast, but not in a hot Jeep like today. It was fine for a short foray into the desert, but for the long drive home, I'd like more comfort."

"Your wish is my command," he said. He did wish he could do anything for her she wanted. An air-conditioned car would be easy. Could he help with selling her artwork? He knew nothing about that. But his mother did. If she'd just warm up to Ella a little, she'd be a tremendous help.

He had a life-size picture of that ever happening. Rashid was head over heels in love with Bethanne, and his mother still chided him for not seeking the woman she had wanted him to marry. He wasn't head over heels in love with Ella. But he liked being with her. Liked hearing her take on things. It gave him a different perspective.

He loved hearing her talk period. Her voice carried a trace of accent. Her Arabic was quite fluent, but softer than most women's. He liked it.

"Khalid!"

He looked at her.

"What?"

"I asked how long it would take to drive back to the coast. Where were you?" She peered up at him.

"Woolgathering. It takes about eight hours. It's a long and boring drive. The road is straight as a stick and there's nothing but sand and scrub bushes as far as the eye can see. We can do it, but I'd rather fly home and spend the afternoon at the beach."

"That does sound nice."

The maître d' appeared and showed them to a secluded table. He presented the menus with a flourish then quietly bowed away.

"No argument? I thought you wanted to drive home," he said.

"Well, you've obviously been across the desert and if it looks all the same, maybe I don't need to experience it for eight hours. You can take me on another trip to the desert if I need more inspiration," she replied, looking at the menu.

"Maybe."

She looked up and grinned. "We are supposed to be engaged, remember?"

"I thought you wanted to talk about that," he said. He had not planned for things to get complicated when he'd told her brother they were engaged. How was he to know it would come out and his mother would make a big production about it?

"So I do. How do we get out of it?"

He stared at her—realizing for the first time he did not want to get out of it. He could understand her haste in ending the agreement. Hadn't his fiancée tossed him over because of the scar? But he wanted Ella to pretend a bit longer.

"We can say we fought on this trip and the deal is off," he said slowly.

She looked at him thoughtfully. "So whose fault was it?"

He met her gaze, almost smiling. "Does it matter?"

"People will ask. And if they don't, they will speculate."

"Have it be mine. It doesn't matter."

"Of course it does," she said passionately. "If you break it off, that's not very nice of you. And if I do, that doesn't reflect well on me."

"So I play the villain. It won't impact my life."

She shook her head slowly. "Not fair. You tried to help me out. And I appreciate it. Antonio would still be here trying to coerce me back to Italy if you hadn't."

"So if I can't break it off and you can't, we don't." Was that the solution? Keep the engagement going long enough for her to feel more comfortable around him. Would she ever see beyond the exterior to what he thought and felt? Could she ever fall in love with him?

Unlikely. She still loved her dead husband. And he sounded like a paragon. Intellectual. A professor. What did an oil field roustabout have to offer in comparison? Granted he had position in the country, but she hadn't been very impressed being seen with a sheikh. He had money, but she came from money herself and was unimpressed. Not like other women he'd dated years ago. In fact, nothing seemed to impress Ella. That was one thing he loved—*liked*—about her. Money and stature and material items others were impressed by seemed inconsequential to her. She liked people—and it didn't seem to matter what they had or did; if they were of interest to her, she was friendly. If not, she was cordial. And someone who knew her well could easily tell the difference.

"So we stay engaged for a while longer," she mused. "Suits me." Her attention turned back to her menu.

Khalid felt a strange relief at her compliance. At least for a while longer, they continued being engaged.

And didn't engaged couples kiss?

The thought sprang to mind and wouldn't leave. He glanced at her. Her attention on the menu, he had ample time to study her lips, imaging them pressed against his again. Imagine feeling her soft body against his, passion rising between them.

If he didn't stop soon, he'd embarrass himself. He wanted dinner ordered eaten and over. They could walk to the square. The day's heat was abating. It would cool down soon as the desert did at night. They could find a secluded spot and watch the stars appear. And he'd hold her and kiss her and pretend for one night everything was normal.

It almost worked that way. They agreed to stroll through town when dinner finished. And when they found a parapet overlooking a city garden, they leaned against the still-warm stone and tried to make out the plants in the garden. But the light faded quickly. Turning, Ella looked up at the sky.

"It's growing darker by the second. Soon a million stars will show."

He nodded and stepped closer, bringing her into his arms. "And you are more beautiful than all of them," he said, and kissed her.

Nothing was normal about that kiss. He felt every inch of his body come alive as he deepened the kiss. She responded like she had been waiting as long as he had. Her mouth was sweet and tender and provocative. Her curves met his muscles and tempted him even more. Her tongue danced with his, inflaming desire to a new level. The parapet disappeared. The stars were forgotten. There remained only the two of them, locked in an embrace that he wanted to go on forever.

Forgotten was the hideous scar that so repulsed others. Gone was the fear he would never find a woman to overlook the distortion even for a night. Khalid felt he was soaring. And he loved every moment.

If only it could last forever.

But it was not fair to Ella to kiss her when he'd coerced her into this engagement. Slowly he broke off the kiss, pleased when she followed him as he pulled back—obviously not wanting to end the kiss.

He was breathing hard when they parted. She was, too.

"Wow," she said, then turned. "I think we should go back to the hotel."

He wanted to agree—if she meant they'd go to

his room. He wanted to make love to her so badly he ached from head to toe. Yet nothing she'd said or done gave him any indication that was where her thoughts were heading.

They turned and walked back toward the hotel.

"Did you arrange for Bethanne to pick us up tomorrow?" she asked as they came into the light spilling into the street from the hotel.

"She'll be here at nine."

"Good."

When they entered the lobby, Ella quickened her pace. She punched the elevator button almost savagely. She hadn't looked at him once since they came into the light.

"Ella, if you're upset—"

"Why would I be upset?" she asked in a brittle tone. "Engaged couples kiss all the time."

The elevator arrived and she stepped in, punching the number for her floor.

Khalid hesitated, then remained where he was. She did look up as the doors began to close.

"See you in the morning," he said before she was lost from view.

Turning, he went back outside. A long walk—like maybe to Alkaahdar—was required. He hoped he had his head on straight come morning.

Stupid, stupid, *stupid!* How could she have responded so freely to Khalid's kiss. No wonder she drove him away. He didn't even want to escort her to her room. Probably thought she'd jump him and drag him inside. Ella paced her room, slapping the wall when she reached it. Turning, she paced to the other wall, slapped it. What could she do to make things come right? She knew he had only helped her out. There was nothing there. How could she have responded so ardently?

Because she loved him and knew he had been lacking in love for years. She wanted to hold him close, pour out her feelings, let him know she loved him beyond anything. But to do so would probably have him running for the nearest exit. A kindness to help her out of a jam didn't mean he was falling for her. He had his life, she had hers.

"Stupid!" she almost shouted the word.

Taking a deep breath, she crossed to the bed and sat down hard. Nothing was going right. She was at odds with her family, had lost her husband—whom she was having trouble remembering when every time she tried her mind saw Khalid. She felt a flare of panic. She couldn't forget Alexander. He'd been her childhood sweetheart. They'd had a nice marriage. At one time she thought he was the only man for her.

Only Khalid had a way of making her forget him. Forget the sweet love they'd shared for the hot and passionate feelings that sprang to life anytime she saw Khalid. Or even thought about him.

Daydreams about what life together could be like. And fears for his safety. She had to get away. Pack her things, face her parents and take complete charge of her life. She didn't have to marry anyone. It wasn't her fault her brother had a gambling problem. Time he faced the music and not expect her to martyr herself on his behalf.

And if she made it big in art, great. If not, maybe she could do stained glass work, or something to keep doing what she loved. It wasn't the same as sharing a life with a man she felt passionately about. But it would have to suffice.

If she could make it on her own. Somehow she must find a way to be self-supporting.

Which meant staying in the cottage was her best bet—the lease was solid for another four years. Khalid would get tired of hanging around and move on. Or sell the estate with the cottage occupied. She could make sure she didn't walk along the beach at night. Or venture outside if she knew he was in residence.

She'd faced worse. She could do this.

"But I don't want to," she wailed, and burst into tears.

The next morning Ella felt more composed. She ate a small breakfast in her room. Made sure no traces of last night's tears showed and descended to the lobby promptly at nine. Khalid was nowhere to be seen. She hadn't gotten the time wrong, had she?

One of the porters saw her and came over. "I will take your bag. You should have called down. The taxi is waiting."

So he wasn't even going back with her. That should help. But Ella felt the loss to her toes. Much as she'd talked herself into staying away from him in the future, she still hoped to fly back with him this morning. Saying goodbye silently so he'd never know, but having a few more hours of his company. Now even that was denied her.

The gleaming white jet sat on the runway with a bevy of men working around it. The cab stopped near the plane and a man rushed over to get her bag. She felt like royalty. Tears stung as she tried to smile and walked to the plane. She missed Khalid and it had been less than ten hours since she'd seen him.

Bethanne popped out of the opened doorway. "Hey, let's get a move on. I've got another run later," she said with a wide smile.

It must not be odd that Khalid wasn't with her, Ella thought as she ran lightly up the stairs.

"Where to later?" she asked, hoping Khalid would not be a topic of conversation.

"To take Khalid and his crew to that fire, of course. Didn't he tell you? Since I was already airborne when the call came in, he's staying here and I'm flying back to get the rest of his crew and then we'll head for Kuwait."

Ella felt her heart freeze. "Another fire?" she said. He had not told her. He had not contacted her at all that morning. Which should show her more than anything how nebulous their connection was. It was not her business after all. He saw no reason to inform her.

"A double from what I understand. Want to sit up in the cockpit? We can talk as I fly."

In a surprisingly short time they were airborne. Ella was so curious about the fire she could hardly sit still. Respecting Bethanne's need for concentration, she kept quiet until the pilot leveled out.

"There, all set. We're heading for the capital city now," Bethanne said.

Ella looked at her. "Tell me about the fire. Khalid didn't say a thing to me about it."

"It's in Kuwait and a bad one. Apparently two wells, connected somehow, ignited. Seven men are known dead and a couple of others are missing. They says it's burning millions of gallons of oil. And hot enough to be felt a half a mile away."

"He can't put it out," Ella said, staggered trying to imagine the puny efforts of men to extinguish such a raging inferno.

"You know Khalid, he'll do his best. And my money's on him."

"Someone should stop him," Ella said.

"What?" Bethanne looked at her. "He'll be okay. He always comes through."

"He got burned pretty badly one time," Ella reminded her.

"Freak accident."

"Which could happen again. Good grief, if the heat is felt so far away, what would it be like close enough to cap it? It's probably melting everything around it and there'd be nothing to cap."

"So they put out the flames, let the oil seep and figure out a way to get into production again. That's what Khalid does, and he's really good at it, according to Rashid. Who, by the way, also wishes he wouldn't do this job. But he knows Khalid is driven to do this and won't stand in his way."

Ella nodded, fear rising like a knot in her throat. She swallowed with difficulty, every fiber of her being wanting to see Khalid again.

She gazed out the window, wishing they'd arranged to ride back together in that air-conditioned car she'd wanted. They would have been out of contact, and someone else would be tapped to try to put out the oil fire. He'd be safe.

"When did the call come?" she asked.

"It happened last night. I suspect they called him once they saw what happened. He's the world's best, you know."

"He should retire."

Bethanne reached out and squeezed Ella's hand. "I know, I'd feel that way if it were Rashid. But women can't change men. My mother told me that fact years ago when explaining how she and my father married and then divorced. She had hoped having a family would be enough for him, but it never was. Some men are meant to do more adventurous things than others."

"I'd hardly call putting out raging oil fires adventurous—more like exceedingly dangerous. Why couldn't he have been a professor or accountant or something?"

Bethanne shrugged. "You might ask yourself why you're engaged to the man. You knew what he did. Yet you plan to marry. It's not going to get easier, but support is important."

Ella couldn't tell her why they were engaged. Apparently Rashid had kept Khalid's secret. Ella couldn't tell anyone she considered leaving Quishari because of Khalid. Maybe the decision would be taken from her. There was nothing she could do now but pray for his safety. She wished they'd ended the evening differently. That she had told him how much she cared. That she'd dare risk everything to let him know she loved him. Would she ever get that chance?

The flight seemed endless. She wanted more information. Could she call Khalid when they landed?

She knew Bethanne was flying his crew back to Quraim Wadi Samil to pick him up and fly them all to Kuwait. He'd still be at the hotel. For a moment her mind went blank. What was the name of the hotel? She had to call him, tell him to be careful.

"Rashid will meet the plane," Bethanne said after responding to flight control. She began descending. Ella could see the city, the blue of the Gulf beyond. But the beauty was lost, fear held her tightly. "He's not going, is he?" Ella asked.

"No, he's taking you home. I'll be back late tonight. He didn't want you to be alone."

"Maybe I can work to take my mind off things," she said. The truth was she couldn't think about anything except Khalid and the danger he was facing.

"Go with Rashid. He'll have the most current information about Khalid and the crew. Besides, he's swinging by his mother's place to update her. Dealing with Madame al Harum is enough to take anyone's mind off troubles. That woman is a piece of work."

Ella smiled despite her worry. "At least we have that in common. Do you think she'll ever come around to accepting you?"

"My guess is once I have a baby or two."

Ella blinked and gazed out the window. What if she and Khalid married and she had a baby? She remembered thinking about a little dark-eyed little girl, or a couple of rambunctious boys that looked just like Khalid. How would she ever stand it if they wanted to grow up to be oil firefighters.

"Madame al Harum must be beside herself with worry," she said. "I would be if it were my son going to fight that fire."

"I would never let a son of mine grow up to do that," Bethanne said.

"Thought you said a woman can't change a man."

"Well, then I'd start with a little boy."

Ella laughed. Then almost cried when she thought more about the danger Khalid faced. How he'd once been an adorable little boy, running at the beach, playing with his twin. How quickly those years must have flown by.

Rashid was standing beside a limo when the plane taxied up to the hangar. There were a half dozen men near him with duffel bags and crates. As soon as the engines were shut down, men began swarming around the plane, loading everything. It was being refueled even as Ella stepped down the stairs. Bethanne followed, then hugged Rashid tightly.

"I wish you'd let someone else fly the plane," he said.

"I'm going. Don't argue. It's Khalid you should be worried about. I'll pick him up and then take them all to Kuwait. I'll be home late tonight. You take care of Ella. I think she's in shock."

"No, I'm fine. I think I should go home."

"You're coming with me," Rashid said.

She looked at him, almost seeing Khalid. Certainly hearing that autocratic tone of his. They looked so alike, yet so different.

"Any news?" she asked.

"Nothing beyond what we learned earlier. Once we reach home we'll call Khalid. He's been talking with the oil field people so will have the latest intel. This all you have?" he asked as one of the men put her bag in the trunk of the limo.

"Yes. It was a short trip." Too short if it was to be the last time she saw Khalid.

Ella went with Rashid to his mother's home. He did not speak on the ride except to try to reassure her that Khalid knew what he was doing and wouldn't take any foolish risks. "Especially now," Rashid said.

Ella nodded, wishing they'd never embarked on this stupid fake engagement. Everyone thought he'd be extra careful, but Rashid knew Khalid had no special reason to be extra cautious. She knew he wouldn't be foolhardy, but so many things could go wrong. What if there was another explosion and his suit was torn again. She couldn't bear to think of the pain he'd go through while healing.

Or what if things went really, really wrong?

"My mother can be a bit difficult. We know she loves us. Sometimes I think it's hard for a mother to realize her children are grown and have their own lives."

Ella thought about her parents. "Sometimes they just want to control children forever."

"Or maybe they get used to it and find it hard to let go."

"Your mother doesn't have to like me," she said.

"No, but it would make family life so much more comfortable in the future, don't you think? We do celebrate happy occasions together—holidays, birthdays."

"Bethanne said once she was a grandmother, she'd come around."

Rashid laughed. "That's our hope. But not right away. I want her to myself for a while."

Would Khalid ever want someone to himself for a while? She wished it would be her.

Madame al Harum was distraught when they arrived. She rushed to the door. "Have you heard anything more?"

"No, Mother," Rashid said, giving her a hug. "He's still in Quraim Wadi Samil. Bethanne just took off to get him. It'll be a few hours before they're in Kuwait."

"Call him. I need to talk to him," she ordered.

"You and Ella."

The older woman looked at Ella as if seeing her for the first time. "Oh." She frowned. "Of course."

"We both want Khalid safely back," Ella said.

Madame al Harum nodded. "Come, we will call him."

Khalid had maps and charts spread around him when the phone rang.

"Al Harum," he said, hoping this was another call from the site, updating the situation.

"Khalid, it's your mother. I wanted to tell you to be careful."

"I always am, Mother." He leaned back in his chair, pressing his thumb and forefinger against his eyes. He'd been studying the layout of the oil field, where the pipes had been drilled and the safety protocols that were in place. He figured he could recite every fact about that field in his sleep.

Glancing at his watch, he noted the plane would be arriving in less than an hour. He had talked to his second in command before he boarded and all the gear they needed was either on the plane or being shipped directly to the fire.

"We will watch over Ella for you," she said.

Khalid's attention snapped back to his mother. Ella. He should have told her this morning before she left, but he'd already been involved in learning all he could from the source. He hadn't wanted to interrupt the phone call to go tell her goodbye.

"She returned safely?" he asked.

"Yes. She's here. Take care of yourself, son."

Before Khalid could say anything, he heard Ella's soft voice.

"Khalid?"

"Yes. You got back all right, I see."

"I didn't know until we were on the plane what was going on. I wished you had told me. You will be careful, won't you?"

"I always am." He was warmed by the concern in her voice.

"From what I've heard, this one is really bad."

He heard a sound from his mother in the background.

"It does seem that way. I'll know more when I get there, but so far, this is probably the most challenging one we've tried."

"I guess I couldn't talk you out of going?" she asked hopefully.

He laughed, picturing her with her pretty brown eyes, hair blowing in the sea breeze. "No, but I wish I didn't have to leave you. Not that I'd take you to a fire. I enjoyed yesterday." He wished he could pull her into his arms this moment and kiss her again. If he hadn't already been on the phone, nothing would have stopped him from explaining this morning—and taking another kiss for luck.

"Me, too."

He waited, hoping she'd say more. The silence on the line was deafening.

"I better go. I'm expecting another call," he finally said. Nothing was going to be decided on the telephone.

"Okay. Take care of yourself. I'll be here when you get back."

He hung up, wondering where else she'd be but at the cottage. She had a lease for another four years. And at this moment, he was grateful for his grandmother's way of doing things.

The phone rang again and this time it was the field manager in Kuwait. Time to push personal agendas on the back burner. He had a conflagration to extinguish.

CHAPTER ELEVEN

ELLA chafed at the way time dragged by. Rashid stayed for a while, then claimed work needed him and took off. Leaving her with Madame al Harum. Ella knew she'd be better off at home. She could try to take her mind off her worry about Khalid with work. Here she had nothing. She rose from the sofa where she'd sat almost since she'd arrived and walked to the window which overlooked the city. It looked hot outside. She'd rather be at the beach.

"I think I'll go home," she said.

"Stay."

Turning, she looked at Khalid's mother. "There's nothing to do here. At home I have work that might distract me from worry."

Sabria al Harum tried to smile. "Nothing will make you forget. I had years of practice with my husband when he went on oil fields. Always worrying about his safety. And he did not try to put out fires. I now worry about Khalid. Rashid assures me he knows his job. But he cannot know what a fire will do."

"It makes it worse since he was injured once," Ella said, looking back out the window.

"Yet you don't seem to mind his scar."

Ella shrugged. "He is not his scar, any more than he is defined by being tall. It's what's inside that counts."

There was a short silence then Sabria said, "Many people don't grasp that concept. He was terribly hurt by the defection of his fiancée when he was still in hospital."

"She either freaked or was not strong enough to be his wife. Khalid is very intense. Not everyone could live with that."

"You could."

Ella nodded, tears filling her eyes. She could. She would love to be the one he picked to share his life. She would match him toe-to-toe if he got autocratic. And she would love to spend the nights in his arms.

"He was like that as a little boy," Sabria said softly.

When Ella turned, she was surprised at the look of love on her hostess's face. "Tell me," she invited. She was eager for every scrap of knowledge she could get of Khalid.

"I have some pictures. Come, I'll tell you all

about my wild twins and show you what I had to put up with." The words were belied by the tone of affection and longing.

Ella was surprised at the number of photo albums in the sitting area of Sabria al Harum's bedroom. The room was bright and airy, decorated in peach and cream colors, feminine and friendly. She would never have suspected the rather austere woman to have this side to her.

Pulling a fat album from the shelves behind the sofa, Sabria sat and patted the cushion next to her for Ella to sit. Placing the album in Ella's lap a moment later, she opened it. For the next hour, the two women looked at all the pictures—from when two adorable babies came home in lacy robes, to the smiling nannies who helped care for them, to the proud parents and on up to adulthood. There were fewer pictures of the two young men, too busy to spend lots of time with their parents. Then she paused over one last picture.

"This was the one taken just before the fire that scarred my son so badly. He has never had his picture taken since. People can be cruel when faced unexpectedly with abnormalities— whether scarring or handicaps. He was doubly injured with the loss of his fiancée. He has so much to offer."

Ella nodded. A mother always said that, but in Khalid's case, it was true.

The phone rang. Sabria rose swiftly and crossed to answer the extension in her sitting room.

"Thank you," she said a moment later.

"That was Rashid. The team has taken off from Quraim Wadi Samil. They'll be in Kuwait in a couple of hours. There's nothing to do but wait."

"Then come with me to my studio. I'll show you my work and you can advise me. Madame Alia al Harum thought I had promise. I want to earn a living by my work, but if it is really impossible, maybe I should find out now, rather than later."

"You will not need to work once married to Khalid."

Ella had no quick response. Only she and Khalid knew there would be no marriage.

"Come and see."

Sabria thought about it for a moment then nodded. "I believe I should like to see what you do."

The afternoon passed slowly. Sabria looked at all the work Ella had done, proclaiming with surprise how beautiful it was. "No wonder my mother-in-law thought you had such promise. You have rare talent. I know just where I'd like to see that rosy vase. It would be perfect in my friend's bedroom. Perhaps I shall buy it for her. When will you begin to sell?"

Ella explained the original plan and then her idea to start earlier. Soon she and Sabria were discussing advantages and disadvantages of going public too soon, yet without the public feedback, how would Ella know which ideas were the most marketable.

Ella wasn't sure if it was the situation, or the fact Sabria was finally receptive to seeing her as an individual—not someone out to capture her son's affections—but she felt the tentative beginning of a friendship. Not that Sabria would necessarily wish to continue when the engagement was broken. Ella could see the dilemma—who took the blame? She didn't want to. Yet in fairness, she needed to be the one. Khalid had been helping her. He did not need any more grief in his life.

They called Rashid for news before eating dinner on the veranda. Nothing new. Ella made a quick spaghetti with sauce she'd prepared a while ago and frozen. The camaraderie in the kitchen was another surprise. Ella thought she could really get to like Khalid's mother.

"I'm going now," Sabria said after they'd enjoyed dinner and some more conversation. Ella could listen to stories about the twins all week. Darkness had fallen. It was getting late. Nothing would change tonight. Khalid had told Rashid they needed to plan carefully since the fire was involved with two wells.

When she took a walk on the beach before going to bed, Ella looked to the north. She could see nothing. The fire was too far away. But she could imagine it. She dealt with fire every day—controlled and beneficial. Raging out of control would be so different. She offered another prayer for Khalid's safety. Her decision to leave was best. She could see about selling what she'd already done and arrange shipping to Italy of her annealer and crucible and glass. She'd establish herself somewhere near enough to see her parents, but far enough away to make sure they knew she was not coming back to the family. Not until her brother's situation was cleared up.

In the meantime, she did her best not to focus on Khalid, but everything from the beach to the house next door reminded her of him. She could picture him standing in her doorway. Looking at the art she had created. Holding the yellow vase in his house that his grandmother had loved. She ached with loneliness and yearning. Could she get by without him over the years ahead?

She had to. There was no future for her in Quishari. That part of her life was over.

Tomorrow she'd begin packing and making arrangements to move.

The next two days were difficult. Ella made Rashid promise to call her the moment he learned of anything—good or bad. There was nothing else she could do, so she began packing. She ordered shipping cartons and crates and enlisted the help of Jalilah to help her. Carefully they wrapped the fragile pieces in packing materials, then in boxes, then crates. It was slow work, but had to be done carefully to insure no breakage during transit.

Every time Khalid's cordless phone rang, Ella's heart dropped, then raced. She'd answer only to hear Rashid's calm voice giving her an update. The materials had arrived. The maps had been updated. The plan was coming together. There was never a personal message for her. What did she expect? Khalid had far more important things to worry about.

But each time Rashid hung up, Ella's heart hurt a bit more. One word, one "tell Ella I'm okay," would have sufficed.

On the third day, Ella could see the progress. She had arranged for the shipping agent to pick up what was already packed. He would hold it at the depot until everything was ready and ship all at once. She and Jalilah were talking when Ella heard a car. Glancing out the window, she saw Rashid and Bethanne get out and hurry toward the cottage.

Fear swamped her as she rushed to the door. "What happened?" she called before they could speak.

Bethanne came to her first, hugging her tightly. "He'll be okay," she said.

"What?" Sick with fear, she looked at Rashid.

"Another well exploded. The fire is worse than ever. Khalid was hit by flying debris. One of the crew was killed, but Khalid's in hospital. He's going to be okay. We're going now. You come with us."

Ella wanted to refuse, but her need to see him was too strong. She had to make sure he was truly okay before leaving.

"I just need my purse and passport," she said. She dashed to the house, Bethanne with her. "Bring a change of clothes and sleepwear. We're planning to stay as long as we need to," she said.

Ella went through the motions, but her thoughts stuck on Khalid. "He's really all right?"

"No, but he will be. So far he's still unconscious. We hope we're there by the time he wakes up," Bethanne said, helping fold clothes and stuffing them in the small travel bag.

Time seemed to stop. Ella felt like she was walking through molasses. She remembered hurrying to Alexander's hospital bed—too late. He had died from the car crash injuries before she was there to see him. She couldn't be too late for Khalid.

She sat on the edge of the bed.

"I can't go," she said.

Bethanne stopped and looked at her. "What?"

"I can't go." She pressed her hands against her chest, wishing she could stop the tearing pain. Khalid. He had to be all right!

"Yes, you can. And will. And greet him with all the love in your heart. He cannot have another fiancée abandon him when he's in the hospital."

Ella looked at Bethanne. "I'm not—" Now was not the time to confess she wasn't really his fiancée. "I'm not abandoning him. But I don't think I can go into a hospital."

"We'll be right with you. Come on. That's all you need. Get your passport and let's go."

Four hours later they entered the hospital. Ella felt physically sick. The few updates Rashid had obtained during the flight had not been encouraging. Entering the new hospital, Ella felt waves of nausea roil over her. "I need a restroom," she said, dashing to the nearest one. Bethanne followed.

After throwing up, Ella leaned limply against the stall wall. "I can't do this again," she said.

"He'll be okay, Ella. He's not Alexander. He'll pull through," Bethanne said, rubbing her back.

"Go on up. I know Rashid needs to see him instantly. I'll clean up and be right behind you." She wanted a few moments to herself. She could do this. She had to. The thought of Khalid lying helpless in bed was almost more than she could stand. But she also wanted to see him. At least one more time. And assure herself he was alive and would recover.

She tried hard to think of this as visiting a sick friend. But as she walked down the corridor, the smells that assailed her reminded her vividly of the frantic dash to see Alexander. Only the times got mixed up. She felt the fear and panic, but it was for Khalid. The door was ajar to the room she'd been directed to. She stood outside, drawing in a deep breath, hoping she wouldn't lose her composure.

Rashid stepped out, smiling when he saw her. "I'm calling Mother. He's awake. And probably wondering where you are." He flipped open his mobile phone and hit a speed-dial number. Walking down the corridor, he began to speak when his mother answered.

Ella turned back to the room, stepping inside. Immediately she saw Khalid, the hospital bed raised so he was sitting. His face was bandaged, both eyes looked blackened. His right shoulder was also bandaged. Bethanne was on the far side, talking a mile a minute in English. Khalid watched her; he hadn't seen Ella yet.

Which was a good thing. It gave her time to get over her shock, give a brief thanks he was awake and seemingly able to recover. Pasting a smile on her face she stepped into the room.

"You scared me to death!" she said.

Khalid swiveled around, groaned at the movement, but looked at her like she was some marvelous creation. Her heart raced. Nothing wrong with his eyes.

"You came," he said.

"You said you'd keep safe." She walked over to the bed. Conscious of Bethanne watching her, she leaned over and kissed him gently on the mouth. His hand came up and kept her head in place as he kissed her back.

"Don't hurt yourself," she said, pulling back a few inches, gazing deep into his eyes.

"I didn't think you'd come," he said, pulling her closer for another brush of lips.

"Why ever not?" Bethanne asked. "If Rashid were injured nothing could keep me away."

"And nothing could keep me away," Ella said. She straightened and took his hand in hers, feeling his grip tighten. Studying him, she shook her head.

"You look horrible," she said.

He laughed, and squeezed her hand. "I feel like a truck ran me over. That was something we didn't expect—another explosion. I think they had the wells linked in a way that didn't show on the maps."

"I heard one of your men died. I'm so sorry."

"Me, too."

She leaned closer. "But I'm glad it wasn't you."

"I'm going to find Rashid. We'll be back." Bethanne waved and headed out of the room.

"When Rashid first came in, I thought you hadn't come," he said.

"Well, some of your fiancées might desert you in hospital, but not all," she said lightly, hating for him to know how much it had taken for her to come. She was so glad she had, but the fear she'd lived with wouldn't easily be forgotten.

He laughed again. Despite his injuries, he seemed the happiest she'd ever seen him.

"Did that blow to the head knock you silly?" she asked.

"Maybe knocked some sense in me. I lay here thinking, after I woke up, what if you didn't come? We haven't known each other that long. What if you didn't care enough to come."

"What if I knocked you up side the head again to stop those rattled brains. Of course I would come. I had to see that you were all right. I couldn't just take Rashid's word for it."

"Why?"

She looked at their linked hands. "I care about you," she said.

"How much?"

She met his gaze. "What do you mean, how much?" she asked.

"I want to know how much you care about me—what's hard about that?"

"Like, more than spinach but less than chocolate?"

His gaze held hers, his demeanor going serious. "Like enough to marry me, stay in Quishari and make a life with me?"

Ella caught her breath. For a moment she forgot to breathe. Did he mean it? Seriously?

"Are you asking me to marry you?" she said. "I mean, for real?"

He nodded. "I am. I hated to say good-night to you in Quraim Wadi Samil. Hated even more leaving for Kuwait without having another kiss. Then I woke up here and realized, life is unexpected. I could die here today, or live for decades. But I knew instantly either way, I wanted you as part of my life. I love you, Ella. I think I have since you touched my cheek on the beach weeks ago. A woman who wasn't horrified by how I look. Who could see me clearer in the dark than anyone in the light. A woman who had been through a lot already, and valued people for who they were, not what they could offer monetarily. Did I also mention who sets my entire body on fire with a single kiss?"

Warmth and love spread through her as she smiled at his words. "You didn't. Maybe we need another check on that." She leaned over and kissed him.

"Are you saying yes?" he prompted a few moments later.

"I am. I love you. I never expected to say those words again after Alexander's death. But you swept into my life, running roughshod over any obstacles I might throw up. I can't pinpoint the moment I fell in love, but I can the moment I realized it. I will love you forever."

"The fire is still going," he said.

"And are you planning to put it out?"

"Might be involved in the planning. But right now I don't feel up to standing to kiss you, so doubt if I'll be leading a foray close to the flames."

"This time," she murmured, remembering what Bethanne had said. She wouldn't want to change a thing about this man.

"This time. But I'm careful. I'm still here, right?"

"Right. Here's hoping there are no more fires in your future."

"Only the one you set with your kisses," he said.

Ella laughed, seeing an entirely different side of the man who had captured her heart. And to think, she almost missed this. She'd have some quick unpacking to do when she got back to the cottage. She couldn't bear for him to think she was leaving. She'd tell him—after a while. After he was convinced of her love as she was already convinced of his.

"I love you, Ella, now and always."

"I love you, Khalid. Now and always."

EPILOGUE

"I'M GETTING car sick riding with my eyes closed," Ella said, still gripping the edge of the door to help with the bouncing. They'd left Quraim Wadi Samil a while ago. In the last ten minutes, Khalid had insisted she close her eyes—he had a surprise for her. It couldn't be the oasis; she'd already seen that. What else was out in this desert?

"Almost there," he said, reaching out to grasp her free hand in his, squeezing it a little.

She felt the car slowing. Then it stopped. The desert wind brought scents of sand, scant vegetation and—was it water?

"Open your eyes," he said.

She did and stared. They were at the oasis. The late afternoon sun cast long shadows against the tall palms, the small pool of water—and the sandstone house that looked as if it had miraculously sprung up from the ground.

"What? Is that a house?"

He left the Jeep and came around to her side, taking her hand to help her out. "It's our house. Ours and Rashid's and Bethanne's. She doesn't know yet. He'll bring her out next week. We have it first."

Ella looked around in astonishment. "You built it here miles and miles from anywhere? How could you get all the materials, how—never mind, money can achieve anything. This is fantastic! I want to see."

He smiled and led her across a flagstone patio to the front door. Lounge chairs rested on the patio, which gave a perfect view of the pool and palms. Opening the door, he swept her into his arms and stepped inside. "Isn't this what newly-weds do?" he asked at her shriek of surprise.

"Yes, in Italy. I didn't know you did it in Quishari." She laughed, traced the new scar on his face and pulled his head down for a kiss. She was so full of love for this husband of hers. And so grateful for his full recovery—with one or two new scars which only made her love him more.

"Why not at our home when we married?" she asked.

"We had the reception there—how could I carry you over the threshold? You were already inside."

"Hmm, good point."

He set her on her feet and turned her around. The small room was furnished with comfortable items. Large windows gave expansive views. Two of her glass pieces were on display. Taking a quick tour, Ella discovered the small kitchen, bath and two large bedrooms.

"This is so lovely," she said, returning to the center of the main room. Khalid had done all he could to make her life wonderful. He'd backed her art exhibit, which turned out wildly successful. She had orders lined up for new pieces.

They'd attended Bethanne and Rashid's wedding in Texas. And then done a quick tour of several larger cities in the United States which Ella had enjoyed with her new husband.

On their way back to Quishari, they'd stopped in Italy so he could meet her parents. Even settled Giacomo's remaining debts, with a stern warning to never gamble again—which only reiterated what her father had decreed. She'd protested, but Khalid had insisted he wanted to have harmonious relations with his new in-laws.

Which she still hoped for with his mother. One day at a time, she reminded herself. At least they'd been married in Quishari, which Madame al Harum liked better than Rashid and Bethanne's wedding.

"The best is outside. Come," Khalid said, drawing her out and around to the side of the house where stairs led to the flat roof.

When they reached the upper level, Ella exclaimed at the loveliness. Pots of flowers dotted the hip-high wall. Several outdoor chairs and sofas provided ample seating. The view was amazing. Slowly she turned around, delight shining in her eyes.

"This is so perfect."

He smiled at her and drew her into his arms. "I wanted something special for us to get away to sometimes, just the two of us. To enjoy the quiet of the desert and the beauty of this oasis."

She smiled, then frowned a little.

"You don't like it?"

"I love it. It's just…" She bit her lower lip and glanced around, then back at Khalid. "It won't be just the two of us."

"Rashid and I plan to keep the other informed when we want to use the house. We won't be here when they are. Or I can just tell him forget it, we want it all ourselves."

"Don't you dare. It's not that. We're having a baby," she blurted out. "Darn, that was not the way I wanted to tell you," she said.

Staring at his stunned face, she almost laughed. "Well, we've been married for four months and not exactly celibate. What do you think?"

"I'm stunned. And thrilled." With a whoop, he lifted her up and spun her around. "How are you feeling? When is it due? Do we know if it's a boy or girl? How long have you known?"

She laughed, feeling light and free and giddy with happiness. She thought he'd be happy; this confirmed it.

"You know Bethanne and Rashid are expecting. She gave me a full rundown on the symptoms she was feeling, from morning sickness to constantly being tired. Only, I don't have any of those. I feel fine. But there are signs and I had it confirmed yesterday. I was going to tell you last night, but then you had that meeting, and then we flew to Quraim Wadi Samil and here we are. Really, this turns out to be the best place to tell you. I loved our picnic here months ago. I'm so thrilled with this new house. We'll have only happy memories here. Do you know we're probably going to have our baby within weeks of Rashid and Bethanne's?"

"So our child will grow up with theirs," he said with quiet satisfaction.

She nodded, already picturing two small children playing on the beach by their home. Or coming here with parents to explore the desert.

"Do you think we'll have twins?" she asked.

"Who cares—one at a time or multiples, we'll love them all."

"All?"

"Don't you want a dozen?" he teased.

She laughed. "No, I do not. A couple, maybe three or four, but not twelve."

"Whatever makes you happy. You have made me happy beyond belief. I love you, Ella." He drew her into his arms and kissed her gently. "You changed everything beyond what I ever expected."

She smiled at him, not seeing the scars, only the love shining from his eyes. "You are all I'll ever want," she said, reaching up to kiss him again on the rooftop of a house made for happy memories.

 ROMANCE 2-in-1

Coming next month

BEAUTY AND THE RECLUSIVE PRINCE
by Raye Morgan

Enjoy the start of *The Brides of Bella Rosa*, a brand new eight-book series where you'll find romance, rivalry and a family reunited. Meet Isabella, who's about to unlock the secrets of reclusive prince Maximilliano...

EXECUTIVE: EXPECTING TINY TWINS
by Barbara Hannay

The Brides of Bella Rosa saga continues. Sparks fly when prim, pampered politician Lizzie meets laid-back cattleman Jack. And there's double trouble on the way – Lizzie's pregnant!

A WEDDING AT LEOPARD TREE LODGE
by Liz Fielding

Events planner Josie has scooped the wildest wedding of the year in Botswana. Crocodiles and creepy crawlies she can handle, it's enigmatic entrepreneur Gideon who's getting under her skin.

THREE TIMES A BRIDESMAID...
by Nicola Marsh

When *another* wedding invitation (+1) arrives, Eve Pemberton organises a date for the day! At such short notice she'll be on billionaire Bryce Gibson's arm – the man who broke a teenage Eve's heart!

On sale 7th May 2010

millsandboon.co.uk Community

Join Us!

The Community is the perfect place to meet and chat to kindred spirits who love books and reading as much as you do, but it's also the place to:

- Get the inside scoop from authors about their latest books
- Learn how to write a romance book with advice from our editors
- Help us to continue publishing the best in women's fiction
- Share your thoughts on the books we publish
- Befriend other users

Forums: Interact with each other as well as authors, editors and a whole host of other users worldwide.

Blogs: Every registered community member has their own blog to tell the world what they're up to and what's on their mind.

Book Challenge: We're aiming to read 5,000 books and have joined forces with The Reading Agency in our inaugural Book Challenge.

Profile Page: Showcase yourself and keep a record of your recent community activity.

Social Networking: We've added buttons at the end of every post to share via digg, Facebook, Google, Yahoo, technorati and de.licio.us.

www.millsandboon.co.uk

2 FREE BOOKS
AND A SURPRISE GIFT

We would like to take this opportunity to thank you for reading this Mills & Boon® book by offering you the chance to take TWO more specially selected books from the Romance series absolutely FREE! We're also making this offer to introduce you to the benefits of the Mills & Boon® Book Club™—

- **FREE home delivery**
- **FREE gifts and competitions**
- **FREE monthly Newsletter**
- **Exclusive Mills & Boon Book Club offers**
- **Books available before they're in the shops**

Accepting these FREE books and gift places you under no obligation to buy, you may cancel at any time, even after receiving your free shipment. Simply complete your details below and return the entire page to the address below. You don't even need a stamp!

YES Please send me 2 free Romance books and a surprise gift. I understand that unless you hear from me, I will receive 5 superb new stories every month including two 2-in-1 books priced at £4.99 each and a single book priced at £3.19, postage and packing free. I am under no obligation to purchase any books and may cancel my subscription at any time. The free books and gift will be mine to keep in any case.

Ms/Mrs/Miss/Mr ——————— Initials ———————

Surname ————————————————————————

Address ————————————————————————

——————————————————— Postcode ————————

E-mail ————————————————————————

Send this whole page to: Mills & Boon Book Club, Free Book Offer, FREEPOST NAT 10298, Richmond, TW9 1BR

Offer valid in UK only and is not available to current Mills & Boon Book Club subscribers to this series. Overseas and Eire please write for details.. We reserve the right to refuse an application and applicants must be aged 18 years or over. Only one application per household. Terms and prices subject to change without notice. Offer expires 30th June 2010. As a result of this application, you may receive offers from Harlequin Mills & Boon and other carefully selected companies. If you would prefer not to share in this opportunity please write to The Data Manager, PO Box 676, Richmond, TW9 1WU.

Mills & Boon® is a registered trademark owned by Harlequin Mills & Boon Limited.
The Mills & Boon® Book Club™ is being used as a trademark.